GREAT ILLUSTRATED CLASSICS

Bret Harte. From the original painting by John Pettie, R.A., 1890.

THE LUCK OF
ROARING CAMP
AND OTHER TALES

BY BRET HARTE

*With pictures of the author and his
environment and illustrations of
the setting of the book together
with an introduction by
Louis B. Salomon*

NEW YORK·DODD, MEAD & COMPANY

INTRODUCTION

"I FIND men and women pretty much the same on Fifth Avenue as in Dutch Flat," Bret Harte wrote in 1877 to William Dean Howells, then editor of the *Atlantic Monthly*. But there was one difference which, as a professional writer in search of material, he had already found out the hard way: while Fifth Avenue readers devoured his stories of people in Dutch (or Poker) Flat and Roaring Camp, they took little interest in his view of the folkways of Fifth Avenue or Boston Common. In Hollywood terms he was type-cast, trapped by the sudden popularity of a form and a subject-vein which he had hit upon in San Francisco some years earlier and which had already spawned so many imitators that the taste for it in this country was beginning to wane. By 1878 he was glad to accept a consular post in Prussia (later, in Scotland) to help support his wife and children while he continued trying to mix the ingredients of his first successful formula, which, luckily for him, still fetched a price in the European market.

That the man who did most to shape the picture of life in the gold-fields for Eastern readers was not himself a real Westerner is hardly surprising; there were precious few literate indigenous Westerners in those days. Bret (born Francis Brett in 1836) Harte grew up in Albany and New York City. In 1854, at the age of eighteen, he moved to California, where he lived by a succession of trades—as teacher, drugstore clerk, prospector, typesetter, and clerical assistant in the United States Mint—while building up a reputation as contributor to journals that also carried stories and sketches by a friend of his who used the pen-name Mark Twain.

As editor of the brand-new *Overland Monthly*, in 1868, Harte was in a position to print his own story "The Luck of Roaring Camp" despite the prudish qualms of a proofreader to such indelicacies as an oblique reference to Cherokee Sal's profession and Kentuck's (to a Victorian eye) salty exclamation "The d---d little cuss!" In the more sophisticated East the story was quickly reprinted and widely acclaimed, and six months later he followed up its success with "Plain Language from Truthful James," a humorous verse account of a "heathen Chinee" that swept the country like a prairie fire and even brought cabled pleas from England for more of his work. In 1871, a full-fledged celebrity, he headed eastward with a fat contract from the prestigious *Atlantic Monthly*.

From this point on, alas, his career ran slowly downhill. A conscientious craftsman, he deprecated the trifling verses that had brought him fame (much as Mark Twain had felt, a few years earlier, about his "Jumping Frog" story). But he lacked Mark Twain's versatility and depth, and even though in a series of parodies called *Condensed Novels* he amusingly burlesqued a number of popular nineteenth century novelists he did not have his more celebrated friend's command of gusty folk-humor. Nor, though he tried lecturing, could he master the inimitable platform manner that brought people flocking to Mark Twain's performances. So, for a few years here, and then in Europe until his death in 1902, Harte continued to turn out tales of lovable scamps and tender hearts concealed by rough exteriors—all this while William Dean Howells was preaching and practising the gospel of homely realism in fiction, Henry James adding new dimensions of psychological subtlety and intricate workmanship to the novel, and Emile Zola exploring with naturalistic zeal the wellsprings of human misery and degradation

The genre to which most of Harte's stories belong, and to the popularity of which he undoubtedly made a powerful contribution, is the "local color" school—dedicated precisely to the proposition that people are not the same on Fifth Avenue as in Dutch Flat. In the disillusioned decades following the Civil War, American readers turned away from both the blatantly sentimental popular romance and the philosophically-oriented fiction of Hawthorne and Melville; instead, they sought what at least seemed to be realistic pictures of the mores, the speech mannerisms, the occupations and amusements of various geographical segments of a rapidly expanding America not yet subjected to the homogenizing influence of jet airliners and mass-communications. In this way the reading public, still largely concentrated in the Boston-New York-Philadelphia zone, vicariously explored the "picturesque" (because unfamiliar) cultures of the deep South, the New England villages, the prairie farms and towns, and the Far West.

But in many cases both readers and writers entered into a conspiracy of self-deception. While the scenery and customs that constitute the local "color" may be more or less faithfully described, the story-plots often merely invert the old melodramatic formula, which equated goodness with social respectability and villainy with hisses; for this they substitute the initially titillating but no less formularized thesis that innate nobility belongs to the outcast and the disreputable and that the pillar of society is a mealy-mouthed hypocrite. Before the end of the story, the tough guy turns Santa Claus, the simpleton puts the shrewd operators to shame.

Even in appearance, the exterior belies the real man. Thus in "Brown of Calaveras" we contrast Jack Hamlin, the half-breed gambler "with his pale Greek face and Homeric gravity" and Bill Masters, "a graduate of Harvard, with his slovenly dress, his overflowing vitality, his intense appreciation of lawlessness and barbarism, and his mouth filled with crackers and cheese." Mliss, in the story named for her, finds encouragement in "a saintly Raphael-face, with blond beard and soft blue eyes, belonging to the biggest scamp in the diggings." Among the crowd of roughs gathered around Cherokee Sal's cabin in Roaring Camp, "the greatest scamp had a Raphael face, with a profusion of blond hair; Oakhurst, a gambler, had the melancholy air and intellectual abstraction of a Hamlet; the coolest and most courageous man was scarcely over five feet in height, with a soft voice and an embarrassed, timid manner. . . . The strongest man had but three fingers on his right hand; the best shot had but one eye." In such a society, a good man who *looked* good, a shiftless character who *looked* shiftless, would have deceived everybody.

Despite the artificiality of this upside-down moral order, Harte's best stories, all of which are included in this volume, handle their material with skill and easy naturalness; and in the very best, we willingly identify ourselves with the central characters, who in fact are acting out the dreams that most of us, in a life increasingly routinized and insulated from violence, weave about ourselves. A sociologist would not find a cross-section of the real West in these stories, but sociologists take little account of our dreams. Romance (why be afraid of the word?) is of the heart, and it comforts us to feel sure, without ever being put to the test, that we would face up to the ultimate challenge as simply and firmly as Kentuck or as nonchalantly as Tennessee. Has one ever known a male poker player who did not, from time to time, picture himself meeting a streak of bad luck with the aplomb of John Oakhurst.

One could choose worse models.

LOUIS B. SALOMON

Brooklyn College

A SELECTED LIST OF WORKS BY BRET HARTE

AND THEIR DATES

Tales
Bohemian Papers, 1867
Condensed Novels, 1867
Mrs. Skagg's Husbands, 1873
Tales of the Argonauts, 1875

Poetry
The Lost Galleon and Other Tales, 1867

Plays
Ah Sin, 1877
Sue, 1896

Novel
Gabriel Conroy, 1876

CONTENTS

ILLUSTRATIONS

THE LUCK OF ROARING CAMP

THERE was commotion in Roaring Camp. It could not have been a fight, for in 1850 that was not novel enough to have called together the entire settlement. The ditches and claims were not only deserted, but "Tuttle's grocery" had contributed its gamblers, who, it will be remembered, calmly continued their game the day that French Pete and Kanaka Joe shot each other to death over the bar in the front room. The whole camp was collected before a rude cabin on the outer edge of the clearing. Conversation was carried on in a low tone, but the name of a woman was frequently repeated. It was a name familiar enough in the camp,—"Cherokee Sal."

Perhaps the less said of her the better. She was a coarse, and, it is to be feared, a very sinful woman. But at that time she was the only woman in Roaring Camp, and was just then lying in sore extremity, when she most needed the ministration of her own sex. Dissolute, abandoned, and irreclaimable, she was yet suffering a martyrdom hard enough to bear even when veiled by sympathizing womanhood, but now terrible in her loneliness. The primal curse had come to her in that original isolation which must have made the punishment of the first transgression so dreadful. It was, perhaps, part of the expiation of her sin, that, at a moment when she most lacked her sex's intuitive tenderness

1

and care, she met only the half-contemptuous faces of her masculine associates. Yet a few of the spectators were, I think, touched by her sufferings. Sandy Tipton thought it was "rough on Sal," and, in the contemplation of her condition, for a moment rose superior to the fact that he had an ace and two bowers in his sleeve.

It will be seen, also, that the situation was novel. Deaths were by no means uncommon in Roaring Camp, but a birth was a new thing. People had been dismissed from the camp effectively, finally, and with no possibility of return; but this was the first time that anybody had been introduced *ab initio*. Hence the excitement.

"You go in there, Stumpy," said a prominent citizen known as "Kentuck," addressing one of the loungers. "Go in there, and see what you kin do. You've had experience in them things."

Perhaps there was a fitness in the selection. Stumpy, in other climes, had been the putative head of two families; in fact, it was owing to some legal informality in these proceedings that Roaring Camp—a city of refuge—was indebted to his company. The crowd approved the choice, and Stumpy was wise enough to bow to the majority. The door closed on the extempore surgeon and midwife, and Roaring Camp sat down outside, smoked its pipe, and awaited the issue.

The assemblage numbered about a hundred men. One or two of these were actual fugitives from justice, some were criminal, and all were reckless. Physically, they exhibited no indication of their past lives and character. The greatest scamp had a Raphael face, with a profusion of blond hair; Oakhurst, a gambler, had the melancholy air and intellectual abstraction of a Hamlet; the coolest and most courageous man was scarcely over five feet in height, with a soft voice and an embarrassed, timid manner. The term "roughs" applied to them was a distinction rather than a definition. Perhaps in the minor details of fingers, toes, ears, etc., the camp may have been deficient, but these slight omissions did not detract from their aggregate force. The strongest man had but three fingers on his right hand; the best shot had but one eye.

Such was the physical aspect of the men that were dispersed around the cabin. The camp lay in a triangular valley, between two hills and a river. The only outlet was a steep trail over the summit of a hill that faced the cabin, now illuminated by the rising moon. The suffering woman might have seen it from the rude bunk whereon she lay,— seen it winding like a silver thread until it was lost in the stars above.

A fire of withered pine-boughs added sociability to the gathering. By degrees the natural levity of Roaring Camp returned. Bets were freely offered and taken regarding the result. Three to five that "Sal would get through with it"; even, that the child would survive; side bets as to the sex and complexion of the coming stranger. In the midst of an excited discussion an exclamation came from those nearest the door, and the camp stopped to listen. Above the swaying and moaning of the pines, the swift rush of the river, and the crackling of the fire, rose a sharp, querulous cry,—a cry unlike anything heard before in the camp. The pines stopped moaning, the river ceased to rush, and the fire to crackle. It seemed as if Nature had stopped to listen too.

The camp rose to its feet as one man! It was proposed to explode a barrel of gunpowder, but, in consideration of the situation of the mother, better counsels prevailed, and

only a few revolvers were discharged; for, whether owing
to the rude surgery of the camp, or some other reason,
Cherokee Sal was sinking fast. Within an hour she had
climbed, as it were, that rugged road that led to the stars,
and so passed out of Roaring Camp, its sin and shame forever. I do not think that the announcement disturbed them
much, except in speculation as to the fate of the child. "Can
he live now?" was asked of Stumpy. The answer was doubtful. The only other being of Cherokee Sal's sex and maternal condition in the settlement was an ass. There was
some conjecture as to fitness, but the experiment was tried.
It was less problematical than the ancient treatment of
Romulus and Remus, and apparently as successful.

When these details were completed, which exhausted another hour, the door was opened, and the anxious crowd of
men who had already formed themselves into a queue, entered in single file. Beside the low bunk or shelf, on which
the figure of the mother was starkly outlined below the
blankets, stood a pine table. On this a candle-box was placed,
and within it, swathed in staring red flannel, lay the last
arrival at Roaring Camp. Beside the candle-box was placed
a hat. Its use was soon indicated. "Gentlemen," said
Stumpy, with a singular mixture of authority and *ex officio*
complacency—"Gentlemen will please pass in at the front
door, round the table, and out at the back door. Them as
wishes to contribute anything toward the orphan will find
a hat handy." The first man entered with his hat on; he
uncovered, however, as he looked about him, and so, unconsciously, set an example to the next. In such communities
good and bad actions are catching. As the procession filed
in, comments were audible,—criticisms addressed, perhaps,
rather to Stumpy, in the character of showman,—"Is that

him?" "mighty small specimen"; "has n't mor'n got the color"; "ain't bigger nor a derringer." The contributions were as characteristic: A silver tobacco-box; a doubloon; a navy revolver, silver mounted; a gold specimen; a very beautifully embroidered lady's handkerchief (from Oakhurst the gambler); a diamond breastpin; a diamond ring (suggested by the pin, with the remark from the giver that he "saw that pin and went two diamonds better"); a slung shot; a Bible (contributor not detected); a golden spur; a silver teaspoon (the initials, I regret to say, were not the giver's); a pair of surgeon's shears; a lancet; a Bank of England note for £5; and about $200 in loose gold and silver coin. During these proceedings Stumpy maintained a silence as impassive as the dead on his left, a gravity as inscrutable as that of the newly born on his right. Only one incident occurred to break the monotony of the curious procession. As Kentuck bent over the candle-box half curiously, the child turned, and, in a spasm of pain, caught at his groping finger, and held it fast for a moment. Kentuck looked foolish and embarrassed. Something like a blush tried to assert itself in his weather-beaten cheek. "The d—d little cuss!" he said, as he extricated his finger, with, perhaps, more tenderness and care than he might have been deemed capable of showing. He held that finger a little apart from its fellows as he went out, and examined it curiously. The examination provoked the same original remark in regard to the child. In fact, he seemed to enjoy repeating it. "He rastled with my finger," he remarked to Tipton, holding up the member, "the d—d little cuss!"

It was four o'clock before the camp sought repose. A light burnt in the cabin where the watchers sat, for Stumpy did not go to bed that night. Nor did Kentuck. He drank quite freely, and related with great gusto his experience, invariably ending with his characteristic condemnation of the new-comer. It seemed to relieve him of any unjust implication of sentiment, and Kentuck had the weaknesses of the nobler sex. When everybody else had gone to bed, he walked down to the river, and whistled reflectingly. Then he walked up the gulch, past the cabin, still whistling with demonstrative unconcern. At a large redwood tree he paused and retraced his steps, and again passed the cabin. Half-way down to the river's bank he again paused, and then returned and knocked at the door. It was opened by Stumpy. "How goes it?" said Kentuck, looking past Stumpy toward the candle-box. "All serene," replied Stumpy. "Anything up?" "Nothing." There was a pause —an embarrassing one—Stumpy still holding the door. Then Kentuck had recourse to his finger, which he held up to Stumpy. "Rastled with it,—the d—d little cuss," he said, and retired.

The next day Cherokee Sal had such rude sepulture as Roaring Camp afforded. After her body had been committed to the hillside, there was a formal meeting of the camp to discuss what should be done with her infant. A resolution to adopt it was unanimous and enthusiastic. But an animated discussion in regard to the manner and feasibility of providing for its wants at once sprung up. It was remarkable that the argument partook of none of those fierce personalities with which discussions were usually conducted at Roaring Camp. Tipton proposed that they should send the child to Red Dog,—a distance of forty miles,—where female attention could be procured. But the unlucky suggestion met with fierce and unanimous opposition. It was evident that no plan which entailed parting from their new acquisition would for a moment be entertained. "Besides," said Tom Ryder, "them fellows at Red Dog would swap it, and ring in somebody else on us." A disbelief in the honesty of other camps prevailed at Roaring Camp as in other places.

The introduction of a female nurse in the camp also met with objection. It was argued that no decent woman could be prevailed to accept Roaring Camp as her home, and the speaker urged that "they didn't want any more of the other kind." This unkind allusion to the defunct mother, harsh as it may seem, was the first spasm of propriety,—the first symptom of the camp's regeneration. Stumpy advanced nothing. Perhaps he felt a certain delicacy in interfering with the selection of a possible successor in office. But when questioned, he averred stoutly that he and "Jinny"—the mammal before alluded to—could manage to rear the child. There was something original, independent, and heroic about the plan that pleased the camp. Stumpy was retained. Certain articles were sent for to Sacramento. "Mind," said the treasurer, as he pressed a bag of gold-dust into the expressman's hand, "the best that can be got,—lace, you know, and filigree-work and frills,—d—m the cost!"

Strange to say, the child thrived. Perhaps the invigorating climate of the mountain camp was compensation for material deficiencies. Nature took the foundling to her broader breast. In that rare atmosphere of the Sierra foothills,—that air pungent with balsamic odor, that ethereal cordial at once bracing and exhilarating,—he may have found food and nourishment, or a subtle chemistry that transmuted asses' milk to lime and phosphorus. Stumpy inclined to the belief that it was the latter and good nursing. "Me and that ass," he would say, "has been father and mother to him! Don't you," he would add, apostrophizing the helpless bundle before him, "never go back on us."

By the time he was a month old, the necessity of giving him a name became apparent. He had generally been known as "the Kid," "Stumpy's boy," "the Cayote" (an allusion to his vocal powers), and even by Kentuck's endearing diminutive of "the d—d little cuss." But these were felt to be vague and unsatisfactory, and were at last dismissed under another influence. Gamblers and adventurers are generally superstitious, and Oakhurst one day declared that the baby had brought "the luck" to Roaring Camp. It was certain that of late they had been successful. "Luck" was the name agreed upon, with the prefix of Tommy for greater convenience. No allusion was made to the mother, and the father was unknown. "It's better," said the philosophical Oakhurst, "to take a fresh deal all round. Call him Luck, and start him fair." A day was accordingly set apart for the christening. What was meant by this ceremony the reader may imagine, who has already gathered some idea of the reckless irreverence of Roaring Camp. The master of ceremonies was one "Boston," a noted wag, and the occasion seemed to promise the greatest facetiousness. This ingenious satirist had spent two days in preparing a burlesque of the church service, with pointed local allusions. The choir was properly trained, and Sandy Tipton was to stand godfather. But after the procession had marched to the grove with music and banners, and the child had been deposited before a mock altar, Stumpy stepped before the expectant crowd. "It ain't my style to spoil fun, boys," said the little man, stoutly, eying the faces around him, "but it strikes me that this thing ain't exactly on the squar. It's playing it pretty low down on this yer baby to ring in

fun on him that he ain't going to understand. And ef there's
going to be any godfathers round, I'd like to see who's got
any better rights than me." A silence followed Stumpy's
speech. To the credit of all humorists be it said, that the
first man to acknowledge its justice was the satirist, thus
stopped of his fun. "But," said Stumpy, quickly, following
up his advantage, "we're here for a christening, and we'll
have it. I proclaim you Thomas Luck, according to the laws
of the United States and the State of California, so help me
God." It was the first time that the name of the Deity had
been uttered otherwise than profanely in the camp. The
form of christening was perhaps even more ludicrous than
the satirist had conceived, but, strangely enough, nobody
saw it and nobody laughed. "Tommy" was christened as
seriously as he would have been under a Christian roof, and
cried and was comforted in as orthodox fashion.

And so the work of regeneration began in Roaring Camp.
Almost imperceptibly a change came over the settlement.
The cabin assigned to "Tommy Luck"—or "The Luck," as
he was more frequently called—first showed signs of improvement. It was kept scrupulously clean and whitewashed. Then it was boarded, clothed, and papered. The
rosewood cradle—packed eighty miles by mule—had, in
Stumpy's way of putting it, "sorter killed the rest of the
furniture." So the rehabilitation of the cabin became a
necessity. The men who were in the habit of lounging in
at Stumpy's to see "how The Luck got on" seemed to appreciate the change, and, in self-defence, the rival establish-
ment of "Tuttle's grocery" bestirred itself, and imported a
carpet and mirrors. The reflections of the latter on the appearance of Roaring Camp tended to produce stricter habits
of personal cleanliness. Again, Stumpy imposed a kind of

quarantine upon those who aspired to the honor and privilege of holding "The Luck." It was a cruel mortification to Kentuck—who, in the carelessness of a large nature and the habits of frontier life, had begun to regard all garments as a second cuticle, which, like a snake's, only sloughed off through decay—to be debarred this privilege from certain prudential reasons. Yet such was the subtle influence of innovation that he thereafter appeared regularly every afternoon in a clean shirt, and face still shining from his ablutions. Nor were moral and social sanitary laws neglected. "Tommy," who was supposed to spend his whole existence in a persistent attempt to repose, must not be disturbed by noise. The shouting and yelling which had gained the camp its infelicitous title were not permitted within hearing distance of Stumpy's. The men conversed in whispers, or smoked with Indian gravity. Profanity was tacitly given up in these sacred precincts, and throughout the camp a popular form of expletive, known as "D—n the luck!" and "Curse the luck!" was abandoned, as having a new personal bearing. Vocal music was not interdicted, being supposed to have a soothing, tranquillizing quality, and one song, sung by "Man-o'-War Jack," an English sailor, from her Majesty's Australian colonies, was quite popular as a lullaby. It was a lugubrious recital of the exploits of "the Arethusa, Seventy-four," in a muffled minor, ending with a prolonged dying fall at the burden of each verse, "On b-o-o-o-ard of the Arethusa." It was a fine sight to see Jack holding The Luck, rocking from side to side as if with the motion of a ship, and crooning forth this naval ditty. Either through the peculiar rocking of Jack or the length of his song,—it contained ninety stanzas, and was continued with conscientious deliberation to the bitter end,—the lullaby generally had the desired effect. At such times the men would lie at full length under the trees, in the soft summer twilight, smoking their pipes and drinking in the melodious utterances. An indistinct idea that this was pastoral happiness pervaded the camp. "This 'ere kind o' think," said the Cockney Simmons, meditatively reclining on his elbow, "is 'evingly." It reminded him of Greenwich.

On the long summer days The Luck was usually carried to the gulch, from whence the golden store of Roaring Camp was taken. There, on a blanket spread over pine-boughs, he would lie while the men were working in the ditches below. Latterly, there was a rude attempt to decorate this bower with flowers and sweet-smelling shrubs, and generally some one would bring him a cluster of wild honeysuckles, azaleas, or the painted blossoms of Las Mariposas. The men had suddenly awakened to the fact that there were beauty and significance in these trifles, which they had so long trodden carelessly beneath their feet. A flake of glittering mica, a fragment of variegated quartz, a bright pebble from the bed of the creek, became beautiful to eyes thus cleared and strengthened, and were invariably put aside for "The Luck." It was wonderful how many treasures the woods and hillsides yielded that "would do for Tommy." Surrounded by playthings such as never child out of fairy-land had before, it is to be hoped that Tommy was content. He appeared to be securely happy—albeit there was an infantine gravity about him—a contemplative light in his round gray eyes—that sometimes worried Stumpy. He was always tractable and quiet, and it is recorded that once, having crept beyond his "corral,"—a hedge of tassellated pine-boughs, which surrounded his bed,—he dropped over the bank on his head in the soft earth, and remained with his mottled legs in the air in that position for at least five minutes with unflinching gravity. He was extricated without a murmur. I hesitate to record the many other instances of his sagacity, which rest, unfortunately, upon the statements of prejudiced friends. Some of them were not without a tinge of superstition. "I crep' up the bank just now," said Kentuck one day, in a breathless state of excitement, "and dern my skin if he wasn't a talking to a jaybird as was a sittin' on his lap. There they was, just as free and sociable as anything you please, a jawin' at each other just like two cherry-bums." Howbeit, whether creeping over the pine-boughs or lying lazily on his back blinking at the leaves above him, to him the birds sang, the squirrels chattered, and the flowers bloomed. Nature was his nurse and play-fellow. For him she would let slip between the leaves golden shafts of sunlight that fell just within his grasp; she would send wandering breezes to visit him with the balm of bay and resinous gums; to him the tall red-woods nodded familiarly and sleepily, the bumble-bees buzzed, and the rooks cawed a slumbrous accompaniment.

Such was the golden summer of Roaring Camp. They were "flush times,"—and the Luck was with them. The claims had yielded enormously. The camp was jealous of its privileges and looked suspiciously on strangers. No encouragement was given to immigration, and, to make their seclusion more perfect, the land on either side of the mountain wall that surrounded the camp they duly pre-empted. This, and a reputation for singular proficiency with the revolver, kept the reserve of Roaring Camp inviolate. The expressman—their only connecting link with the surrounding world—sometimes told wonderful stories of the camp. He would say, "They've a street up there in 'Roaring,' that would lay over any street in Red Dog. They've got vines and flowers round their houses, and they wash themselves twice a day. But they're mighty rough on strangers, and they worship an Ingin baby."

With the prosperity of the camp came a desire for further improvement. It was proposed to build a hotel in the following spring, and to invite one or two decent families to reside there for the sake of "The Luck,"—who might perhaps profit by female companionship. The sacrifice that this concession to the sex cost these men, who were fiercely sceptical in regard to its general virtue and usefulness, can only be accounted for by their affection for Tommy. A few still held out. But the resolve could not be carried into effect for three months, and the minority meekly yielded in the hope that something might turn up to prevent it. And it did.

The winter of 1851 will long be remembered in the foothills. The snow lay deep on the Sierras, and every mountain creek became a river, and every river a lake. Each gorge and gulch was transformed into a tumultuous watercourse that descended the hillsides, tearing down giant trees and scattering its drift and débris along the plain. Red Dog had been twice under water, and Roaring Camp had been forewarned. "Water put the gold into them gulches," said Stumpy. "It's been here once and will be here again!" And that night the North Fork suddenly leaped over its banks, and swept up the triangular valley of Roaring Camp.

In the confusion of rushing water, crushing trees, and crackling timber, and the darkness which seemed to flow with the water and blot out the fair valley, but little could be done to collect the scattered camp. When the morning broke, the cabin of Stumpy nearest the river-bank was gone. Higher up the gulch they found the body of its unlucky owner; but the pride, the hope, the joy, the Luck, of Roaring Camp had disappeared. They were returning with sad hearts, when a shout from the bank recalled them.

It was a relief-boat from down the river. They had picked up, they said, a man and an infant, nearly exhausted, about two miles below. Did anybody know them, and did they belong here?

It needed but a glance to show them Kentuck lying there, cruelly crushed and bruised, but still holding the Luck of Roaring Camp in his arms. As they bent over the strangely assorted pair, they saw that the child was cold and pulseless. "He is dead," said one. Kentuck opened his eyes. "Dead?" he repeated feebly. "Yes, my man, and you are dying too." A smile lit the eyes of the expiring Kentuck. "Dying," he repeated, "he's a taking me with him,—tell the boys I've got the Luck with me now"; and the strong man, clinging to the frail babe as a drowning man is said to cling to a straw, drifted away into the shadowy river that flows forever to the unknown sea.

THE OUTCASTS OF POKER FLAT

As Mr. John Oakhurst, gambler, stepped into the main street of Poker Flat on the morning of the twenty-third of November, 1850, he was conscious of a change in its moral atmosphere since the preceding night. Two or three men, conversing earnestly together, ceased as he approached, and exchanged significant glances. There was a Sabbath lull in the air, which, in a settlement unused to Sabbath influences, looked ominous.

Mr. Oakhurst's calm, handsome face betrayed small concern in these indications. Whether he was conscious of any predisposing cause, was another question. "I reckon they're after somebody," he reflected; "likely it's me." He returned to his pocket the handkerchief with which he had been whipping away the red dust of Poker Flat from his neat boots, and quietly discharged his mind of any further conjecture.

In point of fact, Poker Flat was "after somebody." It had lately suffered the loss of several thousand dollars, two valuable horses, and a prominent citizen. It was experiencing a spasm of virtuous reaction, quite as lawless and ungovernable as any of the acts that had provoked it. A secret committee had determined to rid the town of all improper persons. This was done permanently in regard of two men who were then hanging from the boughs of a sycamore in the gulch, and temporarily in the banishment of certain other objectionable characters. I regret to say that some of these were ladies. It is but due to the sex, however, to state that their impropriety was professional, and it was only in such easily established standards of evil that Poker Flat ventured to sit in judgment.

Mr. Oakhurst was right in supposing that he was included in this category. A few of the committee had urged hanging him as a possible example, and a sure method of reimbursing themselves from his pockets of the sums he had won from them. "It's agin justice," said Jim Wheeler, "to let this yer young man from Roaring Camp—an entire stranger—carry away our money." But a crude sentiment of equity residing in the breasts of those who had been fortunate enough to win from Mr. Oakhurst overruled this narrower local prejudice.

Mr. Oakhurst received his sentence with philosophic

calmness, none the less coolly that he was aware of the hesitation of his judges. He was too much of a gambler not to accept Fate. With him life was at best an uncertain game, and he recognized the usual percentage in favor of the dealer.

A body of armed men accompanied the deported wickedness of Poker Flat to the outskirts of the settlement. Besides Mr. Oakhurst, who was known to be a coolly desperate man, and for whose intimidation the armed escort was intended, the expatriated party consisted of a young woman familiarly known as "The Duchess"; another, who had won the title of "Mother Shipton"; and "Uncle Billy," a suspected sluice-robber and confirmed drunkard. The cavalcade provoked no comments from the spectators, nor was any word uttered by the escort. Only, when the gulch which marked the uttermost limit of Poker Flat was reached, the leader spoke briefly and to the point. The exiles were forbidden to return at the peril of their lives.

As the escort disappeared, their pent-up feelings found vent in a few hysterical tears from the Duchess, some bad language from Mother Shipton, and a Parthian volley of expletives from Uncle Billy. The philosophic Oakhurst alone remained silent. He listened calmly to Mother Shipton's desire to cut somebody's heart out, to the repeated statements of the Duchess that she would die in the road, and to the alarming oaths that seemed to be bumped out of Uncle Billy as he rode forward. With the easy good-humor characteristic of his class, he insisted upon exchanging his own riding-horse, "Five Spot," for the sorry mule which the Duchess rode. But even this act did not draw the party into any closer sympathy. The young woman readjusted her somewhat draggled plumes with a feeble, faded coquetry; Mother Shipton eyed the possessor of "Five Spot" with malevolence, and Uncle Billy included the whole party in one sweeping anathema.

The road to Sandy Bar—a camp that, not having as yet experienced the regenerating influences of Poker Flat, consequently seemed to offer some invitation to the emigrants —lay over a steep mountain range. It was distant a day's severe travel. In that advanced season, the party soon passed out of the moist, temperate regions of the foot-hills into the dry, cold, bracing air of the Sierras. The trail was narrow and difficult. At noon the Duchess, rolling out of her saddle upon the ground, declared her intention of going no farther, and the party halted.

The spot was singularly wild and impressive. A wooded amphitheatre, surrounded on three sides by precipitous cliffs of naked granite, sloped gently toward the crest of another precipice that overlooked the valley. It was, undoubtedly, the most suitable spot for a camp, had camping been advisable. But Mr. Oakhurst knew that scarcely half the journey to Sandy Bar was accomplished, and the party were not equipped or provisioned for delay. This fact he pointed out to his companions curtly, with a philosophic commentary on the folly of "throwing up their hand before the game was played out." But they were furnished with liquor, which in this emergency stood them in place of food, fuel, rest, and prescience. In spite of his remonstrances, it was not long before they were more or less under its influence. Uncle Billy passed rapidly from a bellicose state into one of stupor, the Duchess became maudlin, and Mother Shipton snored. Mr. Oakhurst alone remained erect, leaning against a rock, calmly surveying them.

Mr. Oakhurst did not drink. It interfered with a profession which required coolness, impassiveness, and presence of mind, and, in his own language, he "couldn't afford it." As he gazed at his recumbent fellow-exiles, the loneliness begotten of his pariah-trade, his habits of life, his very vices, for the first time seriously oppressed him. He bestirred himself in dusting his black clothes, washing his hands and face, and other acts characteristic of his studiously neat habits, and for a moment forgot his annoyance. The thought of deserting his weaker and more pitiable companions never perhaps occurred to him. Yet he could not help feeling the want of that excitement which, singularly enough, was most conducive to that calm equanimity for which he was notorious. He looked at the gloomy walls that rose a thousand feet sheer above the circling pines around him; at the sky, ominously clouded; at the valley below, already deepening into shadow. And, doing so, suddenly he heard his own name called.

A horseman slowly ascended the trail. In the fresh, open face of the new-comer Mr. Oakhurst recognized Tom Simson, otherwise known as "The Innocent" of Sandy Bar. He had met him some months before over a "little game," and had, with perfect equanimity, won the entire fortune— amounting to some forty dollars—of that guileless youth. After the game was finished, Mr. Oakhurst drew the youthful speculator behind the door and thus addressed him: "Tommy, you're a good little man, but you can't gamble worth a cent. Don't try it over again." He then handed him his money back, pushed him gently from the room, and so made a devoted slave of Tom Simson.

There was a remembrance of this in his boyish and enthusiastic greeting of Mr. Oakhurst. He had started, he said, to go to Poker Flat to seek his fortune. "Alone?"

No, not exactly alone; in fact (a giggle), he had run away with Piney Woods. Didn't Mr. Oakhurst remember Piney? She that used to wait on the table at the Temperance House? They had been engaged a long time, but old Jake Woods had objected, and so they had run away, and were going to Poker Flat to be married, and here they were. And they were tired out, and how lucky it was they had found a place to camp and company. All this the Innocent delivered rapidly, while Piney, a stout, comely damsel of fifteen, emerged from behind the pine-tree, where she had been blushing unseen, and rode to the side of her lover.

Mr. Oakhurst seldom troubled himself with sentiment, still less with propriety; but he had a vague idea that the situation was not fortunate. He retained, however, his presence of mind sufficiently to kick Uncle Billy, who was about to say something, and Uncle Billy was sober enough to recognize in Mr. Oakhurst's kick a superior power that would not bear trifling. He then endeavored to dissuade Tom Simson from delaying further, but in vain. He even pointed out the fact that there was no provision, nor means of making a camp. But, unluckily, the Innocent met this objection by assuring the party that he was provided with an extra mule loaded with provisions, and by the discovery of a rude attempt at a log-house near the trail. "Piney can stay with Mrs. Oakhurst," said the Innocent, pointing to the Duchess, "and I can shift for myself."

Nothing but Mr. Oakhurst's admonishing foot saved Uncle Billy from bursting into a roar of laughter. As it was, he felt compelled to retire up the cañon until he could recover his gravity. There he confided the joke to the tall pine-trees, with many slaps of his leg, contortions of his face, and the usual profanity. But when he returned to the party, he found them seated by a fire—for the air had grown strangely chill and the sky overcast—in apparently amicable conversation. Piney was actually talking in an impulsive, girlish fashion to the Duchess, who was listening with an interest and animation she had not shown for many days. The Innocent was holding forth, apparently with equal effect, to Mr. Oakhurst and Mother Shipton, who was actually relaxing into amiability. "Is this yer a d—d picnic?" said Uncle Billy, with inward scorn, as he surveyed the sylvan group, the glancing firelight, and the tethered animals in the foreground. Suddenly an idea mingled with the alcoholic fumes that disturbed his brain. It was apparently of a jocular nature, for he felt impelled to slap his leg again and cram his fist into his mouth.

As the shadows crept slowly up the mountain, a slight breeze rocked the tops of the pine-trees, and moaned through their long and gloomy aisles. The ruined cabin, patched and covered with pine-boughs, was set apart for the ladies. As the lovers parted, they unaffectedly exchanged a kiss, so honest and sincere that it might have been heard above the swaying pines. The frail Duchess and the malevolent Mother Shipton were probably too stunned to remark upon this last evidence of simplicity, and so turned without a word to the hut. The fire was replenished, the men lay down before the door, and in a few minutes were asleep.

Mr. Oakhurst was a light sleeper. Toward morning he awoke benumbed and cold. As he stirred the dying fire, the wind, which was now blowing strongly, brought to his cheek that which caused the blood to leave it,—snow!

He started to his feet with the intention of awakening the sleepers, for there was no time to lose. But turning to where Uncle Billy had been lying, he found him gone. A suspicion

"He rastled with my finger, the d—d little cuss!" Illustration by Frederic Remington for *The Luck of Roaring Camp*. (p. 5)

leaped to his brain and a curse to his lips. He ran to the spot where the mules had been tethered; they were no longer there. The tracks were already rapidly disappearing in the snow.

The momentary excitement brought Mr. Oakhurst back to the fire with his usual calm. He did not waken the sleepers. The Innocent slumbered peacefully, with a smile on his good-humored, freckled face; the virgin Piney slept beside her frailer sisters as sweetly as though attended by celestial guardians, and Mr. Oakhurst, drawing his blanket over his shoulders, stroked his mustaches and waited for the dawn. It came slowly in a whirling mist of snow-flakes, that dazzled and confused the eye. What could be seen of the landscape appeared magically changed. He looked over the valley, and summed up the present and future in two words, —"snowed in!"

A careful inventory of the provisions, which, fortunately for the party, had been stored within the hut, and so escaped the felonious fingers of Uncle Billy, disclosed the fact that with care and prudence they might last ten days longer. "That is," said Mr. Oakhurst, *sotto voce* to the Innocent, "if you're willing to board us. If you ain't—and perhaps you'd better not—you can wait till Uncle Billy gets back with provisions." For some occult reason, Mr. Oakhurst could not bring himself to disclose Uncle Billy's rascality, and so offered the hypothesis that he had wandered from the camp and had accidentally stampeded the animals. He dropped a warning to the Duchess and Mother Shipton, who of course knew the facts of their associate's defection. "They'll find out the truth about us *all* when they find out anything," he added, significantly, "and there's no good frightening them now."

Tom Simson not only put all his worldly store at the disposal of Mr. Oakhurst, but seemed to enjoy the prospect of their enforced seclusion. "We'll have a good camp for a week, and then the snow'll melt, and we'll all go back together." The cheerful gayety of the young man, and Mr. Oakhurst's calm infected the others. The Innocent, with the aid of pine-boughs, extemporized a thatch for the roofless cabin, and the Duchess directed Piney in the rearrangement of the interior with a taste and tact that opened the blue eyes of that provincial maiden to their fullest extent. "I reckon now you're used to fine things at Poker Flat," said Piney. The Duchess turned away sharply to conceal something that reddened her cheeks through its professional tint, and Mother Shipton requested Piney not to "chatter." But when Mr. Oakhurst returned from a weary search for the trail, he heard the sound of happy laughter echoed from the rocks. He stopped in some alarm, and his thoughts first naturally reverted to the whiskey, which he had prudently *cachéd*. "And yet it don't somehow sound like whiskey," said the gambler. It was not until he caught sight of the blazing fire through the still-blinding storm and the group around it that he settled to the conviction that it was "square fun."

Whether Mr. Oakhurst had *cachéd* his cards with the whiskey as something debarred the free access of the community, I cannot say. It was certain that, in Mother Shipton's words, he "didn't say cards once" during that evening. Haply the time was beguiled by an accordion, produced somewhat ostentatiously by Tom Simson from his pack. Notwithstanding some difficulties attending the manipulation of this instrument, Piney Woods managed to pluck several reluctant melodies from its keys, to an accompaniment by the Innocent on a pair of bone castinets. But the crowning festivity of the evening was reached in a rude camp-meeting hymn, which the lovers, joining hands, sang with great earnestness and vociferation. I fear that a certain defiant tone and Covenanter's swing to its chorus, rather than any devotional quality, caused it speedily to infect the others, who at last joined in the refrain:—

> "I'm proud to live in the service of the Lord,
> And I'm bound to die in His army."

The pines rocked, the storm eddied and whirled above the miserable group, and the flames of their altar leaped heavenward, as if in token of the snow.

At midnight the storm abated, the rolling clouds parted, and the stars glittered keenly above the sleeping camp. Mr. Oakhurst, whose professional habits had enabled him to live on the smallest possible amount of sleep, in dividing the watch with Tom Simson, somehow managed to take upon himself the greater part of that duty. He excused himself to the Innocent, by saying that he had "often been a week without sleep." "Doing what?" asked Tom. "Poker!" replied Oakhurst, sententiously; "when a man gets a streak of luck,—nigger-luck,—he don't get tired. The luck gives in first. Luck," continued the gambler, reflectively, "is a mighty queer thing. All you know about it for certain is that it's bound to change. And it's finding out when it's going to change that makes you. We've had a streak of bad luck since we left Poker Flat,—you come along, and slap you get into it, too. If you can hold your cards right along you're all right. For," added the gambler, with cheerful irrelevance,—

"'I'm proud to live in the service of the Lord,
And I'm bound to die in His army.'"

The third day came, and the sun, looking through the white-curtained valley, saw the outcasts divide their slowly decreasing store of provisions for the morning meal. It was one of the peculiarities of that mountain climate that its rays diffused a kindly warmth over the wintry landscape, as if in regretful commiseration of the past. But it revealed drift on drift of snow piled high around the hut,—a hopeless, uncharted, trackless sea of white lying below the rocky shores to which the castaways still clung. Through the marvellously clear air the smoke of the pastoral village of Poker Flat rose miles away. Mother Shipton saw it, and from a remote pinnacle of her rocky fastness, hurled in that direction a final malediction. It was her last vituperative attempt, and perhaps for that reason was invested with a certain degree of sublimity. It did her good, she privately informed the Duchess. "Just you go out there and cuss, and see." She then set herself to the task of amusing "the child," as she and the Duchess were pleased to call Piney. Piney was no chicken, but it was a soothing and original theory of the pair thus to account for the fact that she didn't swear and wasn't improper.

When night crept up again through the gorges, the reedy notes of the accordion rose and fell in fitful spasms and long-drawn gasps by the flickering camp-fire. But music failed to fill entirely the aching void left by insufficient food, and a new diversion was proposed by Piney,—story-telling. Neither Mr. Oakhurst nor his female companions caring to relate their personal experiences, this plan would have failed, too, but for the Innocent. Some months before he had chanced upon a stray copy of Mr. Pope's ingenious translation of the Iliad. He now proposed to narrate the principal incidents of that poem—having thoroughly mastered the argument and fairly forgotten the words—in the current vernacular of Sandy Bar. And so for the rest of that night the Homeric demigods again walked the earth. Trojan bully and wily Greek wrestled in the winds, and the great pines in the cañon seemed to bow to the wrath of the son of Peleus. Mr. Oakhurst listened with quiet satisfaction. Most especially was he interested in the fate of "Ash-heels," as the innocent persisted in denominating the "swift-footed Achilles."

So with small food and much of Homer and the accordion, a week passed over the heads of the outcasts. The sun again forsook them, and again from leaden skies the snow-flakes were sifted over the land. Day by day closer around them drew the snowy circle, until at last they looked from their prison over drifted walls of dazzling white, that towered twenty feet above their heads. It became more and more difficult to replenish their fires, even from the fallen trees beside them, now half hidden in the drifts. And yet no one complained. The lovers turned from the dreary prospect and looked into each other's eyes, and were happy. Mr. Oakhurst settled himself coolly to the losing game before him. The Duchess, more cheerful than she had been, assumed the care of Piney. Only Mother Shipton—once the strongest of the party—seemed to sicken and fade. At midnight on the tenth day she called Oakhurst to her side. "I'm going," she said, in a voice of querulous weakness, "but don't say anything about it. Don't waken the kids. Take the bundle from under my head and open it." Mr. Oakhurst did so. It contained Mother Shipton's rations for the last week, untouched. "Give 'em to the child," she said, pointing to the sleeping Piney. "You've starved yourself," said the gambler. "That's what they call it," said the woman, querulously, as she lay down again, and, turning her face to the wall, passed quietly away.

The accordion and the bones were put aside that day, and Homer was forgotten. When the body of Mother Shipton had been committed to the snow, Mr. Oakhurst took the Innocent aside, and showed him a pair of snow-shoes, which he had fashioned from the old pack-saddle. "There's one chance in a hundred to save her yet," he said, pointing to Piney; "but it's there," he added, pointing toward Poker Flat. "If you can reach there in two days she's safe." "And you?" asked Tom Simson. "I'll stay here," was the curt reply.

The lovers parted with a long embrace. "You are not going, too?" said the Duchess, as she saw Mr. Oakhurst apparently waiting to accompany him. "As far as the cañon," he replied. He turned suddenly, kissed the Duchess, leaving her pallid face aflame, and her trembling limbs rigid with amazement.

Night came, but not Mr. Oakhurst. It brought the storm again and the whirling snow. Then the Duchess, feeding the fire, found that some one had quietly piled beside the hut enough fuel to last a few days longer. The tears rose to her eyes, but she hid them from Piney.

The women slept but little. In the morning, looking into each other's faces, they read their fate. Neither spoke; but Piney, accepting the position of the stronger, drew near and placed her arm around the Duchess's waist. They kept this attitude for the rest of the day. That night the storm reached its greatest fury, and, rending asunder the protecting pines, invaded the very hut.

Toward morning they found themselves unable to feed the fire, which gradually died away. As the embers slowly blackened, the Duchess crept closer to Piney, and broke the silence of many hours: "Piney, can you pray?" "No, dear," said Piney, simply. The Duchess, without knowing exactly why, felt relieved, and, putting her head upon Piney's shoulder, spoke no more. And so reclining, the younger and purer pillowing the head of her soiled sister upon her virgin breast, they fell asleep.

The wind lulled as if it feared to waken them. Feathery drifts of snow, shaken from the long pine-boughs, flew like white-winged birds, and settled about them as they slept. The moon through the rifted clouds looked down upon what had been the camp. But all human stain, all trace of earthly travail, was hidden beneath the spotless mantle mercifully flung from above.

They slept all that day and the next, nor did they waken when voices and footsteps broke the silence of the camp. And when pitying fingers brushed the snow from their wan faces, you could scarcely have told from the equal peace that dwelt upon them, which was she that had sinned. Even the law of Poker Flat recognized this, and turned away, leaving them still locked in each other's arms.

But at the head of the gulch, on one of the largest pine-trees, they found the deuce of clubs pinned to the bark with a bowie-knife. It bore the following, written in pencil, in a firm hand:—

†

Beneath This Tree
Lies the Body
of
JOHN OAKHURST,
Who Struck a Streak of Bad Luck
on the 23d of November, 1850,
and
Handed in His Checks
on the 7th December, 1850.

⸸

And pulseless and cold, with a Derringer by his side and a bullet in his heart, though still calm as in life, beneath the snow lay he who was at once the strongest and yet the weakest of the outcasts of Poker Flat.

MIGGLES

WE were eight, including the driver. We had not spoken during the passage of the last six miles, since the jolting of the heavy vehicle over the roughening road had spoiled the Judge's last poetical quotation. The tall man beside the Judge was asleep, his arm passed through the swaying strap and his head resting upon it,—altogether a limp, helpless-looking object, as if he had hanged himself and been cut down too late. The French lady on the back seat was asleep, too, yet in a half-conscious propriety of attitude, shown even in the disposition of the handkerchief which she held to her forehead and which partially veiled her face. The lady from Virginia City, travelling with her husband, had long since lost all individuality in a wild confusion of ribbons, veils, furs, and shawls. There was no sound but the rattling of wheels and the dash of rain upon the roof. Suddenly the stage stopped and we became dimly aware of voices. The driver was evidently in the midst of an exciting colloquy with some one in the road,—a colloquy of which such fragments as "bridge gone," "twenty feet of water," "can't pass," were occasionally distinguishable above the storm. Then came a lull, and a mysterious voice from the road shouted the parting adjuration,—

"Try Miggles's."

We caught a glimpse of our leaders as the vehicle slowly turned, of a horseman vanishing through the rain, and we were evidently on our way to Miggles's.

Who and where was Miggles? The Judge, our authority, did not remember the name, and he knew the country thoroughly. The Washoe traveller thought Miggles must keep a hotel. We only knew that we were stopped by high water in front and rear, and that Miggles was our rock of refuge. A ten minutes' splashing through a tangled by-road, scarcely wide enough for the stage, and we drew up before a barred and boarded gate in a wide stone wall or fence about eight feet high. Evidently Miggles's, and evidently Miggles did not keep a hotel.

The driver got down and tried the gate. It was securely locked.

"Miggles! O Miggles!"

No answer.

"Migg-ells! You Miggles!" continued the driver, with rising wrath.

"Migglesy!" joined in the expressman, persuasively. "O Miggy! Mig!"

But no reply came from the apparently insensate Miggles. The Judge, who had finally got the window down, put his head out and propounded a series of questions, which if answered categorically would have undoubtedly elucidated the whole mystery, but which the driver evaded by replying that "if we didn't want to sit in the coach all night, we had better rise up and sing out for Miggles."

So we rose up and called on Miggles in chorus; then separately. And when we had finished, a Hibernian fellow-passenger from the roof called for "Maygells!" whereat we all laughed. While we were laughing, the driver cried "Shoo!"

We listened. To our infinite amazement the chorus of "Miggles" was repeated from the other side of the wall, even to the final and supplemental "Maygells."

"Extraordinary echo," said the Judge.

"Extraordinary d—d skunk!" roared the driver, contemptuously. "Come out of that, Miggles, and show yourself! Be a man, Miggles! Don't hide in the dark; I wouldn't if I were you, Miggles," continued Yuba Bill, now dancing about in an excess of fury.

"Miggles!" continued the voice, "O Miggles!"

"My good man! Mr. Myghail!" said the Judge, softening the asperities of the name as much as possible. "Consider the inhospitality of refusing shelter from the inclemency of the weather to helpless females. Really, my dear sir—" But a succession of "Miggles," ending in a burst of laughter, drowned his voice.

Yuba Bill hesitated no longer. Taking a heavy stone from the road, he battered down the gate, and with the expressman entered the enclosure. We followed. Nobody was to be seen. In the gathering darkness all that we could distinguish was that we were in a garden—from the rosebushes that scattered over us a minute spray from their

"It was a fine sight to see Jack holding The Luck, rocking from side to side as if with the motion of a ship." Illustration by Pierre Falké for *The Luck of Roaring Camp* in *The Wild West*, published by Harrison of Paris. (*p. 10*)

dripping leaves—and before a long, rambling wooden building.

"Do you know this Miggles?" asked the Judge of Yuba Bill.

"No, nor don't want to," said Bill, shortly, who felt the Pioneer Stage Company insulted in his person by the contumacious Miggles.

"But, my dear sir," expostulated the Judge, as he thought of the barred gate.

"Lookee here," said Yuba Bill, with fine irony, "hadn't you better go back and sit in the coach till yer introduced? I'm going in," and he pushed open the door of the building.

A long room lighted only by the embers of a fire that was dying on the large hearth at its further extremity; the walls curiously papered, and the flickering firelight bringing out its grotesque pattern; somebody sitting in a large arm-chair by the fireplace. All this we saw as we crowded together into the room, after the driver and expressman.

"Hello, be you Miggles?" said Yuba Bill to the solitary occupant.

The figure neither spoke nor stirred. Yuba Bill walked wrathfully toward it, and turned the eye of his coach-lantern upon its face. It was a man's face, prematurely old and wrinkled, with very large eyes, in which there was that expression of perfectly gratuitous solemnity which I had sometimes seen in an owl's. The large eyes wandered from Bill's face to the lantern, and finally fixed their gaze on that luminous object, without further recognition.

Bill restrained himself with an effort.

"Miggles! Be you deaf? You ain't dumb anyhow, you know"; and Yuba Bill shook the insensate figure by the shoulder.

To our great dismay, as Bill removed his hand, the venerable stranger apparently collapsed,—sinking into half his size and an undistinguishable heap of clothing.

"Well, dern my skin," said Bill, looking appealingly at us, and hopelessly retiring from the contest.

The Judge now stepped forward, and we lifted the mysterious invertebrate back into his original position. Bill was dismissed with the lantern to reconnoitre, for it was evident that from the helplessness of this solitary man there must be attendants near at hand, and we all drew around the fire. The Judge, who had regained his authority, and had never lost his conversational amiability,—standing before us with his back to the hearth,—charged us, as an imaginary jury, as follows:—

"It is evident that either our distinguished friend here has reached that condition described by Shakespeare as 'the sere and yellow leaf,' or has suffered some premature abatement of his mental and physical faculties. Whether he is really the Miggles—"

Here he was interrupted by "Miggles! O Miggles! Migglesy! Mig!" and, in fact, the whole chorus of Miggles in very much the same key as it had once before been delivered unto us.

We gazed at each other for a moment in some alarm. The Judge, in particular, vacated his position quickly, as the voice seemed to come directly over his shoulder. The cause, however, was soon discovered in a large magpie who was perched upon a shelf over the fireplace, and who immediately relapsed into a sepulchral silence, which contrasted singularly with his previous volubility. It was, undoubtedly, his voice which we had heard in the road, and our friend in the chair was not responsible for the discourtesy. Yuba

Bill, who re-entered the room after an unsuccessful search, was loath to accept the explanation, and still eyed the helpless sitter with suspicion. He had found a shed in which he had put up his horses, but he came back dripping and sceptical. "Thar ain't nobody but him within ten mile of the shanty, and that 'ar d—d old skeesicks knows it."

But the faith of the majority proved to be securely based. Bill had scarcely ceased growling before we heard a quick step upon the porch, the trailing of a wet skirt, the door was flung open, and with a flash of white teeth, a sparkle of dark eyes, and an utter absence of ceremony or diffidence, a young woman entered, shut the door, and, panting, leaned back against it.

"O, if you please, I'm Miggles!"

And this was Miggles! this bright-eyed, full-throated young woman, whose wet gown of coarse blue stuff could not hide the beauty of the feminine curves to which it clung; from the chestnut crown of whose head, topped by a man's oil-skin sou'wester, to the little feet and ankles, hidden somewhere in the recesses of her boy's brogans, all was grace;—this was Miggles, laughing at us, too, in the most airy, frank, off-hand manner imaginable.

"You see, boys," said she, quite out of breath, and holding one little hand against her side, quite unheeding the speechless discomfiture of our party, or the complete demoralization of Yuba Bill, whose features had relaxed into an expression of gratuitous and imbecile cheerfulness,—"you see, boys, I was mor'n two miles away when you passed down the road. I thought you might pull up here, and so I ran the whole way, knowing nobody was home but Jim,—and—and—I'm out of breath—and—that lets me out."

And here Miggles caught her dripping oil-skin hat from

her head, with a mischievous swirl that scattered a shower
of rain-drops over us; attempted to put back her hair;
dropped two hair-pins in the attempt; laughed and sat down
beside Yuba Bill, with her hands crossed lightly on her lap.

The Judge recovered himself first, and essayed an extravagant compliment.

"I'll trouble you for that thar har-pin," said Miggles,
gravely. Half a dozen hands were eagerly stretched forward; the missing hair-pin was restored to its fair owner;
and Miggles, crossing the room, looked keenly in the face of
the invalid. The solemn eyes looked back at hers with an expression we had never seen before. Life and intelligence
seemed to struggle back into the rugged face. Miggles
laughed again,—it was a singularly eloquent laugh,—and
turned her black eyes and white teeth once more towards us.

"This afflicted person is—" hesitated the Judge.

"Jim," said Miggles.

"Your father?"

"No."

"Brother?"

"No."

"Husband?"

Miggles darted a quick, half-defiant glance at the two
lady passengers who I had noticed did not participate in the
general masculine admiration of Miggles, and said, gravely,
"No; it's Jim."

There was an awkward pause. The lady passengers moved
closer to each other; the Washoe husband looked abstract-
edly at the fire; and the tall man apparently turned his eyes
inward for self-support at this emergency. But Miggles's
laugh, which was very infectious, broke the silence.

"Come," she said briskly, "you must be hungry. Who'll bear a hand to help me get tea?"

She had no lack of volunteers. In a few moments Yuba Bill was engaged like Caliban in bearing logs for this Miranda; the expressman was grinding coffee on the veranda; to myself the arduous duty of slicing bacon was assigned, and the Judge lent each man his good-humored and voluble counsel. And when Miggles, assisted by the Judge and our Hibernian "deck passenger," set the table with all the available crockery, we had become quite joyous, in spite of the rain that beat against windows, the wind that whirled down the chimney, the two ladies who whispered together in the corner, or the magpie who uttered a satirical and croaking commentary on their conversation from his perch above. In the now bright, blazing fire we could see that the walls were papered with illustrated journals, arranged with feminine taste and discrimination. The furniture was extemporized, and adapted from candle-boxes and packing-cases, and covered with gay calico, or the skin of some animal. The arm-chair of the helpless Jim was an ingenious variation of a flour-barrel. There was neatness, and even a taste for the picturesque, to be seen in the few details of the long low room.

The meal was a culinary success. But more, it was a social triumph,—chiefly, I think, owing to the rare tact of Miggles in guiding the conversation, asking all the questions herself, yet bearing throughout a frankness that rejected the idea of any concealment on her own part, so that we talked of ourselves, of our prospects, of the journey, of the weather, of each other,—of everything but our host and hostess. It must be confessed that Miggles's conversation was never elegant, rarely grammatical, and that at times she employed expletives, the use of which had generally been yielded to our sex. But they were delivered with such a lighting up of teeth and eyes, and were usually followed by a laugh—a laugh peculiar to Miggles—so frank and honest that it seemed to clear the moral atmosphere.

Once, during the meal, we heard a noise like the rubbing of a heavy body against the outer walls of the house. This was shortly followed by a scratching and sniffling at the door. "That's Joaquin," said Miggles, in reply to our questioning glances; "would you like to see him?" Before we could answer she had opened the door, and disclosed a half-grown grizzly, who instantly raised himself on his haunches, with his forepaws hanging down in the popular attitude of mendicancy, and looked admiringly at Miggles, with a very singular resemblance in his manner to Yuba Bill. "That's my watch-dog," said Miggles, in explanation. "O, he don't bite," she added, as the two lady passengers fluttered into a corner. "Does he, old Toppy?" (the latter remark being addressed directly to the sagacious Joaquin.) "I tell you what, boys," continued Miggles, after she had fed and closed the door on *Ursa Minor,* "you were in big luck that Joaquin was n't hanging round when you dropped in to-night." "Where was he?" asked the Judge. "With me," said Miggles. "Lord love you; he trots round with me nights like as if he was a man."

We were silent for a few moments, and listened to the wind. Perhaps we all had the same picture before us,—of Miggles walking through the rainy woods, with her savage guardian at her side. The Judge, I remember, said something about Una and her lion; but Miggles received it as she did other compliments, with quiet gravity. Whether she was altogether unconscious of the admiration she excited,—she could hardly have been oblivious of Yuba Bill's adoration,—I know not; but her very frankness suggested a perfect sexual equality that was cruelly humiliating to the younger members of our party.

The incident of the bear did not add anything in Miggles's favor to the opinions of those of her own sex who were present. In fact, the repast over, a chillness radiated from the two lady passengers that no pine-boughs brought in by Yuba Bill and cast as a sacrifice upon the hearth could wholly overcome. Miggles felt it; and, suddenly declaring that it was time to "turn in," offered to show the ladies to their bed in an adjoining room. "You, boys, will have to camp out here by the fire as well as you can," she added, "for thar ain't but the one room."

Our sex—by which, my dear sir, I allude of course to the stronger portion of humanity—has been generally relieved from the imputation of curiosity, or a fondness for gossip. Yet I am constrained to say, that hardly had the door closed on Miggles than we crowded together, whispering, snickering, smiling, and exchanging suspicions, surmises, and a thousand speculations in regard to our pretty hostess and her singular companion. I fear that we even hustled that imbecile paralytic, who sat like a voiceless Memnon in our midst, gazing with the serene indifference of the Past in his passionless eyes upon our wordy counsels. In the midst of an exciting discussion the door opened again, and Miggles re-entered.

But not, apparently, the same Miggles who a few hours before had flashed upon us. Her eyes were downcast, and as she hesitated for a moment on the threshold, with a blanket on her arm, she seemed to have left behind her the frank fearlessness which had charmed us a moment before.

Coming into the room, she drew a low stool beside the paralytic's chair, sat down, drew the blanket over her shoulders, and saying, "If it's all the same to you, boys, as we're rather crowded, I'll stop here to-night," took the invalid's withered hand in her own, and turned her eyes upon the dying fire. An instinctive feeling that this was only premonitory to more confidential relations, and perhaps some shame at our previous curiosity, kept us silent. The rain still beat upon the roof, wandering gusts of wind stirred the embers into momentary brightness, until, in a lull of the elements, Miggles suddenly lifted up her head, and, throwing her hair over her shoulder, turned her face upon the group and asked,—

"Is there any of you that knows me?"

There was no reply.

"Think again! I lived at Marysville in '53. Everybody knew me there, and everybody had the right to know me. I kept the Polka Saloon until I came to live with Jim. That's six years ago. Perhaps I've changed some."

The absence of recognition may have disconcerted her. She turned her head to the fire again, and it was some seconds before she again spoke, and then more rapidly:—

"Well, you see I thought some of you must have known me. There's no great harm done, anyway. What I was going to say was this: Jim here"—she took his hand in both of hers as she spoke—"used to know me, if you didn't, and spent a heap of money upon me. I reckon he spent all he had. And one day—it's six years ago this winter—Jim came into my back room, sat down on my sofy, like as you see him in that chair, and never moved again without help. He was struck all of a heap, and never seemed to know what ailed him. The doctors came and said as how it was

caused all along of his way of life,—for Jim was mighty
free and wild like,—and that he would never get better, and
could n't last long anyway. They advised me to send him
to Frisco to the hospital, for he was no good to any one and
would be a baby all his life. Perhaps it was something in
Jim's eye, perhaps it was that I never had a baby, but I
said 'No.' I was rich then, for I was popular with everybody,—gentlemen like yourself, sir, came to see me,—and
I sold out my business and bought this yer place, because
it was sort of out of the way of travel, you see, and I
brought my baby here."

With a woman's intuitive tact and poetry, she had, as
she spoke, slowly shifted her position so as to bring the mute
figure of the ruined man between her and her audience, hiding in the shadow behind it, as if she offered it as a tacit
apology for her actions. Silent and expressionless, it yet
spoke for her; helpless, crushed, and smitten with the Divine thunderbolt, it still stretched an invisible arm around
her.

Hidden in the darkness, but still holding his hand, she
went on:—

"It was a long time before I could get the hang of things
about yer, for I was used to company and excitement. I
could n't get any woman to help me, and a man I dursent
trust; but what with the Indians hereabout, who'd do odd
jobs for me, and having everything sent from the North
Fork, Jim and I managed to worry through. The Doctor
would run up from Sacramento once in a while. He'd ask
to see 'Miggles's baby,' as he called Jim, and when he'd go
away, he'd say, 'Miggles; you're a trump,—God bless you';
and it did n't seem so lonely after that. But the last time
he was here he said, as he opened the door to go, 'Do you

know, Miggles, your baby will grow up to be a man yet and be an honor to his mother; but not here, Miggles, not here!' And I thought he went away sad,—and—and—" and here Miggles's voice and head was somehow both lost completely in the shadow.

"The folks about here are very kind," said Miggles, after a pause, coming a little into the light again. "The men from the fork used to hang around here, until they found they wasn't wanted, and the women are kind,—and don't call. I was pretty lonely until I picked up Joaquin in the woods yonder one day, when he wasn't so high, and taught him to beg for his dinner; and then thar's Polly—that's the magpie—she knows no end of tricks, and makes it quite sociable of evenings with her talk, and so I don't feel like as I was the only living being about the ranch. And Jim here," said Miggles, with her old laugh again, and coming out quite into the firelight, "Jim—why, boys, you would admire to see how much he knows for a man like him. Sometimes I bring him flowers, and he looks at 'em just as natural as if he knew 'em; and times, when we're sitting alone, I read him those things on the wall. Why, Lord!" said Miggles, with her frank laugh, "I've read him that whole side of the house this winter. There never was such a man for reading as Jim."

"Why," asked the Judge, "do you not marry this man to whom you have devoted your youthful life?"

"Well, you see," said Miggles, "it would be playing it rather low down on Jim, to take advantage of his being so helpless. And then, too, if we were man and wife, now, we'd both know that I was *bound* to do what I do now of my own accord."

"But you are young yet and attractive—"

"It's getting late," said Miggles, gravely, "and you'd better all turn in. Good-night, boys"; and, throwing the blanket over her head, Miggles laid herself down beside Jim's chair, her head pillowed on the low stool that held his feet, and spoke no more. The fire slowly faded from the hearth; we each sought our blankets in silence; and presently there was no sound in the long room but the pattering of the rain upon the roof, and the heavy breathing of the sleepers.

It was nearly morning when I awoke from a troubled dream. The storm had passed, the stars were shining, and through the shutterless window the full moon, lifting itself over the solemn pines without, looked into the room. It touched the lonely figure in the chair with an infinite compassion, and seemed to baptize with a shining flood the lowly head of the woman whose hair, as in the sweet old story, bathed the feet of him she loved. It even lent a kindly poetry to the rugged outline of Yuba Bill, half reclining on his elbow between them and his passengers, with savagely patient eyes keeping watch and ward. And then I fell asleep and only woke at broad day, with Yuba Bill standing over me, and "All aboard" ringing in my ears.

Coffee was waiting for us on the table, but Miggles was gone. We wandered about the house and lingered along after the horses were harnessed, but she did not return. It was evident that she wished to avoid a formal leave-taking, and had so left us to depart as we had come. After we had helped the ladies into the coach, we returned to the house and solemnly shook hands with the paralytic Jim, as solemnly settling him back into position after each hand-shake. Then we looked for the last time around the long low room, at the stool where Miggles had sat, and slowly took our seats in the waiting coach. The whip cracked, and we were off!

But as we reached the high-road, Bill's dexterous hand laid the six horses back on their haunches, and the stage stopped with a jerk. For there, on a little eminence beside the road, stood Miggles, her hair flying, her eyes sparkling, her white handkerchief waving, and her white teeth flashing a last "good-by." We waved our hats in return. And then Yuba Bill, as if fearful of further fascination, madly lashed his horses forward, and we sank back in our seats. We exchanged not a word until we reached the North Fork, and the stage drew up at the Independence House. Then, the Judge leading, we walked into the bar-room and took our places gravely at the bar.

"Are your glasses charged, gentlemen?" said the Judge, solemnly taking off his white hat.

They were.

"Well, then, here's to *Miggles,* GOD BLESS HER!"

Perhaps He had. Who knows?

TENNESSEE'S PARTNER

I DO not think that we ever knew his real name. Our ignorance of it certainly never gave us any social inconvenience, for at Sandy Bar in 1854 most men were christened anew. Sometimes these appellatives were derived from some distinctiveness of dress, as in the case of "Dungaree Jack"; or from some peculiarity of habit, as shown in "Saleratus Bill," so called from an undue proportion of that chemical in his daily bread; or from some unlucky slip, as exhibited in "The Iron Pirate," a mild, inoffensive man, who earned that baleful title by his unfortunate mispronunciation of the term "iron pyrites." Perhaps this may have been the beginning of a rude heraldry; but I am constrained to think that it was because a man's real name in that day rested solely upon his own unsupported statement. "Call yourself Clifford, do you?" said Boston, addressing a timid new-comer with infinite scorn; "hell is full of such Cliffords!" He then introduced the unfortunate man, whose name happened to be really Clifford, as "Jay-bird Charley," —an unhallowed inspiration of the moment that clung to him ever after.

But to return to Tennessee's Partner, whom we never knew by any other than this relative title; that he had ever existed as a separate and distinct individuality we only learned later. It seems that in 1853 he left Poker Flat to go to San Francisco, ostensibly to procure a wife. He never got any farther than Stockton. At that place he was attracted by a young person who waited upon the table at the hotel where he took his meals. One morning he said something to her which caused her to smile not unkindly, to somewhat coquettishly break a plate of toast over his upturned, serious, simple face, and to retreat to the kitchen. He followed her, and emerged a few moments later, covered with more toast and victory. That day week they were married by a Justice of the Peace, and returned to Poker Flat. I am aware that something more might be made of this episode, but I prefer to tell it as it was current at Sandy Bar,—in the gulches and bar-rooms,—where all sentiment was modified by a strong sense of humor.

Of their married felicity but little is known, perhaps for the reason that Tennessee, then living with his partner, one

day took occasion to say something to the bride on his own
account, at which, it is said, she smiled not unkindly and
chastely retreated,—this time as far as Marysville, where
Tennessee followed her, and where they went to housekeep-
ing without the aid of a Justice of the Peace. Tennessee's
Partner took the loss of his wife simply and seriously, as
was his fashion. But to everybody's surprise, when Tennessee one day returned from Marysville, without his partner's
wife,—she having smiled and retreated with somebody
else,—Tennessee's Partner was the first man to shake
his hand and greet him with affection. The boys who had
gathered in the cañon to see the shooting were naturally indignant. Their indignation might have found vent in sarcasm but for a certain look in Tennessee's Partner's eye
that indicated a lack of humorous appreciation. In fact, he
was a grave man, with a steady application to practical detail which was unpleasant in a difficulty.

Meanwhile a popular feeling against Tennessee had
grown up on the Bar. He was known to be a gambler; he
was suspected to be a thief. In these suspicions Tennessee's Partner was equally compromised; his continued intimacy with Tennessee after the affair above quoted could
only be accounted for on the hypothesis of a copartnership
of crime. At last Tennessee's guilt became flagrant. One
day he overtook a stranger on his way to Red Dog. The
stranger afterward related that Tennessee beguiled the time
with interesting anecdote and reminiscence, but illogically
concluded the interview in the following words: "And now,
young man, I'll trouble you for your knife, your pistols, and
your money. You see your weppings might get you into
trouble at Red Dog, and your money's a temptation to the
evilly disposed. I think you said your address was San

Francisco. I shall endeavor to call." It may be stated here that Tennessee had a fine flow of humor, which no business preoccupation could wholly subdue.

This exploit was his last. Red Dog and Sandy Bar made common cause against the highwayman. Tennessee was hunted in very much the same fashion as his prototype, the grizzly. As the toils closed around him, he made a desperate dash through the Bar, emptying his revolver at the crowd before the Arcade Saloon, and so on up Grizzly Cañon; but at its farther extremity he was stopped by a small man on a gray horse. The men looked at each other a moment in silence. Both were fearless, both self-possessed and independent; and both types of a civilization that in the seventeenth century would have been called heroic, but, in the nineteenth, simply "reckless." "What have you got there?—I call," said Tennessee, quietly. "Two bowers and an ace," said the stranger, as quietly, showing two revolvers and a bowie-knife. "That takes me," returned Tennessee; and with this gamblers' epigram, he threw away his useless pistol, and rode back with his captor.

It was a warm night. The cool breeze which usually sprang up with the going down of the sun behind the *chaparral*-crested mountain was that evening withheld from Sandy Bar. The little cañon was stifling with heated resinous odors, and the decaying drift-wood on the Bar sent forth faint, sickening exhalations. The feverishness of day, and its fierce passions, still filled the camp. Lights moved restlessly along the bank of the river, striking no answering reflection from its tawny current. Against the blackness of the pines the windows of the old loft above the express-office stood out staringly bright; and through

their curtainless panes the loungers below could see the
forms of those who were even then deciding the fate of
Tennessee. And above all this, etched on the dark firmament, rose the Sierra, remote and passionless, crowned with
remoter passionless stars.

The trial of Tennessee was conducted as fairly as was
consistent with a judge and jury who felt themselves to
some extent obliged to justify, in their verdict, the previous
irregularities of arrest and indictment. The law of Sandy
Bar was implacable, but not vengeful. The excitement and
personal feeling of the chase was over; with Tennessee safe
in their hands they were ready to listen patiently to any defence, which they were already satisfied was insufficient.
There being no doubt in their own minds, they were willing
to give the prisoner the benefit of any that might exist. Secure in the hypothesis that he ought to be hanged, on general
principles, they indulged him with more latitude of defence
than his reckless hardihood seemed to ask. The Judge appeared to be more anxious than the prisoner, who, otherwise
unconcerned, evidently took a grim pleasure in the responsibility he had created. "I don't take any hand in this yer
game," had been his invariable, but good-humored reply to
all questions. The Judge—who was also his captor—for a
moment vaguely regretted that he had not shot him "on
sight," that morning, but presently dismissed this human
weakness as unworthy of the judicial mind. Nevertheless,
when there was a tap at the door, and it was said that Tennessee's Partner was there on behalf of the prisoner, he was
admitted at once without question. Perhaps the younger
members of the jury, to whom the proceedings were becoming irksomely thoughtful, hailed him as a relief.

For he was not, certainly, an imposing figure. Short and

Bret Harte at seventeen, from a daguerreotype taken shortly before he set out for the gold fields in California.

stout, with a square face, sunburned into a preternatural redness, clad in a loose duck "jumper," and trousers streaked and splashed with red soil, his aspect under any circumstances would have been quaint, and was now even ridiculous. As he stooped to deposit at his feet a heavy carpet-bag he was carrying, it became obvious, from partially developed legends and inscriptions, that the material with which his trousers had been patched had been originally intended for a less ambitious covering. Yet he advanced with great gravity, and after having shaken the hand of each person in the room with labored cordiality, he wiped his serious, perplexed face on a red bandanna handkerchief, a shade lighter than his complexion, laid his powerful hand upon the table to steady himself, and thus addressed the Judge:—

"I was passin' by," he began, by way of apology, "and I thought I'd just step in and see how things was gettin' on with Tennessee thar,—my pardner. It's a hot night. I disremember any sich weather before on the Bar."

He paused a moment, but nobody volunteering any other meteorological recollection, he again had recourse to his pocket-handkerchief, and for some moments mopped his face diligently.

"Have you anything to say in behalf of the prisoner?" said the Judge, finally.

"Thet's it," said Tennessee's Partner, in a tone of relief. "I come yar as Tennessee's pardner,—knowing him nigh on four year, off and on, wet and dry, in luck and out o' luck. His ways ain't allers my ways, but thar ain't any p'ints in that young man, thar ain't any liveliness as he's been up to, as I don't know. And you sez to me, sez you,— confidential-like, and between man and man,—sez you, 'Do you know anything in his behalf?' and I sez to you, sez I,—confidential-like, as between man and man,—'What should a man know of his pardner?'"

"Is this all you have to say?" asked the Judge, impatiently, feeling, perhaps, that a dangerous sympathy of humor was beginning to humanize the Court.

"Thet's so," continued Tennessee's Partner. "It ain't for me to say anything agin' him. And now, what's the case? Here's Tennessee wants money, wants it bad, and does n't like to ask it of his old pardner. Well, what does Tennessee do? He lays for a stranger, and he fetches that stranger. And you lays for *him,* and you fetches *him;* and the honors is easy. And I put it to you, bein' a far-minded man, and to you, gentlemen, all, as far-minded men, ef this isn't so."

"Prisoner," said the Judge, interrupting, "have you any questions to ask this man?"

"No! no!" continued Tennessee's Partner, hastily. "I play this yer hand alone. To come down to the bed-rock, it's just this: Tennessee, thar, has played it pretty rough and expensive-like on a stranger, and on this yer camp. And now, what's the fair thing? Some would say more; some would say less. Here's seventeen hundred dollars in coarse gold and a watch,—it's about all my pile,—and call it square!" And before a hand could be raised to prevent him, he had emptied the contents of the carpet-bag upon the table.

For a moment his life was in jeopardy. One or two men sprang to their feet, several hands groped for hidden weapons, and a suggestion to "throw him from the window" was only overridden by a gesture from the Judge. Tennessee laughed. And apparently oblivious of the excitement, Tennessee's Partner improved the opportunity to mop his face again with his handkerchief.

When order was restored, and the man was made to understand, by the use of forcible figures and rhetoric, that Tennessee's offence could not be condoned by money, his face took a more serious and sanguinary hue, and those who were nearest to him noticed that his rough hand trembled slightly on the table. He hesitated a moment as he slowly returned the gold to the carpet-bag, as if he had not yet entirely caught the elevated sense of justice which swayed the tribunal, and was perplexed with the belief that he had not offered enough. Then he turned to the Judge, and saying, "This yer is a lone hand, played alone, and without my partner," he bowed to the jury and was about to withdraw, when the Judge called him back. "If you have anything to say to Tennessee, you had better say it now." For the first time that evening the eyes of the prisoner and his strange advocate met. Tennessee smiled, showed his white teeth, and, saying, "Euchred, old man!" held out his hand. Tennessee's Partner took it in his own, and saying, "I just dropped in as I was passin' to see how things was gettin' on," let the hand passively fall, and adding that "it was a warm night," again mopped his face with his handkerchief, and without another word withdrew.

The two men never again met each other alive. For the unparalleled insult of a bribe offered to Judge Lynch—who, whether bigoted, weak, or narrow, was at least incorruptible—firmly fixed in the mind of that mythical personage any wavering determination of Tennessee's fate; and at the break of day he was marched, closely guarded, to meet it at the top of Marley's Hill.

How he met it, how cool he was, how he refused to say

anything, how perfect were the arrangements of the committee, were all duly reported, with the addition of a warning moral and example to all future evil-doers, in the Red Dog Clarion, by its editor, who was present, and to whose vigorous English I cheerfully refer the reader. But the beauty of that midsummer morning, the blessed amity of earth and air and sky, the awakened life of the free woods and hills, the joyous renewal and promise of Nature, and above all, the infinite Serenity that thrilled through each, was not reported, as not being a part of the social lesson. And yet, when the weak and foolish deed was done, and a life, with its possibilities and responsibilities, had passed out of the misshapen thing that dangled between earth and sky, the birds sang, the flowers bloomed, the sun shone, as cheerily as before; and possibly the Red Dog Clarion was right.

Tennessee's Partner was not in the group that surrounded the ominous tree. But as they turned to disperse attention was drawn to the singular appearance of a motionless donkey-cart halted at the side of the road. As they approached, they at once recognized the venerable "Jenny" and the two-wheeled cart as the property of Tennessee's Partner,—used by him in carrying dirt from his claim; and a few paces distant the owner of the equipage himself, sitting under a buckeye-tree, wiping the perspiration from his glowing face. In answer to an inquiry, he said he had come for the body of the "diseased," "if it was all the same to the committee." He didn't wish to "hurry anything"; he could "wait." He was not working that day; and when the gentlemen were done with the "diseased," he would take him. "Ef thar is any present," he added, in his simple, serious way, "as would care to jine in the fun'l, they kin come." Perhaps it was from a sense of humor, which I have already intimated was a feature of Sandy Bar,—perhaps it was from something even better than that; but two thirds of the loungers accepted the invitation at once.

It was noon when the body of Tennessee was delivered into the hands of his partner. As the cart drew up to the fatal tree, we noticed that it contained a rough, oblong box, —apparently made from a section of sluicing,—and half filled with bark and the tassels of pine. The cart was further decorated with slips of willow, and made fragrant with buckeye-blossoms. When the body was deposited in the box, Tennessee's Partner drew over it a piece of tarred canvas, and gravely mounting the narrow seat in front, with his feet upon the shafts, urged the little donkey forward. The equipage moved slowly on, at that decorous pace which was habitual with "Jenny" even under less solemn circumstances. The men—half curiously, half jestingly, but all good-humoredly—strolled along beside the cart; some in advance, some a little in the rear of the homely catafalque. But, whether from the narrowing of the road or some present sense of decorum, as the cart passed on, the company fell to the rear in couples, keeping step, and otherwise assuming the external show of a formal procession. Jack Folinsbee, who had at the outset played a funeral march in dumb show upon an imaginary trombone, desisted, from a lack of sympathy and appreciation,—not having, perhaps, your true humorist's capacity to be content with the enjoyment of his own fun.

The way led through Grizzly Cañon,—by this time clothed in funereal drapery and shadows. The redwoods, burying their moccasined feet in the red soil, stood in Indian-file along the track, trailing an uncouth benediction from their bending boughs upon the passing bier. A hare, surprised into helpless inactivity, sat upright and pulsating in the ferns by the roadside, as the *cortége* went by. Squirrels hastened to gain a secure outlook from higher boughs; and the blue-jays, spreading their wings, fluttered before them like outriders, until the outskirts of Sandy Bar were reached, and the solitary cabin of Tennessee's Partner.

Viewed under more favorable circumstances, it would not have been a cheerful place. The unpicturesque site, the rude and unlovely outlines, the unsavory details, which distinguish the nest-building of the California miner, were all here, with the dreariness of decay superadded. A few paces from the cabin there was a rough enclosure, which, in the brief days of Tennessee's Partner's matrimonial felicity, had been used as a garden, but was now overgrown with fern. As we approached it we were surprised to find that what we had taken for a recent attempt at cultivation was the broken soil about an open grave.

The cart was halted before the enclosure; and rejecting the offers of assistance with the same air of simple self-reliance he had displayed throughout, Tennessee's Partner lifted the rough coffin on his back, and deposited it, unaided, within the shallow grave. He then nailed down the board which served as a lid; and mounting the little mound of earth beside it, took off his hat, and slowly mopped his face with his handkerchief. This the crowd felt was a preliminary to speech; and they disposed themselves variously on stumps and boulders, and sat expectant.

"When a man," began Tennessee's Partner, slowly, "has been running free all day, what's the natural thing for him to do? Why, to come home. And if he ain't in a condition to go home, what can his best friend do? Why, bring him home! And here's Tennessee has been running free, and we brings him home from his wandering." He paused, and picked up a fragment of quartz, rubbed it thoughtfully on his sleeve, and went on: "It ain't the first time that I've packed him on my back, as you see'd me now. It ain't the first time that I brought him to this yer cabin when he couldn't help himself; it ain't the first time that I and 'Jinny' have waited for him on yon hill, and picked him up and so fetched him home, when he couldn't speak, and didn't know me. And now that it's the last time, why—" he paused, and rubbed the quartz gently on his sleeve—"you see it's sort of rough on his pardner. And now, gentlemen," he added, abruptly, picking up his long-handled shovel, "the fun'l's over; and my thanks, and Tennessee's thanks, to you for your trouble."

Resisting any proffers of assistance, he began to fill in the grave, turning his back upon the crowd, that after a few moments' hesitation gradually withdrew. As they crossed the little ridge that hid Sandy Bar from view, some, looking back, thought they could see Tennessee's Partner, his work done, sitting upon the grave, his shovel between his knees, and his face buried in his red bandanna handkerchief. But it was argued by others that you couldn't tell his face from his handkerchief at that distance; and this point remained undecided.

In the reaction that followed the feverish excitement of that day, Tennessee's Partner was not forgotten. A secret investigation had cleared him of any complicity in Tennessee's guilt, and left only a suspicion of his general sanity. Sandy Bar made a point of calling on him, and proffering various uncouth, but well-meant kindnesses. But from that day his rude health and great strength seemed visibly to decline; and when the rainy season fairly set in, and the tiny grass-blades were beginning to peep from the rocky mound above Tennessee's grave, he took to his bed.

One night, when the pines beside the cabin were swaying in the storm, and trailing their slender fingers over the roof, and the roar and rush of the swollen river were heard below, Tennessee's Partner lifted his head from the pillow, saying, "It is time to go for Tennessee; I must put 'Jinny' in the cart"; and would have risen from his bed but for the restraint of his attendant. Struggling, he still pursued his singular fancy: "There, now, steady, 'Jinny'—steady, old girl. How dark it is! Look out for the ruts,—and look out for him, too, old gal. Sometimes, you know, when he's blind drunk, he drops down right in the trail. Keep on straight up to the pine on the top of the hill. Thar—I told you so!—thar he is,—coming this way, too,—all by himself, sober, and his face a-shining. Tennessee! Pardner!"

And so they met.

THE IDYL OF RED GULCH

SANDY was very drunk. He was lying under an azalea-bush, in pretty much the same attitude in which he had fallen some hours before. How long he had been lying there he could not tell, and didn't care; how long he should lie there was a matter equally indefinite and unconsidered. A tranquil philosophy, born of his physical condition, suffused and saturated his moral being.

The spectacle of a drunken man, and of this drunken

"Uncle Billy passed rapidly from a bellicose state into one of stupor, the Dutchess became maudlin, and Mother Shipton snored. Mr. Oakhurst alone remained erect." Illustration for an 1872 edition of *The Outcasts of Poker Flat*, published by James R. Osgood & Co., Boston. (*p. 17*)

man in particular, was not, I grieve to say, of sufficient novelty in Red Gulch to attract attention. Earlier in the day some local satirist had erected a temporary tombstone at Sandy's head, bearing the inscription, "Effects of McCorkle's whiskey,—kills at forty rods," with a hand pointing to McCorkle's saloon. But this, I imagine, was, like most local satire, personal; and was a reflection upon the unfairness of the process rather than a commentary upon the impropriety of the result. With this facetious exception, Sandy had been undisturbed. A wandering mule, released from his pack, had cropped the scant herbage beside him, and sniffed curiously at the prostrate man; a vagabond dog, with that deep sympathy which the species have for drunken men, had licked his dusty boots, and curled himself up at his feet, and lay there, blinking one eye in the sunlight, with a simulation of dissipation that was ingenious and dog-like in its implied flattery of the unconscious man beside him.

Meanwhile the shadows of the pine-trees had slowly swung around until they crossed the road, and their trunks barred the open meadow with gigantic parallels of black and yellow. Little puffs of red dust, lifted by the plunging hoofs of passing teams, dispersed in a grimy shower upon the recumbent man. The sun sank lower and lower; and still Sandy stirred not. And then the repose of this philosopher was disturbed, as other philosophers have been, by the intrusion of an unphilosophical sex.

"Miss Mary," as she was known to the little flock that she had just dismissed from the log school-house beyond the pines, was taking her afternoon walk. Observing an unusually fine cluster of blossoms on the azalea-bush opposite, she crossed the road to pluck it,—picking her way through the red dust, not without certain fierce little shivers of disgust, and some feline circumlocution. And then she came suddenly upon Sandy!

Of course she uttered the little *staccato* cry of her sex. But when she had paid that tribute to her physical weakness she became overbold, and halted for a moment,—at least six feet from this prostrate monster,—with her white skirts gathered in her hand, ready for flight. But neither sound nor motion came from the bush. With one little foot she then overturned the satirical head-board, and muttered "Beasts!"—an epithet which probably, at that moment, conveniently classified in her mind the entire male population of Red Gulch. For Miss Mary, being possessed of certain rigid notions of her own, had not, perhaps, properly appreciated the demonstrative gallantry for which the Californian has been so justly celebrated by his brother Californians, and had, as a new-comer, perhaps, fairly earned the reputation of being "stuck up."

As she stood there she noticed, also, that the slant sunbeams were heating Sandy's head to what she judged to be an unhealthy temperature, and that his hat was lying uselessly at his side. To pick it up and to place it over his face was a work requiring some courage, particularly as his eyes were open. Yet she did it and made good her retreat. But she was somewhat concerned, on looking back, to see that the hat was removed, and that Sandy was sitting up and saying something.

The truth was, that in the calm depths of Sandy's mind he was satisfied that the rays of the sun were beneficial and healthful; that from childhood he had objected to lying down in a hat; that no people but condemned fools, past redemption, ever wore hats; and that his right to dispense with them when he pleased was inalienable. This was the

statement of his inner consciousness. Unfortunately, its
outward expression was vague, being limited to a repetition
of the following formula,—"Su'shine all ri'! Wasser maär,
eh? Wass up, su'shine?"

Miss Mary stopped, and, taking fresh courage from her
vantage of distance, asked him if there was anything that he
wanted.

"Wass up? Wasser maär?" continued Sandy, in a very
high key.

"Get up, you horrid man!" said Miss Mary, now thoroughly incensed; "get up, and go home."

Sandy staggered to his feet. He was six feet high, and
Miss Mary trembled. He started forward a few paces and
then stopped.

"Wass I go home for," he suddenly asked, with great
gravity.

"Go and take a bath," replied Miss Mary, eying his
grimy person with great disfavor.

To her infinite dismay, Sandy suddenly pulled off his coat
and vest, threw them on the ground, kicked off his boots,
and, plunging wildly forward, darted headlong over the
hill, in the direction of the river.

"Goodness Heavens!—the man will be drowned!" said
Miss Mary; and then, with feminine inconsistency, she ran
back to the school-house, and locked herself in.

That night, while seated at supper with her hostess, the
blacksmith's wife, it came to Miss Mary to ask, demurely,
if her husband ever got drunk. "Abner," responded Mrs.
Stidger, reflectively, "let's see: Abner hasn't been tight
since last 'lection." Miss Mary would have liked to ask if
he preferred lying in the sun on these occasions, and if a

cold bath would have hurt him; but this would have involved an explanation, which she did not then care to give.
So she contented herself with opening her gray eyes widely
at the red-cheeked Mrs. Stidger,—a fine specimen of Southwestern efflorescence,—and then dismissed the subject altogether. The next day she wrote to her dearest friend, in
Boston: "I think I find the intoxicated portion of this community the least objectionable. I refer, my dear, to the men,
of course. I do not know anything that could make the
women tolerable."

In less than a week Miss Mary had forgotten this episode,
except that her afternoon walks took thereafter, almost unconsciously, another direction. She noticed, however, that
every morning a fresh cluster of azalea-blossoms appeared
among the flowers on her desk. This was not strange, as
her little flock were aware of her fondness for flowers, and
invariably kept her desk bright with anemones, syringas,
and lupines; but, on questioning them, they, one and all,
professed ignorance of the azaleas. A few days later, Master Johnny Stidger, whose desk was nearest to the window,
was suddenly taken with spasms of apparently gratuitous
laughter, that threatened the discipline of the school. All
that Miss Mary could get from him was, that some one had
been "looking in the winder." Irate and indignant, she sallied from her hive to do battle with the intruder. As she
turned the corner of the school-house she came plump upon
the quondam drunkard,—now perfectly sober, and inexpressibly sheepish and guilty-looking.

These facts Miss Mary was not slow to take a feminine
advantage of, in her present humor. But it was somewhat
confusing to observe, also, that the beast, despite some faint

signs of past dissipation, was amiable-looking,—in fact, a kind of blond Samson, whose corn-colored, silken beard apparently had never yet known the touch of barber's razor or Delilah's shears. So that the cutting speech which quivered on her ready tongue died upon her lips, and she contented herself with receiving his stammering apology with supercilious eyelids and the gathered skirts of uncontamination. When she re-entered the school-room, her eyes fell upon the azaleas with a new sense of revelation. And then she laughed, and the little people all laughed, and they were all unconsciously very happy.

It was on a hot day—and not long after this—that two short-legged boys came to grief on the threshold of the school with a pail of water, which they had laboriously brought from the spring, and that Miss Mary compassionately seized the pail and started for the spring herself. At the foot of the hill a shadow crossed her path, and a blue-shirted arm dexterously, but gently relieved her of her burden. Miss Mary was both embarrassed and angry. "If you carried more of that for yourself," she said, spitefully, to the blue arm, without deigning to raise her lashes to its owner, "you'd do better." In the submissive silence that followed she regretted the speech, and thanked him so sweetly at the door that he stumbled. Which caused the children to laugh again,—a laugh in which Miss Mary joined, until the color came faintly into her pale cheek. The next day a barrel was mysteriously placed beside the door, and as mysteriously filled with fresh spring-water every morning.

Nor was this superior young person without other quiet attentions. "Profane Bill," driver of the Slumgullion Stage, widely known in the newspapers for his "gallantry" in invariably offering the box-seat to the fair sex, had excepted Miss Mary from this attention, on the ground that he had a habit of "cussin' on up grades," and gave her half the coach to herself. Jack Hamlin, a gambler, having once silently ridden with her in the same coach, afterward threw a decanter at the head of a confederate for mentioning her name in a bar-room. The over-dressed mother of a pupil whose paternity was doubtful had often lingered near this astute Vestal's temple, never daring to enter its sacred precincts, but content to worship the priestess from afar.

With such unconscious intervals the monotonous procession of blue skies, glittering sunshine, brief twilights, and starlit nights passed over Red Gulch. Miss Mary grew fond of walking in the sedate and proper woods. Perhaps she believed, with Mrs. Stidger, that the balsamic odors of the firs "did her chest good," for certainly her slight cough was less frequent and her step was firmer; perhaps she had learned the unending lesson which the patient pines are never weary of repeating to heedful or listless ears. And so, one day, she planned a picnic on Buckeye Hill, and took the children with her. Away from the dusty road, the straggling shanties, the yellow ditches, the clamor of restless engines, the cheap finery of shop-windows, the deeper glitter of paint and colored glass, and the thin veneering which barbarism takes upon itself in such localities,—what infinite relief was theirs! The last heap of ragged rock and clay passed, the last unsightly chasm crossed,—how the waiting woods opened their long files to receive them! How the children—perhaps because they had not yet grown quite away from the breast of the bounteous Mother—threw themselves face downward on her brown bosom with uncouth

caresses, filling the air with their laughter; and how Miss
Mary herself—felinely fastidious and intrenched as she was
in the purity of spotless skirts, collar, and cuffs—forgot all,
and ran like a crested quail at the head of her brood, until,
romping, laughing, and panting, with a loosened braid of
brown hair, a hat hanging by a knotted ribbon from her
throat, she came suddenly and violently, in the heart of the
forest, upon—the luckless Sandy!

The explanations, apologies, and not overwise conversation that ensued, need not be indicated here. It would seem,
however, that Miss Mary had already established some acquaintance with this ex-drunkard. Enough that he was soon
accepted as one of the party; that the children, with that
quick intelligence which Providence gives the helpless, recognized a friend, and played with his blond beard, and long
silken mustache, and took other liberties,—as the helpless
are apt to do. And when he had built a fire against a tree,
and had shown them other mysteries of wood-craft, their
admiration knew no bounds. At the close of two such foolish, idle, happy hours he found himself lying at the feet of
the schoolmistress, gazing dreamily in her face, as she sat
upon the sloping hillside, weaving wreaths of laurel and
syringa, in very much the same attitude as he had lain when
first they met. Nor was the similitude greatly forced. The
weakness of an easy, sensuous nature, that had found a
dreamy exaltation in liquor, it is to be feared was now finding an equal intoxication in love.

I think that Sandy was dimly conscious of this himself.
I know that he longed to be doing something,—slaying a
grizzly, scalping a savage, or sacrificing himself in some
way for the sake of this sallow-faced, gray-eyed school-

mistress. As I should like to present him in a heroic attitude, I stay my hand with great difficulty at this moment,
being only withheld from introducing such an episode by a
strong conviction that it does not usually occur at such
times. And I trust that my fairest reader, who remembers
that, in a real crisis, it is always some uninteresting stranger
or unromantic policeman, and not Adolphus, who rescues,
will forgive the omission.

So they sat there, undisturbed,—the woodpeckers chat-
tering overhead, and the voices of the children coming pleasantly from the hollow below. What they said matters little.
What they thought—which might have been interesting
—did not transpire. The woodpeckers only learned how
Miss Mary was an orphan; how she left her uncle's house,
to come to California, for the sake of health and independence; how Sandy was an orphan, too; how he came to
California for excitement; how he had lived a wild life, and
how he was trying to reform; and other details, which, from
a woodpecker's view-point, undoubtedly must have seemed
stupid, and a waste of time. But even in such trifles was the
afternoon spent; and when the children were again gathered, and Sandy, with a delicacy which the schoolmistress
well understood, took leave of them quietly at the outskirts
of the settlement, it had seemed the shortest day of her
weary life.

As the long, dry summer withered to its roots, the school
term of Red Gulch—to use a local euphuism—"dried up"
also. In another day Miss Mary would be free; and for a
season, at least, Red Gulch would know her no more. She
was seated alone in the school-house, her cheek resting on
her hand, her eyes half closed in one of those day-dreams in

which Miss Mary—I fear, to the danger of school discipline—was lately in the habit of indulging. Her lap was full of mosses, ferns, and other woodland memories. She was so preoccupied with these and her own thoughts that a gentle tapping at the door passed unheard, or translated itself into the remembrance of far-off woodpeckers. When at last it asserted itself more distinctly, she started up with a flushed cheek and opened the door. On the threshold stood a woman, the self-assertion and audacity of whose dress were in singular contrast to her timid, irresolute bearing.

Miss Mary recognized at a glance the dubious mother of her anonymous pupil. Perhaps she was disappointed, perhaps she was only fastidious; but as she coldly invited her to enter, she half unconsciously settled her white cuffs and collar, and gathered closer her own chaste skirts. It was, perhaps, for this reason that the embarrassed stranger, after a moment's hesitation, left her gorgeous parasol open and sticking in the dust beside the door, and then sat down at the farther end of a long bench. Her voice was husky as she began:—

"I heerd tell that you were goin' down to the Bay to-morrow, and I couldn't let you go until I came to thank you for your kindness to my Tommy."

Tommy, Miss Mary said, was a good boy, and deserved more than the poor attention she could give him.

"Thank you, miss; thank you!" cried the stranger, brightening even through the color which Red Gulch knew facetiously as her "war paint," and striving, in her embarrassment, to drag the long bench nearer the schoolmistress. "I thank you, miss, for that! and if I am his mother, there ain't a sweeter, dearer, better boy lives than him. And if I ain't much as says it, thar ain't a sweeter, dearer, angeler teacher lives than he's got."

Miss Mary, sitting primly behind her desk, with a ruler over her shoulder, opened her gray eyes widely at this, but said nothing.

"It ain't for you to be complimented by the like of me, I know," she went on, hurriedly. "It ain't for me to be comin' here, in broad day, to do it, either; but I come to ask a favor,—not for me, miss,—not for me, but for the darling boy."

Encouraged by a look in the young schoolmistress's eye, and putting her lilac-gloved hands together, the fingers downward, between her knees, she went on, in a low voice:—

"You see, miss, there's no one the boy has any claim on but me, and I ain't the proper person to bring him up. I thought some, last year, of sending him away to 'Frisco to school, but when they talked of bringing a schoolma'am here, I waited till I saw you, and then I knew it was all right, and I could keep my boy a little longer. And O, miss, he loves you so much; and if you could hear him talk about you, in his pretty way, and if he could ask you what I ask you now, you couldn't refuse him.

"It is natural," she went on, rapidly, in a voice that trembled strangely between pride and humility,—"it's natural that he should take to you, miss, for his father, when I first knew him, was a gentleman,—and the boy must forget me, sooner or later,—and so I ain't a goin' to cry about that. For I come to ask you to take my Tommy,—God bless him for the bestest, sweetest boy that lives,—to—to—take him with you."

She had risen and caught the young girl's hand in her own, and had fallen on her knees beside her.

"I've money plenty, and it's all yours and his. Put him in some good school, where you can go and see him, and help him to—to—to forget his mother. Do with him what you like. The worst you can do will be kindness to what he will learn with me. Only take him out of this wicked life, this cruel place, this home of shame and sorrow. You will; I know you will,—won't you? You will,—you must not, you cannot say no! You will make him as pure, as gentle as yourself; and when he has grown up, you will tell him his father's name,—the name that hasn't passed my lips for years,—the name of Alexander Morton, whom they call here Sandy! Miss Mary!—do not take your hand away! Miss Mary, speak to me! You will take my boy? Do not put your face from me. I know it ought not to look on such as me. Miss Mary!—my God, be merciful!—she is leaving me!"

Miss Mary had risen, and, in the gathering twilight, had felt her way to the open window. She stood there, leaning against the casement, her eyes fixed on the last rosy tints that were fading from the western sky. There was still some of its light on her pure young forehead, on her white collar, on her clasped white hands, but all fading, slowly away. The suppliant had dragged herself, still on her knees, beside her.

"I know it takes time to consider. I will wait here all night; but I cannot go until you speak. Do not deny me now. You will!—I see it in your sweet face,—such a face as I have seen in my dreams. I see it in your eyes, Miss Mary!—you will take my boy!"

The last red beam crept higher, suffused Miss Mary's eyes with something of its glory, flickered, and faded, and went out. The sun had set on Red Gulch. In the twilight and silence Miss Mary's voice sounded pleasantly.

"I will take the boy. Send him to me to-night."

The happy mother raised the hem of Miss Mary's skirts to her lips. She would have buried her hot face in its virgin folds, but she dared not. She rose to her feet.

"Does—this man—know of your intention?" asked Miss Mary, suddenly.

"No, nor cares. He has never even seen the child to know it."

"Go to him at once,—to-night,—now! Tell him what you have done. Tell him I have taken his child, and tell him— he must never see—see—the child again. Wherever it may be, he must not come; wherever I may take it, he must not follow! There, go now, please,—I'm weary, and—have much yet to do!"

They walked together to the door. On the threshold the woman turned.

"Good night."

She would have fallen at Miss Mary's feet. But at the same moment the young girl reached out her arms, caught the sinful woman to her own pure breast for one brief moment, and then closed and locked the door.

It was with a sudden sense of great responsibility that Profane Bill took the reins of the Slumgullion Stage the next morning, for the schoolmistress was one of his passengers. As he entered the high-road, in obedience to a pleasant voice from the "inside," he suddenly reined up his horses and respectfully waited, as "Tommy" hopped out at the command of Miss Mary.

"Not that bush, Tommy,—the next."

Tommy whipped out his new pocket-knife, and, cutting a branch from a tall azalea-bush, returned with it to Miss Mary.

"All right now?"

"All right."

And the stage-door closed on the Idyl of Red Gulch.

BROWN OF CALAVERAS

A SUBDUED tone of conversation, and the absence of cigar-smoke and boot-heels at the windows of the Wingdam stage-coach, made it evident that one of the inside passengers was a woman. A disposition on the part of loungers at the stations to congregate before the window, and some concern in regard to the appearance of coats, hats, and collars, further indicated that she was lovely. All of which Mr. Jack Hamlin, on the box-seat, noted with the smile of cynical philosophy. Not that he depreciated the sex, but that he recognized therein a deceitful element, the pursuit of which sometimes drew mankind away from the equally uncertain blandishments of poker,—of which it may be remarked that Mr. Hamlin was a professional exponent.

So that, when he placed his narrow boot on the wheel and leaped down, he did not even glance at the window from which a green veil was fluttering, but lounged up and down with that listless and grave indifference of his class, which

was, perhaps, the next thing to good-breeding. With his
closely buttoned figure and self-contained air he was a
marked contrast to the other passengers, with their feverish
restlessness, and boisterous emotion; and even Bill Masters,
a graduate of Harvard, with his slovenly dress, his overflowing vitality, his intense appreciation of lawlessness and
barbarism, and his mouth filled with crackers and cheese, I
fear cut but an unromantic figure beside this lonely calcu-
lator of chances, with his pale Greek face and Homeric
gravity.

The driver called "All aboard!" and Mr. Hamlin returned
to the coach. His foot was upon the wheel, and his face
raised to the level of the open window, when, at the same
moment, what appeared to him to be the finest eyes in the
world suddenly met his. He quietly dropped down again,
addressed a few words to one of the inside passengers, effected an exchange of seats, and as quietly took his place
inside. Mr. Hamlin never allowed his philosophy to interfere with decisive and prompt action.

I fear that this irruption of Jack cast some restraint upon
the other passengers,—particularly those who were making
themselves most agreeable to the lady. One of them leaned
forward, and apparently conveyed to her information regarding Mr. Hamlin's profession in a single epithet.
Whether Mr. Hamlin heard it, or whether he recognized in
the informant a distinguished jurist, from whom, but a few
evenings before, he had won several thousand dollars, I cannot say. His colorless face betrayed no sign; his black eyes,
quietly observant, glanced indifferently past the legal gentleman, and rested on the much more pleasing features of
his neighbor. An Indian stoicism—said to be an inher-

itance from his maternal ancestor—stood him in good service, until the rolling wheels rattled upon the river-gravel at Scott's Ferry, and the stage drew up at the International Hotel for dinner. The legal gentleman and a member of Congress leaped out, and stood ready to assist the descending goddess, while Colonel Starbottle, of Siskiyou, took charge of her parasol and shawl. In this multiplicity of attention there was a momentary confusion and delay. Jack Hamlin quietly opened the *opposite* door of the coach, took the lady's hand,—with that decision and positiveness which a hesitating and undecided sex know how to admire,—and in an instant had dexterously and gracefully swung her to the ground, and again lifted her to the platform. An audible chuckle on the box, I fear, came from that other cynic, "Yuba Bill," the driver. "Look keerfully arter that baggage, Kernel," said the expressman, with affected concern, as he looked after Colonel Starbottle, gloomily bringing up the rear of the triumphant procession to the waiting-room.

Mr. Hamlin did not stay for dinner. His horse was already saddled, and awaiting him. He dashed over the ford, up the gravelly hill, and out into the dusty perspective of the Wingdam road, like one leaving an unpleasant fancy behind him. The inmates of dusty cabins by the roadside shaded their eyes with their hands, and looked after him, recognizing the man by his horse, and speculating what "was up with Comanche Jack." Yet much of this interest centred in the horse, in a community where the time made by "French Pete's" mare, in his run from the Sheriff of Calaveras, eclipsed all concern in the ultimate fate of that worthy.

The sweating flanks of his gray at length recalled him to himself. He checked his speed, and, turning into a by-road, sometimes used as a cut-off, trotted leisurely along, the reins hanging listlessly from his fingers. As he rode on, the character of the landscape changed, and became more pastoral. Openings in groves of pine and sycamore disclosed some rude attempts at cultivation,—a flowering vine trailed over the porch of one cabin, and a woman rocked her cradled babe under the roses of another. A little farther on Mr. Hamlin came upon some barelegged children, wading in the willowy creek, and so wrought upon them with a badinage peculiar to himself, that they were emboldened to climb up his horse's legs and over his saddle, until he was fain to develop an exaggerated ferocity of demeanor, and to escape, leaving behind some kisses and coin. And then, advancing deeper into the woods, where all signs of habitation failed, he began to sing,—uplifting a tenor so singularly sweet, and shaded by a pathos so subduing and tender, that I wot the robins and linnets stopped to listen. Mr. Hamlin's voice was not cultivated; the subject of his song was some sentimental lunacy, borrowed from the negro minstrels; but there thrilled through all some occult quality of tone and expression that was unspeakably touching. Indeed, it was a wonderful sight to see this sentimental blackleg, with a pack of cards in his pocket and a revolver at his back, sending his voice before him through the dim woods with a plaint about his "Nelly's grave," in a way that overflowed the eyes of the listener. A sparrow-hawk, fresh from his sixth victim, possibly recognizing in Mr. Hamlin a kindred spirit, stared at him in surprise, and was fain to confess the superiority of man. With a superior predatory capacity, *he* couldn't sing.

But Mr. Hamlin presently found himself again on the

high-road, and at his former pace. Ditches and banks of
gravel, denuded hillsides, stumps, and decayed trunks of
trees, took the place of woodland and ravine, and indicated
his approach to civilization. Then a church-steeple came in
sight, and he knew that he had reached home. In a few
moments he was clattering down the single narrow street,
that lost itself in a chaotic ruin of races, ditches, and tail-
ings at the foot of the hill, and dismounted before the gilded
windows of the "Magnolia" saloon. Passing through the
long bar-room, he pushed open a green-baize door, entered
a dark passage, opened another door with a pass-key, and
found himself in a dimly lighted room, whose furniture,
though elegant and costly for the locality, showed signs of
abuse. The inlaid centre-table was overlaid with stained
disks that were not contemplated in the original design. The
embroidered arm-chairs were discolored, and the green velvet lounge, on which Mr. Hamlin threw himself, was soiled
at the foot with the red soil of Wingdam.

Mr. Hamlin did not sing in his cage. He lay still, looking
at a highly colored painting above him, representing a young
creature of opulent charms. It occurred to him then, for the
first time, that he had never seen exactly that kind of a
woman, and that, if he should, he would not, probably, fall
in love with her. Perhaps he was thinking of another style
of beauty. But just then some one knocked at the door.
Without rising, he pulled a cord that apparently shot back a
bolt, for the door swung open, and a man entered.

The new-comer was broad-shouldered and robust,—a
vigor not borne out in the face, which, though handsome,
was singularly weak, and disfigured by dissipation. He appeared to be also under the influence of liquor, for he started

on seeing Mr. Hamlin, and said, "I thought Kate was here"; stammered, and seemed confused and embarrassed.

Mr. Hamlin smiled the smile which he had before worn on the Wingdam coach, and sat up, quite refreshed and ready for business.

"You didn't come up on the stage," continued the new-comer, "did you?"

"No," replied Hamlin; "I left it at Scott's Ferry. It isn't due for half an hour yet. But how's luck, Brown?"

"D—— bad," said Brown, his face suddenly assuming an expression of weak despair; "I'm cleaned out again. Jack," he continued, in a whining tone, that formed a pitiable contrast to his bulky figure, "can't you help me with a hundred till to-morrow's clean-up? You see I've got to send money home to the old woman, and—you've won twenty times that amount from me."

The conclusion was, perhaps, not entirely logical, but Jack overlooked it, and handed the sum to his visitor. "The old woman business is about played out, Brown," he added, by way of commentary; "why don't you say you want to buck agin' faro? You know you ain't married!"

"Fact, sir," said Brown, with a sudden gravity, as if the mere contact of the gold with the palm of the hand had imparted some dignity to his frame. "I've got a wife—a d—— good one, too, if I do say it—in the States. It's three year since I've seen her, and a year since I've writ to her. When things is about straight, and we get down to the lead, I'm going to send for her."

"And Kate?" queried Mr. Hamlin, with his previous smile.

Mr. Brown, of Calaveras, essayed an archness of glance,

to cover his confusion, which his weak face and whisky-muddled intellect but poorly carried out, and said,—

"D—— it, Jack, a man must have a little liberty, you know. But come, what do you say to a little game? Give us a show to double this hundred."

Jack Hamlin looked curiously at his fatuous friend. Perhaps he knew that the man was predestined to lose the money, and preferred that it should flow back into his own coffers rather than any other. He nodded his head, and drew his chair toward the table. At the same moment there came a rap upon the door.

"It's Kate," said Mr. Brown.

Mr. Hamlin shot back the bolt, and the door opened. But, for the first time in his life, he staggered to his feet, utterly unnerved and abashed and for the first time in his life the hot blood crimsoned his colorless cheeks to his forehead. For before him stood the lady he had lifted from the Wingdam coach, whom Brown—dropping his cards with a hysterical laugh—greeted as

"My old woman, by thunder!"

They say that Mrs. Brown burst into tears, and reproaches of her husband. I saw her, in 1857, at Marysville, and disbelieve the story. And the Wingdam Chronicle, of the next week, under the head of "Touching Reunion," said: "One of those beautiful and touching incidents, peculiar to California life, occurred last week in our city. The wife of one of Wingdam's eminent pioneers, tired of the effete civilization of the East and its inhospitable climate, resolved to join her noble husband upon these golden shores. Without informing him of her intention, she undertook the long journey, and arrived last week. The joy of the husband

may be easier imagined than described. The meeting is said
to have been indescribably affecting. We trust her example
may be followed."

Whether owing to Mrs. Brown's influence, or to some
more successful speculations, Mr. Brown's financial fortune
from that day steadily improved. He bought out his part-
ners in the "Nip and Tuck" lead, with money which was
said to have been won at poker, a week or two after his
wife's arrival, but which rumor, adopting Mrs. Brown's
theory that Brown had forsworn the gaming-table, declared
to have been furnished by Mr. Jack Hamlin. He built and
furnished the "Wingdam House," which pretty Mrs.
Brown's great popularity kept overflowing with guests. He
was elected to the Assembly, and gave largess to churches.
A street in Wingdam was named in his honor.

Yet it was noted that in proportion as he waxed wealthy
and fortunate, he grew pale, thin, and anxious. As his
wife's popularity increased, he became fretful and impatient.
The most uxorious of husbands, he was absurdly jealous.
If he did not interfere with his wife's social liberty, it was
because it was maliciously whispered that his first and only
attempt was met by an outburst from Mrs. Brown that ter-
rified him into silence. Much of this kind of gossip came
from those of her own sex whom she had supplanted in the
chivalrous attentions of Wingdam, which, like most popular chivalry, was devoted to an admiration of power, whether
of masculine force or feminine beauty. It should be remembered, too, in her extenuation, that, since her arrival, she
had been the unconscious priestess of a mythological worship, perhaps not more ennobling to her womanhood than

that which distinguished an older Greek democracy. I think that Brown was dimly conscious of this. But his only confidant was Jack Hamlin, whose *infelix* reputation naturally precluded any open intimacy with the family, and whose visits were infrequent.

It was midsummer, and a moonlit night; and Mrs. Brown, very rosy, large-eyed, and pretty, sat upon the piazza, enjoying the fresh incense of the mountain breeze, and, it is to be feared, another incense which was not so fresh, nor quite as innocent. Beside her sat Colonel Starbottle and Judge Boompointer, and a later addition to her court, in the shape of a foreign tourist. She was in good spirits.

"What do you see down the road?" inquired the gallant Colonel, who had been conscious, for the last few minutes, that Mrs. Brown's attention was diverted.

"Dust," said Mrs. Brown, with a sigh. "Only Sister Ann's 'flock of sheep.' "

The Colonel, whose literary recollections did not extend farther back than last week's paper, took a more practical view. "It ain't sheep," he continued; "it's a horseman. Judge, ain't that Jack Hamlin's gray?"

But the Judge didn't know; and, as Mrs. Brown suggested the air was growing too cold for further investigations, they retired to the parlor.

Mr. Brown was in the stable, where he generally retired after dinner. Perhaps it was to show his contempt for his wife's companions; perhaps, like other weak natures, he found pleasure in the exercise of absolute power over inferior animals. He had a certain gratification in the training of a chestnut mare, whom he could beat or caress as pleased him, which he couldn't do with Mrs. Brown. It was here that he recognized a certain gray horse which had just come in, and, looking a little farther on, found his rider. Brown's greeting was cordial and hearty; Mr. Hamlin's somewhat restrained. But at Brown's urgent request, he followed him up the back stairs to a narrow corridor, and thence to a small room looking out upon the stable-yard. It was plainly furnished with a bed, a table, a few chairs, and a rack for guns and whips.

"This yer's my home, Jack," said Brown, with a sigh, as he threw himself upon the bed, and motioned his companion to a chair. "Her room's t'other end of the hall. It's more 'n six months since we've lived together, or met, except at meals. It's mighty rough papers on the head of the house, ain't it?" he said, with a forced laugh. "But I'm glad to see you, Jack, d—— glad," and he reached from the bed, and again shook the unresponsive hand of Jack Hamlin.

"I brought ye up here, for I didn't want to talk in the stable; though, for the matter of that, it's all round town. Don't strike a light. We can talk here in the moonshine. Put up your feet on that winder, and sit here beside me. Thar's whiskey in that jug."

Mr. Hamlin did not avail himself of the information. Brown, of Calaveras, turned his face to the wall, and continued:—

"If I didn't love the woman, Jack, I wouldn't mind. But it's loving her, and seeing her, day arter day, goin' on at this rate, and no one to put down the brake; that's what gits me! But I'm glad to see ye, Jack, d—— glad."

In the darkness he groped about until he had found and wrung his companion's hand again. He would have detained it, but Jack slipped it into the buttoned breast of his coat, and asked, listlessly, "How long has this been going on?"

"Ever since she came here; ever since the day she walked into the Magnolia. I was a fool then; Jack, I'm a fool now; but I didn't know how much I loved her till then. And she hasn't been the same woman since.

"But that ain't all, Jack; and it's what I wanted to see you about, and I'm glad you've come. It ain't that she doesn't love me any more; it ain't that she fools with every chap that comes along, for, perhaps, I staked her love and lost it, as I did everything else at the Magnolia; and, perhaps, foolin' is nateral to some women, and thar ain't no great harm done, 'cept to the fools. But, Jack, I think,—I think she loves somebody else. Don't move, Jack; don't move; if your pistol hurts ye, take it off.

"It's been more'n six months now that she's seemed unhappy and lonesome, and kinder nervous and scared like. And sometimes I've ketched her lookin' at me sort of timid and pitying. And she writes to somebody. And for the last week she's been gathering her own things,—trinkets, and furbelows, and jew'lry,—and, Jack, I think she's goin' off. I could stand all but that. To have her steal away like a thief—" He put his face downward to the pillow, and for a few moments there was no sound but the ticking of a clock on the mantel. Mr. Hamlin lit a cigar, and moved to the open window. The moon no longer shone into the room, and the bed and its occupant were in shadow. "What shall I do, Jack?" said the voice from the darkness.

The answer came promptly and clearly from the window-side,—"Spot the man, and kill him on sight."

"But, Jack?"

"He's took the risk!"

"But will that bring *her* back?"

Jack did not reply, but moved from the window towards the door.

"Don't go yet, Jack; light the candle, and sit by the table. It's a comfort to see ye, if nothin' else."

Jack hesitated, and then complied. He drew a pack of cards from his pocket and shuffled them, glancing at the bed. But Brown's face was turned to the wall. When Mr. Hamlin had shuffled the cards, he cut them, and dealt one card on the opposite side of the table and towards the bed, and another on his side of the table for himself. The first was a deuce; his own card, a king. He then shuffled and cut again. This time "dummy" had a queen, and himself a four-spot. Jack brightened up for the third deal. It brought his adversary a deuce, and himself a king again. "Two out of three," said Jack, audibly.

"What's that, Jack?" said Brown.

"Nothing."

Then Jack tried his hand with dice; but he always threw sixes, and his imaginary opponent aces. The force of habit is sometimes confusing.

Meanwhile, some magnetic influence in Mr. Hamlin's presence, or the anodyne of liquor, or both, brought surcease of sorrow, and Brown slept. Mr. Hamlin moved his chair to the window, and looked out on the town of Wingdam, now sleeping peacefully,—its harsh outlines softened and subdued, its glaring colors mellowed and sobered in the moonlight that flowed over all. In the hush he could hear the gurgling of water in the ditches, and the sighing of the pines beyond the hill. Then he looked up at the firmament, and as he did so a star shot across the twinkling field. Presently another, and then another. The phenomenon suggested to Mr. Hamlin a fresh augury. If in another fifteen minutes another star should fall—He sat there, watch in hand, for twice that time, but the phenomenon was not repeated.

The clock struck two, and Brown still slept. Mr. Hamlin approached the table, and took from his pocket a letter, which he read by the flickering candle-light. It contained only a single line, written in pencil, in a woman's hand,—

"Be at the corral, with the buggy, at three."

The sleeper moved uneasily, and then awoke. "Are you there, Jack?"

"Yes."

"Don't go yet. I dreamed just now, Jack,—dreamed of old times. I thought that Sue and me was being married agin, and that the parson, Jack, was—who do you think?—you!"

The gambler laughed, and seated himself on the bed,—the paper still in his hand.

"It's a good sign, ain't it?" queried Brown.

"I reckon. Say, old man, hadn't you better get up?"

The "old man," thus affectionately appealed to, rose, with the assistance of Hamlin's outstretched hand.

"Smoke?"

Brown mechanically took the proffered cigar.

"Light?"

Jack had twisted the letter into a spiral, lit it, and held it for his companion. He continued to hold it until it was consumed, and dropped the fragment—a fiery star—from the open window. He watched it as it fell, and then returned to his friend.

"Old man," he said, placing his hands upon Brown's shoulders, "in ten minutes I'll be on the road, and gone like that spark. We won't see each other agin; but, before I go, take a fool's advice: sell out all you've got, take your wife with you, and quit the country. It ain't no place for you, nor her. Tell her she must go; make her go, if she won't. Don't whine because you can't be a saint, and she ain't an angel. Be a man,—and treat her like a woman. Don't be a d—— fool. Good by."

He tore himself from Brown's grasp, and leaped down the stairs like a deer. At the stable-door he collared the half-sleeping hostler; and backed him against the wall. "Saddle my horse in two minutes, or I'll—" The ellipsis was frightfully suggestive.

"The missis said you was to have the buggy," stammered the man.

"D——n the buggy!"

The horse was saddled as fast as the nervous hands of the astounded hostler could manipulate buckle and strap.

"Is anything up, Mr. Hamlin?" said the man, who, like all his class, admired the *élan* of his fiery patron, and was really concerned in his welfare.

"Stand aside!"

The man fell back. With an oath, a bound, and clatter, Jack was into the road. In another moment, to the man's half-awakened eyes, he was but a moving cloud of dust in the distance, towards which a star just loosed from its brethren was trailing a stream of fire.

But early that morning the dwellers by the Wingdam turnpike, miles away, heard a voice, pure as a sky-lark's, singing afield. They who were asleep turned over on their

rude couches to dream of youth and love and olden days.
Hard-faced men and anxious gold-seekers, already at work,
ceased their labors and leaned upon their picks, to listen to
a romantic vagabond ambling away against the rosy sunrise.

HIGH-WATER MARK

WHEN the tide was out on the Dedlow Marsh, its extended dreariness was patent. Its spongy, low-lying surface, sluggish, inky pools, and tortuous sloughs, twisting
their slimy way, eel-like, toward the open bay, were all hard
facts. So were the few green tussocks, with their scant
blades, their amphibious flavor, and unpleasant dampness.
And if you choose to indulge your fancy,—although the flat
monotony of the Dedlow Marsh was not inspiring,—the
wavy line of scattered drift gave an unpleasant consciousness of the spent waters, and made the dead certainty of
the returning tide a gloomy reflection, which no present
sunshine could dissipate. The greener meadow-land seemed
oppressed with this idea, and made no positive attempt at
vegetation until the work of reclamation should be complete. In the bitter fruit of the low cranberry-bushes one
might fancy he detected a naturally sweet disposition cur-
dled and soured by an injudicious course of too much regular cold water.

The vocal expression of the Dedlow Marsh was also
melancholy and depressing. The sepulchral boom of the bit-
tern, the shriek of the curlew, the scream of passing brent,
the wrangling of quarrelsome teal, the sharp, querulous

protest of the startled crane, and syllabled complaint of the
"killdeer" plover were beyond the power of written expression. Nor was the aspect of these mournful fowls at all
cheerful and inspiring. Certainly not the blue heron standing midleg deep in the water, obviously catching cold in a
reckless disregard of wet feet and consequences; nor the
mournful curlew, the dejected plover, or the low-spirited
snipe, who saw fit to join him in his suicidal contemplation; nor the impassive kingfisher—an ornithological
Marius—reviewing the desolate expanse; nor the black
raven that went to and fro over the face of the marsh continually, but evidently couldn't make up his mind whether
the waters had subsided, and felt low-spirited in the reflection that, after all this trouble, he wouldn't be able to give
a definite answer. On the contrary, it was evident at a
glance that the dreary expanse of Dedlow Marsh told unpleasantly on the birds, and that the season of migration
was looked forward to with a feeling of relief and satisfaction by the full-grown, and of extravagant anticipation by
the callow, brood. But if Dedlow Marsh was cheerless at
the slack of the low tide, you should have seen it when the
tide was strong and full. When the damp air blew chilly
over the cold, glittering expanse, and came to the faces of
those who looked seaward like another tide; when a steel-
like glint marked the low hollows and the sinuous line of
slough; when the great shell-incrusted trunks of fallen trees
arose again, and went forth on their dreary, purposeless
wanderings, drifting hither and thither, but getting no farther toward any goal at the falling tide or the day's decline
than the cursed Hebrew in the legend; when the glossy
ducks swung silently, making neither ripple nor furrow on

the shimmering surface; when the fog came in with the tide and shut out the blue above, even as the green below had been obliterated; when boatmen, lost in that fog, paddling about in a hopeless way, started at what seemed the brushing of mermen's fingers on the boat's keel, or shrank from the tufts of grass spreading around like the floating hair of a corpse, and knew by these signs that they were lost upon Dedlow Marsh, and must make a night of it, and a gloomy one at that,—then you might know something of Dedlow Marsh at high water.

Let me recall a story connected with this latter view which never failed to recur to my mind in my long gunning excursions upon Dedlow Marsh. Although the event was briefly recorded in the county paper, I had the story, in all its eloquent detail, from the lips of the principal actor. I cannot hope to catch the varying emphasis and peculiar coloring of feminine delineation, for my narrator was a woman; but I'll try to give at least its substance.

She lived midway of the great slough of Dedlow Marsh and a good-sized river, which debouched four miles beyond into an estuary formed by the Pacific Ocean, on the long sandy peninsula which constituted the southwestern boundary of a noble bay. The house in which she lived was a small frame cabin raised from the marsh a few feet by stout piles, and was three miles distant from the settlements upon the river. Her husband was a logger,—a profitable business in a county where the principal occupation was the manufacture of lumber.

It was the season of early spring, when her husband left on the ebb of a high tide, with a raft of logs for the usual transportation to the lower end of the bay. As she stood by the door of the little cabin when the voyagers departed she noticed a cold look in the southeastern sky, and she remembered hearing her husband say to his companions that they must endeavor to complete their voyage before the coming of the southwesterly gale which he saw brewing. And that night it began to storm and blow harder than she had ever before experienced, and some great trees fell in the forest by the river, and the house rocked like her baby's cradle.

But however the storm might roar about the little cabin, she knew that one she trusted had driven bolt and bar with his own strong hand, and that had he feared for her he would not have left her. This, and her domestic duties, and the care of her little sickly baby, helped to keep her mind from dwelling on the weather, except, of course, to hope that he was safely harbored with the logs at Utopia in the dreary distance. But she noticed that day, when she went out to feed the chickens and look after the cow, that the tide was up to the little fence of their garden-patch, and the roar of the surf on the south beach, though miles away, she could hear distinctly. And she began to think that she would like to have some one to talk with about matters, and she believed that if it had not been so far and so stormy, and the trail so impassable, she would have taken the baby and have gone over to Ryckman's, her nearest neighbor. But then, you see, he might have returned in the storm, all wet, with no one to see to him; and it was a long exposure for baby, who was croupy and ailing.

But that night, she never could tell why, she didn't feel like sleeping or even lying down. The storm had somewhat abated, but she still "sat and sat," and even tried to read.

I don't know whether it was a Bible or some profane magazine that this poor woman read, but most probably the latter, for the words all ran together and made such sad nonsense that she was forced at last to put the book down and turn to that dearer volume which lay before her in the cradle, with its white initial leaf as yet unsoiled, and try to look forward to its mysterious future. And, rocking the cradle, she thought of everything and everybody, but still was wide awake as ever.

It was nearly twelve o'clock when she at last lay down in her clothes. How long she slept she could not remember, but she awoke with a dreadful choking in her throat, and found herself standing, trembling all over, in the middle of the room, with her baby clasped to her breast, and she was "saying something." The baby cried and sobbed, and she walked up and down trying to hush it, when she heard a scratching at the door. She opened it fearfully, and was glad to see it was only old Pete, their dog, who crawled, dripping with water, into the room. She would like to have looked out, not in the faint hope of her husband's coming, but to see how things looked; but the wind shook the door so savagely that she could hardly hold it. Then she sat down a little while, and then walked up and down a little while, and then she lay down again a little while. Lying close by the wall of the little cabin, she thought she heard once or twice something scrape slowly against the clapboards, like the scraping of branches. Then there was a little gurgling sound, "like the baby made when it was swallowing"; then something went "click-click" and "cluck-cluck," so that she sat up in bed. When she did so she was attracted by something else that seemed creeping from the back door towards the centre of the room. It wasn't much wider than her little finger, but soon it swelled to the width of her hand, and began spreading all over the floor. It was water.

She ran to the front door and threw it wide open, and saw nothing but water. She ran to the back door and threw it open, and saw nothing but water. She ran to the side window, and throwing that open, she saw nothing but water. Then she remembered hearing her husband once say that there was no danger in the tide, for that fell regularly, and people could calculate on it, and that he would rather live near the bay than the river, whose banks might overflow at any time. But was it the tide? So she ran again to the back door, and threw out a stick of wood. It drifted away towards the bay. She scooped up some of the water and put it eagerly to her lips. It was fresh and sweet. It was the river, and not the tide!

It was then—O, God be praised for his goodness! she did neither faint nor fall; it was then—blessed be the Saviour for it was his merciful hand that touched and strengthened her in this awful moment—that fear dropped from her like a garment, and her trembling ceased. It was then and thereafter that she never lost her self-command, through all the trials of that gloomy night.

She drew the bedstead towards the middle of the room, and placed a table upon it and on that she put the cradle. The water on the floor was already over her ankles, and the house once or twice moved so perceptibly, and seemed to be rocked so, that the closet doors all flew open. Then she heard the same rasping and thumping against the wall, and, looking out, saw that a large uprooted tree, which had lain near the road at the upper end of the pasture, had floated

"Beneath the snow lay he who was at once the strongest and yet the weakest of the outcasts of Poker Flat." Illustration by Pierre Falké for *The Outcasts of Poker Flat* in *The Wild West*, published by Harrison of Paris. (*p. 28*)

down to the house. Luckily its long roots dragged in the soil and kept it from moving as rapidly as the current, for had it struck the house in its full career, even the strong nails and bolts in the piles could not have withstood the shock. The hound had leaped upon its knotty surface, and crouched near the roots shivering and whining. A ray of hope flashed across her mind. She drew a heavy blanket from the bed, and, wrapping it about the babe, waded in the deepening waters to the door. As the tree swung again, broadside on, making the little cabin creak and tremble, she leaped on to its trunk. By God's mercy she succeeded in obtaining a footing on its slippery surface, and, twining an arm about its roots, she held in the other her moaning child. Then something cracked near the front porch, and the whole front of the house she had just quitted fell forward,—just as cattle fall on their knees before they lie down—and at the same moment the great redwood-tree swung round and drifted away with its living cargo into the black night.

For all the excitement and danger, for all her soothing of her crying babe, for all the whistling of the wind, for all the uncertainty of her situation, she still turned to look at the deserted and water-swept cabin. She remembered even then, and she wonders how foolish she was to think of it at that time, that she wished she had put on another dress and the baby's best clothes; and she kept praying that the house would be spared so that he, when he returned, would have something to come to, and it wouldn't be quite so desolate, and—how could he ever know what had become of her and baby? And at the thought she grew sick and faint. But she had something else to do besides worrying, for whenever the long roots of her ark struck an obstacle,

the whole trunk made half a revolution, and twice dipped
her in the black water. The hound, who kept distracting her
by running up and down the tree and howling, at last fell
off at one of these collisions. He swam for some time beside her, and she tried to get the poor beast upon the tree,
but he "acted silly" and wild, and at last she lost sight of
him forever. Then she and her baby were left alone. The
light which had burned for a few minutes in the deserted
cabin was quenched suddenly. She could not then tell whither
she was drifting. The outline of the white dunes on the
peninsula showed dimly ahead, and she judged the tree was
moving in a line with the river. It must be about slack
water, and she had probably reached the eddy formed by the
confluence of the tide and the overflowing waters of the
river. Unless the tide fell soon, there was present danger
of her drifting to its channel, and being carried out to sea
or crushed in the floating drift. That peril averted, if she
were carried out on the ebb toward the bay, she might hope
to strike one of the wooded promontories of the peninsula,
and rest till daylight. Sometimes she thought she heard
voices and shouts from the river, and the bellowing of cattle
and bleating of sheep. Then again it was only the ringing
in her ears and throbbing of her heart. She found at about
this time that she was so chilled and stiffened in her cramped
position that she could scarcely move, and the baby cried
so when she put it to her breast that she noticed the milk
refused to flow; and she was so frightened at that, that she
put her head under her shawl, and for the first time cried
bitterly.

When she raised her head again, the boom of the surf
was behind her, and she knew that her ark had again swung

round. She dipped up the water to cool her parched throat, and found that it was salt as her tears. There was a relief, though, for by this sign she knew that she was drifting with the tide. It was then the wind went down, and the great and awful silence oppressed her. There was scarcely a ripple against the furrowed sides of the great trunk on which she rested, and around her all was black gloom and quiet. She spoke to the baby just to hear herself speak, and to know that she had not lost her voice. She thought then,—it was queer, but she could not help thinking it,—how awful must have been the night when the great ship swung over the Asiatic peak, and the sounds of creation were blotted out from the world. She thought, too, of mariners clinging to spars, and of poor women who were lashed to rafts, and beaten to death by the cruel sea. She tried to thank God that she was thus spared, and lifted her eyes from the baby who had fallen into a fretful sleep. Suddenly, away to the southward, a great light lifted itself out of the gloom, and flashed and flickered, and flickered and flashed again. Her heart fluttered quickly against the baby's cold cheek. It was the lighthouse at the entrance of the bay. As she was yet wondering, the tree suddenly rolled a little, dragged a little, and then seemed to lie quiet and still. She put out her hand and the current gurgled against it. The tree was aground, and, by the position of the light and the noise of the surf, aground upon the Dedlow Marsh.

Had it not been for her baby, who was ailing and croupy, had it not been for the sudden drying up of that sensitive fountain, she would have felt safe and relieved. Perhaps it was this which tended to make all her impressions mournful and gloomy. As the tide rapidly fell, a great flock of

black brent fluttered by her, screaming and crying. Then
the plover flew up and piped mournfully, as they wheeled
around the trunk, and at last fearlessly lit upon it like a gray
cloud. Then the heron flew over and around her, shrieking
and protesting, and at last dropped its gaunt legs only a few
yards from her. But, strangest of all, a pretty white bird,
larger than a dove,—like a pelican, but not a pelican,—
circled around and around her. At last it lit upon a rootlet
of the tree, quite over her shoulder. She put out her hand
and stroked its beautiful white neck, and it never appeared
to move. It stayed there so long that she thought she would
lift up the baby to see it, and try to attract her attention.
But when she did so, the child was so chilled and cold, and
had such a blue look under the little lashes which it didn't
raise at all, that she screamed aloud, and the bird flew away,
and she fainted.

Well, that was the worst of it, and perhaps it was not so
much, after all, to any but herself. For when she recovered
her senses it was bright sunlight, and dead low water. There
was a confused noise of guttural voices about her, and an
old squaw, singing an Indian "hushaby," and rocking herself from side to side before a fire built on the marsh, before
which she, the recovered wife and mother, lay weak and
weary. Her first thought was for her baby, and she was
about to speak, when a young squaw, who must have been
a mother herself, fathomed her thought and brought her
the "mowitch," pale but living, in such a queer little willow
cradle all bound up, just like the squaw's own young one,
that she laughed and cried together, and the young squaw
and the old squaw showed their big white teeth and glinted
their black eyes and said, "Plenty get well, skeena mowitch,"

"wagee man come plenty soon," and she could have kissed their brown faces in her joy. And then she found that they had been gathering berries on the marsh in their queer, comical baskets, and saw the skirt of her gown fluttering on the tree from afar, and the old squaw couldn't resist the temptation of procuring a new garment, and came down and discovered the "wagee" woman and child. And of course she gave the garment to the old squaw, as you may imagine, and when *he* came at last and rushed up to her, looking about ten years older in his anxiety, she felt so faint again that they had to carry her to the canoe. For, you see, he knew nothing about the flood until he met the Indians at Utopia, and knew by the signs that the poor woman was his wife. And at the next high-tide he towed the tree away back home, although it wasn't worth the trouble, and built another house, using the old tree for the foundation and props, and called it after her, "Mary's Ark!" But you may guess the next house was built above High-water mark. And that's all.

Not much, perhaps, considering the malevolent capacity of the Dedlow Marsh. But you must tramp over it at low water, or paddle over it at high tide, or get lost upon it once or twice in the fog, as I have, to understand properly Mary's adventure, or to appreciate duly the blessings of living beyond High-Water Mark.

A LONELY RIDE

As I stepped into the Slumgullion stage I saw that it was a dark night, a lonely road, and that I was the only passenger. Let me assure the reader that I have no ulterior design in making this assertion. A long course of light reading has forewarned me what every experienced intelligence must confidently look for from such a statement. The story-teller who wilfully tempts Fate by such obvious beginnings; who is to the expectant reader in danger of being robbed or half murdered, or frightened by an escaped lunatic, or introduced to his lady-love for the first time, deserves to be detected. I am relieved to say that none of these things occurred to me. The road from Wingdam to Slumgullion knew no other banditti than the regularly licensed hotel-keepers; lunatics had not yet reached such depth of imbecility as to ride of their own free-will in California stages; and my Laura, amiable and long-suffering as she always is, could not, I fear, have borne up against these depressing circumstances long enough to have made the slightest impression on me.

I stood with my shawl and carpet-bag in hand, gazing doubtingly on the vehicle. Even in the darkness the red dust of Wingdam was visible on its roof and sides, and the red slime of Slumgullion clung tenaciously to its wheels. I opened the door; the stage creaked uneasily, and in the gloomy abyss the swaying straps beckoned me, like ghostly hands, to come in now, and have my sufferings out at once.

I must not omit to mention the occurrence of a circumstance which struck me as appalling and mysterious. A lounger on the steps of the hotel, whom I had reason to suppose was not in any way connected with the stage company, gravely descended, and, walking toward the conveyance, tried the handle of the door, opened it, expectorated in the carriage, and returned to the hotel with a serious demeanor. Hardly had he resumed his position, when another individual, equally disinterested, impassively walked down the steps, proceeded to the back of the stage, lifted it, expectorated carefully on the axle, and returned slowly and pensively to the hotel. A third spectator wearily disengaged himself from one of the Ionic columns of the portico and walked to the box, remained for a moment in serious and expectorative contemplation of the boot, and then returned to his column. There was something so weird in this baptism that I grew quite nervous.

Perhaps I was out of spirits. A number of infinitesimal annoyances, winding up with the resolute persistency of the clerk at the stage-office to enter my name misspelt on the way-bill, had not predisposed me to cheerfulness. The inmates of the Eureka House, from a social view-point, were not attractive. There was the prevailing opinion—so common to many honest people—that a serious style of deportment and conduct toward a stranger indicates high gentility and elevated station. Obeying this principle, all hilarity ceased on my entrance to supper, and general mark merged into the safer and uncompromising chronicle of several bad cases of diphtheria, then epidemic at Wingdam. When I left the dining-room, with an odd feeling that I had been supping exclusively on mustard and tea-leaves, I stopped a moment at the parlor door. A piano, harmoniously related to the dinner-bell, tinkled responsive to a diffident and uncertain touch. On the white wall the shadow of an old and sharp profile was bending over several symmetrical and shadowy curls. "I sez to Mariar, Mariar, sez I, 'Praise to the face is open disgrace'." I heard no more. Dreading some susceptibility to sincere expression on the subject of female loveliness, I walked away, checking the compliment that otherwise might have risen unbidden to my lips, and have brought shame and sorrow to the household.

It was with the memory of these experiences resting heavily upon me, that I stood hesitatingly before the stage door. The driver, about to mount, was for a moment illuminated by the open door of the hotel. He had the wearied look which was the distinguishing expression of Wingdam. Satisfied that I was properly way-billed and receipted for, he took no further notice of me. I looked longingly at the box-seat, but he did not respond to the appeal. I flung my carpet-bag into the chasm, dived recklessly after it, and—before I was fairly seated—with a great sigh, a creaking of unwilling springs, complaining bolts, and harshly expostulating axle, we moved away. Rather the hotel door slipped behind, the sound of the piano sank to rest, and the night and its shadows moved solemnly upon us.

To say it was dark expressed but faintly the pitchy obscurity that encompassed the vehicle. The roadside trees were scarcely distinguishable as deeper masses of shadow; I knew them only by the peculiar sodden odor that from time to time sluggishly flowed in at the open window as we rolled by. We proceeded slowly; so leisurely that, leaning from the carriage, I more than once detected the fragrant sigh of some astonished cow, whose ruminating repose upon the highway we had ruthlessly disturbed. But in the dark-

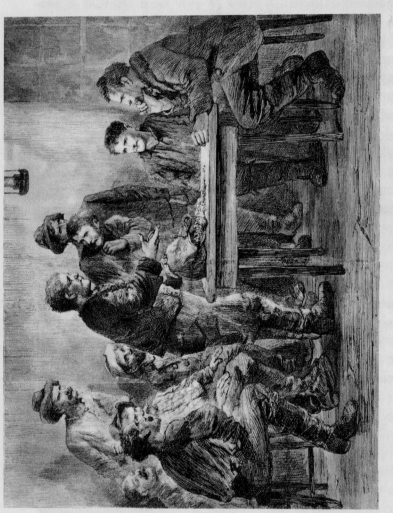

"And before a hand could be raised to prevent him, he had emptied the contents of the carpet-bag upon the table." Illustration for an 1872 edition of *Tennessee's Partner*, published by James R. Osgood & Co. (*p. 48*)

ness our progress, more the guidance of some mysterious instinct than any apparent volition of our own, gave an indefinable charm of security to our journey, that a moment's hesitation or indecision on the part of the driver would have destroyed.

I had indulged a hope that in the empty vehicle I might obtain that rest so often denied me in its crowded condition. It was a weak delusion. When I stretched out my limbs it was only to find that the ordinary conveniences for making several people distinctly uncomfortable were distributed throughout my individual frame. At last, resting my arms on the straps, by dint of much gymnastic effort I became sufficiently composed to be aware of a more refined species of torture. The springs of the stage, rising and falling regularly, produced a rhythmical beat, which began painfully to absorb my attention. Slowly this thumping merged into a senseless echo of the mysterious female of the hotel parlor, and shaped itself into this awful and benumbing axiom,—"Praise-to-the-face-is-open-disgrace. Praise-to-the-face-is-open-disgrace." Inequalities of the road only quickened its utterance or drawled it to an exasperating length.

It was of no use seriously to consider the statement. It was of no use to except to it indignantly. It was of no use to recall the many instances where praise to the face had redounded to the everlasting honor of praiser and bepraised; of no use to dwell sentimentally on modest genius and courage lifted up and strengthened by open commendation; of no use to except to the mysterious female,—to picture her as rearing a thin-blooded generation on selfish and mechanically repeated axioms,—all this failed to counteract the monotonous repetition of this sentence. There was nothing

to do but to give in,—and I was about to accept it weakly,
as we too often treat other illusions of darkness and necessity, for the time being,—when I became aware of some
other annoyance that had been forcing itself upon me for
the last few moments. How quiet the driver was!

Was there any driver? Had I any reason to suppose that
he was not lying, gagged and bound on the roadside, and
the highwayman, with blackened face who did the thing so
quietly, driving me—whither? The thing is perfectly feas-
ible. And what is this fancy now being jolted out of me?
A story? It's of no use to keep it back,—particularly in this
abysmal vehicle, and here it comes: I am a Marquis,—a
French Marquis; French, because the peerage is not so well
known, and the country is better adapted to romantic incident,—a Marquis, because the democratic reader delights
in the nobility. My name is something *ligny*. I am coming
from Paris to my country-seat at St. Germain. It is a dark
night, and I fall asleep and tell my honest coachman, André,
not to disturb me, and dream of an angel. The carriage at
last stops at the chateau. It is so dark that when I alight
I do not recognize the face of the footman who holds the
carriage door. But what of that?—*peste!* I am heavy with
sleep. The same obscurity also hides the old familiar inde-
cencies of the statues on the terrace; but there is a door,
and it opens and shuts behind me smartly. Then I find myself in a trap, in the presence of the brigand who has quietly
gagged poor André and conducted the carriage thither.
There is nothing for me to do, as a gallant French Marquis,
but to say, *"Parbleu!"* draw my rapier, and die valorously!
I am found a week or two after, outside a deserted *cabaret*
near the barrier, with a hole through my ruffled linen and
my pockets stripped. No; on second thoughts, I am res-

cued,—rescued by the angel I have been dreaming of, who
is the assumed daughter of the brigand, but the real daughter of an intimate friend.

Looking from the window again, in the vain hope of distinguishing the driver, I found my eyes were growing accustomed to the darkness. I could see the distant horizon,
defined by India-inky woods, relieving a lighter sky. A few
stars widely spaced in this picture glimmered sadly. I noticed
again the infinite depth of patient sorrow in their serene
faces; and I hope that the Vandal who first applied the
flippant "twinkle" to them may not be driven melancholy
mad by their reproachful eyes. I noticed again the mystic
charm of space that imparts a sense of individual solitude
to each integer of the densest constellation, involving the
smallest star with immeasurable loneliness. Something of
this calm and solitude crept over me, and I dozed in my
gloomy cavern. When I awoke the full moon was rising.
Seen from my window, it had an indescribably unreal and
theatrical effect. It was the full moon of Norma,—that
remarkable celestial phenomenon which rises so palpably to
a hushed audience and a sublime *andante* chorus, until the
Casta Diva is sung,—the "inconstant moon" that then and
thereafter remains fixed in the heavens as though it were a
part of the solar system inaugurated by Joshua. Again the
white-robed Druids filed past me, again I saw that improbable mistletoe cut from that impossible oak, and again cold
chills ran down my back with the first strain of the recita-
tive. The thumping springs essayed to beat time, and the
private-box-like obscurity of the vehicle lent a cheap en-
chantment to the view. But it was a vast improvement upon
my past experience, and I hugged the fond delusion.

My fears for the driver were dissipated with the rising

moon. A familiar sound had assured me of his presence in the full possession of at least one of his most important functions. Frequent and full expectoration convinced me that his lips were as yet not sealed by the gag of highwaymen, and soothed my anxious ear. With this load lifted from my mind, and assisted by the mild presence of Diana, who left, as when she visited Endymion, much of her splendor outside my cavern,—I looked around the empty vehicle. On the forward seat lay a woman's hair-pin. I picked it up with an interest that, however, soon abated. There was no scent of the roses to cling to it still, not even of hair-oil. No bend or twist in its rigid angles betrayed any trait of its wearer's character. I tried to think that it might have been "Mariar's." I tried to imagine that, confining the symmetrical curls of that girl, it might have heard the soft compliments whispered in her ears, which provoked the wrath of the aged female. But in vain. It was reticent and unswerving in its upright fidelity, and at last slipped listlessly through my fingers.

I had dozed repeatedly,—waked on the threshold of oblivion by contact with some of the angles of the coach, and feeling that I was unconsciously assuming, in imitation of a humble insect of my childish recollection, that spherical shape which could best resist those impressions, when I perceived that the moon, riding high in the heavens, had begun to separate the formless masses of the shadowy landscape. Trees isolated, in clumps and assemblages, changed places before my window. The sharp outlines of the distant hills came back, as in daylight, but little softened in the dry, cold, dewless air of a California summer night. I was wondering how late it was, and thinking that if the horses of the night travelled as slowly as the team before us, Faustus might have been spared his agonizing prayer, when a sudden spasm of activity attacked my driver. A succession of whip-snappings, like a pack of Chinese crackers, broke from the box before me. The stage leaped forward, and when I could pick myself from under the seat, a long white building had in some mysterious way rolled before my window. It must be Slumgullion! As I descended from the stage I addressed the driver:—

"I thought you changed horses on the road?"

"So we did. Two hours ago."

"That's odd. I didn't notice it."

"Must have been asleep, sir. Hope you had a pleasant nap. Bully place for a nice quiet snooze,—empty stage, sir!"

THE MAN OF NO ACCOUNT

His name was Fagg,—David Fagg. He came to California in '52 with us, in the "Skyscraper." I don't think he did it in an adventurous way. He probably had no other place to go to. When a knot of us young fellows would recite what splendid opportunities we resigned to go, and how sorry our friends were to have us leave, and show daguerreotypes and locks of hair, and talk of Mary and Susan, the man of no account used to sit by and listen with a pained, mortified expression on his plain face, and say nothing. I think he had nothing to say. He had no associates except when we patronized him; and, in point of fact, he was a good deal of sport to us. He was always sea-sick whenever we had a capful of wind. He never got his sea-legs on either. And I never shall forget how we all laughed when Rattler took him the piece of pork on a string, and—But you know that time-honored joke. And then we had such a splendid lark with him. Miss Fanny Twinkler couldn't bear the sight of him, and we used to make Fagg think that she had taken a fancy to him, and send him little delicacies and books from the cabin. You ought to have witnessed the rich scene that took place when he came up, stammering and very sick, to thank her! Didn't she flash up grandly and beautifully and scornfully? So like "Medora," Rattler said,—Rattler knew Byron by heart,—and wasn't old Fagg awfully cut up? But he got over it, and when Rattler fell sick at Valparaiso, old Fagg used to nurse him. You see he was a good sort of fellow, but he lacked manliness and spirit.

He had absolutely no idea of poetry. I've seen him sit stolidly by, mending his old clothes, when Rattler delivered that stirring apostrophe of Byron's to the ocean. He asked Rattler once, quite seriously, if he thought Byron was ever sea-sick. I don't remember Rattler's reply, but I know we all laughed very much, and I have no doubt it was something good, for Rattler was smart.

When the "Skyscraper" arrived at San Francisco we had a grand "feed." We agreed to meet every year and perpetuate the occasion. Of course we didn't invite Fagg. Fagg was a steerage-passenger, and it was necessary, you see, now we were ashore, to exercise a little discretion. But Old Fagg, as we called him,—he was only about twenty-five years old, by the way,—was the source of immense amusement to us that day. It appeared that he had conceived the idea that he could walk to Sacramento, and actually started off afoot. We had a good time, and shook hands with one another all around, and so parted. Ah me! only eight years ago, and yet some of those hands then clasped in amity have been clenched at each other, or have dipped furtively in one another's pockets. I know that we didn't dine together the next year, because young Barker swore he wouldn't put his feet under the same mahogany with such a very contempti-ble scoundrel as that Mixer; and Nibbles, who borrowed money at Valparaiso of young Stubbs, who was then a waiter in a restaurant, didn't like to meet such people.

When I bought a number of shares in the Coyote Tunnel at Mugginsville, in '54, I thought I'd take a run up there and see it. I stopped at the Empire Hotel, and after dinner I got a horse and rode round the town and out to the claim. One of those individuals whom newspaper correspondents call "our intelligent informant," and to whom in all small communities the right of answering questions is tacitly yielded, was quietly pointed out to me. Habit had enabled him to work and talk at the same time, and he never pre-termitted either. He gave me a history of the claim, and added: "You see, stranger" (he addressed the bank before him), "gold is sure to come out 'er that theer claim (he put in a comma with his pick), but the old pro-pri-e-tor (he wriggled out the word and the point of his pick) warn't of much account (a long stroke of the pick for a period). He was green, and let the boys about here jump him,"—and the rest of his sentence was confided to his hat, which he had removed to wipe his manly brow with his red bandanna.

I asked him who was the original proprietor.

"His name war Fagg."

I went to see him. He looked a little older and plainer. He had worked hard, he said, and was getting on "so, so." I took quite a liking to him and patronized him to some ex-tent. Whether I did so because I was beginning to have a distrust for such fellows as Rattler and Mixer is not necessary for me to state.

You remember how the Coyote Tunnel went in, and how awfully we shareholders were done! Well, the next thing I heard was that Rattler, who was one of the heaviest shareholders, was up at Mugginsville keeping bar for the proprietor of the Mugginsville Hotel, and that old Fagg had struck it rich, and didn't know what to do with his money. All this was told me by Mixer, who had been there, settling up matters, and likewise that Fagg was sweet upon the daughter of the proprietor of the aforesaid hotel. And so by hearsay and letter I eventually gathered that old Robins, the hotel man, was trying to get up a match between Nellie Robins and Fagg. Nellie was a pretty, plump, and foolish little thing, and would do just as her father wished. I thought it would be a good thing for Fagg if he should marry and settle down; that as a married man he might be of some account. So I ran up to Mugginsville one day to look after things.

It did me an immense deal of good to make Rattler mix my drinks for me,—Rattler! the gay, brilliant, and unconquerable Rattler, who had tried to snub me two years ago. I talked to him about old Fagg and Nellie, particularly as I thought the subject was distasteful. He never liked Fagg, and he was sure, he said, that Nellie didn't. Did Nellie like anybody else? He turned around to the mirror behind the bar and brushed up his hair! I understood the conceited wretch. I thought I'd put Fagg on his guard and get him to hurry up matters. I had a long talk with him. You could see by the way the poor fellow acted that he was badly stuck. He sighed, and promised to pluck up courage to hurry matters to a crisis. Nellie was a good girl, and I think had a sort of quiet respect for old Fagg's unobtrusiveness. But her fancy was already taken captive by Rattler's superficial qualities, which were obvious and pleasing. I don't think Nellie was any worse than you or I. We are more apt to take acquaintances at their apparent value than their intrinsic worth. It's less trouble, and, except when we want to trust them, quite as convenient. The difficulty with women is that their feelings are apt to get interested sooner than ours, and then, you know, reasoning is out of the question. That is what old Fagg would have known had he been of any account. But he wasn't. So much the worse for him.

It was a few months afterward, and I was sitting in my office when in walked old Fagg. I was surprised to see him down, but we talked over the current topics in that mechanical manner of people who know that they have something else to say, but are obliged to get at it in that formal way. After an interval Fagg in his natural manner said,—

"I'm going home!"

"Going home?"

"Yes,—that is, I think I'll take a trip to the Atlantic States. I came to see you, as you know I have some little property, and I have executed a power of attorney for you to manage my affairs. I have some papers I'd like to leave with you. Will you take charge of them?"

"Yes," I said. "But what of Nellie?"

His face fell. He tried to smile, and the combination resulted in one of the most startling and grotesque effects I ever beheld. At length he said,—

"I shall not marry Nellie,—that is,"—he seemed to apologize internally for the positive form of expression,—"I think that I had better not."

"David Fagg," I said with sudden severity, "you're of no account!"

To my astonishment his face brightened. "Yes," said he, "that's it!—I'm of no account! But I always knew it. You see I thought Rattler loved that girl as well as I did, and I knew she liked him better than she did me, and would be happier I dare say with him. But then I knew that old Robins would have preferred me to him, as I was better off,—and the girl would do as he said,—and, you see, I thought I was kinder in the way,—and so I left. But," he continued, as I was about to interrupt him, "for fear the old man might object to Rattler, I've lent him enough to set him up in business for himself in Dogtown. A pushing, active, brilliant fellow, you know, like Rattler can get along, and will soon be in his old position again,—and you need not be hard on him, you know, if he doesn't. Good by."

I was too much disgusted with his treatment of that Rattler to be at all amiable, but as his business was profitable, I promised to attend to it, and he left. A few weeks passed. The return steamer arrived, and a terrible incident occupied the papers for days afterward. People in all parts of the State conned eagerly the details of an awful shipwreck, and those who had friends aboard went away by themselves, and read the long list of the lost under their breath. I read of the gifted, the gallant, the noble, and loved ones who had perished, and among them I think I was the first to read the name of David Fagg. For the "man of no account" had "gone home!"

MLISS

CHAPTER I

JUST where the Sierra Nevada begins to subside in gentler undulations, and the rivers grow less rapid and yellow, on the side of a great red mountain, stands "Smith's Pocket." Seen from the red road at sunset, in the red light and the red dust, its white houses look like the outcroppings of quartz on the mountain-side. The red stage topped with red-shirted passengers is lost to view half a dozen times in the tortuous descent, turning up unexpectedly in out-of-the-way places, and vanishing altogether within a hundred yards of the town. It is probably owing to this sudden twist in the road that the advent of a stranger at Smith's Pocket is usually attended with a peculiar circumstance. Dismounting from the vehicle at the stage-office, the too confident traveller is apt to walk straight out of town under the impression that it lies in quite another direction. It is related that one of the tunnel-men, two miles from town, met one of these self-reliant passengers with a carpet-bag, umbrella, Harper's Magazine, and other evidences of "Civilization and Refinement," plodding along over the road he had just ridden, vainly endeavoring to find the settlement of Smith's Pocket.

An observant traveller might have found some compensation for his disappointment in the weird aspect of that vicinity. There were huge fissures on the hillside, and displacements of the red soil, resembling more the chaos of some primary elemental upheaval than the work of man; while, half-way down, a long flume straddled its narrow body and disproportionate legs over the chasm, like an enormous fossil of some forgotten antediluvian. At every step smaller ditches crossed the road, hiding in their sallow depths unlovely streams that crept away to a clandestine union with the great yellow torrent below, and here and there were the ruins of some cabin with the chimney alone left intact and the hearthstone open to the skies.

The settlement of Smith's Pocket owed its origin to the finding of a "pocket" on its site by a veritable Smith. Five thousand dollars were taken out of it in one half-hour by Smith. Three thousand dollars were expended by Smith and others in erecting a flume and in tunnelling. And then Smith's Pocket was found to be only a pocket, and subject like other pockets to depletion. Although Smith pierced the bowels of the great red mountain, that five thousand dollars was the first and last return of his labor. The mountain grew reticent of its golden secrets, and the flume steadily ebbed away the remainder of Smith's fortune. Then Smith went into quartz-mining; then into quartz-milling; then into hydraulics and ditching, and then by easy degrees into saloon-keeping. Presently it was whispered that Smith was drinking a great deal; then it was known that Smith was a habitual drunkard, and then people began to think, as they are apt to, that he had never been anything else. But the settlement of Smith's Pocket, like that of most discoveries, was happily not dependent on the fortune of its pioneer, and other parties projected tunnels and found pockets. So Smith's Pocket became a settlement with its two fancy stores, its two hotels, its one express-office, and its two first families. Occasionally its one long straggling street was overawed by the assumption of the latest San Francisco fashions, imported per express, exclusively to the first families; making outraged Nature, in the ragged outline of her furrowed surface, look still more homely, and putting personal insult on that greater portion of the population to whom the Sabbath, with a change of linen, brought merely the necessity of cleanliness, without the luxury of adornment. Then there was a Methodist Church, and hard by a Monte Bank, and a little beyond, on the mountain-side, a graveyard; and then a little school-house.

"The Master," as he was known to his little flock, sat alone one night in the school-house, with some open copybooks before him, carefully making those bold and full characters which are supposed to combine the extremes of chirographical and moral excellence, and had got as far as "Riches are deceitful," and was elaborating the noun with an insincerity of flourish that was quite in the spirit of his text, when he heard a gentle tapping. The woodpeckers had been busy about the roof during the day, and the noise did not disturb his work. But the opening of the door, and the tapping continuing from the inside, caused him to look up. He was slightly startled by the figure of a young girl, dirty and shabbily clad. Still, her great black eyes, her coarse, uncombed, lustreless black hair falling over her sun-burned face, her red arms and feet streaked with the red soil, were all familiar to him. It was Melissa Smith,—Smith's motherless child.

"What can she want here?" thought the master. Everybody knew "Mliss," as she was called, throughout the length and height of Red Mountain. Everybody knew her as an incorrigible girl. Her fierce, ungovernable disposition, her mad freaks and lawless character, were in their way as proverbial as the story of her father's weaknesses, and as philosophically accepted by the townsfolk. She wrangled with and fought the school-boys with keener invective and quite as powerful arm. She followed the trails with a woodman's craft, and the master had met her before, miles away, shoeless, stockingless, and bareheaded on the mountain road. The miners' camps along the stream supplied her with subsistence during these voluntary pilgrimages, in freely offered alms. Not but that a larger protection had been previously extended to Mliss. The Rev. Joshua McSnagley, "stated" preacher, had placed her in the hotel as servant, by way of preliminary refinement, and had introduced her to his scholars at Sunday school. But she threw plates occasionally at the landlord, and quickly retorted to the cheap witticisms of the guests, and created in the Sabbath school a sensation that was so inimical to the orthodox dulness and placidity of that institution, that, with a decent regard for the starched frocks and unblemished morals of the two pink-and-white-faced children of the first families, the reverend gentleman had her ignominiously expelled. Such were the antecedents, and such the character of Mliss, as she stood before the master. It was shown in the ragged dress, the unkempt hair, and bleeding feet, and asked his pity. It flashed from her black, fearless eyes, and commanded his respect.

"I come here to-night," she said rapidly and boldly, keeping her hard glance on his, "because I knew you was alone. I wouldn't come here when them gals was here. I hate 'em and they hates me. That's why. You keep school, don't you? I want to be teached!"

If to the shabbiness of her apparel and uncomeliness of her tangled hair and dirty face she had added the humility

of tears, the master would have extended to her the usual
moiety of pity, and nothing more. But with the natural,
though illogical instincts of his species, her boldness awakened in him something of that respect which all original
natures pay unconsciously to one another in any grade.
And he gazed at her the more fixedly as she went on still
rapidly, her hand on that door-latch and her eyes on his:—

"My name's Mliss,—Mliss Smith! You can bet your life
on that. My father's Old Smith,—Old Bummer Smith,—
that's what's the matter with him. Mliss Smith,—and I'm
coming to school!"

"Well?" said the master.

Accustomed to be thwarted and opposed, often wantonly
and cruelly, for no other purpose than to excite the violent
impulses of her nature, the master's phlegm evidently took
her by surprise. She stopped; she began to twist a lock of
her hair between her fingers; and the rigid line of upper
lip, drawn over the wicked little teeth, relaxed and quivered
slightly. Then her eyes dropped, and something like a blush
struggled up to her cheek, and tried to assert itself through
the splashes of redder soil, and the sunburn of years. Suddenly she threw herself forward, calling on God to strike
her dead, and fell quite weak and helpless, with her face on
the master's desk, crying and sobbing as if her heart would
break.

The master lifted her gently and waited for the paroxysm
to pass. When with face still averted, she was repeating
between her sobs the *mea culpa* of childish penitence,—that
"she'd be good, she didn't mean to," etc., it came to him
to ask her why she had left Sabbath school.

Why had she left the Sabbath school?—why? O yes.
What did he (McSnagley) want to tell her she was wicked

for? What did he tell her that God hated her for? If God hated her, what did she want to go to Sabbath school for? *She* didn't want to be "beholden" to anybody who hated her.

Had she told McSnagley this?

Yes, she had.

The master laughed. It was a hearty laugh, and echoed so oddly in the little school-house, and seemed so inconsist= ent and discordant with the sighing of the pines without, that he shortly corrected himself with a sigh. The sigh was quite as sincere in its way, however, and after a moment of serious silence he asked about her father.

Her father? What father? Whose father? What had he ever done for her? Why did the girls hate her? Come now! what made the folks say, "Old Bummer Smith's Mliss!" when she passed? Yes; O yes. She wished he was dead,—she was dead,—everybody was dead; and her sobs broke forth anew.

The master then, leaning over her, told her as well as he could what you or I might have said after hearing such unnatural theories from childish lips; only bearing in mind perhaps better than you or I the unnatural facts of her ragged dress, her bleeding feet, and the omnipresent shadow of her drunken father. Then, raising her to her feet, he wrapped his shawl around her, and, bidding her come early in the morning, he walked with her down the road. There he bade her "good night." The moon shone brightly on the narrow path before them. He stood and watched the bent little figure as it staggered down the road, and waited until it had passed the little graveyard and reached the curve of the hill, where it turned and stood for a moment, a mere atom of suffering outlined against the far-off patient stars. Then he went back to his work. But the lines of the copy=

Bret Harte at the height of his literary fame, showing the fashionable clothes which he liked to wear.

book thereafter faded into long parallels of never-ending road, over which childish figures seemed to pass sobbing and crying into the night. Then, the little school-house seeming lonelier than before, he shut the door and went home.

The next morning Mliss came to school. Her face had been washed, and her coarse black hair bore evidence of recent struggles with the comb, in which both had evidently suffered. The old defiant look shone occasionally in her eyes, but her manner was tamer and more subdued. Then began a series of little trials and self-sacrifices, in which master and pupil bore an equal part, and which increased the confidence and sympathy between them. Although obedient under the master's eye, at times during recess, if thwarted or stung by a fancied slight, Mliss would rage in ungovernable fury, and many a palpitating young savage, finding himself matched with his own weapons of torment, would seek the master with torn jacket and scratched face, and complaints of the dreadful Mliss. There was a serious division among the townspeople on the subject; some threatening to withdraw their children from such evil companionship, and others as warmly upholding the course of the master in his work of reclamation. Meanwhile, with a steady persistence that seemed quite astonishing to him on looking back afterward, the master drew Mliss gradually out of the shadow of her past life, as though it were but her natural progress down the narrow path on which he had set her feet the moonlit night of their first meeting. Remembering the experience of the evangelical McSnagley, he carefully avoided that Rock of Ages on which that unskilful pilot had shipwrecked her young faith. But if, in the course of her reading, she chanced to stumble upon those

few words which have lifted such as she above the level of
the older, the wiser, and the more prudent,—if she learned
something of a faith that is symbolized by suffering, and
the old light softened in her eyes, it did not take the shape
of a lesson. A few of the plainer people had made up a
little sum by which the ragged Mliss was enabled to assume
the garments of respect and civilization; and often a rough
shake of the hand, and words of homely commendation
from a red-shirted and burly figure, sent a glow to the cheek
of the young master, and set him to thinking if it was
altogether deserved.

Three months had passed from the time of their first
meeting, and the master was sitting late one evening over
the moral and sententious copies, when there came a tap
at the door, and again Mliss stood before him. She was
neatly clad and clean-faced, and there was nothing perhaps
but the long black hair and bright black eyes to remind him
of his former apparition. "Are you busy?" she asked.
"Can you come with me?"—and on his signifying his readiness, in her old wilful way she said, "Come, then, quick!"

They passed out of the door together and into the dark
road. As they entered the town the master asked her
whither she was going. She replied, "To see my father."

It was the first time he had heard her call him by that
filial title, or indeed anything more than "Old Smith" or
the "Old Man." It was the first time in three months that
she had spoken of him at all, and the master knew she had
kept resolutely aloof from him since her great change.
Satisfied from her manner that it was fruitless to question
her purpose, he passively followed. In out-of-the-way
places, low groggeries, restaurants, and saloons; in gam-
bling-hells and dance-houses, the master, preceded by Mliss,

came and went. In the reeking smoke and blasphemous
outcries of low dens, the child, holding the master's hand,
stood and anxiously gazed, seemingly unconscious of all
in the one absorbing nature of her pursuit. Some of the
revellers, recognizing Mliss, called to the child to sing and
dance for them, and would have forced liquor upon her but
for the interference of the master. Others, recognizing
him mutely, made way for them to pass. So an hour slipped
by. The child whispered in his ear that there was a cabin
on the other side of the creek crossed by the long flume,
where she thought he still might be. Thither they crossed,
—a toilsome half-hour's walk,—but in vain. They were
returning by the ditch at the abutment of the flume, gazing
at the lights of the town on the opposite bank, when, suddenly, sharply, a quick report rang out on the clear night
air. The echoes caught it, and carried it round and round
Red Mountain, and set the dogs to barking all along the
streams. Lights seemed to dance and move quickly on the
outskirts of the town for a few moments, the stream rippled
quite audibly beside them, a few stones loosened themselves
from the hillside and splashed into the stream, a heavy wind
seemed to surge the branches of the funereal pines, and then
the silence seemed to fall thicker, heavier, and deadlier. The
master turned towards Mliss with an unconscious gesture
of protection, but the child had gone. Oppressed by a
strange fear, he ran quickly down the trail to the river's
bed, and jumping from boulder to boulder, reached the base
of Red Mountain and the outskirts of the village. Midway
of the crossing he looked up and held his breath in awe.
For high above him on the narrow flume he saw the
fluttering little figure of his late companion crossing swiftly
in the darkness.

He climbed the bank, and, guided by a few lights moving about a central point on the mountain, soon found himself breathless among a crowd of awe-stricken and sorrowful men. Out from among them the child appeared, and, taking the master's hand, led him silently before what seemed a ragged hole in the mountain. Her face was quite white, but her excited manner gone, and her look that of one to whom some long-expected event had at last happened,—an expression that to the master in his bewilderment seemed almost like relief. The walls of the cavern were partly propped by decaying timbers. The child pointed to what appeared to be some ragged, cast-off clothes left in the hole by the late occupant. The master approached nearer with his flaming dip, and bent over them. It was Smith, already cold, with a pistol in his hand and a bullet in his heart, lying beside his empty pocket.

CHAPTER II

THE opinion which McSnagley expressed in reference to a "change of heart" supposed to be experienced by Mliss was more forcibly described in the gulches and tunnels. It was thought there that Mliss had "struck a good lead." So when there was a new grave added to the little enclosure, and at the expense of the master a little board and inscription put above it, the Red Mountain Banner came out quite handsomely, and did the fair thing to the memory of one of "our oldest Pioneers," alluding gracefully to that "bane of noble intellects," and otherwise genteelly shelving our dear brother with the past. "He leaves an only child to mourn his loss," says the Banner, "who is now an exemplary scholar, thanks to the efforts of the Rev. Mr. Mc-Snagley." The Rev. McSnagley, in fact, made a strong point of Mliss's conversion, and, indirectly attributing to the unfortunate child the suicide of her father, made affecting allusions in Sunday school to the beneficial effects of the "silent tomb," and in this cheerful contemplation drove most of the children into speechless horror, and caused the pink-and-white scions of the first families to howl dismally and refuse to be comforted.

The long dry summer came. As each fierce day burned itself out in little whiffs of pearl-gray smoke on the mountain summits, and the upspringing breeze scattered its red embers over the landscape, the green wave which in early spring upheaved above Smith's grave grew sere and dry and hard. In those days the master, strolling in the little churchyard of a Sabbath afternoon, was sometimes surprised to find a few wild-flowers plucked from the damp pine-forests scattered there, and oftener rude wreaths hung upon the little pine cross. Most of these wreaths were formed of a sweet-scented grass, which the children loved to keep in their desks, intertwined with the plumes of the buckeye, the syringa, and the wood-anemone; and here and there the master noticed the dark blue cowl of the monk's-hood, or deadly aconite. There was something in the odd association of this noxious plant with these memorials which occasioned a painful sensation to the master deeper than his aesthetic sense. One day, during a long walk, in crossing a wooded ridge he came upon Mliss in the heart of the forest, perched upon a prostrate pine, on a fantastic throne formed by the hanging plumes of lifeless branches, her lap full of grasses and pine-burrs, and crooning to herself one of the negro melodies of her younger life. Recognizing him at a distance, she made room for him on her elevated throne, and with a grave assumption of hospitality and patronage that would have been ridiculous had it not been so terribly earnest, she fed him with pine-nuts and crab-apples. The master took that opportunity to point out to her the noxious and deadly qualities of the monk's-hood, whose dark blossoms he saw in her lap, and extorted from her a promise not to meddle with it as long as she remained his pupil. This done,—as the master had tested her integrity before,—he rested satisfied, and the strange feeling which had overcome him on seeing them died away.

Of the homes that were offered Mliss when her conversion became known, the master preferred that of Mrs. Morpher, a womanly and kind-hearted specimen of Southwestern efflorescence, known in her maidenhood as the "Per-rairie Rose." Being one of those who contend resolutely against their own natures, Mrs. Morpher, by a long series of self-sacrifices and struggles, had at last subjugated her naturally careless disposition to principles of "order," which she considered, in common with Mr. Pope, as "Heaven's first law." But she could not entirely govern the orbits of her satellites, however regular her own movements, and even her own "Jeemes" sometimes collided with her. Again her old nature asserted itself in her children. Lycurgus dipped into the cupboard "between meals," and Aristides came home from school without shoes, leaving those important articles on the threshold, for the delight of a barefooted walk down the ditches. Octavia and Cassandra were "keerless" of their clothes. So with but one exception, however much the "Prairie Rose" might have trimmed and pruned and trained her own matured luxuriance, the little shoots came up defiantly wild and straggling. That one exception was Clytemnestra Morpher, aged fifteen. She was the realization of her mother's immaculate conception,—neat, orderly, and dull.

It was an amiable weakness of Mrs. Morpher to imagine that "Clytie" was a consolation and model for Mliss. Following this fallacy, Mrs. Morpher threw Clytie at the head of Mliss when she was "bad," and set her up before the child for adoration in her penitential moments. It was not, therefore, surprising to the master to hear that Clytie was coming to school, obviously as a favor to the master and as an example for Mliss and others. For "Clytie" was quite a young lady. Inheriting her mother's physical peculiarities, and in obedience to the climatic laws of the Red Mountain region, she was an early bloomer. The youth of Smith's Pocket, to whom this kind of flower was rare, sighed for her in April and languished in May. Enamored swains haunted the school-house at the hour of dismissal. A few were jealous of the master.

Perhaps it was this latter circumstance that opened the master's eyes to another. He could not help noticing that Clytie was romantic; that in school she required a great deal of attention; that her pens were uniformly bad and wanted fixing; that she usually accompanied the request with a certain expectation in her eye that was somewhat disproportionate to the quality of service she verbally required; that she sometimes allowed the curves of a round, plump white arm to rest on his when he was writing her copies; that she always blushed and flung back her blond curls when she did so. I don't remember whether I have stated that the master was a young man,—it's of little consequence, however; he had been severely educated in the school in which Clytie was taking her first lesson, and, on the whole, withstood the flexible curves and factitious glance like the fine young Spartan that he was. Perhaps an insufficient quality of food may have tended to this asceticism. He generally avoided Clytie; but one evening, when she returned to the school-house after something she had forgotten, and did not find it until the master walked home with her, I hear that he endeavored to make himself particularly agreeable,—partly from the fact, I imagine, that his conduct was adding gall and bitterness to the already overcharged hearts of Clytemnestra's admirers.

The morning after this affecting episode Mliss did not come to school. Noon came, but not Mliss. Questioning Clytie on the subject, it appeared that they had left the school together, but the wilful Mliss had taken another road. The afternoon brought her not. In the evening he called on Mrs. Morpher, whose motherly heart was really alarmed. Mr. Morpher had spent all day in search of her, without discovering a trace that might lead to her discovery. Aristides was summoned as a probable accomplice, but that equitable infant succeeded in impressing the household with his innocence. Mrs. Morpher entertained a vivid impression that the child would yet be found drowned in a ditch, or, what was almost as terrible, muddied and soiled beyond the redemption of soap and water. Sick at heart, the master returned to the school-house. As he lit his lamp and seated himself at his desk, he found a note lying before him addressed to himself, in Mliss's handwriting. It seemed to be written on a leaf torn from some old memorandum-book, and, to prevent sacrilegious trifling, had been sealed with six broken wafers. Opening it almost tenderly, the master read as follows:—

"He found himself lying at the feet of the schoolmistress, gazing dreamily in her face, as she sat upon the sloping hillside." Illustration by Mary Hallock Foote for *The Idyl of Red Gulch. (p. 61)*

Respected Sir,—When you read this, I am run away. Never to come back. *Never,* Never, NEVER. You can give my beeds to Mary Jennings, and my Amerika's Pride [a highly colored lithograph from a tobacco-box] to Sally Flanders. But don't you give anything to Clytie Morpher. Don't you dare to. Do you know what my oppinion is of her, it is this, she is perfekly disgustin. That is all and no more at present from

Yours respectfully,
Melissa Smith.

The master sat pondering on this strange epistle till the moon lifted its bright face above the distant hills, and illuminated the trail that led to the school-house, beaten quite hard with the coming and going of little feet. Then, more satisfied in mind, he tore the missive into fragments and scattered them along the road.

At sunrise the next morning he was picking his way through the palm-like fern and thick underbrush of the pine-forest, starting the hare from its form, and awakening a querulous protest from a few dissipated crows, who had evidently been making a night of it, and so came to the wooded ridge where he had once found Mliss. There he found the prostrate pine and tasselled branches, but the throne was vacant. As he drew nearer, what might have been some frightened animal started through the crackling limbs. It ran up the tossed arms of the fallen monarch, and sheltered itself in some friendly foliage. The master, reaching the old seat, found the nest still warm; looking up in the intertwining branches, he met the black eyes of the errant Mliss. She was first to break the silence.

"What do you want?" she asked curtly.

The master had decided on a course of action. "I want some crab-apples," he said humbly.

"Sha' n't have 'em! go away. Why don't you get 'em of Clytemnerestera?" (It seemed to be a relief to Mliss to express her contempt in additional syllables to that classical young woman's already long-drawn title.) "O you wicked thing!"

"I am hungry, Lissy. I have eaten nothing since dinner yesterday. I am famished!" and the young man in a state of remarkable exhaustion leaned against the tree.

Melissa's heart was touched. In the bitter days of her gypsy life she had known the sensation he so artfully simulated. Overcome by his heartbroken tone, but not entirely divested of suspicion, she said,—

"Dig under the tree near the roots, and you'll find lots; but mind you don't tell," for Mliss had *her* hoards as well as the rats and squirrels.

But the master, of course, was unable to find them; the effects of hunger probably blinding his senses. Mliss grew uneasy. At length she peered at him through the leaves in an elfish way, and questioned,—

"If I come down and give you some, you'll promise you won't touch me?"

The master promised.

"Hope you'll die if you do!"

The master accepted instant dissolution as a forfeit. Mliss slid down the tree. For a few moments nothing transpired but the munching of the pine-nuts. "Do you feel better?" she asked, with some solicitude. The master confessed to a recuperated feeling, and then, gravely thanking her, proceeded to retrace his steps. As he expected, he had not gone far before she called him. He turned. She

was standing there quite white, with tears in her widely
opened orbs. The master felt that the right moment had
come. Going up to her, he took both her hands, and, looking in her tearful eyes, said, gravely, "Lissy, do you remember the first evening you came to see me?"

Lissy remembered.

"You asked me if you might come to school, for you
wanted to learn something and be better, and I said—"

"Come," responded the child, promptly.

"What would *you* say if the master now came to you and
said that he was lonely without his little scholar, and that
he wanted her to come and teach him to be better?"

The child hung her head for a few moments in silence.
The master waited patiently. Tempted by the quiet, a hare
ran close to the couple, and raising her bright eyes and
velvet forepaws, sat and gazed at them. A squirrel ran
half-way down the furrowed bark of the fallen tree, and
there stopped.

"We are waiting, Lissy," said the master, in a whisper,
and the child smiled. Stirred by a passing breeze, the tree-
tops rocked, and a long pencil of light stole through their
interlaced boughs full on the doubting face and irresolute
little figure. Suddenly she took the master's hand in her
quick way. What she said was scarcely audible, but the
master, putting the black hair back from her forehead,
kissed her; and so, hand in hand, they passed out of the
damp aisles and forest odors into the open sunlit road.

CHAPTER III

SOMEWHAT less spiteful in her intercourse with other
scholars, Mliss still retained an offensive attitude in regard

to Clytemnestra. Perhaps the jealous element was not entirely lulled in her passionate little breast. Perhaps it was only that the round curves and plump outline offered more extended pinching surface. But while such ebullitions were under the master's control, her enmity occasionally took a new and irrepressible form.

The master in his first estimate of the child's character could not conceive that she had ever possessed a doll. But the master, like many other professed readers of character, was safer in a *posteriori* than a *priori* reasoning. Mliss had a doll, but then it was emphatically Mliss's doll,—a smaller copy of herself. Its unhappy existence had been a secret discovered accidentally by Mrs. Morpher. It had been the old-time companion of Mliss's wanderings, and bore evident marks of suffering. Its original complexion was long since washed away by the weather and anointed by the slime of ditches. It looked very much as Mliss had in days past. Its one gown of faded stuff was dirty and ragged as hers had been. Mliss had never been known to apply to it any childish term of endearment. She never exhibited it in the presence of other children. It was put severely to bed in a hollow tree near the school-house, and only allowed exercise during Mliss's rambles. Fulfilling a stern duty to her doll, as she would to herself, it knew no luxuries.

Now Mrs. Morpher, obeying a commendable impulse, bought another doll and gave it to Mliss. The child received it gravely and curiously. The master on looking at it one day fancied he saw a slight resemblance in its round red cheeks and mild blue eyes to Clytemnestra. It became evident before long that Mliss had also noticed the same resemblance. Accordingly she hammered its waxen head on the rocks when she was alone, and sometimes dragged it with a string round its neck to and from school. At other times, setting it up on her desk, she made a pin-cushion of its patient and inoffensive body. Whether this was done in revenge of what she considered a second figurative obtrusion of Clytie's excellences upon her, or whether she had an intuitive appreciation of the rites of certain other heathens, and, indulging in that "Fetish" ceremony, imagined that the original of her wax model would pine away and finally die, is a metaphysical question I shall not now consider.

In spite of these moral vagaries, the master could not help noticing in her different tasks the working of a quick, restless, and vigorous perception. She knew neither the hesitancy nor the doubts of childhood. Her answers in class were always slightly dashed with audacity. Of course she was not infallible. But her courage and daring in passing beyond her own depth and that of the floundering little swimmers around her, in their minds outweighed all errors of judgment. Children are not better than grown people in this respect, I fancy; and whenever the little red hand flashed above her desk, there was a wondering silence, and even the master was sometimes oppressed with a doubt of his own experience and judgment.

Nevertheless, certain attributes which at first amused and entertained his fancy began to afflict him with grave doubts. He could not but see that Mliss was revengeful, irreverent, and wilful. That there was but one better quality which pertained to her semi-savage disposition,—the faculty of physical fortitude and self-sacrifice, and another, though not always an attribute of the noble savage,—Truth. Mliss was both fearless and sincere; perhaps in such a character the adjectives were synonymous.

The master had been doing some hard thinking on this subject, and had arrived at that conclusion quite common to all who think sincerely, that he was generally the slave of his own prejudices, when he determined to call on the Rev. McSnagley for advice. This decision was somewhat humiliating to his pride, as he and McSnagley were not friends. But he thought of Mliss, and the evening of their first meeting; and perhaps with a pardonable superstition that it was not chance alone that had guided her wilful feet to the school-house, and perhaps with a complacent consciousness of the rare magnanimity of the act, he choked back his dislike and went to McSnagley.

The reverend gentleman was glad to see him. Moreover, he observed that the master was looking "peartish," and hoped he had got over the "neuralgy" and "rheumatiz." He himself had been troubled with a dumb "ager" since last conference. But he had learned to "rastle and pray."

Pausing a moment to enable the master to write his certain method of curing the dumb "ager" upon the book and volume of his brain, Mr. McSnagley proceeded to inquire after Sister Morpher. "She is an adornment to Christewanity, and has a likely growin' young family," added Mr. McSnagley; "and there's that mannerly young gal,—so well behaved,—Miss Clytie." In fact, Clytie's perfections seemed to affect him to such an extent that he dwelt for several minutes upon them. The master was doubly embarrassed. In the first place, there was an enforced contrast with poor Mliss in all this praise of Clytie. Secondly, there was something unpleasantly confidential in his tone of speaking of Mrs. Morpher's earliest born. So that the master, after a few futile efforts to say something natural, found it convenient to recall another engagement, and left without asking the information required, but in his after reflections somewhat unjustly giving the Rev. Mr. McSnagley the full benefit of having refused it.

Perhaps this rebuff placed the master and pupil once more in the close communion of old. The child seemed to notice the change in the master's manner, which had of late been constrained, and in one of their long post-prandial walks she stopped suddenly, and, mounting a stump, looked full in his face with big, searching eyes. "You ain't mad?" said she, with an interrogative shake of the black braids. "No." "Nor bothered?" "No." "Nor hungry?" (Hunger was to Mliss a sickness that might attack a person at any moment.) "No." "Nor thinking of her?" "Of whom, Lissy?" "That white girl." (This was the latest epithet invented by Mliss, who was a very dark brunette, to express Clytemnestra.) "No." "Upon your word?" (A substitute for "Hope you'll die!" proposed by the master.) "Yes." "And sacred honor?" "Yes." Then Mliss gave him a fierce little kiss, and, hopping down, fluttered off. For two or three days after that she condescended to appear more like other children, and be, as she expressed it, "good."

Two years had passed since the master's advent at Smith's Pocket, and as his salary was not large, and the prospects of Smith's Pocket eventually becoming the capital of the State not entirely definite, he contemplated a change. He had informed the school trustees privately of his intentions, but, educated young men of unblemished moral character being scarce at that time, he consented to continue his school term through the winter to early spring. None else knew of his intention except his one friend, a Dr. Duchesne, a young Creole physician known to the people of Wingdam as "Duchesny." He never mentioned it to Mrs. Morpher,

Clytie, or any of his scholars. His reticence was partly the result of a constitutional indisposition to fuss, partly a desire to be spared the questions and surmises of vulgar curiosity, and partly that he never really believed he was going to do anything before it was done.

He did not like to think of Mliss. It was a selfish instinct, perhaps, which made him try to fancy his feeling for the child was foolish, romantic, and unpractical. He even tried to imagine that she would do better under the control of an older and sterner teacher. Then she was nearly eleven, and in a few years, by the rules of Red Mountain, would be a woman. He had done his duty. After Smith's death he addressed letters to Smith's relatives, and received one answer from a sister of Melissa's mother. Thanking the master, she stated her intention of leaving the Atlantic States for California with her husband in a few months. This was a slight superstructure for the airy castle which the master pictured for Mliss's home, but it was easy to fancy that some loving, sympathetic woman, with the claims of kindred, might better guide her wayward nature. Yet, when the master had read the letter, Mliss listened to it carelessly, received it submissively, and afterwards cut figures out of it with her scissors, supposed to represent Clytemnestra, labelled "the white girl," to prevent mistakes, and impaled them upon the outer walls of the school-house.

When the summer was about spent, and the last harvest had been gathered in the valleys, the master bethought him of gathering in a few ripened shoots of the young idea, and of having his Harvest-Home, or Examination. So the savants and professionals of Smith's Pocket were gathered to witness that time-honored custom of placing timid children in a constrained position, and bullying them as in a witness-box. As usual in such cases, the most audacious and self-possessed were the lucky recipients of the honors. The reader will imagine that in the present instance Mliss and Clytie were pre-eminent, and divided public attention; Mliss with her clearness of material perception and self-reliance, Clytie with her placid self-esteem and saint-like correctness of deportment. The other little ones were timid and blundering. Mliss's readiness and brilliancy, of course, captivated the greatest number and provoked the greatest applause. Mliss's antecedents had unconsciously awakened the strongest sympathies of a class whose athletic forms were ranged against the walls, or whose handsome bearded faces looked in at the windows. But Mliss's popularity was overthrown by an unexpected circumstance.

McSnagley had invited himself, and had been going through the pleasing entertainment of frightening the more timid pupils by the vaguest and most ambiguous questions delivered in an impressive funereal tone; and Mliss had soared into Astronomy, and was tracking the course of our spotted ball through space, and keeping time with the music of the spheres, and defining the tethered orbits of the planets, when McSnagley impressively arose. "Meelissy! ye were speaking of the revolutions of this yere yearth and the move-*ments* of the sun, and I think ye said it had been a doing of it since the creashun, eh?" Mliss nodded a scornful affirmative. "Well, war that the truth?" said McSnagley, folding his arms. "Yes," said Mliss, shutting up her little red lips tightly. The handsome outlines at the windows peered further in the school-room, and a saintly Raphael-face, with blond beard and soft blue eyes, belonging to the biggest scamp in the diggings, turned toward the child and whispered, "Stick to it, Mliss!" The reverend gentleman heaved a deep sigh, and cast a compassionate glance at the master, then at the children, and then rested his look on Clytie. That young woman softly elevated her round, white arm. Its seductive curves were enhanced by a gorgeous and massive specimen bracelet, the gift of one of her humblest worshippers, worn in honor of the occasion. There was a momentary silence. Clytie's round cheeks were very pink and soft. Clytie's big eyes were very bright and blue. Clytie's low-necked white book-muslin rested softly on Clytie's white, plump shoulders. Clytie looked at the master, and the master nodded. Then Clytie spoke softly:—

"Joshua commanded the sun to stand still, and it obeyed him!" There was a low hum of applause in the school-room, a triumphant expression on McSnagley's face, a grave shadow on the master's, and a comical look of disappointment reflected from the windows. Mliss skimmed rapidly over her Astronomy, and then shut the book with a loud snap. A groan burst from McSnagley, an expression of astonishment from the school-room, a yell from the windows, as Mliss brought her red fist down on the desk, with the emphatic declaration,—

"It's a d—n lie. I don't believe it!"

CHAPTER IV

THE long wet season had drawn near its close. Signs of spring were visible in the swelling buds and rushing torrents. the pine-forests exhaled the fresher spicery. The azaleas were already budding, the Ceanothus getting ready its lilac livery for spring. On the green upland which climbed Red Mountain at its southern aspect the long spike of the monk's-hood shot up from its broad-leaved stool, and once more shook its dark-blue bells. Again the billow above Smith's grave was soft and green, its crest just tossed with the foam of daisies and buttercups. The little graveyard had gathered a few new dwellers in the past year, and the mounds were placed two by two by the little paling until they reached Smith's grave, and there there was but one. General superstition had shunned it, and the plot beside Smith was vacant.

There had been several placards posted about the town, intimating that, at a certain period, a celebrated dramatic company would perform, for a few days, a series of "side-splitting" and "screaming farces"; that, alternating pleasantly with this, there would be some melodrama and a grand divertisement, which would include singing, dancing, etc. These announcements occasioned a great fluttering among the little folk, and were the theme of much excitement and great speculation among the master's scholars. The master had promised Mliss, to whom this sort of thing was sacred and rare, that she should go, and on that momentous evening the master and Mliss "assisted."

The performance was the prevalent style of heavy mediocrity; the melodrama was not bad enough to laugh at nor good enough to excite. But the master, turning wearily to the child, was astonished, and felt something like self-accusation in noticing the peculiar effect upon her excitable nature. The red blood flushed in her cheeks at each stroke of her panting little heart. Her small passionate lips were slightly parted to give vent to her hurried breath. Her widely opened lids threw up and arched her black eyebrows. She did not laugh at the dismal comicalities of the funny man, for Mliss seldom laughed. Nor was she discreetly affected to the delicate extremes of the corner of a white handkerchief, as was the tender-hearted "Clytie," who was talking with her "feller" and ogling the master at the same moment. But when the performance was over, and the green curtain fell on the little stage, Mliss drew a long deep breath, and turned to the master's grave face with a half-apologetic smile and wearied gesture. Then she said, "Now take me home!" and dropped the lids of her black eyes, as if to dwell once more in fancy on the mimic stage.

On their way to Mrs. Morpher's the master thought proper to ridicule the whole performance. Now he shouldn't wonder if Mliss thought that the young lady who acted so beautifully was really in earnest, and in love with the gentleman who wore such fine clothes. Well, if she were in love with him it was a very unfortunate thing! "Why?" said Mliss, with an upward sweep of the drooping lid. "Oh! well, he couldn't support his wife at his present salary, and pay so much a week for his fine clothes, and then they wouldn't receive as much wages if they were married as if they were merely lovers,—that is," added the master, "if they are not already married to somebody else; but I think the husband of the pretty young countess takes the tickets at the door, or pulls up the curtain, or snuffs the candles, or does something equally refined and elegant. As to the young man with nice clothes, which are really nice now, and must cost at least two and a half or three dollars, not to speak of that mantle of red drugget which I happen to know the price of, for I bought some of it for my room once,—as to this young man, Lissy, he is a pretty good fellow, and if he does drink occasionally, I don't think people ought to take advantage of it and give him black eyes and throw him in the mud. Do you? I am sure he might owe me two dollars and a half a long time, before I would throw it up in his face, as the fellow did the other night at Wingdam."

Mliss had taken his hand in both of hers and was trying to look in his eyes, which the young man kept as resolutely averted. Mliss had a faint idea of irony, indulging herself sometimes in a species of sardonic humor, which was equally visible in her actions and her speech. But the young man continued in this strain until they had reached Mrs. Morpher's, and he had deposited Mliss in her maternal charge. Waiving the invitation of Mrs. Morpher to refreshment and rest, and shading his eyes with his hand to keep out the blue-eyed Clytemnestra's siren glances, he excused himself, and went home.

For two or three days after the advent of the dramatic company, Mliss was late at school, and the master's usual Friday afternoon ramble was for once omitted, owing to the absence of his trustworthy guide. As he was putting away his books and preparing to leave the school-house, a small voice piped at his side, "Please, sir?" The master turned and there stood Aristides Morpher.

"Well, my little man," said the master, impatiently, "what is it? quick!"

"Please, sir, me and 'Kerg' thinks that Mliss is going to run away agin."

"What's that, sir?" said the master, with that unjust testiness with which we always receive disagreeable news.

"Why, sir, she don't stay home any more, and 'Kerg' and me see her talking with one of those actor fellers, and she's with him now; and please, sir, yesterday she told 'Kerg' and me she could make a speech as well as Miss Cellerstina

Montmoressy, and she spouted right off by heart," and the little fellow paused in a collapsed condition.

"What actor?" asked the master.

"Him as wears the shiny hat. And hair. And gold pin. And gold chain," said the just Aristides, putting periods for commas to eke out his breath.

The master put on his gloves and hat, feeling an unpleasant tightness in his chest and thorax, and walked out in the road. Aristides trotted along by his side, endeavoring to keep pace with his short legs to the master's strides, when the master stopped suddenly, and Aristides bumped up against him. "Where were they talking?" asked the master, as if continuing the conversation.

"At the Arcade," said Aristides.

When they reached the main street the master paused. "Run down home," said he to the boy. "If Mliss is there, come to the Arcade and tell me. If she isn't there, stay home; run!" And off trotted the short-legged Aristides.

The Arcade was just across the way,—a long, rambling building containing a bar-room, billiard-room, and restaurant. As the young man crossed the plaza he noticed that two or three of the passers-by turned and looked after him. He looked at his clothes, took out his handkerchief and wiped his face, before he entered the bar-room. It contained the usual number of loungers, who stared at him as he entered. One of them looked at him so fixedly and with such a strange expression that the master stopped and looked again, and then saw it was only his own reflection in a large mirror. This made the master think that perhaps he was a little excited, and so he took up a copy of the Red Mountain Banner from one of the tables, and tried to recover his composure by reading the column of advertisements.

He then walked through the bar-room, through the restaurant, and into the billiard-room. The child was not there. In the latter apartment a person was standing by one of the tables with a broad-brimmed glazed hat on his head. The master recognized him as the agent of the dramatic company; he had taken a dislike to him at their first meeting, from the peculiar fashion of wearing his beard and hair. Satisfied that the object of his search was not there, he turned to the man with the glazed hat. He had noticed the master, but tried that common trick of unconsciousness, in which vulgar natures always fail. Balancing a billiard-cue in his hand, he pretended to play with a ball in the centre of the table. The master stood opposite to him until he raised his eyes; when their glances met, the master walked up to him.

He had intended to avoid a scene or quarrel, but when he began to speak, something kept rising in his throat and retarded his utterance, and his own voice frightened him, it sounded so distant, low, and resonant. "I understand," he began, "that Melissa Smith, an orphan, and one of my scholars, has talked with you about adopting your profession. Is that so?"

The man with the glazed hat leaned over the table, and made an imaginary shot, that sent the ball spinning round the cushions. Then walking round the table he recovered the ball and placed it upon the spot. This duty discharged, getting ready for another shot, he said,—

"S'pose she has?"

The master choked up again, but, squeezing the cushion of the table in his gloved hand, he went on:—

"If you are a gentleman, I have only to tell you that I am her guardian, and responsible for her career. You know as well as I do the kind of life you offer her. As you may learn of any one here, I have already brought her out of an existence worse than death,—out of the streets and the contamination of vice. I am trying to do so again. Let us talk like men. She has neither father, mother, sister, or brother. Are you seeking to give her an equivalent for these?"

The man with the glazed hat examined the point of his cue, and then looked around for somebody to enjoy the joke with him.

"I know that she is a strange, wilful girl," continued the master, "but she is better than she was. I believe that I have some influence over her still. I beg and hope, therefore, that you will take no further steps in this matter, but as a man, as a gentleman, leave her to me. I am willing—" But here something rose again in the master's throat, and the sentence remained unfinished.

The man with the glazed hat, mistaking the master's silence, raised his head with a coarse, brutal laugh, and said in a loud voice,—

"Want her yourself, do you? That cock won't fight here, young man!"

The insult was more in the tone than the words, more in the glance than tone, and more in the man's instinctive nature than all these. The best appreciable rhetoric to this kind of animal is a blow. The master felt this, and, with his pent-up, nervous energy finding expression in the one act, he struck the brute full in his grinning face. The blow sent the glazed hat one way and the cue another, and tore the glove and skin from the master's hand from knuckle to joint. It opened up the corners of the fellow's mouth, and spoilt the peculiar shape of his beard for some time to come.

There was a shout, an imprecation, a scuffle, and the trampling of many feet. Then the crowd parted right and left, and two sharp quick reports followed each other in rapid succession. Then they closed again about his opponent, and the master was standing alone. He remembered picking bits of burning wadding from his coat-sleeve with his left hand. Some one was holding his other hand. Looking at it, he saw it was still bleeding from the blow, but his fingers were clenched around the handle of a glittering knife. He could not remember when or how he got it.

The man who was holding his hand was Mr. Morpher. He hurried the master to the door, but the master held back, and tried to tell him as well as he could with his parched throat about "Mliss." "It's all right, my boy," said Mr. Morpher. "She's home!" And they passed out into the street together. As they walked along Mr. Morpher said that Mliss had come running into the house a few moments before, and had dragged him out, saying that somebody was trying to kill the master at the Arcade. Wishing to be alone, the master promised Mr. Morpher that he would not seek the Agent again that night, and parted from him, taking the road toward the school-house. He was surprised in nearing it to find the door open,—still more surprised to find Mliss sitting there.

The master's nature, as I have hinted before, had, like most sensitive organizations, a selfish basis. The brutal taunt thrown out by his late adversary still rankled in his heart. It was possible, he thought, that such a construction might be put upon his affection for the child, which at best was foolish and Quixotic. Besides, had she not voluntarily abnegated his authority and affection? And what had everybody else said about her? Why should he alone combat the opinion of all, and be at last obliged tacitly to confess the truth of all they had predicted? And he had been a participant in a low bar-room fight with a common boor, and risked his life, to prove what? What had he proved? Nothing? What would the people say? What would his friends say? What would McSnagley say?

In his self-accusation the last person he should have wished to meet was Mliss. He entered the door, and, going up to his desk, told the child, in a few cold words, that he was busy, and wished to be alone. As she rose he took her vacant seat, and, sitting down, buried his head in his hands. When he looked up again she was still standing there. She was looking at his face with an anxious expression.

"Did you kill him?" she asked.

"No!" said the master.

"That's what I gave you the knife for!" said the child, quickly.

"Gave me the knife?" repeated the master, in bewilderment.

"Yes, gave you the knife. I was there under the bar. Saw you hit him. Saw you both fall. He dropped his old knife. I gave it to you. Why didn't you stick him?" said Mliss rapidly, with an expressive twinkle of the black eyes and a gesture of the little red hand.

The master could only look his astonishment.

"Yes," said Mliss. "If you'd asked me, I'd told you I was off with the play-actors. Why was I off with the play-actors? Because you wouldn't tell me you was going away. I knew it. I heard you tell the Doctor so. I wasn't a goin' to stay here alone with those Morphers. I'd rather die first."

With a dramatic gesture which was perfectly consistent with her character, she drew from her bosom a few limp green leaves, and, holding them out at arm's-length, said in her quick vivid way, and in the queer pronunciation of her old life, which she fell into when unduly excited,—

"That's the poison plant you said would kill me. I'll go with the play-actors, or I'll eat this and die here. I don't care which. I won't stay here, where they hate and despise me! Neither would you let me, if you didn't hate and despise me too!"

The passionate little breast heaved, and two big tears peeped over the edge of Mliss's eyelids, but she whisked them away with the corner of her apron as if they had been wasps.

"If you lock me up in jail," said Mliss, fiercely, "to keep me from the play-actors, I'll poison myself. Father killed himself,—why shouldn't I? You said a mouthful of that root would kill me, and I always carry it here," and she struck her breast with her clenched fist.

The master thought of the vacant plot beside Smith's grave, and of the passionate little figure before him. Seizing her hands in his and looking full into her truthful eyes, he said,—

"Lissy, will you go with *me?*"

The child put her arms around his neck, and said joyfully, "Yes."

"But now—to-night?"

"To-night."

And, hand in hand, they passed into the road,—the narrow road that had once brought her weary feet to the master's door, and which it seemed she should not tread again alone. The stars glittered brightly above them. For good or ill the lesson had been learned, and behind them the school of Red Mountain closed upon them forever.

THE RIGHT EYE OF THE COMMANDER

THE year of grace 1797 passed away on the coast of California in a southwesterly gale. The little bay of San Carlos, albeit sheltered by the headlands of the blessed Trinity, was rough and turbulent; its foam clung quivering to the seaward wall of the Mission garden; the air was filled with flying sand and spume, and as the Señor Comandante, Hermenegildo Salvatierra, looked from the deep embrasured window of the Presidio guard-room, he felt the salt breath of the distant sea buffet a color into his smoke-dried cheeks.

The Commander, I have said, was gazing thoughtfully from the window of the guard-room. He may have been reviewing the events of the year now about to pass away. But, like the garrison at the Presidio, there was little to review; the year, like its predecessors, had been uneventful, —the days had slipped by in a delicious monotony of simple duties, unbroken by incident or interruption. The regularly recurring feasts and saints' days, the half-yearly courier from San Diego, the rare transport-ship and rarer foreign vessel, were the mere details of his patriarchal life. If there was no achievement, there was certainly no failure. Abundant harvests and patient industry amply supplied the wants of Presidio and Mission. Isolated from the family of nations, the wars which shook the world concerned them not so much as the last earthquake; the struggle that emancipated their sister colonies on the other side of the continent to them had no suggestiveness. In short, it was that glori-

ous Indian summer of California history, around which so
much poetical haze still lingers,—that bland, indolent autumn of Spanish rule, so soon to be followed by the wintry
storms of Mexican independence and the reviving spring of
American conquest.

The Commander turned from the window and walked
toward the fire that burned brightly on the deep oven-like
hearth. A pile of copy-books, the work of the Presidio
school, lay on the table. As he turned over the leaves with a
paternal interest, and surveyed the fair round Scripture
text,—the first pious pot-hooks of the pupils of San Carlos,
—an audible commentary fell from his lips: "Abimelech
took her from Abraham,—ah, little one, excellent!—'Jacob
sent to see his brother'—body of Christ! that up-stroke of
thine, Paquita, is marvellous; the Governor shall see it!"
A film of honest pride dimmed the Commander's left eye,—
the right, alas! twenty years before had been sealed by an
Indian arrow. He rubbed it softly with the sleeve of his
leather jacket, and continued: " 'The Ishmaelites having
arrived—' "

He stopped, for there was a step in the courtyard, a foot
upon the threshold, and a stranger entered. With the instinct of an old soldier, the Commander, after one glance
at the intruder, turned quickly toward the wall, where his
trusty Toledo hung, or should have been hanging. But it
was not there, and as he recalled that the last time he had
seen that weapon it was being ridden up and down the
gallery by Pepito, the infant son of Bautista, the tortilio-
maker, he blushed and then contented himself with frown-
ing upon the intruder.

But the stranger's air, though irreverent, was decidedly
peaceful. He was unarmed, and wore the ordinary cape of

tarpauling and sea-boots of a mariner. Except a villainous smell of codfish, there was little about him that was peculiar.

His name, as he informed the Commander, in Spanish that was more fluent than elegant or precise,—his name was Peleg Scudder. He was master of the schooner "General Court," of the port of Salem, in Massachusetts, on a trading-voyage to the South Seas, but now driven by stress of weather into the bay of San Carlos. He begged permission to ride out the gale under the headlands of the blessed Trinity, and no more. Water he did not need, having taken in a supply at Bodega. He knew the strict surveillance of the Spanish port regulations in regard to foreign vessels, and would do nothing against the severe discipline and good order of the settlement. There was a slight tinge of sarcasm in his tone as he glanced toward the desolate parade-ground of the Presidio and the open unguarded gate. The fact was that the sentry, Felipe Gomez, had discreetly retired to shelter at the beginning of the storm, and was then sound asleep in the corridor.

The Commander hesitated. The port regulations were severe, but he was accustomed to exercise individual authority, and beyond an old order issued ten years before, regarding the American ship "Columbia," there was no precedent to guide him. The storm was severe, and a sentiment of humanity urged him to grant the stranger's request. It is but just to the Commander to say, that his inability to enforce a refusal did not weigh with his decision. He would have denied with equal disregard of consequences that right to a seventy-four gun ship which he now yielded so gracefully to this Yankee trading-schooner. He stipulated only, that there should be no communication between the ship and shore. "For yourself, Señor Captain," he continued, "accept my hospitality. The fort is yours as long as you shall grace it with your distinguished presence"; and with old-fashioned courtesy, he made the semblance of withdrawing from the guard-room.

Master Peleg Scudder smiled as he thought of the half-dismantled fort, the two mouldy brass cannon, cast in Manila a century previous, and the shiftless garrison. A wild thought of accepting the Commander's offer literally, conceived in the reckless spirit of a man who never let slip an offer for trade, for a moment filled his brain, but a timely reflection of the commercial unimportance of the transaction checked him. He only took a capacious quid of tobacco, as the Commander gravely drew a settle before the fire, and in honor of his guest untied the black silk handkerchief that bound his grizzled brows.

What passed between Salvatierra and his guest that night it becomes me not, as a grave chronicler of the salient points of history, to relate. I have said that Master Peleg Scudder was a fluent talker, and under the influence of divers strong waters, furnished by his host, he became still more loquacious. And think of a man with a twenty years' budget of gossip! The Commander learned, for the first time, how Great Britain lost her colonies; of the French Revolution; of the great Napoleon, whose achievements, perhaps, Peleg colored more highly than the Commander's superiors would have liked. And when Peleg turned questioner, the Commander was at his mercy. He gradually made himself master of the gossip of the Mission and Presidio, the "small-beer" chronicles of that pastoral age, the conversion of the heathen, the Presidio schools, and even asked the Commander how he had lost his eye! It is said that at this point of the conversation Master Peleg produced from about his person divers small trinkets, kick-shaws and new-fangled trifles, and even forced some of them upon his host. It is further alleged that under the malign influence of Peleg and several glasses of *aguardiente,* the Commander lost somewhat of his decorum, and behaved in a manner unseemly for one in his position, reciting high-flown Spanish poetry, and even piping in a thin, high voice, divers madrigals and heathen canzonets of an amorous complexion; chiefly in regard to a "little one" who was his, the Commander's, "soul"! These allegations, perhaps unworthy the notice of a serious chronicler, should be received with great caution, and are introduced here as simple hearsay. That the Commander, however, took a handkerchief and attempted to show his guest the mysteries of the *sembi cuacua,* capering in an agile but indecorous manner about the apartment, has been denied. Enough for the purposes of this narrative, that at midnight Peleg assisted his host to bed with many protestations of undying friendship, and then, as the gale had abated, took his leave of the Presidio and hurried aboard the "General Court." When the day broke the ship was gone.

I know not if Peleg kept his word with his host. It is said that the holy fathers at the Mission that night heard a loud chanting in the plaza, as of the heathens singing psalms through their noses; that for many days after an odor of salt codfish prevailed in the settlement; that a dozen hard nutmegs, which were unfit for spice or seed, were found in the possession of the wife of the baker, and that several bushels of shoe-pegs, which bore a pleasing resemblance to oats, but were quite inadequate to the purposes of provender, were discovered in the stable of the blacksmith. But when the reader reflects upon the sacredness of a Yankee trader's word, the stringent discipline of the Spanish port regulations, and the proverbial indisposition of my countrymen to impose upon the confidence of a simple people, he will at once reject this part of the story.

A roll of drums, ushering in the year 1798, awoke the Commander. The sun was shining brightly, and the storm had ceased. He sat up in bed, and through the force of habit rubbed his left eye. As the remembrance of the previous night came back to him, he jumped from his couch and ran to the window. There was no ship in the bay. A sudden thought seemed to strike him, and he rubbed both of his eyes. Not content with this, he consulted the metallic mirror which hung beside his crucifix. There was no mistake; the Commander had a visible second eye,—a right one, —as good, save for the purposes of vision, as the left.

Whatever might have been the true secret of this transformation, but one opinion prevailed at San Carlos. It was one of those rare miracles vouchsafed a pious Catholic community as an evidence to the heathen, through the intercession of the blessed San Carlos himself. That their beloved Commander, the temporal defender of the Faith, should be the recipient of this miraculous manifestation was most fit and seemly. The Commander himself was reticent; he could not tell a falsehood,—he dared not tell the truth. After all, if the good folk of San Carlos believed that the powers of his right eye were actually restored, was it wise and discreet for him to undeceive them? For the first time in his life the Commander thought of policy,—for the first time he quoted that text which has been the lure of so many well-meaning but easy Christians, of being "all things to all men." Infeliz Hermenegildo Salvatierra!

For by degrees an ominous whisper crept through the little settlement. The Right Eye of the Commander, although miraculous, seemed to exercise a baleful effect upon the beholder. No one could look at it without winking. It was cold, hard, relentless and unflinching. More than that, it seemed to be endowed with a dreadful prescience,—a faculty of seeing through and into the inarticulate thoughts of those it looked upon. The soldiers of the garrison obeyed the eye rather than the voice of their commander, and answered his glance rather than his lips in questioning. The servants could not evade the ever-watchful, but cold attention that seemed to pursue them. The children of the Presidio School smirched their copy-books under the awful supervision, and poor Paquita, the prize pupil, failed utterly in that marvellous up-stroke when her patron stood beside her. Gradually distrust, suspicion, self-accusation, and timidity took the place of trust, confidence, and security throughout San Carlos. Whenever the Right Eye of the Commander fell, a shadow fell with it.

Nor was Salvatierra entirely free from the baleful influence of his miraculous acquisition. Unconscious of its effect upon others, he only saw in their actions evidence of certain things that the crafty Peleg had hinted on that eventful New Year's eve. His most trusty retainers stammered, blushed, and faltered before him. Self-accusations, confessions of minor faults and delinquencies, or extravagant excuses and apologies met his mildest inquiries. The very children that he loved—his pet pupil, Paquita—seemed to be conscious of some hidden sin. The result of this constant irritation showed itself more plainly. For the first half-year the Commander's voice and eye were at variance. He was still kind, tender, and thoughtful in speech. Gradually, however, his voice took upon itself the hardness of his glance and its sceptical, impassive quality, and as the year again neared its close it was plain that the Commander had fitted himself to the eye, and not the eye to the Commander.

It may be surmised that these changes did not escape the watchful solicitude of the Fathers. Indeed, the few who were first to ascribe the right eye of Salvatierra to miraculous origin and the special grace of the blessed San Carlos, now talked openly of witchcraft and the agency of Luzbel, the evil one. It would have fared ill with Hermenegildo Salvatierra had he been aught but Commander or amenable to local authority. But the reverend father, Friar Manuel de Cortes, had no power over the political executive, and all attempts at spiritual advice failed signally. He retired baffled and confused from his first interview with the Commander, who seemed now to take a grim satisfaction in the fateful power of his glance. The holy father contradicted himself, exposed the fallacies of his own arguments, and even, it is asserted, committed himself to several undoubted heresies. When the Commander stood up at mass, if the officiating priest caught that sceptical and searching eye, the service was inevitably ruined. Even the power of the Holy Church seemed to be lost, and the last hold upon the affections of the people and the good order of the settlement departed from San Carlos.

As the long dry summer passed, the low hills that surrounded the white walls of the Presidio grew more and more to resemble in hue the leathern jacket of the Commander, and Nature herself seemed to have borrowed his dry, hard glare. The earth was cracked and seamed with drought; a blight had fallen upon the orchards and vineyards, and the rain, long delayed and ardently prayed for, came not. The sky was as tearless as the right eye of the Commander. Murmurs of discontent, insubordination, and plotting among the Indians reached his ears; he only set his teeth the more firmly, tightened the knot of his black silk handkerchief, and looked up his Toledo.

The last day of the year 1798 found the Commander sitting, at the hour of evening prayers, alone in the guardroom. He no longer attended the services of the Holy Church, but crept away at such times to some solitary spot, where he spent the interval in silent meditation. The firelight played upon the low beams and rafters, but left the bowed figure of Salvatierra in darkness. Sitting thus, he felt a small hand touch his arm, and, looking down, saw the figure of Paquita, his little Indian pupil, at his knee. "Ah, littlest of all," said the Commander, with something of his old tenderness, lingering over the endearing diminutives of his native speech,—"sweet one, what doest thou here? Art thou not afraid of him whom every one shuns and fears?"

"No," said the little Indian, readily, "not in the dark. I hear your voice,—the old voice; I feel your touch,—the old touch; but I see not your eye, Señor Comandante. That only I fear,—and that, O Señor, O my father," said the child, lifting her little arms towards his,—"that I know is not thine own!"

The Commander shuddered and turned away. Then, recovering himself, he kissed Paquita gravely on the forehead and bade her retire. A few hours later, when silence had fallen upon the Presidio, he sought his own couch and slept peacefully.

At about the middle watch of the night a dusky figure crept through the low embrasure of the Commander's apartment. Other figures were flitting through the parade-ground, which the Commander might have seen had he not slept so quietly. The intruder stepped noiselessly to the couch and listened to the sleeper's deep-drawn inspiration. Something glittered in the firelight as the savage lifted his arm; another moment and the sore perplexities of Hermenegildo Salvatierra would have been over, when suddenly the savage started and fell back in a paroxysm of terror. The Commander slept peacefully, but his right eye, widely opened, fixed and unaltered, glared coldly on the would-be assassin. The man fell to the earth in a fit, and the noise awoke the sleeper.

To rise to his feet, grasp his sword, and deal blows thick and fast upon the mutinous savages who now thronged the room, was the work of a moment. Help opportunely arrived, and the undisciplined Indians were speedily driven beyond the walls, but in the scuffle the Commander received a blow upon his right eye, and, lifting his hand to that mysterious organ, it was gone. Never again was it found, and never again, for bale or bliss, did it adorn the right orbit of the Commander.

With it passed away the spell that had fallen upon San Carlos. The rain returned to invigorate the languid soil, harmony was restored between priest and soldier, the green grass presently waved over the sere hillsides, the children flocked again to the side of their martial preceptor, a *Te Deum* was sung in the Mission Church, and pastoral content once more smiled upon the gentle valleys of San Carlos. And far southward crept the "General Court" with its master, Peleg Scudder, trafficking in beads and peltries with the Indians, and offering glass eyes, wooden legs, and other Boston notions to the chiefs.

NOTES BY FLOOD AND FIELD

PART I—IN THE FIELD

IT was near the close of an October day that I began to be disagreeably conscious of the Sacramento Valley. I had been riding since sunrise, and my course through the depressing monotony of the long level landscape affected me more like a dull dyspeptic dream than a business journey, performed under that sincerest of natural phenomena,—a California sky. The recurring stretches of brown and baked fields, the gaping fissures in the dusty trail, the hard outline of the distant hills, and the herds of slowly moving cattle, seemed like features of some glittering stereoscopic picture that never changed. Active exercise might have removed this feeling, but my horse by some subtle instinct had long since given up all ambitious effort, and had lapsed into a dogged trot.

It was autumn, but not the season suggested to the Atlantic reader under that title. The sharply defined boundaries of the wet and dry seasons were prefigured in the clear outlines of the distant hills. In the dry atmosphere the decay of vegetation was too rapid for the slow hectic which overtakes an Eastern landscape, or else Nature was too practical for such thin disguises. She merely turned the Hippocratic face to the spectator, with the old diagnosis of Death in her sharp, contracted features.

In the contemplation of such a prospect there was little

148

to excite any but a morbid fancy. There were no clouds in the flinty blue heavens, and the setting of the sun was accompanied with as little ostentation as was consistent with the dryly practical atmosphere. Darkness soon followed, with a rising wind, which increased as the shadows deepened on the plain. The fringe of alder by the watercourse began to loom up as I urged my horse forward. A half-hour's active spurring brought me to a *corral,* and a little beyond a house, so low and broad it seemed at first sight to be half buried in the earth.

My second impression was that it had grown out of the soil, like some monstrous vegetable, its dreary proportions were so in keeping with the vast prospect. There were no recesses along its roughly boarded walls for vagrant and unprofitable shadows to lurk in the daily sunshine. No projection for the wind by night to grow musical over, to wail, whistle, or whisper to; only a long wooden shelf containing a chilly-looking tin basin, and a bar of soap. Its uncurtained windows were red with the sinking sun, as though bloodshot and inflamed from a too long unlidded existence. The tracks of cattle led to its front door, firmly closed against the rattling wind.

To avoid being confounded with this familiar element, I walked to the rear of the house, which was connected with a smaller building by a slight platform. A grizzled, hard-faced old man was standing there, and met my salutation with a look of inquiry, and, without speaking, led the way to the principal room. As I entered, four young men, who were reclining by the fire, slightly altered their attitudes of perfect repose, but beyond that betrayed neither curiosity nor interest. A hound started from a dark corner with a growl, but was immediately kicked by the old man into obscurity, and silenced again. I can't tell why, but I instantly received the impression that for a long time the group by the fire had not uttered a word or moved a muscle. Taking a seat, I briefly stated my business.

Was a United States surveyor. Had come on account of the Espíritu Santo Rancho. Wanted to correct the exterior boundaries of township lines, so as to connect with the near exteriors of private grants. There had been some intervention to the old survey by a Mr. Tryan who had pre-empted adjacent—"settled land warrants," interrupted the old man. "Ah, yes! Land Warrants,—and then this was Mr. Tryan?"

I had spoken mechanically, for I was preoccupied in connecting other public lines with private surveys, as I looked in his face. It was certainly a hard face, and reminded me of the singular effect of that mining operation known as "ground sluicing"; the harder lines of underlying character were exposed, and what were once plastic curves and soft outlines were obliterated by some powerful agency.

There was a dryness in his voice not unlike the prevailing atmosphere of the valley, as he launched into an *ex parte* statement of the contest, with a fluency, which, like the wind without, showed frequent and unrestrained expression. He told me—what I had already learned—that the boundary line of the old Spanish grant was a creek, described in the loose phraseology of the *deseño* as beginning in the *valda* or skirt of the hill, its precise location long the subject of litigation. I listened and answered with little interest, for my mind was still distracted by the wind which swept violently by the house, as well as by his odd face, which was again reflected in the resemblance that the silent group by the fire bore toward him. He was still talking, and the wind

A photograph of Bret Harte, around 1880, as Consul at Grefeld, Germany, which is inscribed "The Herr Consul."

was yet blowing, when my confused attention was aroused by a remark addressed to the recumbent figures.

"Now, then, which on ye'll see the stranger up the creek to Altascar's, to-morrow?"

There was a general movement of opposition in the group, but no decided answer.

"Kin you go, Kerg?"

"Who's to look up stock in Strarberry per-ar-ie?"

This seemed to imply a negative, and the old man turned to another hopeful, who was pulling the fur from a mangy bear-skin on which he was lying, with an expression as though it were somebody's hair.

"Well, Tom, wot's to hinder you from goin'?"

"Mam's goin' to Brown's store at sun-up, and I s'pose I've got to pack her and the baby agin."

I think the expression of scorn this unfortunate youth exhibited for the filial duty into which he had been evidently beguiled, was one of the finest things I had ever seen.

"Wise?"

Wise deigned no verbal reply, but figuratively thrust a worn and patched boot into the discourse. The old man flushed quickly.

"I told ye to get Brown to give you a pair the last time you war down the river."

"Said he wouldn't without'en order. Said it was like pulling gum-teeth to get the money from you even then."

There was a grim smile at this local hit at the old man's parsimony, and Wise, who was clearly the privileged wit of the family, sank back in honorable retirement.

"Well, Joe, ef your boots are new, and you aren't pestered with wimmin and children, p'r'aps you'll go," said

Tryan, with a nervous twitching, intended for a smile, about a mouth not remarkably mirthful.

Tom lifted a pair of bushy eyebrows, and said shortly,—

"Got no saddle."

"Wot's gone of your saddle?"

"Kerg, there,"—indicating his brother with a look such as Cain might have worn at the sacrifice.

"You lie!" returned Kerg, cheerfully.

Tryan sprang to his feet, seizing the chair, flourishing it around his head and gazing furiously in the hard young faces which fearlessly met his own. But it was only for a moment; his arm soon dropped by his side, and a look of hopeless fatality crossed his face. He allowed me to take the chair from his hand, and I was trying to pacify him by the assurance that I required no guide, when the impressible Wise again lifted his voice:—

"Theer's George comin'! why don't ye ask him? He'll go and introduce you to Don Fernandy's darter, too, ef you ain't pertickler."

The laugh which followed this joke, which evidently had some domestic allusion (the general tendency of rural pleasantry), was followed by a light step on the platform, and the young man entered. Seeing a stranger present, he stopped and colored; made a shy salute and colored again, and then, drawing a box from the corner, sat down, his hands clasped lightly together and his very handsome bright blue eyes turned frankly on mine.

Perhaps I was in a condition to receive the romantic impression he made upon me, and I took it upon myself to ask his company as guide, and he cheerfully assented. But some domestic duty called him presently away.

The fire gleamed brightly on the hearth, and, no longer

resisting the prevailing influence, I silently watched the spirting flame, listening to the wind which continually shook the tenement. Besides the one chair which had acquired a new importance in my eyes, I presently discovered a crazy table in one corner, with an ink-bottle and pen; the latter in that greasy state of decomposition peculiar to country taverns and farm-houses. A goodly array of rifles and double-barrelled guns stocked the corner; half a dozen saddles and blankets lay near, with a mild flavor of the horse about them. Some deer and bear skins completed the inventory. As I sat there, with the silent group around me, the shadowy gloom within and the dominant wind without, I found it difficult to believe I had ever known a different existence. My profession had often led me to wilder scenes, but rarely among those whose unrestrained habits and easy unconsciousness made me feel so lonely and uncomfortable. I shrank closer to myself, not without grave doubts—which I think occur naturally to people in like situations—that this was the general rule of humanity, and I was a solitary and somewhat gratuitous exception.

It was a relief when a laconic announcement of supper by a weak-eyed girl caused a general movement in the family. We walked across the dark platform, which led to another low-ceiled room. Its entire length was occupied by a table, at the farther end of which a weak-eyed woman was already taking her repast, as she, at the same time, gave nourishment to a weak-eyed baby. As the formalities of introduction had been dispensed with, and as she took no notice of me, I was enabled to slip into a seat without discomposing or interrupting her. Tryan extemporized a grace, and the attention of the family became absorbed in bacon, potatoes, and dried apples.

The meal was a sincere one. Gentle gurglings at the upper end of the table often betrayed the presence of the "well-spring of pleasure." The conversation generally referred to the labors of the day, and comparing notes as to the where-abouts of missing stock. Yet the supper was such a vast improvement upon the previous intellectual feast, that when a chance allusion of mine to the business of my visit brought out the elder Tryan, the interest grew quite exciting. I remember he inveighed bitterly against the system of ranch-holding by the "greasers," as he was pleased to term the native Californians. As the same ideas have been sometimes advanced under more pretentious circumstances, they may be worthy of record.

"Look at 'em holdin' the finest grazin' land that ever lay outer doors? Whar's the papers for it? Was it grants? Mighty fine grants,—most of 'em made arter the 'Merri-kans got possession. More fools the 'Merrikans for lettin' 'em hold 'em. Wat paid for 'em? 'Merrikan blood and money.

"Didn't they oughter have suthin out of their native country? Wot for? Did they ever improve? Got a lot of yaller-skinned diggers, not so sensible as niggers to look arter stock, and they a sittin' home and smokin'. With their gold and silver candlesticks, and missions, and crucifixens, priests and graven idols, and sich? Them sort things wurent allowed in Mizzoori."

At the mention of improvements, I involuntarily lifted my eyes, and met the half-laughing, half-embarrassed look of George. The act did not escape detection, and I had at once the satisfaction of seeing that the rest of the family had formed an offensive alliance against us.

"It was agin Nater, and agin God," added Tryan. "God

never intended gold in the rocks to be made into heathen candlesticks and crucifixens. That's why he sent 'Merrikans here. Nater never intended such a climate for lazy lopers. She never gin six months' sunshine to be slept and smoked away."

How long he continued, and with what further illustration I could not say, for I took an early opportunity to escape to the sitting-room. I was soon followed by George, who called me to an open door leading to a smaller room, and pointed to a bed.

"You'd better sleep there to-night," he said; "you'll be more comfortable, and I'll call you early."

I thanked him, and would have asked him several questions which were then troubling me, but he shyly slipped to the door and vanished.

A shadow seemed to fall on the room when he had gone. The "boys" returned, one by one, and shuffled to their old places. A larger log was thrown on the fire, and the huge chimney glowed like a furnace, but it did not seem to melt or subdue a single line of the hard faces that it lit. In half an hour later, the furs which had served as chairs by day undertook the nightly office of mattresses, and each received its owner's full-length figure. Mr. Tryan had not returned, and I missed George. I sat there, until, wakeful and nervous, I saw the fire fall and shadows mount the wall. There was no sound but the rushing of the wind and the snoring of the sleepers. At last, feeling the place insupportable, I seized my hat and, opening the door, ran out briskly into the night.

The acceleration of my torpid pulse in the keen fight with the wind, whose violence was almost equal to that of a tornado, and the familiar faces of the bright stars above me,

I felt as a blessed relief. I ran not knowing whither, and when I halted, the square outline of the house was lost in the alder-bushes. An uninterrupted plain stretched before me, like a vast sea beaten flat by the force of the gale. As I kept on I noticed a slight elevation toward the horizon, and presently my progress was impeded by the ascent of an Indian mound. It struck me forcibly as resembling an island in the sea. Its height gave me a better view of the expanding plain. But even here I found no rest. The ridiculous interpretation Tryan had given the climate was somehow sung in my ears, and echoed in my throbbing pulse, as, guided by the star, I sought the house again.

But I felt fresher and more natural as I stepped upon the platform. The door of the lower building was open, and the old man was sitting beside the table, thumbing the leaves of a Bible with a look in his face as though he were hunting up prophecies against the "Greaser." I turned to enter, but my attention was attracted by a blanketed figure lying beside the house, on the platform. The broad chest heaving with healthy slumber, and the open, honest face were familiar. It was George, who had given up his bed to the stranger among his people. I was about to wake him, but he lay so peaceful and quiet, I felt awed and hushed. And I went to bed with a pleasant impression of his handsome face and tranquil figure soothing me to sleep.

I was awakened the next morning from a sense of lulled repose and grateful silence by the cheery voice of George, who stood beside my bed, ostentatiously twirling a "riata," as if to recall the duties of the day to my sleep-bewildered eyes. I looked around me. The wind had been magically laid, and the sun shone warmly through the windows. A dash of cold water, with an extra chill on from the tin basin, helped to brighten me. It was still early, but the family had already breakfasted and dispersed, and a wagon winding far in the distance showed that the unfortunate Tom had already "packed" his relatives away. I felt more cheerful, —there are few troubles Youth cannot distance with the start of a good night's rest. After a substantial breakfast, prepared by George, in a few moments we were mounted and dashing down the plain.

We followed the line of alder that defined the creek, now dry and baked with summer's heat, but which in winter, George told me, overflowed its banks. I still retain a vivid impression of that morning's ride, the far-off mountains, like *silhouettes,* against the steel-blue sky, the crisp dry air, and the expanding track before me, animated often by the well-knit figure of George Tryan, musical with jingling spurs, and picturesque with flying "riata." He rode a powerful native roan, wild-eyed, untiring in stride and unbroken in nature. Alas! the curves of beauty were concealed by the cumbrous *machillas* of the Spanish saddle, which levels all equine distinctions. The single rein lay loosely on the cruel bit that can gripe, and, if need be, crush the jaw it controls.

Again the illimitable freedom of the valley rises before me, as we again bear down into sunlit space. Can this be "Chu-Chu," staid and respectable filly of American pedigree,—"Chu-Chu," forgetful of plank-roads and cobblestones, wild with excitement, twinkling her small white feet beneath me? George laughs out of a cloud of dust, "Give her her head; don't you see she likes it?" and "Chu-Chu" seems to like it, and, whether bitten by native tarantula into native barbarism or emulous of the roan, "blood" asserts itself, and in a moment the peaceful servitude of years is beaten out in the music of her clattering hoofs. The creek widens to a deep gully. We dive into it and up on the opposite side, carrying a moving cloud of impalpable powder with us. Cattle are scattered over the plain, grazing quietly, or banded together in vast restless herds. George makes a wide, indefinite sweep with the "riata," as if to include them all in his *vaquero's* loop, and says, "Ours!"

"About how many, George?"

"Don't know."

"How many?"

"Well, p'r'aps three thousand head," says George, reflecting. "We don't know, takes five men to look 'em up and keep run."

"What are they worth?"

"About thirty dollars a head."

I make a rapid calculation, and look my astonishment at the laughing George. Perhaps a recollection of the domestic economy of the Tryan household is expressed in that look, for George averts his eye and says, apologetically,—

"I've tried to get the old man to sell and build, but you know he says it ain't no use to settle down, just yet. We must keep movin'. In fact, he built the shanty for that purpose, lest titles should fall through, and we'd have to get up and move stakes further down."

Suddenly his quick eye detects some unusual sight in a herd we are passing, and with an exclamation he puts his roan into the centre of the mass. I follow, or rather "Chu-Chu" darts after the roan, and in a few moments we are in the midst of apparently inextricable horns and hoofs. "Toro!" shouts George, with vaquero enthusiasm, and the band opens a way for the swinging "riata." I can feel their steaming breaths, and their spume is cast on "Chu-Chu's" quivering flank.

Wild, devilish-looking beasts are they; not such shapes as Jove might have chosen to woo a goddess, nor such as peacefully range the downs of Devon, but lean and hungry Cassius-like bovines, economically got up to meet the exigencies of a six months' rainless climate, and accustomed to wrestle with the distracting wind and the blinding dust.

"That's not our brand," says George; "they're strange stock," and he points to what my scientific eye recognizes as the astrological sign of Venus deeply seared in the brown flanks of the bull he is chasing. But the herd are closing round us with low mutterings, and George has again recourse to the authoritative "Toro," and with swinging "riata" divides the "bossy bucklers" on either side. When we are free, and breathing somewhat more easily, I venture to ask George if they ever attack any one.

"Never horsemen,—sometimes footmen. Not through rage, you know, but curiosity. They think a man and his horse are one, and if they meet a chap afoot, they run him down and trample him under hoof, in the pursuit of knowledge. But," adds George, "here's the lower bench of the foot-hills, and here's Altascar's corral, and that white building you see yonder is the *casa*."

A whitewashed wall enclosed a court containing another adobe building, baked with the solar beams of many summers. Leaving our horses in the charge of a few peons in the courtyard, who were basking lazily in the sun, we entered a low doorway, where a deep shadow and an agreeable coolness fell upon us, as sudden and grateful as a plunge in cool water, from its contrast with the external glare and heat. In the centre of a low-ceiled apartment sat an old man with a black silk handkerchief tied about his head; the few gray hairs that escaped from its folds relieving his gamboge-colored face. The odor of cigarritos was as incense added to the cathedral gloom of the building.

As Señor Altascar rose with well-bred gravity to receive us, George advanced with such a heightened color, and such a blending of tenderness and respect in his manner, that I was touched to the heart by so much devotion in the careless youth. In fact, my eyes were still dazzled by the effect of the outer sunshine, and at first I did not see the white teeth and black eyes of Pepita, who slipped into the corridor as we entered.

It was no pleasant matter to disclose particulars of business which would deprive the old Señor of the greater part of that land we had just ridden over, and I did it with great embarrassment. But he listened calmly,—not a muscle of his dark face stirring,—and the smoke curling placidly from his lips showed his regular respiration. When I had finished, he offered quietly to accompany us to the line of demarcation. George had meanwhile disappeared, but a suspicious conversation in broken Spanish and English, in the corridor, betrayed his vicinity. When he returned again, a little absent-minded, the old man, by far the coolest and most self-possessed of the party, extinguished his black silk cap beneath that stiff, uncomely *sombrero* which all native Californians affect. A *serapa* thrown over his shoulders hinted that he was waiting. Horses are always ready saddled in Spanish ranchos, and in half an hour from the time of our arrival we were again "loping" in the staring sunlight.

But not as cheerfully as before. George and myself were weighed down by restraint, and Altascar was gravely quiet.

To break the silence, and by way of a consolatory essay, I hinted to him that there might be further intervention or appeal, but the proffered oil and wine were returned with a careless shrug of the shoulders and a sententious *"Que bueno?*—Your courts are always just."

The Indian mound of the previous night's discovery was a bearing monument of the new line, and there we halted. We were surprised to find the old man Tryan waiting us. For the first time during our interview the old Spaniard seemed moved, and the blood rose in his yellow cheek. I was anxious to close the scene, and pointed out the corner boundaries as clearly as my recollection served.

"The deputies will be here to-morrow to run the lines from this initial point, and there will be no further trouble, I believe, gentlemen."

Señor Altascar had dismounted and was gathering a few tufts of dried grass in his hands. George and I exchanged glances. He presently arose from his stooping posture, and, advancing to within a few paces of Joseph Tryan, said, in a voice broken with passion,—

"And I, Fernando Jesus Maria Altascar, put you in possession of my land in the fashion of my country."

He threw a sod to each of the cardinal points.

"I don't know your courts, your judges, or your *corregidores*. Take the *llano!*—and take this with it. May the drought seize your cattle till their tongues hang down as long as those of your lying lawyers! May it be the curse and torment of your old age, as you and yours have made it of mine!"

We stepped between the principal actors in this scene, which only the passion of Altascar made tragical, but

Tryan, with a humility but ill concealing his triumph, interrupted:—

"Let him curse on. He'll find 'em coming home to him sooner than the cattle he has lost through his sloth and pride. The Lord is on the side of the just, as well as agin all slanderers and revilers."

Altascar but half guessed the meaning of the Missourian, yet sufficiently to drive from his mind all but the extravagant power of his native invective.

"Stealer of the Sacrament! Open not!—open not, I say, your lying, Judas lips to me! Ah! half-breed, with the soul of a cayote!—Car-r-r-ramba!"

With his passion reverberating among the consonants like distant thunder, he laid his hand upon the mane of his horse as though it had been the gray locks of his adversary, swung himself into the saddle and galloped away.

George turned to me:—

"Will you go back with us to-night?"

I thought of the cheerless walls, the silent figures by the fire, and the roaring wind, and hesitated.

"Well then, good-by."

"Good-by, George."

Another wring of the hands, and we parted. I had not ridden far, when I turned and looked back. The wind had risen early that afternoon, and was already sweeping across the plain. A cloud of dust travelled before it, and a picturesque figure occasionally emerging therefrom was my last indistinct impression of George Tryan.

PART II—IN THE FLOOD

THREE months after the survey of the Espíritu Santo Rancho, I was again in the valley of the Sacramento. But a general and terrible visitation had erased the memory of that event as completely as I supposed it had obliterated the boundary monuments I had planted. The great flood of 1861-62 was at its height, when, obeying some indefinite yearning, I took my carpet-bag and embarked for the inundated valley.

There was nothing to be seen from the bright cabin windows of the "Golden City" but night deepening over the water. The only sound was the pattering rain, and that had grown monotonous for the past two weeks, and did not disturb the national gravity of my countrymen as they silently sat around the cabin stove. Some on errands of relief to friends and relatives wore anxious faces, and conversed soberly on the one absorbing topic. Others, like myself, attracted by curiosity, listened eagerly to newer details. But with that human disposition to seize upon any circumstance that might give chance event the exaggerated importance of instinct, I was half conscious of something more than curiosity as an impelling motive.

The dripping of rain, the low gurgle of water, and a leaden sky greeted us the next morning as we lay beside the half-submerged levee of Sacramento. Here, however, the novelty of boats to convey us to the hotels was an appeal that was irresistible. I resigned myself to a dripping rubber-cased mariner called "Joe," and, wrapping myself in a shining cloak of the like material, about as suggestive of warmth as court-plaster might have been, took my seat in the stern-sheets of his boat. It was no slight inward struggle to part from the steamer, that to most of the passengers was the only visible connecting link between us and the dry and habitable earth, but we pulled away and entered the city, stemming a rapid current as we shot the levee.

We glided up the long level of K Street,—once a cheerful, busy thoroughfare, now distressing in its silent desolation. The turbid water which seemed to meet the horizon edge before us flowed at right angles in sluggish rivers through the streets. Nature had revenged herself on the local taste by disarraying the regular rectangles by huddling houses on street corners, where they presented abrupt gables to the current, or by capsizing them in compact ruin. Crafts of all kinds were gliding in and out of low-arched doorways. The water was over the top of the fences surrounding well-kept gardens, in the first stories of hotels and private dwellings, trailing its slime on velvet carpets as well as roughly boarded floors. And a silence quite as suggestive as the visible desolation was in the voiceless streets that no longer echoed to carriage-wheel or footfall. The low ripple of water, the occasional splash of oars, or the warning cry of boatmen were the few signs of life and habitation.

With such scenes before my eyes and such sounds in my ears, as I lie lazily in the boat, is mingled the song of my gondolier who sings to the music of his oars. It is not quite as romantic as his brother of the Lido might improvise, but my Yankee "Giuseppe" has the advantage of earnestness and energy, and gives a graphic description of the terrors of the past week and of noble deeds of self-sacrifice and devotion, occasionally pointing out a balcony from which some California Bianca or Laura had been snatched, half clothed and famished. Giuseppe is otherwise peculiar, and refuses the proffered fare, for—am I not a citizen of San Francisco, which was first to respond to the suffering cry of Sacramento? and is not he, Giuseppe, a member of the Howard Society? No! Giuseppe is poor, but cannot take my money. Still, if I must spend it, there is the Howard Society, and the women and children without food and clothes at the Agricultural Hall.

I thank the generous gondolier, and we go to the Hall,— a dismal, bleak place, ghastly with the memories of last year's opulence and plenty, and here Giuseppe's fare is swelled by the stranger's mite. But here Giuseppe tells me of the "Relief Boat" which leaves for the flooded district in the interior, and here, profiting by the lesson he has taught me, I make the resolve to turn my curiosity to the account of others, and am accepted of those who go forth to succor and help the afflicted. Giuseppe takes charge of my carpet-bag, and does not part from me until I stand on the slippery deck of "Relief Boat No. 3."

An hour later I am in the pilot-house, looking down upon what was once the channel of a peaceful river. But its banks are only defined by tossing tufts of willow washed by the long swell that breaks over a vast inland sea. Stretches of "tule" land fertilized by its once regular channel and dotted by flourishing ranchos are now cleanly erased. The cultivated profile of the old landscape had faded. Dotted lines in symmetrical perspective mark orchards that are buried and chilled in the turbid flood. The roofs of a few farm-houses are visible, and here and there the smoke curling from chimneys of half-submerged tenements show an undaunted life within. Cattle and sheep are gathered on Indian mounds waiting the fate of their companions whose carcasses drift by us, or swing in eddies with the wrecks of barns and out-houses. Wagons are stranded everywhere where the tide could carry them. As I wipe the moistened glass, I see nothing but water, pattering on the deck from the lowering clouds, dashing against the window, dripping from the willows, hissing by the wheels, everywhere washing, coiling, sapping, hurrying in rapids, or swelling at last into deeper and vaster lakes, awful in their suggestive quiet and concealment.

As day fades into night the monotony of this strange prospect grows oppressive. I seek the engine-room, and in the company of some of the few half-drowned sufferers we have already picked up from temporary rafts, I forget the general aspect of desolation in their individual misery. Later we meet the San Francisco packet, and transfer a number of our passengers. From them we learn how inward-bound vessels report to having struck the well-defined channel of the Sacramento, fifty miles beyond the bar. There is a voluntary contribution taken among the generous travellers for the use of our afflicted, and we part company with a hearty "God speed" on either side. But our signal-lights are not far distant before a familiar sound comes back to us,—an indomitable Yankee cheer,—which scatters the gloom.

Our course is altered, and we are steaming over the obliterated banks far in the interior. Once or twice black objects loom up near us,—the wrecks of houses floating by. There is a slight rift in the sky towards the north, and a few bearing stars to guide us over the waste. As we penetrate into shallower water, it is deemed advisable to divide our party into smaller boats, and diverge over the submerged prairie. I borrow a pea-coat of one of the crew, and in that practical disguise am doubtfully permitted to pass into one of the boats. We give way northerly. It is quite dark yet, although the rift of cloud has widened.

It must have been about three o'clock, and we were lying upon our oars in an eddy formed by a clump of cottonwood, and the light of the steamer is a solitary, bright star in the distance, when the silence is broken by the "bow oar":—

"Light ahead."

All eyes are turned in that direction. In a few seconds a twinkling light appears, shines steadily, and again disappears as if by the shifting position of some black object apparently drifting close upon us.

"Stern, all; a steamer!"

"Hold hard there! Steamer be d—d!" is the reply of the coxswain. "It's a house, and a big one too."

It is a big one, looming in the starlight like a huge fragment of the darkness. The light comes from a single candle, which shines through a window as the great shape swings by. Some recollection is drifting back to me with it, as I listen with beating heart.

"There's some one in it, by Heavens! Give way, boys,— lay her alongside. Handsomely, now! The door's fastened; try the window; no! here's another!"

In another moment we are trampling in the water, which washes the floor to the depth of several inches. It is a large room, at the further end of which an old man is sitting wrapped in a blanket, holding a candle in one hand, and apparently absorbed in the book he holds with the other. I spring toward him with an exclamation:—

"Joseph Tryan!"

He does not move. We gather closer to him, and I lay my hand gently on his shoulder, and say:—

"Look up, old man, look up! Your wife and children,

where are they? The boys,—George! Are they here? are they safe?"

He raises his head slowly, and turns his eyes to mine, and we involuntarily recoil before his look. It is a calm and quiet glance, free from fear, anger, or pain; but it somehow sends the blood curdling through our veins. He bowed his head over his book again, taking no further notice of us. The men look at me compassionately, and hold their peace. I make one more effort:—

"Joseph Tryan, don't you know me? the surveyor who surveyed your ranch,—the Espíritu Santo? Look up, old man!"

He shuddered and wrapped himself closer in his blanket. Presently he repeated to himself, "The surveyor who surveyed your ranch,—Espíritu Santo," over and over again, as though it were a lesson he was trying to fix in his memory.

I was turning sadly to the boatmen, when he suddenly caught me fearfully by the hand and said,—

"Hush!"

We were silent.

"Listen!" He puts his arm around my neck and whispers in my ear, "I'm a *moving off!*"

"Moving off?"

"Hush! Don't speak so loud. Moving off. Ah! wot's that? Don't you hear?—there! listen!"

We listen, and hear the water gurgle and click beneath the floor.

"It's them wot he sent!—Old Altascar sent. They've been here all night. I heard 'em first in the creek, when they came to tell the old man to move farther off. They came nearer and nearer. They whispered under the door, and I saw their eyes on the step,—their cruel, hard eyes. Ah, why don't they quit?"

I tell the men to search the room and see if they can find any further traces of the family, while Tryan resumes his old attitude. It is so much like the figure I remember on the breezy night that a superstitious feeling is fast overcoming me. When they have returned, I tell them briefly what I know of him, and the old man murmurs again,—

"Why don't they quit, then? They have the stock,—all gone—gone, gone for the hides and hoofs," and he groans bitterly.

"There are other boats below us. The shanty cannot have drifted far, and perhaps the family are safe by this time," says the coxswain, hopefully.

We lift the old man up, for he is quite helpless, and carry him to the boat. He is still grasping the Bible in his right hand, though its strengthening grace is blank to his vacant eye, and he cowers in the stern as we pull slowly to the steamer, while a pale gleam in the sky shows the coming day.

I was weary with excitement, and when we reached the steamer, and I had seen Joseph Tryan comfortably bestowed, I wrapped myself in a blanket near the boiler and presently fell asleep. But even then the figure of the old man often started before me, and a sense of uneasiness about George made a strong undercurrent to my drifting dreams. I was awakened at about eight o'clock in the morning by the engineer, who told me one of the old man's sons had been picked up and was now on board.

"Is it George Tryan?" I ask quickly.

"Don't know; but he's a sweet one, whoever he is," adds

the engineer, with a smile at some luscious remembrance. "You'll find him for'ard."

I hurry to the bow of the boat, and find, not George, but the irrepressible Wise, sitting on a coil of rope, a little dirtier and rather more dilapidated than I can remember having seen him.

He is examining, with apparent admiration, some rough, dry clothes that have been put out for his disposal. I cannot help thinking that circumstances have somewhat exalted his usual cheerfulness. He puts me at my ease by at once addressing me:—

"These are high old times, ain't they? I say, what do you reckon's become o' them thar bound'ry moniments you stuck? Ah!"

The pause which succeeds this outburst is the effect of a spasm of admiration at a pair of high boots, which, by great exertion, he has at last pulled on his feet.

"So you've picked up the ole man in the shanty, clean crazy? He must have been soft to have stuck there instead o' leavin' with the old woman. Didn't know me from Adam; took me for George!"

At this affecting instance of paternal forgetfulness, Wise was evidently divided between amusement and chagrin. I took advantage of the contending emotions to ask about George.

"Don't know whar he is! If he'd tended stock instead of running about the prairie, packin' off wimmin and children, he might have saved suthin. He lost every hoof and hide, I'll bet a cookey! Say you," to a passing boatman, "when are you goin' to give us some grub? I'm hungry 'nough to skin and eat a hoss. Reckon I'll turn butcher when things is dried up, and save hides, horns, and taller."

I could not but admire this indomitable energy, which under softer climatic influences might have borne such goodly fruit.

"Have you any idea what you'll do, Wise?" I ask.

"Thar ain't much to do now," says the practical young man. "I'll have to lay over a spell, I reckon, till things comes straight. The land ain't worth much now, and won't be, I dessay, for some time. Wonder whar the ole man'll drive stakes next?"

"I meant as to your father and George, Wise."

"O, the ole man and I'll go on to 'Miles's,' whar Tom packed the old woman and babies last week. George'll turn up somewhar atween this and Altascar's, ef he ain't thar now."

I ask how the Altascars have suffered.

"Well, I reckon he ain't lost much in stock. I shouldn't wonder if George helped him drive 'em up the foot-hills. And his 'casa's' built too high. O, thar ain't any water thar, you bet. Ah," says Wise, with reflective admiration, "those greasers ain't the darned fools people thinks 'em. I'll bet thar ain't one swamped out in all 'er Californy." But the appearance of "grub" cut this rhapsody short.

"I shall keep on a little farther," I say, "and try to find George."

Wise stared a moment at this eccentricity until a new light dawned upon him.

"I don't think you'll save much. What's the percentage, —workin' on shares, eh!"

I answer that I am only curious, which I feel lessens his opinion of me, and with a sadder feeling than his assurance of George's safety might warrant, I walked away.

From others whom we picked up from time to time we

heard of George's self-sacrificing devotion, with the praises of the many he had helped and rescued. But I did not feel disposed to return until I had seen him, and soon prepared myself to take a boat to the lower "valda" of the foot-hills, and visit Altascar. I soon perfected my arrangements, bade farewell to Wise, and took a last look at the old man, who was sitting by the furnace-fires quite passive and composed. Then our boat-head swung round, pulled by sturdy and willing hands.

It was again raining, and a disagreeable wind had risen. Our course lay nearly west, and we soon knew by the strong current that we were in the creek of the Espíritu Santo. From time to time the wrecks of barns were seen, and we passed many half-submerged willows hung with farming implements.

We emerge at last into a broad silent sea. It is the "llano de Espíritu Santo." As the wind whistles by me, piling the shallower fresh water into mimic waves, I go back, in fancy, to the long ride of October over that boundless plain, and recall the sharp outlines of the distant hills which are now lost in the lowering clouds. The men are rowing silently, and I find my mind, released from its tension, growing benumbed and depressed as then. The water, too, is getting more shallow as we leave the banks of the creek, and with my hand dipped listlessly over the thwarts, I detect the tops of chimisal, which shows the tide to have somewhat fallen. There is a black mound, bearing to the north of the line of alder, making an adverse current, which, as we sweep to the right to avoid, I recognize. We pull close alongside and I call to the men to stop.

There was a stake driven near its summit with the initials, "L. E. S. I." Tied half-way down was a curiously worked

"riata." It was George's. It had been cut with some sharp
instrument, and the loose gravelly soil of the mound was
deeply dented with horse's hoofs. The stake was covered
with horse-hairs. It was a record, but no clew.

The wind had grown more violent, as we still fought our
way forward, resting and rowing by turns, and oftener
"poling" the shallower surface, but the old "valda," or
bench, is still distant. My recollection of the old survey en-
ables me to guess the relative position of the meanderings
of the creek, and an occasional simple professional experiment to determine the distance gives my crew the fullest
faith in my ability. Night overtakes us in our impeded progress. Our condition looks more dangerous than it really is,
but I urge the men, many of whom are still new in this mode
of navigation, to greater exertion by assurance of perfect
safety and speedy relief ahead. We go on in this way until
about eight o'clock, and ground by the willows. We have a
muddy walk for a few hundred yards before we strike a dry
trail, and simultaneously the white walls of Altascar's appear like a snow-bank before us. Lights are moving in the
courtyard; but otherwise the old tomb-like repose charac-
terizes the building.

One of the peons recognized me as I entered the court,
and Altascar met me on the corridor.

I was too weak to do more than beg his hospitality for
the men who had dragged wearily with me. He looked at
my hand, which still unconsciously held the broken "riata."
I began, wearily, to tell him about George and my fears, but
with a gentler courtesy than was even his wont, he gravely
laid his hand on my shoulder.

"*Poco a poco* Señor,—not now. You are tired, you have

hunger, you have cold. Necessary it is you should have peace."

He took us into a small room and poured out some French cognac, which he gave to the men that had accompanied me. They drank and threw themselves before the fire in the larger room. The repose of the building was intensified that night, and I even fancied that the footsteps on the corridor were lighter and softer. The old Spaniard's habitual gravity was deeper; we might have been shut out from the world as well as the whistling storm, behind those ancient walls with their time-worn inheritor.

Before I could repeat my inquiry he retired. In a few minutes two smoking dishes of "chupa" with coffee were placed before us, and my men ate ravenously. I drank the coffee, but my excitement and weariness kept down the instincts of hunger.

I was sitting sadly by the fire when he re-entered.

"You have eat?"

I said, "Yes," to please him.

"*Bueno,* eat when you can,—food and appetite are not always."

He said this with that Sancho-like simplicity with which most of his countrymen utter a proverb, as though it were an experience rather than a legend, and, taking the "riata" from the floor, held it almost tenderly before him.

"It was made by me, Señor."

"I kept it as a clew to him, Don Altascar," I said. "If I could find him—"

"He is here."

"Here! and"—but I could not say, "well!" I understood the gravity of the old man's face, the hushed footfalls, the tomb-like repose of the building in an electric flash of consciousness; I held the clew to the broken riata at last. Altascar took my hand, and we crossed the corridor to a sombre apartment. A few tall candles were burning in sconces before the window.

In an alcove there was a deep bed with its counterpane, pillows, and sheets heavily edged with lace, in all that splendid luxury which the humblest of these strange people lavish upon this single item of their household. I stepped beside it and saw George lying, as I had seen him once before, peacefully at rest. But a greater sacrifice than that he had known was here, and his generous heart was stilled forever.

"He was honest and brave," said the old man, and turned away.

There was another figure in the room; a heavy shawl drawn over her graceful outline, and her long black hair hiding the hands that buried her downcast face. I did not seem to notice her, and, retiring presently, left the loving and loved together.

When we were again beside the crackling fire, in the shifting shadows of the great chamber, Altascar told me how he had that morning met the horse of George Tryan swimming on the prairie; how that, farther on, he found him lying, quite cold and dead, with no marks or bruises on his person; that he had probably become exhausted in fording the creek, and that he had as probably reached the mound only to die for want of that help he had so freely given to others; that, as a last act, he had freed his horse. These incidents were corroborated by many who collected in the great chamber that evening,—women and children,—most of them succored through the devoted energies of him who lay cold and lifeless above.

He was buried in the Indian mound,—the single spot of

strange perennial greenness, which the poor aborigines had raised above the dusty plain. A little slab of sandstone with the initials "G. T." is his monument, and one of the bearings of the initial corner of the new survey of the "Espíritu Santo Rancho."

THE MISSION DOLORES

THE Mission Dolores is destined to be "The Last Sigh" of the native Californian. When the last "Greaser" shall indolently give way to the bustling Yankee, I can imagine he will, like the Moorish King, ascend one of the Mission hills to take his last lingering look at the hilled city. For a long time he will cling tenaciously to Pacific Street. He will delve in the rocky fastnesses of Telegraph Hill until progress shall remove it. He will haunt Vallejo Street, and those back slums which so vividly typify the degradation of a people; but he will eventually make way for improvement. The Mission will be last to drop from his nerveless fingers.

As I stand here this pleasant afternoon, looking up at the old chapel,—its ragged senility contrasting with the smart spring sunshine, its two gouty pillars with the plaster dropping away like tattered bandages, its rayless windows, its crumbling entrances, the leper spots on its whitewashed wall eating through the dark adobe,—I give the poor old mendicant but a few years longer to sit by the highway and ask alms in the names of the blessed saints. Already the vicinity is haunted with the shadows of its dissolution. The shriek of the locomotive discords with the Angelus bell. An Episcopal church, of a green Gothic type, with massive buttresses of Oregon pine, even now mocks its hoary age with imitation and supplants it with a sham. Vain, alas! were those rural accessories, the nurseries and market-gardens, that once gathered about its walls and resisted civic encroachment. They, too, are passing away. Even those queer little adobe buildings with tiled roofs like longitudinal slips of cinnamon, and walled enclosures sacredly guarding a few bullock horns and strips of hide. I look in vain for the half-reclaimed Mexican, whose respectability stopped at his waist, and whose red sash under his vest was the utter undoing of his black broadcloth. I miss, too, those black-haired women, with swaying unstable busts, whose dresses were always unseasonable in texture and pattern; whose wearing of a shawl was a terrible awakening from the poetic dream of the Spanish mantilla. Traces of another nationality are visible. The railroad "navvy" has builded his shanty near the chapel, and smokes his pipe in the Posada. Gutturals have taken the place of linguals and sibilants; I miss the half-chanted, half-drawled cadences that used to mingle with the cheery "All aboard" of the stage-driver, in those good old days when the stages ran hourly to the Mission, and a trip thither was an excursion. At the very gates of the temple, in the place of those "who sell doves for sacrifice," a vender of mechanical spiders has halted with his unhallowed wares. Even the old Padre—last type of the Missionary, and descendant of the good Junipero—I cannot find to-day; in his stead a light-haired Celt is reading a lesson from a Vulgate that is wonderfully replete with double r's. Gentle priest, in thy orisons, let the stranger and heretic be remembered.

I open a little gate and enter the Mission Churchyard. There is no change here, though perhaps the graves lie closer together. A willow-tree, growing beside the deep, brown wall, has burst into tufted plumes in the fulness of spring. The tall grass-blades over each mound show a strange quickening of the soil below. It is pleasanter here than on the bleak mountain seaward, where distracting winds continually bring the strife and turmoil of the ocean. The Mission hills lovingly embrace the little cemetery, whose decorative taste is less ostentatious. The foreign flavor is strong; here are never-failing garlands of *immortelles,* with their sepulchral spicery; here are little cheap medallions of pewter, with the adornment of three black tears, that would look like the three of clubs, but that the simple humility of the inscription counterbalances all sense of the ridiculous. Here are children's graves with guardian angels of great specific gravity; but here, too, are the little one's toys in a glass case beside them. Here is the average quantity of execrable original verses; but one stanza—over a sailor's grave—is striking, for it expresses a hope of salvation through the "Lord High Admiral Christ!" Over the foreign graves there is a notable lack of scriptural quotation, and an increase, if I may say it, of humanity and tenderness. I cannot help thinking that too many of my countrymen are influenced by a morbid desire to make a practical point of this occasion, and are too apt hastily to crowd a whole life of omission into the culminating act. But when I see the gray *immortelles* crowning a tombstone, I know I shall find the mysteries of the resurrection shown rather in symbols, and only the love taught in His new commandment left for the graphic touch. But "they manage these things better in France."

During my purposeless ramble the sun has been steadily

climbing the brown wall of the church, and the air seems to grow cold and raw. The bright green dies out of the grass, and the rich bronze comes down from the wall. The willow-tree seems half inclined to doff its plumes, and wears the dejected air of a broken faith and violated trust. The spice of the *immortelles* mixes with the incense that steals through the open window. Within, the barbaric gilt and crimson look cold and cheap in this searching air; by this light the church certainly is old and ugly. I cannot help wondering whether the old Fathers, if they ever revisit the scene of their former labors, in their larger comprehensions, view with regret the impending change, or mourn over the day when the Mission Dolores shall appropriately come to grief.

JOHN CHINAMAN

The expression of the Chinese face in the aggregate is neither cheerful nor happy. In an acquaintance of half a dozen years, I can only recall one or two exceptions to this rule. There is an abiding consciousness of degradation,— a secret pain or self-humiliation visible in the lines of the mouth and eye. Whether it is only a modification of Turkish gravity, or whether it is the dread Valley of the Shadow of the Drug through which they are continually straying, I cannot say. They seldom smile, and their laughter is of such an extraordinary and sardonic nature—so purely a mechanical spasm, quite independent of any mirthful attribute— that to this day I am doubtful whether I ever saw a Chinaman laugh. A theatrical representation by natives, one might think, would have set my mind at ease on this point; but it did not. Indeed, a new difficulty presented itself,—

the impossibility of determining whether the performance was a tragedy or farce. I thought I detected the low comedian in an active youth who turned two somersaults, and knocked everybody down on entering the stage. But, unfortunately, even this classic resemblance to the legitimate farce of our civilization was deceptive. Another brocaded actor, who represented the hero of the play, turned three somersaults, and not only upset my theory and his fellow-actors at the same time, but apparently run a-muck behind the scenes for some time afterward. I looked around at the glinting white teeth to observe the effect of these two palpable hits. They were received with equal acclamation, and apparently equal facial spasms. One or two beheadings which enlivened the play produced the same sardonic effect, and upon my mind a painful anxiety to know what was the serious business of life in China. It was noticeable, however, that my unrestrained laughter had a discordant effect, and that triangular eyes sometimes turned ominously toward the "Fanqui devil"; but as I retired discreetly before the play was finished, there were no serious results. I have only given the above as an instance of the impossibility of deciding upon the outward and superficial expression of Chinese mirth. Of its inner and deeper existence I have some private doubts. An audience that will view with a serious aspect the hero, after a frightful and agonizing death, get up and quietly walk off the stage, cannot be said to have remarkable perceptions of the ludicrous.

I have often been struck with the delicate pliability of the Chinese expression and taste, that might suggest a broader and deeper criticism than is becoming these pages. A Chinaman will adopt the American costume, and wear it with a taste of color and detail that will surpass those "native, and to the manner born." To look at a Chinese slipper, one might imagine it impossible to shape the original foot to anything less cumbrous and roomy, yet a neater-fitting boot than that belonging to the Americanized Chinaman is rarely seen on this side of the Continent. When the loose sack or paletot takes the place of his brocade blouse, it is worn with a refinement and grace that might bring a jealous pang to the exquisite of our more refined civilization. Pantaloons fall easily and naturally over legs that have known unlimited freedom and bagginess, and even garrote collars meet correctly around sun-tanned throats. The new expression seldom overflows in gaudy cravats. I will back my Americanized Chinaman against any neophyte of European birth in the choice of that article. While in our own State, the Greaser resists one by one the garments of the Northern invader, and even wears the livery of his conqueror with a wild and buttonless freedom, the Chinaman, abused and degraded as he is, changes by correctly graded transition to the garments of Christian civilization. There is but one article of European wear that he avoids. These Bohemian eyes have never yet been pained by the spectacle of a tall hat on the head of an intelligent Chinaman.

My acquaintance with John has been made up of weekly interviews, involving the adjustment of the washing accounts, so that I have not been able to study his character from a social view-point or observe him in the privacy of the domestic circle. I have gathered enough to justify me in believing him to be generally honest, faithful, simple, and painstaking. Of his simplicity let me record an instance where a sad and civil young Chinaman brought me certain shirts with most of the buttons missing and others hanging on delusively by a single thread. In a moment of unguarded irony I informed him that unity would at least have been preserved if the buttons were removed altogether. He smiled sadly and went away. I thought I had hurt his feelings, until the next week when he brought me my shirts with a look of intelligence, and the buttons carefully and totally erased. At another time, to guard against his general disposition to carry off anything as soiled clothes that he thought could hold water, I requested him to always wait until he saw me. Coming home late one evening, I found the household in great consternation, over an immovable Celestial who had remained seated on the front door-step during the day, sad and submissive, firm but also patient, and only betraying any animation or token of his mission when he saw me coming. This same Chinaman evinced some evidences of regard for a little girl in the family, who in her turn reposed such faith in his intellectual qualities as to present him with a preternaturally uninteresting Sunday-school book, her own property. This book John made a point of carrying ostentatiously with him in his weekly visits. It appeared usually on the top of the clean clothes, and was sometimes painfully clasped outside of the big bundle of soiled linen. Whether John believed he unconsciously imbibed some spiritual life through its pasteboard cover, as the Prince in the Arabian Nights imbibed the medicine through the handle of the mallet, or whether he wished to exhibit a due sense of gratitude, or whether he hadn't any pockets, I have never been able to ascertain. In his turn he would sometimes cut marvellous imitation roses from carrots for his little friend. I am inclined to think that the few roses strewn in John's path were such scentless imitations. The thorns only were real. From the persecutions of the young and old of a certain class, his life was a torment. I don't know what was the

"He drew a pack of cards from his pocket and shuffled them, glancing at the bed. But Brown's face was turned to the wall." Illustration for an 1872 edition of *Brown of Calaveras*, published by James R. Osgood & Co. (*p. 78*)

exact philosophy that Confucius taught, but it is to be hoped that poor John in his persecution is still able to detect the conscious hate and fear with which inferiority always regards the possibility of even-handed justice, and which is the key-note to the vulgar clamor about servile and degraded races.

FROM A BACK WINDOW

I REMEMBER that long ago, as a sanguine and trustful child, I became possessed of a highly colored lithograph, representing a fair Circassian sitting by a window. The price I paid for this work of art may have been extravagant, even in youth's fluctuating slate-pencil currency; but the secret joy I felt in its possession knew no pecuniary equivalent. It was not alone that Nature in Circassia lavished alike upon the cheek of beauty and the vegetable kingdom that most expensive of colors,—Lake; nor was it that the rose which bloomed beside the fair Circassian's window had no visible stem, and was directly grafted upon a marble balcony; but it was because it embodied an idea. That idea was a hinting of my Fate. I felt that somewhere a young and fair Circassian was sitting by a window looking out for me. The idea of resisting such an array of charms and color never occurred to me, and to my honor be it recorded, that during the feverish period of adolescence I never thought of averting my destiny. But as vacation and holiday came and went, and as my picture at first grew blurred, and then faded quite away between the Eastern and Western continents in my atlas, so its charm seemed mysteriously to pass away. When I became convinced that few females, of Cir-

cassian or other origin, sat pensively resting their chins on
their henna-tinged nails, at their parlor windows, I turned
my attention to back windows. Although the fair Circassian
has not yet burst upon me with open shutters, some peculiarities not unworthy of note have fallen under my observation.
This knowledge has not been gained without sacrifice. I
have made myself familiar with back windows and their
prospects, in the weak disguise of seeking lodgings, heed-
less of the suspicious glances of landladies and their evident
reluctance to show them. I have caught cold by long exposure to draughts. I have become estranged from friends by
unconsciously walking to their back windows during a visit,
when the weekly linen hung upon the line, or where Miss
Fanny (ostensibly indisposed) actually assisted in the laun-
dry, and Master Bobby, in scant attire, disported himself on
the area railings. But I have thought of Galileo, and the
invariable experience of all seekers and discovers of truth
has sustained me.

Show me the back windows of a man's dwelling, and I
will tell you his character. The rear of a house only is sincere. The attitude of deception kept up at the front windows leaves the back area defenceless. The world enters at
the front door, but nature comes out at the back passage.
That glossy, well-brushed individual, who lets himself in
with a latch-key at the front door at night, is a very different being from the slipshod wretch who growls of mornings
for hot water at the door of the kitchen. The same with
Madame, whose contour of figure grows angular, whose
face grows pallid, whose hair comes down, and who looks
some ten years older through the sincere medium of a back
window. No wonder that intimate friends fail to recognize
each other in this *dos à dos* position. You may imagine your-

self familiar with the silver door-plate and bow-windows
of the mansion where dwells your Saccharissa; you may
even fancy you recognize her graceful figure between the
lace curtains of the upper chamber which you fondly imagine to be hers; but you shall dwell for months in the rear
of her dwelling and within whispering distance of her
bower, and never know it. You shall see her with a handkerchief tied round her head in confidential discussion with
the butcher, and know her not. You shall hear her voice in
shrill expostulation with her younger brother, and it shall
awaken no familiar response.

I am writing at a back window. As I prefer the warmth
of my coal-fire to the foggy freshness of the afternoon
breeze that rattles the leafless shrubs in the garden below
me, I have my window-sash closed; consequently, I miss
much of the shrill altercation that has been going on in the
kitchen of No. 7 just opposite. I have heard fragments of
an entertaining style of dialogue usually known as "chaffing," which has just taken place between Biddy in No. 9
and the butcher who brings the dinner. I have been pitying
the chilled aspect of a poor canary, put out to taste the fresh
air, from the window of No. 5. I have been watching—
and envying, I fear—the real enjoyment of two children
raking over an old dust-heap in the alley, containing the
waste and *débris* of all the back yards in the neighborhood.
What a wealth of soda-water bottles and old iron they
have acquired! But I am waiting for an even more familiar
prospect from my back window. I know that later in the
afternoon, when the evening paper comes, a thickset, gray-
haired man will appear in his shirt-sleeves at the back door
of No. 9, and, seating himself on the door-step, begin to
read. He lives in a pretentious house, and I hear he is a

rich man. But there is such humility in his attitude, and such evidence of gratitude at being allowed to sit outside of his own house and read his paper in his shirt-sleeves, that I can picture his domestic history pretty clearly. Perhaps he is following some old habit of humbler days. Perhaps he has entered into an agreement with his wife not to indulge his disgraceful habit indoors. He does not look like a man who could be coaxed into a dressing-gown. In front of his own palatial residence, I know him to be a quiet and respectable middle-aged business-man, but it is from my back window that my heart warms toward him in his shirt-sleeved simplicity. So I sit and watch him in the twilight as he reads gravely, and wonder sometimes, when he looks up, squares his chest, and folds his paper thoughtfully over his knee, whether he doesn't fancy he hears the letting down of bars, or the tinkling of bells, as the cows come home and stand lowing for him at the gate.

BOONDER

I NEVER knew how the subject of this memoir came to attach himself so closely to the affections of my family. He was not a prepossessing dog. He was not a dog of even average birth and breeding. His pedigree was involved in the deepest obscurity. He may have had brothers and sisters, but in the whole range of my canine acquaintance (a pretty extensive one), I never detected any of Boonder's peculiarities in any other of his species. His body was long, and his forelegs and hindlegs were very wide apart, as though Nature originally intended to put an extra pair between them, but had unwisely allowed herself to be persuaded out of it. This peculiarity was annoying on cold nights, as it always prolonged the interval of keeping the door open for Boonder's ingress long enough to allow two or three dogs of a reasonable length to enter. Boonder's feet were decided; his toes turned out considerably, and in repose his favorite attitude was the first position of dancing. Add to a pair of bright eyes ears that seemed to belong to some other dog, and a symmetrically pointed nose that fitted all apertures like a pass-key, and you have Boonder as we knew him.

I am inclined to think that his popularity was mainly owing to his quiet impudence. His advent in the family was that of an old member, who had been absent for a short time, but had returned to familiar haunts and associations. In a Pythagorean point of view this might have been the case, but I cannot recall any deceased member of the family who was in life partial to bone-burying (though it might be *post-mortem* a consistent amusement), and this was Boonder's great weakness. He was at first discovered coiled up on a rug in an upper chamber, and was the least disconcerted of the entire household. From that moment Boonder became one of its recognized members, and privileges, often denied the most intelligent and valuable of his species, were quietly taken by him and submitted to by us. Thus, if he were found coiled up in a clothes-basket, or any article of clothing assumed locomotion on its own account, we only said, "O, it's Boonder," with a feeling of relief that it was nothing worse.

I have spoken of his fondness for bone-burying. It could not be called an economical faculty, for he invariably forgot the locality of his treasure, and covered the garden with

purposeless holes; but although the violets and daisies were
not improved by Boonder's gardening, no one ever thought
of punishing him. He became a synonym for Fate; a
Boonder to be grumbled at, to be accepted philosophically,—
but never to be averted. But although he was not an intelligent dog, nor an ornamental dog, he possessed some gentlemanly instincts. When he performed his only feat,—
begging upon his hindlegs (and looking remarkably like a
penguin),—ignorant strangers would offer him crackers or
cake, which he didn't like, as a reward of merit. Boonder
always made a great show of accepting the proffered dain-
ties, and even made hypocritical contortions as if swallowing, but always deposited the morsel when he was
unobserved in the first convenient receptacle,—usually the
visitor's overshoes.

In matters that did not involve courtesy, Boonder was
sincere in his likes and dislikes. He was instinctively opposed to the railroad. When the track was laid through our
street, Boonder maintained a defiant attitude toward every
rail as it went down, and resisted the cars shortly after to
the fullest extent of his lungs. I have a vivid recollection
of seeing him, on the day of the trial trip, come down the
street in front of the car, barking himself out of all shape,
and thrown back several feet by the recoil of each bark.
But Boonder was not the only one who has resisted innova-
tions, or has lived to see the innovation prosper and even
crush—But I am anticipating. Boonder had previously resisted the gas, but although he spent one whole day in angry
altercation with the workmen,—leaving his bones unburied
and bleaching in the sun,—somehow the gas went in. The
Spring Valley water was likewise unsuccessfully opposed,

and the grading of an adjoining lot was for a long time a personal matter between Boonder and the contractor.

These peculiarities seemed to evince some decided character and embody some idea. A prolonged debate in the family upon this topic resulted in an addition to his name, —we called him "Boonder the Conservative," with a faint acknowledgment of his fateful power. But, although Boonder had his own way, his path was not entirely of roses. Thorns sometimes pricked his sensibilities. When certain minor chords were struck on the piano, Boonder was always painfully affected and howled a remonstrance. If he were removed for company's sake to the back yard, at the recurrence of the provocation, he would go his whole length (which was something) to improvise a howl that should reach the performer. But we got accustomed to Boonder, and as we were fond of music the playing went on.

One morning Boonder left the house in good spirits with his regular bone in his mouth, and apparently the usual intention of burying it. The next day he was picked up lifeless on the track,—run over apparently by the first car that went out of the depot.

HOW SANTA CLAUS CAME TO SIMPSON'S BAR

It had been raining in the valley of the Sacramento. The North Fork had overflowed its bank, and Rattlesnake Creek was impassable. The few boulders that had marked the summer ford at Simpson's Crossing were obliterated by a vast sheet of water stretching to the foothills. The up-stage was stopped at Granger's; the last mail had been abandoned in the *tules,* the rider swimming for his life. "An area," remarked the "Sierra Avalanche," with pensive local pride, "as large as the State of Massachusetts is now under water."

Nor was the weather any better in the foothills. The mud lay deep on the mountain road; wagons that neither physical force nor moral objurgation could move from the evil ways into which they had fallen encumbered the track, and the way to Simpson's Bar was indicated by broken-down teams and hard swearing. And farther on, cut off and inaccessible, rained upon and bedraggled, smitten by high winds and threatened by high water, Simpson's Bar, on the eve of Christmas Day, 1862, clung like a swallow's nest to the rocky entablature and splintered capitals of Table Mountain, and shook in the blast.

As night shut down on the settlement, a few lights gleamed through the mist from the windows of cabins on either side of the highway, now crossed and gullied by lawless streams and swept by marauding winds. Happily, most of the population were gathered at Thompson's store, clustered around a red-hot stove, at which they silently spat in some accepted sense of social communion that perhaps rendered conversation unnecessary. Indeed, most methods of diversion had long since been exhausted on Simpson's Bar; high water had suspended the regular occupations on gulch and on river, and a consequent lack of money and whisky had taken the zest from most illegitimate recreation. Even Mr. Hamlin was fain to leave the Bar with fifty dollars in his pocket—the only amount actually realized of the large sums won by him in the successful exercise of his arduous profession. "Ef I was asked," he remarked somewhat later,—"ef I was asked to pint out a purty little village where a retired sport as didn't care for money could exercise hisself, frequent and lively, I'd say Simpson's Bar; but for a young man with a large family depending on his exertions it don't pay." As Mr. Hamlin's family consisted mainly of female adults, this remark is quoted rather to show the breadth of his humor than the exact extent of his responsibilities.

Howbeit, the unconscious objects of this satire sat that evening in the listless apathy begotten of idleness and lack of excitement. Even the sudden splashing of hoofs before the door did not arouse them. Dick Bullen alone paused in the act of scraping out his pipe, and lifted his head, but no other one of the group indicated any interest in, or recognition of, the man who entered.

It was a figure familiar enough to the company, and known in Simpson's Bar as "The Old Man." A man of perhaps fifty years; grizzled and scant of hair, but still fresh and youthful of complexion. A face full of ready but not very powerful sympathy, with a chameleon-like aptitude for taking on the shade and color of contiguous moods and feelings. He had evidently just left some hilarious companions, and did not at first notice the gravity of the group, but clapped the shoulder of the nearest man jocularly, and threw himself into a vacant chair.

"Jest heard the best thing out, boys! Ye know Smiley, over yar—Jim Smiley—funniest man in the Bar? Well, Jim was jest telling the richest yarn about"——

"Smiley's a —— fool," interrupted a gloomy voice.

"A particular —— skunk," added another in sepulchral accents.

A silence followed these positive statements. The Old Man glanced quickly around the group. Then his face slowly changed. "That's so," he said reflectively, after a pause, "certainly a sort of a skunk and suthin' of a fool. In course." He was silent for a moment as in painful contemplation of the unsavoriness and folly of the unpopular Smiley. "Dismal weather, ain't it?" he added, now fully embarked on the current of prevailing sentiment. "Mighty rough papers on the boys, and no show for money this season. And to-morrow's Christmas."

There was a movement among the men at this announcement, but whether of satisfaction or disgust was not plain. "Yes," continued the Old Man in the lugubrious tone he had, within the last few moments, unconsciously adopted, —"yes, Christmas, and to-night's Christmas Eve. Ye see, boys, I kinder thought—that is, I sorter had an idea, jest passin' like, you know—that maybe ye'd all like to come over to my house to-night and have a sort of tear round. But I suppose, now, you wouldn't? Don't feel like it, maybe?" he added with anxious sympathy, peering into the faces of his companions.

"Well, I don't know," responded Tom Flynn with some cheerfulness. "P'r'aps we may. But how about your wife, Old Man? What does *she* say to it?"

The Old Man hesitated. His conjugal experience had not been a happy one, and the fact was known to Simpson's Bar. His first wife, a delicate, pretty little woman, had suffered keenly and secretly from the jealous suspicions of her husband, until one day he invited the whole Bar to his house to expose her infidelity. On arriving, the party found the shy, *petite* creature quietly engaged in her household duties, and retired abashed and discomfited. But the sensitive woman did not easily recover from the shock of this extraordinary outrage. It was with difficulty she regained her equanimity sufficiently to release her lover from the closet in which he was concealed, and escape with him. She left a boy of three years to comfort her bereaved husband. The Old Man's present wife had been his cook. She was large, loyal, and aggressive.

Before he could reply, Joe Dimmick suggested with great directness that it was the "Old Man's house," and that, invoking the Divine Power, if the case were his own, he would invite whom he pleased, even if in so doing he imperiled his salvation. The Powers of Evil, he further remarked, should contend against him vainly. All this delivered with a terseness and vigor lost in this necessary translation.

"In course. Certainly. Thet's it," said the Old Man with a sympathetic frown. "Thar's no trouble about *thet*. It's my own house, built every stick on it myself. Don't you be afeard o' her, boys. She *may* cut up a trifle rough —ez wimmin do—but she'll come round." Secretly the Old Man trusted to the exaltation of liquor and the power of courageous example to sustain him in such an emergency.

As yet, Dick Bullen, the oracle and leader of Simpson's Bar, had not spoken. He now took his pipe from his lips. "Old Man, how's that yer Johnny gettin' on? Seems to me he didn't look so peart last time I seed him on the bluff heavin' rocks at Chinamen. Didn't seem to take much interest in it. Thar was a gang of 'em by yar yesterday— drownded out up the river—and I kinder thought o' Johnny, and how he'd miss 'em! Maybe now, we'd be in the way ef he wus sick?"

The father, evidently touched not only by this pathetic picture of Johnny's deprivation, but by the considerate delicacy of the speaker, hastened to assure him that Johnny

was better and that a "little fun might 'liven him up."
Whereupon Dick arose, shook himself, and saying, "I'm
ready. Lead the way, Old Man: here goes," himself led
the way with a leap, a characteristic howl, and darted out
into the night. As he passed through the outer room he
caught up a blazing brand from the hearth. The action
was repeated by the rest of the party, closely following and
elbowing each other, and before the astonished proprietor
of Thompson's grocery was aware of the intention of his
guests, the room was deserted.

The night was pitchy dark. In the first gust of wind
their temporary torches were extinguished, and only the red
brands dancing and flitting in the gloom like drunken
will-o'-the-wisps indicated their whereabouts. Their way
led up Pine-Tree Cañon, at the head of which a broad, low,
bark-thatched cabin burrowed in the mountain side. It was
the home of the Old Man, and the entrance to the tunnel
in which he worked when he worked at all. Here the
crowd paused for a moment, out of delicate deference to
their host, who came up panting in the rear.

"P'r'aps ye'd better hold on a second out yer, whilst I
go in and see that things is all right," said the Old Man,
with an indifference he was far from feeling. The suggestion was graciously accepted, the door opened and closed on
the host, and the crowd leaning their backs against the
wall and cowering under the eaves, waited and listened.

For a few moments there was no sound but the dripping
of water from the eaves, and the stir and rustle of wrestling
boughs above them. Then the men became uneasy, and
whispered suggestion and suspicion passed from the one to
the other. "Reckon she's caved in his head the first lick!"
"Decoyed him inter the tunnel and barred him up, likely."

"Got him down and sittin' on him." "Prob'ly biling suthin' to heave on us: stand clear the door, boys!" For just then the latch clicked, the door slowly opened, and a voice said, "Come in out o' the wet."

The voice was neither that of the Old Man nor of his wife. It was the voice of a small boy, its weak treble broken by that preternatural hoarseness which only vagabondage and the habit of premature self-assertion can give. It was the face of a small boy that looked up at theirs,—a face that might have been pretty, and even refined, but that it was darkened by evil knowledge from within, and dirt and hard experience from without. He had a blanket around his shoulders, and had evidently just risen from his bed. "Come in," he repeated, "and don't make no noise. The Old Man's in there talking to Mar," he continued, pointing to an adjacent room which seemed to be a kitchen, from which the Old Man's voice came in deprecating accents. "Let me be," he added querulously, to Dick Bullen, who had caught him up, blanket and all, and was affecting to toss him into the fire, "let go o' me, you d—d old fool, d'ye hear?"

Thus adjured, Dick Bullen lowered Johnny to the ground with a smothered laugh, while the men, entering quietly, ranged themselves around a long table of rough boards which occupied the center of the room. Johnny then gravely proceeded to a cupboard and brought out several articles, which he deposited on the table. "Thar's whisky. And crackers. And red herons. And cheese." He took a bite of the latter on his way to the table. "And sugar." He scooped up a mouthful *en route* with a small and very dirty hand. "And terbacker. Thar's dried appils too on the shelf, but I don't admire 'em. Appils is swellin'.

Thar," he concluded, "now wade in, and don't be afeard. *I* don't mind the old woman. She don't b'long to *me*. S'long."

He had stepped to the threshold of a small room, scarcely larger than a closet, partitioned off from the main apartment, and holding in its dim recess a small bed. He stood there a moment looking at the company, his bare feet peeping from the blanket, and nodded.

"Hello, Johnny! You ain't goin' to turn in agin, are ye?" said Dick.

"Yes, I are," responded Johnny decidedly.

"Why, wot's up, old fellow?"

"I'm sick."

"How sick?"

"I've got a fevier. And childblains. And roomatiz," returned Johnny, and vanished within. After a moment's pause, he added in the dark, apparently from under the bedclothes,—"And biles!"

There was an embarrassing silence. The men looked at each other and at the fire. Even with the appetizing banquet before them, it seemed as if they might again fall into the despondency of Thompson's grocery, when the voice of the Old Man, incautiously lifted, came deprecatingly from the kitchen.

"Certainly! Thet's so. In course they is. A gang o' lazy, drunken loafers, and that ar Dick Bullen's the ornariest of all. Didn't hev no more *sabe* than to come round yar with sickness in the house and no provision. Thet's what I said: 'Bullen,' sez I, 'it's crazy drunk you are, or a fool,' sez I, 'to think o' such a thing.' 'Staples,' I sez, 'be you a man, Staples, and 'spect to raise h—ll under my roof and invalids lyin' round?' But they would come,

—they would. Thet's wot you must 'spect o' such trash as lays round the Bar."

A burst of laughter from the men followed this unfortunate exposure. Whether it was overheard in the kitchen, or whether the Old Man's irate companion had just then exhausted all other modes of expressing her contemptuous indignation, I cannot say, but a back door was suddenly slammed with great violence. A moment later and the Old Man reappeared, haply unconscious of the cause of the late hilarious outburst, and smiled blandly.

"The old woman thought she'd jest run over to Mrs. MacFadden's for a sociable call," he explained with jaunty indifference as he took a seat at the board.

Oddly enough it needed this untoward incident to relieve the embarrassment that was beginning to be felt by the party, and their natural audacity returned with their host. I do not propose to record the convivialities of that evening. The inquisitive reader will accept the statement that the conversation was characterized by the same intellectual exaltation, the same cautious reverence, the same fastidious delicacy, the same rhetorical precision, and the same logical and coherent discourse somewhat later in the evening, which distinguish similar gatherings of the masculine sex in more civilized localities and under more favorable auspices. No glasses were broken in the absence of any; no liquor was uselessly spilt on the floor or table in the scarcity of that article.

It was nearly midnight when the festivities were interrupted. "Hush," said Dick Bullen, holding up his hand. It was the querulous voice of Johnny from his adjacent closet: "O dad!"

The Old Man arose hurriedly and disappeared in the

closet. Presently he reappeared. "His rheumatiz is coming on agin bad," he explained, "and he wants rubbin'."
He lifted the demijohn of whisky from the table and shook
it. It was empty. Dick Bullen put down his tin cup with an
embarrassed laugh. So did the others. The Old Man examined their contents and said hopefully, "I reckon that's
enough; he don't need much. You hold on all o' you for a
spell, and I'll be back;" and vanished in the closet with an
old flannel shirt and the whisky. The door closed but imperfectly, and the following dialogue was distinctly audible:

"Now, sonny, whar does she ache worst?"

"Sometimes over yar and sometimes under yer; but it's
most powerful from yer to yer. Rub yer, dad."

A silence seemed to indicate a brisk rubbing. Then
Johnny:

"Hevin' a good time out thar, dad?"

"Yes, sonny."

"To-morrer's Chrismiss,—ain't it?"

"Yes, sonny. How does she feel now?"

"Better. Rub a little furder down. Wot's Chrismiss,
anyway? Wot's it all about?"

"Oh, it's a day."

This exhaustive definition was apparently satisfactory,
for there was a silent interval of rubbing. Presently Johnny
again:

"Mar sez that everywhere else but yer everybody gives
things to everybody Chrismiss, and then she jist waded inter
you. She sez thar's a man they call Sandy Claws, not a
white man, you know, but a kind o' Chinemin, comes down
the chimbley night afore Chrismiss and gives things to
chillern,—boys like me. Puts 'em in their butes! Thet's
what she tried to play upon me. Easy now, pop, whar are

you rubbin' to,—thet's a mile from the place. She jest made that up, didn't she, jest to aggrewate me and you? Don't rub thar. . . . Why, dad!"

In the great quiet that seemed to have fallen upon the house the sigh of the near pines and the drip of leaves without was very distinct. Johnny's voice, too, was lowered as he went on, "Don't you take on now, for I'm gettin' all right fast. Wot's the boys doin' out thar?"

The Old Man partly opened the door and peered through. His guests were sitting there sociably enough, and there were a few silver coins and a lean buckskin purse on the table. "Bettin' on suthin'—some little game or 'nother. They're all right," he replied to Johnny, and recommenced his rubbing.

"I'd like to take a hand and win some money," said Johnny reflectively after a pause.

The Old Man glibly repeated what was evidently a familiar formula, that if Johnny would wait until he struck it rich in the tunnel he'd have lots of money, &c., &c.

"Yes," said Johnny, "but you don't. And whether you strike it or I win it, it's about the same. It's all luck. But it's mighty cur'o's about Chrismiss—ain't it? Why do they call it Chrismiss?"

Perhaps from some instinctive deference to the overhearing of his guests, or from some vague sense of incongruity, the Old Man's reply was so low as to be inaudible beyond the room.

"Yes," said Johnny, with some slight abatement of interest, "I've heerd o' *him* before. Thar, that'll do, dad. I don't ache near so bad as I did. Now wrap me tight in this yer blanket. So. Now," he added in a muffled whisper, "sit down yer by me till I go asleep." To assure himself of obedience, he disengaged one hand from the blanket and, grasping his father's sleeve, again composed himself to rest.

For some moments the Old Man waited patiently. Then the unwonted stillness of the house excited his curiosity, and without moving from the bed he cautiously opened the door with his disengaged hand, and looked into the main room. To his infinite surprise it was dark and deserted. But even then a smoldering log on the hearth broke, and by the upspringing blaze he saw the figure of Dick Bullen sitting by the dying embers.

"Hello!"

Dick started, rose, and came somewhat unsteadily toward him.

"Whar's the boys?" said the Old Man.

"Gone up the cañon on a little *pasear*. They're coming back for me in a minit. I'm waitin' round for 'em. What are you starin' at, Old Man?" he added with a forced laugh; "do you think I'm drunk?"

The Old Man might have been pardoned the supposition, for Dick's eyes were humid and his face flushed. He loitered and lounged back to the chimney, yawned, shook himself, buttoned up his coat and laughed. "Liquor ain't so plenty as that, Old Man. Now don't you git up," he continued, as the Old Man made a movement to release his sleeve from Johnny's hand. "Don't you mind manners. Sit jest whar you be; I'm goin' in a jiffy. Thar, that's them now."

There was a low tap at the door. Dick Bullen opened it quickly, nodded "Good night" to his host, and disappeared. The Old Man would have followed him but for the hand that still unconsciously grasped his sleeve. He could have easily disengaged it: it was small, weak, and emaciated. But perhaps because it *was* small, weak, and emaciated he changed his mind, and, drawing his chair closer to the bed, rested his head upon it. In this defenseless attitude the potency of his earlier potations surprised him. The room flickered and faded before his eyes, reappeared, faded again, went out, and left him—asleep.

Meantime Dick Bullen, closing the door, confronted his companions. "Are you ready?" said Staples. "Ready," said Dick; "what's the time?" "Past twelve," was the reply; "can you make it?—it's nigh on fifty miles, the round trip hither and yon." "I reckon," returned Dick shortly. "Whar's the mare?" "Bill and Jack's holdin' her at the crossin'." "Let 'em hold on a minit longer," said Dick.

He turned and re-entered the house softly. By the light of the guttering candle and dying fire he saw that the door of the little room was open. He stepped toward it on tiptoe and looked in. The Old Man had fallen back in his chair, snoring, his helpless feet thrust out in a line with his collapsed shoulders, and his hat pulled over his eyes. Beside him, on a narrow wooden bedstead, lay Johnny, muffled tightly in a blanket that hid all save a strip of forehead and a few curls damp with perspiration. Dick Bullen made a step forward, hesitated, and glanced over his shoulder into the deserted room. Everything was quiet. With a sudden resolution he parted his huge moustaches with both hands and stooped over the sleeping boy. But even as he did so a mischievous blast, lying in wait, swooped down the chimney, rekindled the hearth, and lit up the room with a shameless glow from which Dick fled in bashful terror.

His companions were already waiting for him at the

crossing. Two of them were struggling in the darkness with some strange misshapen bulk, which as Dick came nearer took the semblance of a great yellow horse.

It was the mare. She was not a pretty picture. From her Roman nose to her rising haunches, from her arched spine hidden by the stiff *machillas* of a Mexican saddle, to her thick, straight, bony legs, there was not a line of equine grace. In her half-blind but wholly vicious white eyes, in her protruding under-lip, in her monstrous color, there was nothing but ugliness and vice.

"Now then," said Staples, "stand cl'ar of her heels, boys, and up with you. Don't miss your first holt of her mane, and mind ye get your off stirrup *quick*. Ready!"

There was a leap, a scrambling struggle, a bound, a wild retreat of the crowd, a circle of flying hoofs, two springless leaps that jarred the earth, a rapid play and jingle of spurs, a plunge, and then the voice of Dick somewhere in the darkness. "All right!"

"Don't take the lower road back onless you're hard pushed for time! Don't hold her in down hill. We'll be at the ford at five. G'lang! Hoopa! Mula! GO!"

A splash, a spark struck from the ledge in the road, a clatter in the rocky cut beyond, and Dick was gone.

.　.　.　.　.　.　.　.　.

Sing, O Muse, the ride of Richard Bullen! Sing, O Muse, of chivalrous men! the sacred quest, the doughty deeds, the battery of low churls, the fearsome ride and gruesome perils of the Flower of Simpson's Bar! Alack! she is dainty, this Muse! She will have none of this bucking brute and swaggering, ragged rider, and I must follow him in prose, afoot!

It was one o'clock, and yet he had only gained Rattle-snake Hill. For in that time Jovita had rehearsed to him all her imperfections and practised all her vices. Thrice had she stumbled. Twice had she thrown up her Roman nose in a straight line with the reins, and, resisting bit and spur, struck out madly across country. Twice had she reared, and rearing, fallen backward; and twice had the agile Dick, unharmed, regained his seat before she found her vicious legs again. And a mile beyond them, at the foot of a long hill, was Rattlesnake Creek. Dick knew that here was the crucial test of his ability to perform his enterprise, set his teeth grimly, put his knees well into her flanks, and changed his defensive tactics to brisk aggression. Bullied and maddened, Jovita began the descent of the hill. Here the artful Richard pretended to hold her in with ostentatious objurgation and well-feigned cries of alarm. It is unnecessary to add that Jovita instantly ran away. Nor need I state the time made in the descent; it is written in the chronicles of Simpson's Bar. Enough that in another moment, as it seemed to Dick, she was splashing on the overflowed banks of Rattlesnake Creek. As Dick expected, the momentum she had acquired carried her beyond the point of balking, and, holding her well together for a mighty leap, they dashed into the middle of the swiftly flowing current. A few moments of kicking, wading, and swimming, and Dick drew a long breath on the opposite bank.

The road from Rattlesnake Creek to Red Mountain was tolerably level. Either the plunge in Rattlesnake Creek had dampened her baleful fire, or the art which led to it had shown her the superior wickedness of her rider, for Jovita no longer wasted her surplus energy in wanton con-

ceits. Once she bucked, but it was from force of habit;
once she shied, but it was from a new, freshly-painted meeting-house at the crossing of the county road. Hollows,
ditches, gravelly deposits, patches of freshly-springing
grasses, flew from beneath her rattling hoofs. She began to
smell unpleasantly, once or twice she coughed slightly, but
there was no abatement of her strength or speed. By two
o'clock he had passed Red Mountain and begun the descent
to the plain. Ten minutes later the drive of the fast Pioneer
coach was overtaken and passed by a "man on a Pinto
hoss,"—an event sufficiently notable for remark. At half
past two Dick rose in his stirrups with a great shout. Stars
were glittering through the rifted clouds, and beyond him,
out of the plain, rose two spires, a flagstaff, and a straggling
line of black objects. Dick jingled his spurs and swung
his *riata*, Jovita bounded forward, and in another moment
they swept into Tuttleville, and drew up before the wooden
piazza of "The Hotel of All Nations."

What transpired that night at Tuttleville is not strictly a
part of this record. Briefly I may state, however, that after
Jovita had been handed over to a sleepy ostler, whom she
at once kicked into unpleasant consciousness, Dick sallied
out with the barkeeper for a tour of the sleeping town.
Lights still gleamed from a few saloons and gambling-
houses; but, avoiding these, they stopped before several
closed shops, and by persistent tapping and judicious outcry
roused the proprietors from their beds, and made them un-
bar the doors of their magazines and expose their wares.
Sometimes they were met by curses, but oftener by interest
and some concern in their needs, and the interview was invariably concluded by a drink. It was three o'clock before
this pleasantry was given over, and with a small waterproof

bag of indiarubber strapped on his shoulders Dick returned to the hotel. But here he was waylaid by Beauty,—Beauty opulent in charms, affluent in dress, persuasive in speech, and Spanish in accent! In vain she repeated the invitation in "Excelsior," happily scorned by all Alpine-climbing youth, and rejected by this child of the Sierras,—a rejection softened in this instance by a laugh and his last gold coin. And then he sprang to the saddle and dashed down the lonely street and out into the lonelier plain, where presently the lights, the black line of houses, the spires, and the flag-staff sank into the earth behind him again and were lost in the distance.

The storm had cleared away, the air was brisk and cold, the outlines of adjacent landmarks were distinct, but it was half past four before Dick reached the meeting-house and the crossing of the county road. To avoid the rising grade he had taken a longer and more circuitous road, in whose viscid mud Jovita sank fetlock deep at every bound. It was a poor preparation for a steady ascent of five miles more; but Jovita, gathering her legs under her, took it with her usual blind, unreasoning fury, and a half-hour later reached the long level that led to Rattlesnake Creek. Another half-hour would bring him to the creek. He threw the reins lightly upon the neck of the mare, chirruped to her, and began to sing.

Suddenly Jovita shied with a bound that would have unseated a less practised rider. Hanging to her rein was a figure that had leaped from the bank, and at the same time from the road before her arose a shadowy horse and rider. "Throw up your hands," commanded the second apparition, with an oath.

Dick felt the mare tremble, quiver, and apparently sink under him. He knew what it meant and was prepared.

"Stand aside, Jack Simpson. I know you, you d—d thief! Let me pass, or"——

He did not finish the sentence. Jovita rose straight in the air with a terrific bound, throwing the figure from her bit with a single shake of her vicious head, and charged with deadly malevolence down on the impediment before her. An oath, a pistol-shot, horse and highwayman rolled over in the road, and the next moment Jovita was a hundred yards away. But the good right arm of her rider, shattered by a bullet, dropped helplessly at his side.

Without slacking his speed he shifted the reins to his left hand. But a few moments later he was obliged to halt and tighten the saddle-girths that had slipped in the onset. This in his crippled condition took some time. He had no fear of pursuit, but looking up he saw that the eastern stars were already paling, and that the distant peaks had lost their ghostly whiteness, and now stood out blackly against a lighter sky. Day was upon him. Then completely absorbed in a single idea, he forgot the pain of his wound, and mounting again dashed on toward Rattlesnake Creek. But now Jovita's breath came broken by gasps, Dick reeled in his saddle, and brighter and brighter grew the sky.

Ride, Richard; run Jovita; linger O day!

For the last few rods there was a roaring in his ears. Was it exhaustion from loss of blood, or what? He was dazed and giddy as he swept down the hill, and did not recognize his surroundings. Had he taken the wrong road, or was this Rattlesnake Creek?

It was. But the brawling creek he had swam a few hours before had risen, more than doubled its volume, and now rolled a swift and resistless river between him and Rattle-snake Hill. For the first time that night Richard's heart sank within him. The river, the mountain, the quickening east, swam before his eyes. He shut them to recover his self-control. In that brief interval, by some fantastic mental process, the little room at Simpson's Bar and the figures of the sleeping father and son rose upon him. He opened his eyes wildly, cast off his coat, pistol, boots, and saddle, bound his precious pack tightly to his shoulders, grasped the bare flanks of Jovita with his bared knees, and with a shout dashed into the yellow water. A cry rose from the opposite bank as the head of a man and horse struggled for a few moments against the battling current, and then were swept away amidst uprooted trees and whirling driftwood.

.   .   .   .

The Old Man started and woke. The fire on the hearth was dead, the candle in the outer room flickering in its socket, and somebody was rapping at the door. He opened it, but fell back with a cry before the dripping, half-naked figure that reeled against the doorpost.

"Dick?"

"Hush! Is he awake yet?"

"No; but, Dick?"——

"Dry up, you old fool! Get me some whisky, *quick!*" The Old Man flew and returned with—an empty bottle! Dick would have sworn, but his strength was not equal to the occasion. He staggered, caught at the handle of the door, and motioned to the Old Man.

"Thar's suthin' in my pack yer for Johnny. Take it off.
I can't."

The Old Man unstrapped the pack, and laid it before
the exhausted man.

"Open it, quick."

He did so with trembling fingers. It contained only a few
poor toys—cheap and barbaric enough, goodness knows, but
bright with paint and tinsel. One of them was broken; another, I fear, was irretrievably ruined by water, and on the
third—ah me! there was a cruel spot.

"It don't look like much, that's a fact," said Dick rue-
fully. . . . "But it's the best we could do. . . . Take 'em,
Old Man, and put 'em in his stocking, and tell him—tell
him, you know—hold me, Old Man"——The Old Man
caught at his sinking figure. "Tell him," said Dick, with
a weak little laugh,—"tell him Sandy Claus has come."

And even so, bedraggled, ragged, unshaven and unshorn,
with one arm hanging helplessly at his side, Santa Claus
came to Simpson's Bar and fell fainting on the first threshold. The Christmas dawn came slowly after touching the
remoter peaks with the rosy warmth of ineffable love. And it
looked so tenderly on Simpson's Bar that the whole mountain, as if caught in a generous action, blushed to the skies.

WAN LEE, THE PAGAN

As I opened Hop Sing's letter there fluttered to the
ground a square strip of yellow paper covered with hiero-
glyphics, which at first glance I innocently took to be the
label from a pack of Chinese fire-crackers. But the same

envelope also contained a smaller strip of rice paper, with two Chinese characters traced in India ink, that I at once knew to be Hop Sing's visiting card. The whole, as afterwards literally translated, ran as follows:—

"To the stranger the gates of my house are not closed; the rice jar is on the left, and the sweetmeats on the right as you enter.
Two sayings of the Master:
Hospitality is the virtue of the son and the wisdom of the ancestor.
The superior man is light-hearted after the crop-gathering; he makes a festival.
When the stranger is in your melon patch observe him not too closely; inattention is often the highest form of civility.
Happiness, Peace, and Prosperity.
HOP SING."

Admirable, certainly, as was this morality and proverbial wisdom, and although this last axiom was very characteristic of my friend Hop Sing, who was that most sombre of all humorists, a Chinese philosopher, I must confess that, even after a very free translation, I was at a loss to make any immediate application of the message. Luckily I discovered a third enclosure in the shape of a little note in English and Hop Sing's own commercial hand. It ran thus—

"The pleasure of your company is requested at No.—, Sacramento Street, on Friday Evening at 8 o'clock. A cup of tea at 9—sharp. HOP SING."

This explained all. It meant a visit to Hop Sing's warehouse, the opening and exhibition of some rare Chinese novelties and *curios,* a chat in the back office, a cup of tea of a perfection unknown beyond these sacred precincts, cigars, and a visit to the Chinese Theatre or Temple. This was in fact the favorite program of Hop Sing when he exercised his functions of hospitality as the chief factor or Superintendent of the Ning Foo Company.

At eight o'clock on Friday evening I entered the warehouse of Hop Sing. There was that deliciously commingled mysterious foreign odor that I had so often noticed; there was the old array of uncouth looking objects, the long procession of jars and crockery, the same singular blending of the grotesque and the mathematically neat and exact, the same endless suggestions of frivolity and fragility, the same want of harmony in colours that were each, in themselves, beautiful and rare. Kites in the shape of enormous dragons and gigantic butterflies; kites so ingeniously arranged as to utter at intervals, when facing the wind, the cry of a hawk; kites so large as to be beyond any boy's power of restraint —so large that you understood why kite-flying in China was an amusement for adults; gods of china and bronze so gratuitously ugly as to be beyond any human interest or sympathy from their very impossibility; jars of sweetmeats covered all over with moral sentiments from Confucius; hats that looked like baskets, and baskets that looked like hats; silks so light that I hesitate to record the incredible number of square yards that you might pass through the ring on your little finger—these and a great many other indescribable objects were all familiar to me. I pushed my way through the dimly-lighted warehouse until I reached the back office or parlor, where I found Hop Sing waiting to receive me.

Before I describe him I want the average reader to discharge from his mind any idea of a Chinaman that he may have gathered from the pantomime. He did not wear beautifully scalloped drawers fringed with little bells —I never met a Chinaman who did; he did not habitually carry his forefinger extended before him at right angles with his body, nor did I ever hear him utter the mysterious sentence, "Ching a ring a ring chaw," nor dance under any provocation. He was, on the whole, a rather grave, decorous, handsome gentleman. His complexion, which extended all over his head except where his long pig-tail grew, was like a very nice piece of glazed brown paper muslin. His eyes were black and bright, and his eyelids set at an angle of 15°; his nose straight and delicately formed, his mouth small, and his teeth white and clean. He wore a dark blue silk blouse, and in the streets on cold days a short jacket of Astrakhan fur. He wore also a pair of drawers of blue brocade gathered tightly over his calves and ankles, offering a general sort of suggestion that he had forgotten his trousers that morning, but that, so gentlemanly were his manners, his friends had forborne to mention the fact to him. His manner was urbane, although quite serious. He spoke French and English fluently. In brief, I doubt if you could have found the equal of this Pagan shopkeeper among the Christian traders of San Francisco.

There were a few others present: a Judge of the Federal Court, an editor, a high government official, and a prominent merchant. After we had drunk our tea, and tasted a few sweetmeats from a mysterious jar, that looked as if it might contain a preserved mouse among its other nondescript treasures, Hop Sing arose, and gravely beckoning us to follow him, began to descend to the basement. When we got there, we were amazed at finding it brilliantly lighted, and that a number of chairs were arranged in a half-circle on the asphalt pavement. When he had courteously seated us, he said—

"I have invited you to witness a performance which I can at least promise you no other foreigners but yourselves have ever seen. Wang, the court juggler, arrived here yesterday morning. He has never given a performance outside of the palace before. I have asked him to entertain my friends this evening. He requires no theatre, stage, accessories, or any confederate—nothing more than you see here. Will you be pleased to examine the ground yourselves, gentlemen."

Of course we examined the premises. It was the ordinary basement or cellar of the San Francisco storehouse, cemented to keep out the damp. We poked our sticks into the pavement and rapped on the walls to satisfy our polite host, but for no other purpose. We were quite content to be the victims of any clever deception. For myself, I knew I was ready to be deluded to any extent, and if I had been offered an explanation of what followed, I should have probably declined it.

Although I am satisfied that Wang's general performance was the first of that kind ever given on American soil, it has probably since become so familiar to many of my readers that I shall not bore them with it here. He began by setting to flight, with the aid of his fan, the usual number of butterflies made before our eyes of little bits of tissue paper, and kept them in the air during the remainder of the performance. I have a vivid recollection of the judge trying to catch one that had lit on his knee, and of its evading him with the pertinacity of a living insect. And even at this time Wang, still plying his fan, was taking chickens out of hats, making oranges disappear, pulling endless yards of silk from his sleeve, apparently filling the whole area of the basement with goods that appeared mysteriously from the ground, from his own sleeves, from nowhere! He swallowed knives to the ruin of his digestion for years to come; he dislocated every limb of his body; he reclined in the air, apparently upon nothing. But his crowning performance, which I have never yet seen repeated, was the most weird, mysterious, and astounding. It is my apology for this long introduction, my sole excuse for writing this article, the genesis of this veracious history.

He cleared the ground of its encumbering articles for a space of about fifteen feet square, and then invited us all to walk forward and again examine it. We did so gravely; there was nothing but the cemented pavement below to be seen or felt. He then asked for the loan of a handkerchief, and, as I chanced to be nearest him, I offered mine. He took it and spread it open upon the floor. Over this he spread a large square of silk, and over this again a large shawl nearly covering the space he had cleared. He then took a position at one of the points of this rectangle, and began a monotonous chant, rocking his body to and fro in time with the somewhat lugubrious air.

We sat still and waited. Above the chant we could hear the striking of the city clocks, and the occasional rattle of a cart in the street overhead. The absolute watchfulness and expectation, the dim, mysterious half-light of the cellar, falling in a gruesome way upon the misshapen bulk of a Chinese diety in the background, a faint smell of opium smoke mingling with spice, and the dreadful uncertainty of what we were really waiting for, sent an uncomfortable thrill down our backs, and made us look at each other with a forced and unnatural smile. This feeling was heightened when Hop Sing slowly rose, and, without a word, pointed with his finger to the center of the shawl.

There was something beneath the shawl! Surely—and something that was not there before. At first a mere suggestion in relief, a faint outline, but growing more and more distinct and visible every moment. The chant still continued, the perspiration began to roll from the singer's face, gradually the hidden object took upon itself a shape and bulk that raised the shawl in its center some five or six inches. It was now unmistakably the outline of a small but perfect human figure, with extended arms and legs. One or two of us turned pale, there was a feeling of general uneasiness, until the editor broke the silence by a gibe that, poor as it was, was received with spontaneous enthusiasm. Then the chant suddenly ceased, Wang arose, and, with a quick, dexterous movement, stripped both shawl and silk away, and discovered, sleeping peacefully upon my handkerchief, a tiny Chinese baby!

The applause and uproar which followed this revelation ought to have satisfied Wang, even if his audience was a small one; it was loud enough to awaken the baby—a pretty little boy about a year old, looking like a Cupid cut out of sandalwood. He was whisked away almost as mysteriously as he appeared. When Hop Sing returned my handkerchief to me with a bow, I asked if the juggler was the father of the baby. "No sabe!" said the imperturbable Hop Sing, taking refuge in that Spanish form of non-committalism so common in California.

"But does he have a new baby for every performance?" I asked.

A family group taken about 1900 showing standing, Bret Harte and Mrs. Francis King Bret Harte, his daughter-in-law; and seated, his youngest daughter, Ethel, and his wife, Anna.

"Perhaps; who knows?"

"But what will become of this one?"

"Whatever you choose, gentlemen," replied Hop Sing, with a courteous inclination; "it was born here—you are its godfathers."

There were two characteristic peculiarities of any Californian assemblage in 1856: it was quick to take a hint, and generous to the point of prodigality in its response to any charitable appeal. No matter how sordid or avaricious the individual, he could not resist the infection of sympathy. I doubled the points of my handkerchief into a bag, dropped a coin into it, and, without a word, passed it to the judge. He quietly added a twenty-dollar gold piece, and passed it to the next; when it was returned to me it contained over a hundred dollars. I knotted the money in the handkerchief, and gave it to Hop Sing.

"For the baby, from its godfathers."

"But what name?" said the judge. There was a running fire of "Erebus," "Nox," "Plutus," "Terra Cotta," "Antæus," &c., &c. Finally the question was referred to our host.

"Why not keep his own name," he said quietly—"Wan Lee?" And he did.

And thus was Wan Lee, on the night of Friday the 5th of March 1856, born into this veracious chronicle.

The last form of the "Northern Star" for the 19th of July 1865—the only daily paper published in Klamath County—had just gone to press, and at three A. M. I was putting aside my proofs and manuscripts, preparatory to going home, when I discovered a letter lying under some sheets of paper which I must have overlooked. The envelope was considerably soiled, it had no post-mark, but I had no difficulty in recognizing the hand of my friend Hop Sing. I opened it hurriedly and read as follows:—

"MY DEAR SIR,—I do not know whether the bearer will suit you, but unless the office of 'devil' in your newspaper is a purely technical one, I think he has all the qualities required. He is very quick, active, and intelligent; understands English better than he speaks it, and makes up for any defect by his habits of observation and imitation. You have only to show him how to do a thing once, and he will repeat it, whether it is an offence or a virtue. But you certainly know him already; your are one of his godfathers, for is he not Wan Lee, the reputed son of Wang the conjurer, to whose performances I had the honor to introduce you? But, perhaps, you have forgotten it.

"I shall send him with a gang of coolies to Stockton, thence by express to your town. If you can use him there, you will do me a favor, and probably save his life, which is at present in great peril from the hands of the younger members of your Christian and highly civilized race who attend the enlightened schools in San Francisco.

"He has acquired some singular habits and customs from his experience of Wang's profession, which he followed for some years, until he became too large to go in a hat, or be produced from his father's sleeve. The money you left with me has been expended on his education; he has gone through the Tri-literal Classics, but, I think, without much benefit. He knows but little of Confucius, and absolutely nothing of Mencius. Owing to the negligence of his father, he associated, perhaps, too much with American children.

"I should have answered your letter before, by post, but I thought that Wan Lee himself would be a better messenger for this.

"Yours respectfully,

"Hop Sing."

And this was the long-delayed answer to my letter to Hop Sing. But where was "the bearer"? How was the letter delivered? I summoned hastily the foreman, printers, and office-boy, but without eliciting anything; no one had seen the letter delivered, nor knew anything of the bearer. A few days later I had a visit from my laundry-man, Ah Ri.

"You wantee debbil? All lightee; me catchee him."

He returned in a few moments with a bright-looking Chinese boy, about ten years old, with whose appearance and general intelligence I was so greatly impressed that I engaged him on the spot. When the business was concluded, I asked his name.

"Wan Lee," said the boy.

"What! Are you the boy sent out by Hop Sing? What the devil do you mean by not coming here before, and how did you deliver that letter?"

Wan Lee looked at me and laughed. "Me pitchee in top side window."

I did not understand. He looked for a moment perplexed, and then, snatching the letter out of my hand, ran down the stairs. After a moment's pause, to my great astonishment, the letter came flying in at the window, circled twice around the room, and then dropped gently like a bird upon my table. Before I had got over my surprise Wan Lee reappeared, smiled, looked at the letter and then at me, said, "So, John," and then remained gravely silent.

I said nothing further, but it was understood that this was his first official act.

His next performance, I grieve to say, was not attended with equal success. One of our regular paper-carriers fell sick, and, at a pinch, Wan Lee was ordered to fill his place. To prevent mistakes he was shown over the route the previous evening, and supplied at about daylight with the usual number of subscribers' copies. He returned after an hour, in good spirits and without the papers. He had delivered them all, he said.

Unfortunately for Wan Lee, at about eight o'clock indignant subscribers began to arrive at the office. They had received their copies; but how? In the form of hard-pressed cannon balls, delivered by a single shot and a mere *tour de force* through the glass of bedroom windows. They had received them full in the face, like a base ball, if they happened to be up and stirring; they had received them in quarter sheets, tucked in at separate windows; they had found them in the chimney, pinned against the door, shot through attic windows, delivered in long slips through convenient keyholes, stuffed into ventilators, and occupying the same can with the morning's milk. One subscriber, who waited for some time at the office door, to have a personal interview with Wan Lee (then comfortably locked in my bedroom), told me, with tears of rage in his eyes, that he had been awakened at five o'clock by a most hideous yelling below his windows; that on rising, in great agitation, he was startled by the sudden appearance of the "Northern Star," rolled hard and bent into the form of a boomerang or East India club, that sailed into the window, described a number of fiendish circles in the room, knocked over the light, slapped the baby's face, "took" him (the subscriber) "in the jaw," and then returned out of the window, and dropped helplessly in the area. During the rest of the day wads and strips of soiled paper, purporting to be copies of the "Northern Star" of that morning's issue were brought indignantly to the office. An admirable editorial on "The Resources of Humboldt County," which I had constructed the evening before, and which, I have reason to believe, might have changed the whole balance of trade during the ensuing year, and left San Francisco bankrupt at her wharves, was in this way lost to the public.

It was deemed advisable for the next three weeks to keep Wan Lee closely confined to the printing-office and the purely mechanical part of the business. Here he developed a surprising quickness and adaptability, winning even the favor and goodwill of the printers and foreman, who at first looked upon his introduction into the secrets of their trade as fraught with the gravest political significance. He learned to set type readily and neatly, his wonderful skill in manipulation aiding him in the mere mechanical act, and his ignorance of the language confining him simply to the mechanical effort—confirming the printer's axiom that the printer who considers or follows the ideas of his copy makes a poor compositor. He would set up deliberately long diatribes against himself, composed by his fellow-printers, and hung on his hook as copy, and even such short sentences as "Wan Lee is the devil's own imp," "Wan Lee is a Mongolian rascal," and bring the proof to me with happiness beaming from every tooth and satisfaction shining in his huckleberry eyes.

It was not long, however, before he learned to retaliate on his mischievous persecutors. I remember one instance in which his reprisal came very near involving me in a serious misunderstanding. Our foreman's name was Webster, and Wan Lee presently learned to know and recognize the individual and combined letters of his name. It was during a political campaign, and the eloquent and fiery Colonel Starbottle, of Siskiyou, had delivered an effective speech, which was reported especially for the "Northern Star." In a very sublime peroration Colonel Starbottle had said, "In the language of the godlike Webster, I repeat,"—and here followed the quotation, which I have forgotten. Now, it chanced that Wan Lee, looking over the galley after it had been revised, saw the name of his chief persecutor, and, of course, imagined the quotation his. After the form was locked up, Wan Lee took advantage of Webster's absence to remove the quotation, and substitute a thin piece of lead, of the same size as the type, engraved with Chinese characters, making a sentence, which, I had reason to believe, was an utter and abject confession of the incapacity and offensiveness of the Webster family generally, and exceedingly eulogistic of Wan Lee himself personally.

The next morning's paper contained Colonel Starbottle's speech in full, in which it appeared that the "godlike" Webster had on one occasion uttered his thoughts in excellent but perfectly enigmatical Chinese. The rage of Colonel Starbottle knew no bounds. I have a vivid recollection of that admirable man walking into my office and demanding a retraction of the statement.

"But, my dear sir," I asked, "are you willing to deny,

over your own signature, that Webster ever uttered such a sentence? Dare you deny that, with Mr. Webster's well-known attainments, a knowledge of Chinese might not have been among the number? Are you willing to submit a translation suitable to the capacity of our readers, and deny, upon your honor as a gentleman, that the late Mr. Webster ever uttered such a sentiment? If you are, sir, I am willing to publish your denial."

The Colonel was not, and left, highly indignant.

Webster, the foreman, took it more coolly. Happily he was unaware that for two days after, Chinamen from the laundries, from the gulches, from the kitchens, looked in the front office door with faces beaming with sardonic delight; that three hundred extra copies of the "Star" were ordered for the wash-houses on the river. He only knew that during the day Wan Lee occasionally went off into convulsive spasms, and that he was obliged to kick him into consciousness again. A week after the occurrence I called Wan Lee into my office.

"Wan," I said gravely, "I should like you to give me, for my own personal satisfaction, a translation of that Chinese sentence which my gifted countryman, the late godlike Webster, uttered upon a public occasion." Wan Lee looked at me intently, and then the slightest possible twinkle crept into his black eyes. Then he replied, with equal gravity—

"Mishtel Webstel,—he say: 'China boy makee me belly much foolee. China boy makee me heap sick.'" Which I have reason to think was true.

But I fear I am giving but one side, and not the best, of Wan Lee's character. As he imparted it to me, his had been a hard life. He had known scarcely any childhood— he had no recollection of a father or mother. The conjurer Wang had brought him up. He had spent the first seven years of his life in appearing from baskets, in dropping out of hats, in climbing ladders, in putting his little limbs out of joint in posturing. He had lived in an atmosphere of trickery and deception; he had learned to look upon mankind as dupes of their senses; in fine, if he had thought at all, he would have been a sceptic, if he had been a little older, he would have been a cynic, if he had been older still, he would have been a philosopher. As it was, he was a little imp! A good-natured imp it was, too—an imp whose moral nature had never been awakened, an imp up for a holiday, and willing to try virtue as a diversion. I don't know that he had any spiritual nature; he was very superstitious: he carried about with him a hideous little porcelain god, which he was in the habit of alternately reviling and propitiating. He was too intelligent for the commoner Chinese vices of stealing or gratuitous lying. Whatever discipline he practised was taught by his intellect.

I am inclined to think that his feelings were not altogether unimpressible—although it was almost impossible to extract an expression from him—and I conscientiously believe he became attached to those that were good to him. What he might have become under more favorable conditions than the bondsman of an over-worked, under-paid literary man, I don't know; I only know that the scant, irregular, impulsive kindnesses that I showed him were gratefully received. He was very loyal and patient—two qualities rare in the average American servant. He was like Malvolio, "sad and civil" with me; only once, and then under great provo-

"The water on the floor was already over her ankles." Illustration by
B. West Clinedinst for *High-Water Mark. (p. 86)*

cation, do I remember of his exhibiting any impatience. It was my habit, after leaving the office at night, to take him with me to my rooms, as the bearer of any supplemental or happy after-thought in the editorial way, that might occur to me before the paper went to press. One night I had been scribbling away past the usual hour of dismissing Wan Lee, and had become quite oblivious of his presence in a chair near my door, when suddenly I became aware of a voice saying, in plaintive accents, something that sounded like "Chy Lee."

I faced around sternly.

"What did you say?"

"Me say, 'Chy Lee.'"

"Well?" I said impatiently.

"You sabe, 'How do, John'?"

"Yes."

"You sabe, 'So long, John'?"

"Yes."

"Well, 'Chy Lee' allee same!"

I understood him quite plainly. It appeared that "Chy Lee" was a form of "good-night," and that Wan Lee was anxious to go home. But an instinct of mischief which I fear I possessed in common with him, impelled me to act as if oblivious of the hint. I muttered something about not understanding him, and again bent over my work. In a few minutes I heard his wooden shoes pattering pathetically over the floor. I looked up. He was standing near the door.

"You no sabe, 'Chy Lee'?"

"No," I said sternly.

"You sabe muchee big foolee!—allee same!"

And with this audacity upon his lips he fled. The next morning, however, he was as meek and patient as before, and I did not recall his offence. As a probable peace-offering, he blacked all my boots—a duty never required of him—including a pair of buff deerskin slippers and an immense pair of horseman's jack-boots, on which he indulged his remorse for two hours.

I have spoken of his honesty as being a quality of his intellect rather than his principle, but I recall about this time two exceptions to the rule. I was anxious to get some fresh eggs, as a change to the heavy diet of a mining town, and knowing that Wan Lee's countrymen were great poultry raisers, I applied to him. He furnished me with them regularly every morning, but refused to take any pay, saying that the man did not sell them—a remarkable instance of self-abnegation, as eggs were then worth half a dollar apiece. One morning, my neighbor, Foster, dropped in upon me at breakfast, and took occasion to bewail his own ill fortune as his hens had lately stopped laying, or wandered off in the bush. Wan Lee, who was present during our colloquy, preserved his characteristic sad taciturnity. When my neighbor had gone, he turned to me with a slight chuckle—"Flostel's hens—Wan Lee's hens—allee same!" His other offence was more serious and ambitious. It was a season of great irregularities in the mails, and Wan Lee had heard me deplore the delay in the delivery of my letters and newspapers. On arriving at my office one day, I was amazed to find my table covered with letters, evidently just from the post-office, but unfortunately not one was addressed to me. I turned to Wan Lee, who was surveying them with a calm satisfaction, and demanded an explanation. To my horror he pointed to an empty mail-bag in the corner, and said—"Postman he say 'No lettee, John—no lettee, John.' Postman plentee lie! Postman no good. Me catchee lettee last night—allee same!" Luckily it was still early; the mails had not been distributed; I had a hurried interview with the Postmaster, and Wan Lee's bold attempt at robbing the U.S. Mail was finally condoned, by the purchase of a new mail-bag, and the whole affair thus kept a secret.

If my liking for my little pagan page had not been sufficient, my duty to Hop Sing was enough to cause me to take Wan Lee with me when I returned to San Francisco, after my two years' experience with the "Northern Star." I do not think he contemplated the change with pleasure. I attributed his feelings to a nervous dread of crowded public streets—when he had to go across town for me on an errand, he always made a long circuit of the outskirts— to his dislike for the discipline of the Chinese and English school to which I proposed to send him, to his fondness for the free, vagrant life of the mines, to sheer wilfulness! That it might have been a superstitious premonition did not occur to me until long after.

Nevertheless it really seemed as if the opportunity I had long looked for and confidently expected had come—the opportunity of placing Wan Lee under gently restraining influences, of subjecting him to a life and experience that would draw out of him what good my superficial care and ill-regulated kindness could not reach. Wan Lee was placed at the school of a Chinese missionary—an intelligent and kind-hearted clergyman, who had shown great interest in the boy, and who, better than all, had a wonderful faith in him. A home was found for him in the family of a widow, who had a bright and interesting daughter about two years younger than Wan Lee. It was this bright, cheery, innocent and artless child that touched and reached a depth in the boy's nature that hitherto had been unsuspected—that awakened a moral susceptibility which had lain for years insensible alike to the teachings of society or the ethics of the theologian.

These few brief months, bright with a promise that we never saw fulfilled, must have been happy ones to Wan Lee. He worshipped his little friend with something of the same superstition, but without any of the caprice, that he bestowed upon his porcelain god. It was his delight to walk behind her to school carrying her books—a service always fraught with danger to him from the little hands of his Caucasian Christian brothers. He made her the most marvellous toys, he would cut out of carrots and turnips the most astonishing roses and tulips, he made lifelike chickens out of melon-seeds, he constructed fans and kites, and was singularly proficient in the making of dolls' paper dresses. On the other hand she played and sang to him, taught him a thousand little prettinesses and refinements only known to girls, gave him a yellow ribbon for his pigtail, as best suiting his complexion, read to him, showed him wherein he was original and valuable, took him to Sunday School with her, against the precedents of the school, and, small-womanlike, triumphed. I wish I could add here, that she effected his conversion, and made him give up his porcelain idol, but I am telling a true story, and this little girl was quite content to fill him with her own Christian goodness, without letting him know that he was changed. So they got along very well together—this little Christian girl with her shining cross hanging around her plump, white, little neck, and this dark little pagan, with his hideous porcelain god hidden away in his blouse.

There were two days of that eventful year which will long be remembered in San Francisco—two days when a mob of her citizens set upon and killed unarmed, defenceless foreigners, because they were foreigners and of another race, religion, and color, and worked for what wages they could get. There were some public men so timid, that, seeing this, they thought that the end of the world had come; there were some eminent statesmen whose names I am ashamed to write here, who began to think that the passage in the Constitution which guarantees civil and religious liberty to every citizen or foreigner was a mistake. But there were also some men who were not so easily frightened, and in twenty-four hours we had things so arranged that the timid men could wring their hands in safety, and the eminent statemen utter their doubts without hurting anybody or anything. And in the midst of this I got a note from Hop Sing, asking me to come to him immediately.

I found his warehouse closed and strongly guarded by the police against any possible attack of the rioters. Hop Sing admitted me through a barred grating with his usual imperturbable calm, but, as it seemed to me, with more than his usual seriousness. Without a word he took my hand and led me to the rear of the room, and thence downstairs into the basement. It was dimly lighted, but there was something lying on the floor covered by a shawl. As I approached he drew the shawl away with a sudden gesture, and revealed Wan Lee, the Pagan, lying there dead!

Dead, my reverend friends, dead! Stoned to death in the streets of San Francisco, in the year of grace, eighteen hundred and sixty-nine, by a mob of half-grown boys and Christian schoolchildren!

As I put my hand reverently upon his breast, I felt something crumbling beneath his blouse. I looked inquiringly at Hop Sing. He put his hand between the folds of silk and drew out something with the first bitter smile I had ever seen on the face of that pagan gentleman.

It was Wan Lee's porcelain god, crushed by a stone from the hands of those Christian iconoclasts!

TWO SAINTS OF THE FOOTHILLS

IT never was clearly ascertained how long they had been there. The first settler of Rough-and-Ready—one Low, playfully known to his familiars as "The Poor Indian"— declared that the Saints were afore his time, and occupied a cabin in the brush when he "blazed" his way to the North Fork. It is certain that the two were present when the water was first turned on the Union Ditch, and then and there received the designation of Daddy Downey and Mammy Downey, which they kept to the last. As they tottered toward the refreshment tent, they were welcomed with the greatest enthusiasm by the boys; or, to borrow the more refined language of the "Union Recorder,"—"Their gray hairs and bent figures, recalling as they did the happy paternal eastern homes of the spectators, and the blessings that fell from venerable lips when they left those homes to journey in quest of the Golden Fleece on Occidental Slopes, caused many to burst into tears." The nearer facts, that many of these spectators were orphans, that a few were unable to establish any legal parentage whatever, that others had enjoyed a State's guardianship and discipline, and that

a majority had left their parental roofs without any embarrassing preliminary formula, were mere passing clouds that
did not dim the golden imagery of the writer. From that
day the Saints were adopted as historical lay figures, and
entered at once into possession of uninterrupted gratuities
and endowments.

It was not strange that, in a country largely made up of
ambitious and reckless youth, these two—types of conservative and settled forms—should be thus celebrated. Apart
from any sentiment or veneration, they were admirable foils
to the community's youthful progress and energy. They
were put forward at every social gathering, occupied prominent seats on the platform at every public meeting, walked
first in every procession, were conspicuous at the frequent
funeral and rarer wedding, and were godfather and godmother to the first baby born in Rough-and-Ready. At the
first poll opened in that precinct, Daddy Downey cast the
first vote, and, as was his custom on all momentous occasions, became volubly reminiscent. "The first vote I ever
cast," said Daddy, "was for Andrew Jackson—the father
o' some on you peart young chaps wasn't born then; he! he!
—that was 'way long in '33, wasn't it? I disremember now,
but if Mammy was here, she bein' school-gal at the time,
she could say. But my memory's failin' me. I'm an old man,
boys; yet I likes to see the young ones go ahead. I recklect
that thar vote from a suckumstance. Squire Adams was
present, and seein' it was my first vote, he put a goold piece
into my hand, and, sez he, sez Squire Adams, 'Let that
always be a reminder of the exercise of a glorious freeman's
privilege!' He did; he! he! Lord, boys! I feel so proud of
ye, that I wish I had a hundred votes to cast for ye all."

It is hardly necessary to say that the memorial tribute of

Squire Adams was increased tenfold by the judges, inspectors, and clerks, and that the old man tottered back to Mammy considerably heavier than he came. As both of the rival candidates were equally sure of his vote, and each had called upon him and offered a conveyance, it is but fair to presume they were equally beneficent. But Daddy insisted upon walking to the polls,—a distance of two miles,—as a moral example, and a text for the Californian paragraphers, who hastened to record that such was the influence of the foothill climate, that "a citizen of Rough-and-Ready, aged eighty-four, rose at six o'clock, and, after milking two cows, walked a distance of twelve miles to the polls, and returned in time to chop a cord of wood before dinner." Slightly exaggerated as this statement may have been, the fact that Daddy was always found by the visitor to be engaged at his wood-pile, which seemed neither to increase nor diminish under his axe, a fact, doubtless, owing to the activity of Mammy, who was always at the same time making pies, seemed to give some credence to the story. Indeed, the wood-pile of Daddy Downey was a standing reproof to the indolent and sluggish miner.

"Ole Daddy must use up a pow'ful sight of wood; every time I've passed by his shanty he's been makin' the chips fly. But what gets me is, that the pile don't seem to come down," said Whisky Dick to his neighbor.

"Well, you derned fool!" growled his neighbor, "spose some chap happens to pass by thar, and sees the ole man doin' at man's work at eighty, and slouches like you and me lying round drunk, and that chap, feelin' kinder humped, goes up some dark night and heaves a load of cut pine over his fence, who's got anything to say about it? say?"

Certainly not the speaker, who had done the act suggested, nor the penitent and remorseful hearer, who repeated it next day.

The pies and cakes made by the old woman were, I think, remarkable rather for their inducing the same loyal and generous spirit than for their intrinsic excellence, and, it may be said, appealed more strongly to the nobler aspirations of humanity than its vulgar appetite. Howbeit, everybody ate Mammy Downey's pies, and thought of his childhood. "Take 'em, dear boys," the old lady would say; "it does me good to see you eat 'em; reminds me kinder of my poor Sammy, that ef he'd lived, would hev been ez strong and big ez you be, but was taken down with lung fever at Sweetwater. I kin see him yet; that's forty year ago, dear! comin' out o' the lot to the bakehouse, and smilin' such a beautiful smile, like yours, dear boy, as I handed him a mince or a lemming turnover. Dear, dear, how I do run on! and those days is past! but I seems to live in you again!" The wife of the hotel-keeper, actuated by a low jealousy, had suggested that she "seemed to live *off* *t*hem;" but as that person tried to demonstrate the truth of her statement by reference to the cost of the raw material used by the old lady, it was considered by the camp as too practical and economical for consideration. "Besides," added Cy Perkins, "ef old Mammy wants to turn an honest penny in her old age, let her do it. How would you like your old mother to make pies on grub wages? eh?" A suggestion that so affected his hearer (who had no mother) that he bought three on the spot. The quality of these pies had never been discussed but once. It is related that a young lawyer from San Francisco, dining at the Palmetto restaurant, pushed away one of Mammy Downey's pies with every expression of disgust and dissatisfaction. At this juncture, Whisky

Dick considerably affected by his favorite stimulant, approached the stranger's table, and, drawing up a chair, sat uninvited before him.

"Mebbee, young man," he began gravely, "ye don't like Mammy Downey's pies?"

The stranger replied curtly, and in some astonishment, that he did not, as a rule, "eat pie."

"Young man," continued Dick with drunken gravity, "mebbee you're accustomed to Charlotte rusks and blue mange; mebbee ye can't eat unless your grub is got up by one o' them French cooks? Yet *we*—us boys yar in this camp—calls that pie—a good—a com-pe-tent pie!"

The stranger again disclaimed anything but a general dislike of that form of pastry.

"Young man," continued Dick, utterly unheeding the explanation,—"young man, mebbee you onst had an ole— a very ole mother, who, tottering down the vale o' years, made pies. Mebbee, and it's like your blank epicurean soul, ye turned up your nose on the ole woman, and went back on the pies, and on her! She that dandled ye when ye woz a baby,—a little baby! Mebbee ye went back on her, and shook her, and played off on her, and gave her away—dead away! And now, mebbee young man—I wouldn't hurt ye for the world, but mebbee, afore ye leave this yar table, YE'LL EAT THAT PIE!"

The stranger rose to his feet, but the muzzle of a dragoon revolver in the unsteady hands of Whisky Dick caused him to sit down again. He ate the pie, and lost his case likewise before a Rough-and-Ready jury.

Indeed, far from exhibiting the cynical doubts and distrusts of age, Daddy Downey received always with childlike delight the progress of modern improvement and ener-

gy. "In my day, long back in the twenties, it took us nigh
a week—a week, boys—to get up a barn, and all the young
ones—I was one then—for miles round at the raisin'; and
yer's you boys—rascals ye are, too—runs up this yer shanty
for Mammy and me 'twixt sun-up and dark! Eh, eh, you're
teachin' the old folks new tricks, are ye? Ah, get along,
you!" and in playful simulation of anger he would shake his
white hair and his hickory staff at the "rascals." The only
indication of the conservative tendencies of age was visible
in his continual protest against the extravagance of the boys.
"Why," he would say, "a family, a hull family,—leavin'
alone me and the old woman,—might be supported on what
you young rascals throw away in a single spree. Ah, you
young dogs, didn't I hear about your scattering half-dollars
on the stage the other night when that Eyetalian Papist was
singin'. And that money goes out of Ameriky—ivry cent!"

There was little doubt that the old couple were saving, if
not avaricious. But when it was known, through the indis-
creet volubility of Mammy Downey, that Daddy Downey
sent the bulk of their savings, gratuities, and gifts, to a
dissipated and prodigal son in the East,—whose photograph
the old man always carried with him, it rather elevated him
in their regard. "When ye write to that gay and festive son
o' yourn, Daddy," said Joe Robinson, "send him this yer
specimen. Give him my compliments, and tell him, ef he kin
spend money faster than I can, I call him! Tell him, ef he
wants a first-class jamboree, to kem out here, and me and
the boys will show him what a square drunk is!" In vain
would the old man continue to protest against the spirit of
the gift; the miner generally returned with his pockets that
much the lighter, and it is not improbable a little less intoxicated than he otherwise might have been. It may be premised

that Daddy Downey was strictly temperate. The only way he managed to avoid hurting the feelings of the camp was by accepting the frequent donations of whisky to be used for the purposes of liniment.

"Next to snake-oil, my son," he would say, "and dilberry-juice,—and ye don't seem to produce 'em hereabouts,—whisky is good for rubbin' onto old bones to make 'em limber. But pure cold water, 'sparklin' and bright in its liquid light,' and, so to speak, reflectin' of God's own linyments on its surnss, is the best, onless, like poor ol Mammy and me, ye gets the dumb-agur from over-use."

The fame of the Downey couple was not confined to the foothills. The Rev. Henry Gushington, D.D., of Boston, making a bronchial tour of California, wrote to the "Christian Pathfinder" an affecting account of his visit to them, placed Daddy Downey's age at 102, and attributed the recent conversions in Rough-and-Ready to their influence. That gifted literary Hessian, Bill Smith, travelling in the interests of various capitalists, and the trustworthy correspondent of four "only independent American journals," quoted him as an evidence of the longevity superinduced by the climate, offered him as an example of the security of helpless life and property in the mountains, used him as an advertisement of the Union Ditch, and it is said, in some vague way, cited him as proving the collateral facts of a timber and ore-producing region existing in the foothills worthy the attention of Eastern capitalists.

Praised thus by the lips of distinguished report, fostered by the care and sustained by the pecuniary offerings of their fellow-citizens, the Saints led for two years a peaceful life of gentle absorption. To relieve them from the embarrassing appearance of eleemosynary receipts,—an embarrassment felt more by the givers than the recipients,—the post-mastership of Rough-and-Ready was procured for Daddy, and the duty of receiving and delivering the United States mails performed by him, with the advice and assistance of the boys. If a few letters went astray at this time, it was easily attributed to this undisciplined aid, and the boys themselves were always ready to make up the value of a missing money-letter and "keep the old man's accounts square." To these functions presently were added the treasurerships of the Masons' and Odd Fellows' charitable funds,—the old man being far advanced in their respective degrees,—and even the position of almoner of their bounties was super-added. Here, unfortunately, Daddy's habits of economy and avaricious propensity came near making him unpopular, and very often needy brothers were forced to object to the quantity and quality of the help extended. They always met with more generous relief from the private hands of the brothers themselves, and the remark, "that the ol' man was trying to set an example,—that he meant well,"—and that they would yet be thankful for his zealous care and economy. A few, I think, suffered in noble silence, rather than bring the old man's infirmity to the public notice.

And so with this honor of Daddy and Mammy, the days of the miners were long and profitable in the land of the foothills. The mines yielded their abundance, the winters were singularly open, and yet there was no drouth nor lack of water, and peace and plenty smiled on the Sierrean foot-hills, from their highest sunny upland to the trailing *falda* of wild oats and poppies. If a certain superstition got abroad among the other camps, connecting the fortunes of Rough-and-Ready with Daddy and Mammy, it was a gentle, harm-less fancy, and was not, I think, altogether rejected by the old people. A certain large, patriarchal, bountiful manner, of late visible in Daddy, and the increase of much white hair and beard, kept up the poetic illusion, while Mammy, day by day, grew more and more like somebody's fairy godmother. An attempt was made by a rival camp to emulate these paying virtues of reverence, and an aged mariner was procured from the Sailor's Snug Harbor in San Francisco on trial. But the unfortunate seaman was more or less diseased, was not always presentable, through a weakness for ardent spirits, and finally, to use the powerful idiom of one of his disappointed foster-children, "up and died in a week, without slinging ary blessin'."

But vicissitude reaches young and old alike. Youthful Rough-and-Ready and the Saints had climbed to their meridian together, and it seemed fit that they should together decline. The first shadow fell with the immigration to Rough-and-Ready of a second aged pair. The landlady of the Independence Hotel had not abated her malevolence towards the Saints, and had imported at considerable expense her grand-aunt and grand-uncle, who had been enjoying for some years a sequestered retirement in the poorhouse at East Machias. They were indeed very old. By what miracle, even as anatomical specimens, they had been preserved during their long journey was a mystery to the camp. In some respects they had superior memories and reminiscences. The old man—Abner Trix—had shouldered a musket in the war of 1812; his wife, Abigail, had seen Lady Washington. She could sing hymns; he knew every text between "the leds" of a Bible. There is little doubt but that in many respects, to the superficial and giddy crowd of youthful spectators, they were the more interesting spectacle.

Whether it was jealousy, distrust, or timidity that overcame the Saints, was never known, but they studiously declined to meet the strangers. When directly approached upon the subject, Daddy Downey pleaded illness, kept himself in close seclusion, and the Sunday that the Trixes attended church in the schoolhouse on the hill, the triumph of the Trix party was mitigated by the fact that the Downeys were not in their accustomed pew. "You bet that Daddy and Mammy is lying low jest to ketch them old mummies yet," explained a Downeyite. For by this time schism and division had crept into the camp; the younger and later members of the settlement adhering to the Trixes, while the older pioneers stood not only loyal to their own favorites, but even, in the true spirit of partisanship, began to seek for a principle underlying their personal feelings. "I tell ye what, boys," observed Sweetwater Joe, "if this yer camp is goin' to be run by greenhorns, and old pioneers, like Daddy and the rest of us, must take back seats, it's time we emigrated and shoved out, and tuk Daddy with us. Why, they're talkin' of rotation in offiss, and of putting that skeleton that Ma'am Decker sets up at the table to take her boarders' appetites away, into the post office in place o' Daddy. And, indeed, there were some fears of such a conclusion; the newer men of Rough-and-Ready were in the majority, and wielded a more than equal influence of wealth and outside enterprise. "Frisco," as a Downeyite bitterly remarked, "already owned half the town." The old friends that rallied around Daddy and Mammy were, like most loyal friends in adversity, in bad case themselves, and were beginning to look and act, it was observed, not unlike their old favorites.

At this juncture Mammy died.

The sudden blow for a few days seemed to reunite dissevered Rough-and-Ready. Both factions hastened to the bereaved Daddy with condolements, and offers of aid and assistance. But the old man received them sternly. A change had come over the weak and yielding octogenarian. Those who expected to find him maudlin, helpless, disconsolate, shrank from the cold, hard eyes and truculent voice that bade them "begone," and "leave him with his dead." Even his own friends failed to make him respond to their sympathy, and were fain to content themselves with his cold intimation that both the wishes of his dead wife and his own instincts were against any display, or the reception of any favor from the camp that might tend to keep up the divisions they had innocently created. The refusal of Daddy to accept any service offered was so unlike him as to have but one dreadful meaning! The sudden shock had turned his brain! Yet so impressed were they with his resolution that they permitted him to perform the last sad offices himself, and only a select few of his nearer neighbors assisted him in carrying the plain deal coffin from his lonely cabin in the woods to the still lonelier cemetery on the hill-top. When the shallow grave was filled, he dismissed even these curtly, shut himself up in his cabin, and for days remained unseen. It was evident that he was no longer in his right mind.

His harmless aberration was accepted and treated with a degree of intelligent delicacy hardly to be believed of so rough a community. During his wife's sudden and severe illness, the safe containing the funds intrusted to his care by the various benevolent associations was broken into and robbed, and although the act was clearly attributable to his carelessness and preoccupation, all allusion to the fact was

The Red House, Camberley, Surrey, the house in England where Bret Harte died.

withheld from him in his severe affliction. When he appeared again before the camp, and the circumstances were considerately explained to him, with the remark that "the boys had made it all right," the vacant, hopeless, unintelligent eye that he turned upon the speaker showed too plainly that he had forgotten all about it. "Don't trouble the old man," said Whisky Dick, with a burst of honest poetry. "Don't ye see his memory's dead, and lying there in the coffin with Mammy?" Perhaps the speaker was nearer right than he imagined.

Failing in religious consolation, they took various means of diverting his mind with worldly amusements, and one was a visit to a travelling variety troupe, then performing in the town. The result of the visit was briefly told by Whisky Dick. "Well, sir, we went in, and I sot the old man down in a front seat, and kinder propped him up with some other of the fellers round him, and there he sot as silent and awful ez the grave. And then that fancy dancer, Miss Grace Somerset, comes in, and dern my skin, ef the old man didn't get to trembling and fidgeting all over, as she cut them pidgin wings. I tell ye what, boys, men is men, way down to their boots,—whether they're crazy or not! Well, he took on so, that I'm blamed if at last that gal *herself* didn't notice him! and she ups, suddenly, and blows him a kiss—so! with her fingers!"

Whether this narration were exaggerated or not, it is certain that the old man Downey every succeeding night of the performance was a spectator. That he may have aspired to more than that was suggested a day or two later in the following incident: A number of the boys were sitting around the stove in the Magnolia saloon, listening to the onset of a winter storm against the windows, when Whisky

Dick, tremulous, excited, and bristling with rain-drops and information, broke in upon them.

"Well, boys, I've got just the biggest thing out. Ef I hadn't seed it myself, I wouldn't hev believed it!"

"It ain't thet ghost ag'in?" growled Robinson, from the depths of his arm-chair; "thet ghost's about played."

"Wot ghost?" asked a new-comer.

"Why, ole Mammy's ghost, that every feller about yer sees when he's half full and out late o' nights."

"Where?"

"Where? Why, where should a ghost be? Meanderin' round her grave on the hill, yander, in course."

"It's suthin bigger nor thet, pard," said Dick confidently; "no ghost kin rake down the pot ag'in the keerds I've got here. This ain't no bluff!"

"Well, go on!" said a dozen excited voices.

Dick paused a moment diffidently, with the hesitation of an artistic *raconteur*.

"Well," he said, with affected deliberation, "let's see! It's nigh onto an hour ago ez I was down thar at the variety show. When the curtain was down betwixt the ax, I looks round fer Daddy. No Daddy thar! I goes out and asks some o' the boys. 'Daddy *was* there a minnit ago,' they say; 'must hev gone home.' Bein' kinder responsible for the old man, I hangs around, and goes out in the hall and sees a passage leadin' behind the scenes. Now the queer thing about this, boys, ez that suthin in my bones tells me the old man is *thar*. I pushes in, and, sure as a gun, I hear his voice. Kinder pathetic, kinder pleadin', kinder"——

"Love makin'!" broke in the impatient Robinson.

"You've hit it, pard,—you've rung the bell every time! But she says, 'I wants thet money down, or I'll'—and here

I couldn't get to hear the rest. And then he kinder coaxes, and she says, sorter sassy, but listenin' all the time,—woman like, ye know, Eve and the sarpint!—and she says, 'I'll see to-morrow.' And he says, 'You won't blow on me?' and I gets excited and peeps in, and may I be teetotally durned ef I didn't see"——

"What?" yelled the crowd.

"Why, *Daddy on his knees to that there fancy dancer,* Grace Somerset! Now, if Mammy's ghost is meanderin' round, why, et's about time she left the cemetery and put in an appearance in Jackson's Hall. Thet's all!"

"Look yar, boys," said Robinson, rising, "I don't know ez it's the square thing to spile Daddy's fun. I don't object to it, provided she ain't takin' in the old man, and givin' him dead away. But ez we're his guardeens, I propose that we go down thar and see the lady, and find out ef her intentions is honorable. If she means marry, and the old man persists, why, I reckon we kin give the young couple a send-off that won't disgrace this yer camp! Hey, boys?"

It is unnecessary to say that the proposition was received with acclamation, and that the crowd at once departed on their discreet mission. But the result was never known, for the next morning brought a shock to Rough-and-Ready before which all other interest paled to nothingness.

The grave of Mammy Downey was found violated and despoiled; the coffin opened, and half filled with the papers and accounts of the robbed benevolent associations; but the body of Mammy was gone! Nor, on examination, did it appear that the sacred and ancient form of that female had ever reposed in its recesses!

Daddy Downey was not to be found, nor is it necessary to say that the ingenuous Grace Somerset was also missing.

For three days the reason of Rough-and-Ready trembled in the balance. No work was done in the ditches, in the flume, nor in the mills. Groups of men stood by the grave of the lamented relict of Daddy Downey, as open-mouthed and vacant as that sepulchre. Never since the great earthquake of '52 had Rough-and-Ready been so stirred to its deepest foundations.

On the third day the sheriff of Calaveras—a quiet, gentle, thoughtful man—arrived in town, and passed from one to the other of excited groups, dropping here and there detached but concise and practical information.

"Yes, gentlemen, you are right, Mrs. Downey is not dead, because there wasn't any Mrs. Downey! Her part was played by George F. Fenwick, of Sydney,—a 'ticket-of-leave-man,' who was, they say, a good actor. Downey? Oh yes! Downey was Jem Flanigan, who, in '52, used to run the variety troupe in Australia, where Miss Somerset made her *début*. Stand back a little, boys. Steady! The money? Oh yes, they've got away with that, sure! How are ye, Joe? Why, you're looking well and hearty! I rather expected ye court week. How's things your way?"

"Then they were only play-actors, Joe Hall?" broke in a dozen voices.

"I reckon!" returned the sheriff coolly.

"And for a matter o' five blank years," said Whisky Dick sadly, "they played this camp!"

THE FOOL OF FIVE FORKS

HE lived alone. I do not think this peculiarity arose from any wish to withdraw his foolishness from the rest of the

camp, nor was it probable that the combined wisdom of Five
Forks ever drove him into exile. My impression is, that he
lived alone from choice—a choice he made long before the
camp indulged in any criticism of his mental capacity. He
was much given to moody reticence, and although to outward appearances a strong man, was always complaining
of ill health. Indeed, one theory of his isolation was that it
afforded him better opportunities for taking medicine, of
which he habitually consumed large quantities.

His folly first dawned upon Five Forks through the Post
Office windows. He was for a long time the only man who
wrote home by every mail, his letters being always directed
to the same person—a woman. Now it so happened that the
bulk of the Five Forks' correspondence was usually the
other way; there were many letters received—the majority
being in the female hand—but very few answered.

The men received them indifferently, or as a matter of
course; a few opened and read them on the spot with a
barely repressed smile of self-conceit, or quite as frequently
glanced over them with undisguised impatience. Some of
the letters began with "my dear husband," and some were
never called for. But the fact that the only regular correspondent of Five Forks never received any reply became
at last quite notorious. Consequently, when an envelope was
received bearing the stamp of the "Dead Letter Office," addressed to the Fool under the more conventional title of
"Cyrus Hawkins," there was quite a fever of excitement. I
do not know how the secret leaked out, but it was eventually
known to the camp that the envelope contained Hawkins'
own letters returned. This was the first evidence of his
weakness; any man who repeatedly wrote to a woman who
did not reply must be a fool. I think Hawkins suspected that

his folly was known to the camp, but he took refuge in symptoms of chills and fever, which he at once developed, and
effected a diversion with three bottles of Indian chologogue
and two boxes of pills. At all events, at the end of a week
he resumed a pen, stiffened by tonics, with all his old epis-
tolatory pertinacity. This time the letters had a new address.

In those days a popular belief obtained in the mines that
Luck particularly favored the foolish and unscientific.
Consequently, when Hawkins struck a "pocket" in the hillside near his solitary cabin, there was but little surprise.
"He will sink it all in the next hole," was the prevailing
belief, predicated upon the usual manner in which the possessor of "nigger luck" disposed of his fortune. To everybody's astonishment, Hawkins, after taking out about eight
thousand dollars and exhausting the pocket, did not prospect
for another. The camp then waited patiently to see what
he would do with his money. I think, however, that it was
with the greatest difficulty their indignation was kept from
taking the form of a personal assault, when it became known
that he had purchased a draft for eight thousand dollars in
favor of "that woman." More than this, it was finally
whispered that the draft was returned to him as his letters
had been, and that he was ashamed to reclaim the money at
the express office. "It wouldn't be a bad specilation to go
East, get some smart gal for a hundred dollars to dress herself up and represent that hag, and jest freeze onto that
eight thousand," suggested a far-seeing financier. I may
state here that we always alluded to Hawkins' fair unknown
as "The Hag," without having, I am confident, the least
justification for that epithet.

That the Fool should gamble seemed eminently fit and
proper. That he should occasionally win a large stake,

according to that popular theory which I have recorded in the preceding paragraph, appeared also a not improbable or inconsistent fact. That he should, however, break the faro bank which Mr. John Hamlin had set up in Five Forks, and carry off a sum variously estimated at from ten to twenty thousand dollars, and not return the next day and lose the money at the same table, really appeared incredible. Yet such was the fact. A day or two passed withwithout any known investment of Mr. Hawkins' recently-acquired capital. "Ef he allows to send it to that Hag," said one prominent citizen, "suthin' ought to be done! It's jest ruinin' the reputation of this yer camp—this sloshin' around o' capital on non-residents ez don't claim it!" "It's settin' an example o' extravagance," said another, "ez is little better nor a swindle. Thars mor'n five men in this camp thet, hearin' thet Hawkins had sent home eight thousand dollars, must jest rise up and send home their hard earnings, too! And then to think that eight thousand was only a bluff, after all, and thet it's lyin' there on call in Adams & Co.'s bank! Well! I say it's one o' them things a vigilance committee oughter look into!"

When there seemed no possibility of this repetition of Hawkins' folly, the anxiety to know what he had really done with his money became intense. At last a self-appointed committee of four citizens dropped artfully, but to outward appearances carelessly, upon him in his seclusion. When some polite formalities had been exchanged, and some easy vituperation of a backward season offered by each of the parties, Tom Wingate approached the subject—

'Sorter dropped heavy on Jack Hamlin the other night, didn't ye? He allows you didn't give him no show for revenge. I said you wasn't no such d—d fool—didn't I, Dick?" continued the artful Wingate, appealing to a confederate.

"Yes," said Dick promptly. "You said twenty thousand dollars wasn't goin' to be thrown around recklessly. You said Cyrus had suthin' better to do with his capital," superadded Dick, with gratuitous mendacity. "I disremember now what partickler investment you said he was goin' to make with it," he continued, appealing with easy indifference to his friend.

Of course Wingate did not reply, but looked at the Fool, who with a troubled face, was rubbing his legs softly. After a pause he turned deprecatingly toward his visitors.

"Ye didn't enny of ye ever hev a sort of tremblin' in your legs—a kind o' shakiness from the knee down? Suthin'," he continued, slightly brightening with his topic, "suthin' that begins like chills, and yet ain't chills. A kind o' sensation of goneness here, and a kind o' feelin' as if you might die suddent! When Wright's Pills don't somehow reach the spot, and Quinine don't fetch you?"

"No!" said Wingate, with a curt directness, and the air of authoritatively responding for his friends. "No, never had. You was speakin' of this yer investment."

"And your bowels all the time irregular!" continued Hawkins, blushing under Wingate's eye, and yet clinging despairingly to his theme like a shipwrecked mariner to his plank.

Wingate did not reply, but glanced significantly at the rest. Hawkins evidently saw this recognition of his mental deficiency, and said apologetically, "You was saying suthin' about my investment?"

"Happily, most of the population were gathered at Thompson's store, clustered around a red-hot stove." Wood engraving by Paul Landacre for *How Santa Claus Came to Simpson's Bar*, published in a limited edition by the Ward Ritchie Press. *(p. 190)*

"Yes," said Wingate, so rapidly as to almost take Hawkins' breath away—"the investment you made in"—

"Rafferty's Ditch," said the Fool, timidly.

For a moment the visitors could only stare blankly at each other. "Rafferty's Ditch," the one notorious failure of Five Forks! Rafferty's Ditch, the impracticable scheme of an utterly unpractical man; Rafferty's Ditch, a ridiculous plan for taking water that could not be got to a place where it wasn't wanted! Rafferty's Ditch, that had buried the fortunes of Rafferty and twenty wretched stockholders in its muddy depths!

"And thet's it—is it?" said Wingate, after a gloomy pause. "Thet's it! I see it all now, boys. That's how ragged Pat Rafferty went down to San Francisco yesterday in store clothes, and his wife and four children went off in a kerridge to Sacramento. Thet's why them ten workmen of his, ez hedn't a cent to bless themselves with, was playin' billiards last night and eatin' isters. Thet's whar that money kum frum—one hundred dollars—to pay for thet long advertisement of the new issue of Ditch stock in the *Times* yesterday. Thet's why them six strangers were booked at the Magnolia Hotel yesterday. Don't you see—it's thet money and thet Fool!"

The Fool sat silent. The visitors rose without a word.

"You never took any of them Indian Vegetable Pills?" asked Hawkins timidly, of Wingate.

"No," roared Wingate, as he opened the door.

"They tell me that took with the Panacea—they was out o' the Panacea when I went to the drug store last week—they say that, took with the Panacea, they always effect a certing cure."—But by this time Wingate and his disgusted friends had retreated, slamming the door on the Fool and his ailments.

Nevertheless in six months the whole affair was forgotten, the money had been spent—the "Ditch" had been purchased by a company of Boston capitalists, fired by the glowing description of an Eastern tourist, who had spent one drunken night at Five Forks—and I think even the mental condition of Hawkins might have remained undisturbed by criticism, but for a singular incident.

It was during an exciting political campaign, when party feeling ran high, that the irascible Captain McFadden, of Sacramento, visited Five Forks. During a heated discussion in the Prairie Rose Saloon words passed between the Captain and the Honorable Calhoun Bungstarter, ending in a challenge. The Captain bore the infelix reputation of being a notorious duellist and a dead shot: the Captain was unpopular; the Captain was believed to have been sent by the opposition for a deadly purpose, and the Captain was, moreover, a stranger. I am sorry to say that with Five Forks this latter condition did not carry the quality of sanctity or reverence that usually obtains among other nomads. There was consequently some little hesitation when the Captain turned upon the crowd and asked for some one to act as his friend. To everybody's astonishment, and to the indignation of many, the Fool stepped forward and offered himself in that capacity. I do not know whether Captain McFadden would have chosen him voluntarily, but he was constrained, in the absence of a better man, to accept his services.

The duel never took place! The preliminaries were all arranged, the spot indicated, the men were present with their seconds, there was no interruption from without, there was no explanation or apology passed—but the duel did *not* take place. It may be readily imagined that these facts, which were all known to Five Forks, threw the whole community into a fever of curiosity. The principals, the surgeon, and one second left town the next day. Only the Fool remained. *He* resisted all questioning—declaring himself held in honor not to divulge—in short, conducted himself with consistent but exasperating folly. It was not until six months had passed that Colonel Starbottle, the second of Calhoun Bungstarter, in a moment of weakness superinduced by the social glass, condescended to explain. I should not do justice to the parties if I did not give that explanation in the Colonel's own words. I may remark, in passing, that the characteristic dignity of Colonel Starbottle always became intensified by stimulants, and that by the same process all sense of humor was utterly eliminated.

"With the understanding that I am addressing myself confidentially to men of honor," said the Colonel, elevating his chest above the bar-room counter of the Prairie Rose Saloon, "I trust that it will not be necessary for me to protect myself from levity, as I was forced to do in Sacramento on the only other occasion when I entered into an explanation of this delicate affair by—er—er—calling the individual to a personal account—er! I do not believe," added the Colonel, slightly waving his glass of liquor in the air with a graceful gesture of courteous deprecation —"knowing what I do of the present company—that such a course of action is required here. Certainly not—Sir—in the home of Mr. Hawkins—er—the gentleman who represented Mr. Bungstarter, whose conduct, ged, Sir, is worthy of praise, blank me!"

Apparently satisfied with the gravity and respectful

attention of his listeners, Colonel Starbottle smiled relent-
ingly and sweetly, closed his eyes half dreamily, as if to
recall his wandering thoughts, and began—

"As the spot selected was nearest the tenement of Mr.
Hawkins, it was agreed that the parties should meet there.
They did so promptly at half past six. The morning being
chilly, Mr. Hawkins extended the hospitalities of his house
with a bottle of Bourbon whisky—of which all partook but
myself. The reason for that exception is, I believe, well
known. It is my invariable custom to take brandy—a wine-
glassful in a cup of strong coffee, immediately on rising.
It stimulates the functions, sir, without producing any blank
derangement of the nerves."

The barkeeper, to whom, as an expert, the Colonel had
graciously imparted this information, nodded approvingly,
and the Colonel, amid a breathless silence, went on—

"We were about twenty minutes in reaching the spot.
The ground was measured, the weapons were loaded, when
Mr. Bungstarter confided to me the information that he
was unwell and in great *pain!* On consultation with Mr.
Hawkins, it appeared that his principal in a distant part of
the field was also suffering and in great pain. The symptoms were such as a medical man would pronounce 'chol-
eric.' I say *would* have pronounced, for on examination
the surgeon was also found to be—er—in pain, and I regret
to say, expressing himself in language unbecoming the
occasion. His impression was that some powerful drug
had been administered. On referring the question to Mr.
Hawkins, he remembered that the bottle of whiskey partaken
by them contained a medicine which he had been in the habit
of taking, but which, having failed to act upon him, he had
concluded to be generally ineffective, and had forgotten.

His perfect willingness to hold himself personally responsible to each of the parties, his genuine concern at the disas-
trous effect of the mistake, mingled with his own alarm at
the state of his system, which—er—failed to—er—respond
to the peculiar qualities of the medicine, was most becoming to him as a man of honor and a gentleman! After an
hour's delay, both principals being completely exhausted,
and abandoned by the surgeon, who was unreasonably
alarmed at his own condition, Mr. Hawkins and I agreed
to remove our men to Markleville. There, after a further
consultation with Mr. Hawkins, an amicable adjustment
of all difficulties, honorable to both parties, and governed
by profound secrecy, was arranged. I believe," added the
Colonel, looking around and setting down his glass, "no
gentleman has yet expressed himself other than satisfied
with the result."

Perhaps it was the Colonel's manner, but whatever was
the opinion of Five Forks regarding the intellectual display
of Mr. Hawkins in this affair, there was very little out-
spoken criticism at the moment. In a few weeks the whole
thing was forgotten, except as part of the necessary record
of Hawkins' blunders, which was already a pretty full one.
Again some later follies conspired to obliterate the past,
until, a year later, a valuable lead was discovered in the
"Blazing Star" Tunnel, in the hill where he lived, and a
large sum was offered him for a portion of his land on the
hill-top. Accustomed as Five Forks had become to the
exhibition of his folly, it was with astonishment that they
learned that he resolutely and decidedly refused the offer.
The reason that he gave was still more astounding. He
was about to build!

To build a house upon property available for mining

purposes was preposterous; to build at all with a roof already covering him, was an act of extravagance; to build a house of the style he proposed was simply madness!

Yet here were facts. The plans were made and the lumber for the new building was already on the ground, while the shaft of the "Blazing Star" was being sunk below. The site was, in reality, a very picturesque one—the building itself of a style and quality hitherto unknown in Five Forks. The citizens, at first sceptical, during their moments of recreation and idleness gathered doubtingly about the locality. Day by day, in that climate of rapid growths, the building, pleasantly known in the slang of Five Forks as "the Idiot Asylum," rose beside the green oaks and clustering firs of Hawkins' Hill, as if it were part of the natural phenomena. At last it was completed. Then Mr. Hawkins proceeded to furnish it with an expensiveness and extravagance of outlay quite in keeping with his former idiocy. Carpets, sofas, mirrors, and finally a piano—the only one known in the county, and brought at great expense from Sacramento—kept curiosity at a fever heat. More than that, there were articles and ornaments which a few married experts declared only fit for women. When the furnishing of the house was complete—it had occupied two months of the speculative and curious attention of the camp—Mr. Hawkins locked the front door, put the key in his pocket, and quietly retired to his more humble roof, lower on the hill-side.

I have not deemed it necessary to indicate to the intelligent reader all of the theories which obtained in Five Forks during the erection of the building. Some of them may be readily imagined. That "the Hag" had by artful coyness and systematic reticence at last completely subjugated the

Fool, and that the new house was intended for the nuptial bower of the (predestined) unhappy pair, was of course the prevailing opinion. But when, after a reasonable time had elapsed, and the house still remained untenanted, the more exasperating conviction forced itself upon the general mind that the Fool had been for the third time imposed upon. When two months had elapsed and there seemed no prospect of a mistress for the new house, I think public indignation became so strong that had "the Hag" arrived, the marriage would have been publicly prevented. But no one appeared that seemed to answer to this idea of an available tenant, and all inquiry of Mr. Hawkins as to his intention in building a house and not renting it or occupying it, failed to elicit any further information. The reasons that he gave were felt to be vague, evasive, and unsatisfactory. He was in no hurry to move, he said; when he *was* ready, it surely was not strange that he should like to have his house all ready to receive him. He was often seen upon the veranda of a summer evening smoking a cigar. It is reported that one night the house was observed to be brilliantly lighted from garret to basement; that a neighbour, observing this, crept toward the open parlor window, and, looking in, espied the Fool accurately dressed in evening costume, lounging upon a sofa in the drawing-room, with the easy air of socially entertaining a large party. Notwithstanding this, the house was unmistakably vacant that evening, save for the presence of the owner, as the witnesses afterward testified. When this story was first related, a few practical men suggested the theory that Mr. Hawkins was simply drilling himself in the elaborate duties of hospitality against a probable event in his history. A few ventured the belief that the house was haunted. The imaginative editor of the

Five Forks "Record" evolved from the depths of his professional consciousness a story that Hawkins' sweetheart had died, and that he regularly entertained her spirit in this beautifully-furnished mausoleum. The occasional spectacle of Hawkins' tall figure pacing the veranda on moonlight nights lent some credence to this theory, until an unlooked-for incident diverted all speculation into another channel.

It was about this time that a certain wild, rude valley, in the neighborhood of Five Forks, had become famous as a picturesque resort. Travellers had visited it, and declared that there were more cubic yards of rough stone cliff and a waterfall of greater height, than any they had visited. Correspondents had written it up with extravagant rhetoric and inordinate poetical quotation. Men and women who had never enjoyed a sunset, a tree, or a flower—who had never appreciated the graciousness or meaning of the yellow sunlight that flecked their homely doorways, or the tenderness of a midsummer's night, to whose moonlight they bared their shirt-sleeves or their *tulle* dresses—came from thousands of miles away to calculate the height of this rock, to observe the depth of this chasm, to remark upon the enormous size of this unsightly tree, and to believe with ineffable self-complacency that they really admired nature. And so it came to pass that, in accordance with the tastes or weaknesses of the individual, the more prominent and salient points of the valley were christened, and there was a "Lace Handkerchief Fall," and the "Tears of Sympathy Cataract," and one distinguished orator's "Peak," and several "Mounts" of various noted people, living or dead; and an "Exclamation Point," and a "Valley of Silent Adoration." And, in course of time, empty soda-water bottles were found at the base of the cataract, and greasy newspapers and fragments of ham sandwiches lay at the dusty roots of giant trees. With this, there were frequent irruptions of closely-shaven and tightly-cravated men and delicate-faced women in the one long street of Five Forks, and a scampering of mules, and an occasional procession of dusty brown-linen cavalry.

A year after "Hawkins' Idiot Asylum" was completed, one day there drifted into the valley a riotous cavalcade of "school-marms," teachers of the San Francisco public schools, out for a holiday. Not severely-spectacled Minervas and chastely armed and mailed Pallases, but, I fear for the security of Five Forks, very human, charming, and mischievous young women. At least, so the men thought, working in the ditches and tunnelling on the hill-side; and when, in the interests of Science and the mental advancement of Juvenile Posterity, it was finally settled that they should stay in Five Forks two or three days for the sake of visiting the various mines, and particularly the "Blazing Star" Tunnel, there was some flutter of masculine anxiety. There was a considerable inquiry for "store clothes," a hopeless overhauling of old and disused raiment, and a general demand for "boiled shirts" and the barber.

Meanwhile, with that supreme audacity and impudent hardihood of the sex when gregarious, the school-marms rode through the town, admiring openly the handsome faces and manly figures that looked up from the ditches or rose behind the cars of ore at the mouths of tunnels. Indeed, it is alleged that Jenny Forester, backed and supported by seven other equally shameless young women, had openly and publicly waved her handkerchief to the florid Hercules of Five Forks—one Tom Flynn, formerly of Virginia—

leaving that good-natured but not over-bright giant pulling his blonde moustaches in bashful amazement.

It was a pleasant June afternoon that Miss Nelly Arnot, Principal of the primary department of one of the public schools of San Francisco, having evaded her companions, resolved to put into operation a plan which had lately sprung up in her courageous and mischief-loving fancy. With that wonderful and mysterious instinct of her sex, from whom no secrets of the affections are hid and to whom all hearts are laid open, she had heard the story of Hawkins' folly and the existence of the "Idiot Asylum." Alone, on Hawkins' Hill, she had determined to penetrate its seclusion. Skirting the underbush at the foot of the hill, she managed to keep the heaviest timber between herself and the "Blazing Star" Tunnel at its base, as well as the cabin of Hawkins, half-way up the ascent, until, by a circuitous route, at last she reached, unobserved, the summit. Before her rose, silent, darkened, and motionless, the object of her search. Here her courage failed her, with all the characteristic inconsequence of her sex. A sudden fear of all the dangers she had safely passed—bears, tarantulas, drunken men, and lizards—came upon her. For a moment, as she afterwards expressed it, "She thought she should die." With this belief, probably, she gathered three large stones, which she could hardly lift, for the purpose of throwing a great distance; put two hairpins in her mouth, and carefully readjusted with both hands two stray braids of her lovely blue-black mane which had fallen in gathering the stones. Then she felt in the pockets of her linen duster for her card-case, handkerchief, pocket-book, and smelling-bottle, and finding them intact, suddenly assumed an air of easy, ladylike unconcern, went up the steps of the veranda, and

demurely pulled the front door-bell, which she knew would
not be answered. After a decent pause, she walked around
the encompassing veranda, examining the closed shutters of
the French windows until she found one that yielded to her
touch. Here she paused again to adjust her coquettish hat
by the mirror-like surface of the long sash window that
reflected the full length of her pretty figure. And then she
opened the window and entered the room.

Although long closed, the house had a smell of newness
and of fresh paint that was quite unlike the mouldiness of
the conventional haunted house. The bright carpets, the
cheerful walls, the glistening oil-cloths were quite inconsistent with the idea of a ghost. With childish curiosity
she began to explore the silent house, at first timidly—
opening the doors with a violent push, and then stepping
back from the threshold to make good a possible retreat; and
then more boldly, as she became convinced of her security
and absolute loneliness. In one of the chambers, the largest,
there were fresh flowers in a vase—evidently gathered that
morning; and what seemed still more remarkable, the
pitchers and ewers were freshly filled with water. This
obliged Miss Nelly to notice another singular fact, namely,
that the house was free from dust—the one most obtrusive
and penetrating visitor of Five Forks. The floors and
carpets had been recently swept, the chairs and furniture
carefully wiped and dusted. If the house *was* haunted, it
was possessed by a spirit who had none of the usual indifference to decay and mould. And yet the beds had evidently
never been slept in, the very springs of the chair in which
she sat creaked stiffly at the novelty, the closet doors opened
with the reluctance of fresh paint and varnish, and in spite
of the warmth, cleanliness, and cheerfulness of furniture

and decoration, there was none of the ease of tenancy and occupation. As Miss Nelly afterwards confessed, she longed to "tumble things around," and when she reached the parlor or drawing-room again, she could hardly resist the desire. Particularly was she tempted by a closed piano, that stood mutely against the wall. She thought she would open it just to see who was the maker. That done, it would be no harm to try its tone. She did so, with one little foot on the soft pedal. But Miss Nelly was too good a player, and too enthusiastic a musician, to stop at half measures. She tried it again—this time so sincerely that the whole house seemed to spring into voice. Then she stopped and listened. There was no response—the empty rooms seemed to have relapsed into their old stillness. She stepped out on the veranda—a woodpecker recommenced his tapping on an adjacent tree, the rattle of a cart in the rocky gulch below the hill came faintly up. No one was to be seen far or near. Miss Nelly, reassured, returned. She again ran her fingers over the keys—stopped, caught at a melody running in her mind, half played it, and then threw away all caution. Before five minutes had elapsed she had entirely forgotten herself, and with her linen duster thrown aside, her straw hat flung on the piano, her white hands bared, and a black loop of her braided hair hanging upon her shoulder, was fairly embarked upon a flowing sea of musical recollection.

She had played perhaps half-an-hour, when, having just finished an elaborate symphony and resting her hands on the keys, she heard very distinctly and unmistakably the sound of applause from without. In an instant the fires of shame and indignation leaped into her cheeks, and she rose from the instrument and ran to the window, only in time to catch sight of a dozen figures in blue and red flannel shirts vanishing hurriedly through the trees below.

Miss Nelly's mind was instantly made up. I think I have already intimated that under the stimulus of excitement she was not wanting in courage, and as she quietly resumed her gloves, hat, and duster, she was not perhaps exactly the young person that it would be entirely safe for the timid, embarrassed, or inexperienced of my sex to meet alone. She shut down the piano, and having carefully reclosed all the windows and doors, and restored the house to its former desolate condition, she stepped from the veranda, and proceeded directly to the cabin of the unintellectual Hawkins, that reared its adobe chimney above the umbrage a quarter of a mile below.

The door opened instantly to her impulsive knock, and the Fool of Five Forks stood before her. Miss Nelly had never before seen the man designated by this infelicitous title, and as he stepped backward in half courtesy and half astonishment she was for the moment disconcerted. He was tall, finely formed, and dark-bearded. Above cheeks a little hollowed by care and ill-health shone a pair of hazel eyes, very large, very gentle, but inexpressibly sad and mournful. This was certainly not the kind of man Miss Nelly had expected to see, yet after her first embarrassment had passed, the very circumstance, oddly enough, added to her indignation, and stung her wounded pride still more deeply. Nevertheless, the arch hypocrite instantly changed her tactics with the swift intuition of her sex.

"I have come," she said with a dazzling smile, infinitely more dangerous than her former dignified severity, "I have come to ask your pardon for a great liberty I have just taken. I believe the new house above us on the hill is yours. I was so much pleased with its exterior that I left my friends for a moment below here," she continued artfully, with a slight wave of the hand, as if indicating a band of fearless Amazons without, and waiting to avenge any possible insult offered to one of their number, "and ventured to enter it. Finding it unoccupied, as I had been told, I am afraid I had the audacity to sit down and amuse myself for a few moments at the piano—while waiting for my friends."

Hawkins raised his beautiful eyes to hers. He saw a very pretty girl, with frank gray eyes glistening with excitement, with two red, slightly freckled cheeks, glowing a little under his eyes, with a short scarlet upper lip turned back, like a rose leaf, over a little line of white teeth, as she breathed somewhat hurriedly in her nervous excitement. He saw all this calmly, quietly, and, save for the natural uneasiness of a shy, reticent man, I fear without a quickening of his pulse.

"I knowed it," he said simply. "I heerd ye as I kem up."

Miss Nelly was furious at his grammar, his dialect, his coolness, and still more at the suspicion that he was an active member of her invisible *claque*.

"Ah," she said, still smiling, "then I think I heard *you*"——

"I reckon not," he interrupted gravely. "I didn't stay long. I found the boys hanging round the house, and I allowed at first I'd go in and kinder warn you, but they promised to keep still, and you looked so comfortable and wrapped up in your music, that I hadn't the heart to disturb you, and kem away. I hope," he added earnestly, "they didn't let on ez they heerd you. They ain't a bad lot—them Blazin' Star boys—though they're a little hard at times.

But they'd no more hurt ye then they would a—a—a cat!"
continued Mr. Hawkins, blushing with a faint apprehension
of the inelegance of his simile.

"No! no!" said Miss Nelly, feeling suddenly very angry
with herself, the Fool, and the entire male population of
Five Forks. "No! I have behaved foolishly, I suppose—and
if they *had* it would have served me right. But I only
wanted to apologize to you. You'll find everything as you
left it. Good day!"

She turned to go. Mr. Hawkins began to feel embarrassed. "I'd have asked ye to sit down," he said, finally, "if
it hed been a place fit for a lady. I oughter done so, enny
way. I don't know what kept me from it. But I ain't well,
Miss. Times I get a sort o' dumb ager—it's the ditches, I
think, Miss—and I don't seem to hev my wits about me."

Instantly Miss Arnot was all sympathy—her quick
woman's heart was touched.

"Can I—can anything be done?" she asked, more timidly
than she had before spoken.

"No!—not onless ye remember suthin' about these pills."
He exhibited a box containing about half-a-dozen. "I forget the direction—I don't seem to remember much, any way,
these times—they're 'Jones' Vegetable Compound.' If ye've
ever took 'em ye'll remember whether the reg'lar dose is
eight. They ain't but six here. But perhaps ye never tuk
any," he added deprecatingly.

"No," said Miss Nelly, curtly. She had usually a keen
sense of the ludicrous, but somehow Mr. Hawkins' eccentricity only pained her.

"Will you let me see you to the foot of the hill?" he said
again, after another embarrassing pause.

Miss Arnot felt instantly that such an act would condone

her trespass in the eyes of the world. She might meet some of her invisible admirers—or even her companions—and, with all her erratic impulses, she was nevertheless a woman, and did not entirely despise the verdict of conventionality. She smiled sweetly and assented, and in another moment the two were lost in the shadows of the wood.

Like many other apparently trivial acts in an uneventful life, it was decisive. As she expected, she met two or three of her late applauders, whom, she fancied, looked sheepish and embarrassed; she met also her companions looking for her in some alarm, who really appeared astonished at her escort, and, she fancied, a trifle envious of her evident success. I fear that Miss Arnot, in response to their anxious inquiries, did not state entirely the truth, but, without actual assertion, led them to believe that she had at a very early stage of the proceeding completely subjugated this weak-minded giant, and had brought him triumphantly to her feet. From telling this story two or three times she got finally to believing that she had some foundation for it; then to a vague sort of desire that it would eventually prove to be true, and then to an equally vague yearning to hasten that consummation. That it would redound to any satisfaction of the Fool she did not stop to doubt. That it would cure him of his folly she was quite confident. Indeed, there are very few of us—men or women—who do not believe that even a hopeless love for ourselves is more conducive to the salvation of the lover than a requited affection for another.

The criticism of Five Forks was, as the reader may imagine, swift and conclusive. When it was found out that Miss Arnot was not "the Hag" masquerading as a young and pretty girl, to the ultimate deception of Five Forks in general and the Fool in particular, it was decided at once that nothing but the speedy union of the Fool and the "pretty school-marm" was consistent with ordinary common sense. The singular good fortune of Hawkins was quite in accordance with the theory of his luck as propounded by the camp. That after "the Hag" failed to make her appearance he should "strike a lead" in his own house, without the trouble of "prospectin'," seemed to these casuists as a wonderful but inevitable law. To add to these fateful probabilities, Miss Arnot fell and sprained her ankle in the ascent of Mount Lincoln, and was confined for some weeks to the hotel after her companions had departed. During this period Hawkins was civilly but grotesquely attentive. When, after a reasonable time had elapsed, there still appeared to be no immediate prospect of the occupancy of the new house, public opinion experienced a singular change in regard to its theories of Mr. Hawkins' conduct. "The Hag" was looked upon as a saint-like and long-suffering martyr to the weaknesses and inconsistency of the Fool. That, after erecting this new house at her request, he had suddenly "gone back" on her; that his celibacy was the result of a long habit of weak proposal and subsequent shameless rejection, and that he was now trying his hand on the helpless school-marm, was perfectly plain to Five Forks. That he should be frustrated in his attempts at any cost was equally plain. Miss Nelly suddenly found herself invested with a rude chivalry that would have been amusing had it not been at times embarrassing; that would have been impertinent but for the almost superstitious respect with which it was proffered. Every day somebody from Five Forks rode out to inquire the health of the fair patient. "Hez Hawkins bin over yer to-day?" queried Tom Flynn, with artful ease and indifference as he leaned over Miss Nelly's easy-chair on the veranda. Miss Nelly, with a faint pink flush on her cheek, was constrained to answer "No." "Well, he sorter sprained his foot agin a rock yesterday," continued Flynn, with shameless untruthfulness. "You mus'n't think anything o' that, Miss Arnot. He'll be over yer to-morrer, and meantime he told me to hand ye this yer bookay with his regards, and this yer specimen!" And Mr. Flynn laid down the flowers he had picked *en route* against such an emergency, and presented respectfully a piece of quartz and gold which he had taken that morning from his own sluice-box. "You mus'n't mind Hawkins' ways, Miss Nelly," said another sympathizing miner. "There ain't a better man in camp than that theer Cy Hawkins!—but he don't understand the ways o' the world with wimen. He hasn't mixed as much with society as the rest of us," he added, with an elaborate Chesterfieldian ease of manner, "but he means well." Meanwhile a few other sympathetic tunnel-men were impressing upon Mr. Hawkins the necessity of the greatest attention to the invalid. "It won't do, Hawkins," they explained, "to let that there gal go back to San Francisco and say that when she was sick and alone, the only man in Five Forks under whose roof she had rested, and at whose table she had sat"—this was considered a natural but pardonable exaggeration of rhetoric—"ever threw off on her; and it shan't be done. It ain't the square thing to Five Forks." And then the Fool would rush away to the valley, and be received by Miss Nelly with a certain reserve of manner that finally disappeared in a flush of color, some increased vivacity, and a pardonable coquetry. And so the days passed; Miss Nelly grew better in health and more troubled in mind, and Mr. Hawkins became more and more embarrassed, and Five Forks smiled and rubbed its hands, and waited for the approaching denouement. And then it came. But not perhaps in the manner that Five Forks had imagined.

It was a lovely afternoon in July that a party of Eastern tourists rode into Five Forks. They had just "done" the Valley of Big Things, and there being one or two Eastern capitalists among the party, it was deemed advisable that a proper knowledge of the practical mining resources of California should be added to their experience of the merely picturesque in Nature. Thus far everything had been satisfactory; the amount of water which passed over the Fall was large, owing to a backward season; some snow still remained in the cañons near the highest peaks; they had ridden round one of the biggest trees, and through the prostrate trunk of another. To say that they were delighted is to express feebly the enthusiasm of these ladies and gentlemen, drunk with the champagny hospitality of their entertainers, the utter novelty of scene, and the dry, exhilarating air of the valley. One or two had already expressed themselves ready to live and die there; another had written a glowing account to the Eastern press, depreciating all other scenery in Europe and America; and under these circumstances it was reasonably expected that Five Forks would do its duty, and equally impress the stranger after its own fashion.

Letters to this effect were sent from San Francisco by prominent capitalists there, and under the able superintendence of one of their agents, the visitors were taken in hand, shown "what was to be seen," carefully restrained from observing what ought not to be visible, and so kept in a blissful and enthusiastic condition. And so the graveyard of Five Forks, in which but two of the occupants had

died natural deaths, the dreary, ragged cabins on the hillsides, with their sad-eyed, cynical, broken-spirited occupants, toiling on, day by day, for a miserable pittance and
a fare that a self-respecting Eastern mechanic would have
scornfully rejected, were not a part of the Eastern visitors'
recollection. But the hoisting works and machinery of the
"Blazing Star Tunnel Company" was—the Blazing Star
Tunnel Company, whose "gentlemanly Superintendent" had
received private information from San Francisco to do the
"proper thing" for the party. Wherefore the valuable heaps
of ore in the company's works were shown, the oblong bars
of gold—ready for shipment—were playfully offered to
the ladies who could lift and carry them away unaided, and
even the tunnel itself, gloomy, fateful, and peculiar, was
shown as part of the experience; and, in the noble language
of one correspondent, "the wealth of Five Forks and the
peculiar inducements that it offered to Eastern capitalists"
were established beyond a doubt. And then occurred a
little incident which, as an unbiased spectator, I am free
to say, offered no inducements to anybody whatever, but
which, for its bearing upon the central figure of this
veracious chronicle, I cannot pass over.

It had become apparent to one or two more practical
and sober-minded in the party that certain portions of the
"Blazing Star" Tunnel—(owing, perhaps, to the exigencies
of a flattering annual dividend)—were economically and
imperfectly "shored" and supported, and were consequently
unsafe, insecure, and to be avoided. Nevertheless, at a
time when champagne corks were popping in dark corners,
and enthusiastic voices and happy laughter rang through
the half-lighted levels and galleries, there came a sudden
and mysterious silence. A few lights dashed swiftly by in

the direction of a distant part of the gallery, and then there
was a sudden sharp issuing of orders and a dull, ominous
rumble. Some of the visitors turned pale—one woman
fainted!

Something had happened. What? "Nothing"—the
speaker is fluent but uneasy—"one of the gentlemen in
trying to dislodge a 'specimen' from the wall had knocked
away a support. There had been a 'cave'—the gentleman
was caught and buried below his shoulders. It was all
right—they'd get him out in a moment—only it required
great care to keep from extending the 'cave.' Didn't know
his name—it was that little man—the husband of that lively
lady with the black eyes. Eh! Hullo there! Stop her.
For God's sake!—not that way! She'll fall from that shaft.
She'll be killed!"

But the lively lady was already gone. With staring black
eyes, imploringly trying to pierce the gloom, with hands and
feet that sought to batter and break down the thick darkness, with incoherent cries and supplications, following the
moving of *ignis fatuus* lights ahead, she ran and ran
swiftly! Ran over treacherous foundations, ran by yawning
gulfs, ran past branching galleries and arches, ran wildly,
ran despairingly, ran blindly, and at last ran into the arms
of the Fool of Five Forks.

In an instant she caught at his hand. "Oh, save him!"
she cried; "you belong here—you know this dreadful place;
bring me to him. Tell me where to go and what to do, I
implore you! Quick, he is dying. Come!"

He raised his eyes to hers, and then, with a sudden cry,
dropped the rope and crowbar he was carrying, and reeled
against the wall. "Annie!" he gasped, slowly, "is it you?"

She caught at both his hands, brought her face to his

with staring eyes, murmured "Good God, Cyrus!" and
sank upon her knees before him.

He tried to disengage the hand that she wrung with
passionate entreaty.

"No, no! Cyrus, you will forgive me—you will forget
the past! God has sent you here to-day. You will come
with me. You will—you must—save him!"

"Save who?" cried Cyrus hoarsely.

"My husband!"

The blow was so direct—so strong and overwhelming—
that even through her own stronger and more selfish absorption she saw it in the face of the man, and pitied him.

"I thought—you—knew—it!" she faltered. He did not
speak, but looked at her with fixed, dumb eyes. And then
the sound of distant voices and hurrying feet started her
again into passionate life. She once more caught his hand.

"O Cyrus! hear me! If you have loved me through all
these years, you will not fail me now. You must save him!
You can! You are brave and strong—you always were,
Cyrus! You will save him, Cyrus, for my sake—for the
sake of your love for me! You will—I know it! God
bless you!"

She rose as if to follow him, but at a gesture of command she stood still. He picked up the rope and crowbar
slowly, and in a dazed, blinded way that, in her agony of
impatience and alarm, seemed protracted to cruel infinity.
Then he turned, and raising her hand to his lips, he kissed
it slowly, looked at her again—and the next moment was
gone.

He did not return. For at the end of the next half-hour,
when they laid before her the half-conscious breathing
body of her husband, safe and unharmed but for exhaus-

tion and some slight bruises, she learned that the worst fears of the workmen had been realized. In releasing him a second "cave" had taken place. They had barely time to snatch away the helpless body of her husband before the strong frame of his rescuer, Cyrus Hawkins, was struck and smitten down in his place.

For two hours he lay there, crushed and broken-limbed, with a heavy beam lying across his breast, in sight of all, conscious and patient. For two hours they had labored around him, wildly, despairingly, hopefully, with the wills of gods and the strength of giants, and at the end of that time they came to an upright timber, which rested its base upon the beam. There was a cry for axes, and one was already swinging in the air, when the dying man called to them, feebly—

"Don't cut that upright!"

"Why?"

"It will bring down the whole gallery with it."

"How?"

"It's one of the foundations of my house."

The axe fell from the workman's hand, and with a blanched face he turned to his fellows. It was too true. They were in the uppermost gallery, and the "cave" had taken place directly below the new house. After a pause the Fool spoke again more feebly.

"The lady!—quick."

They brought her—a wretched, fainting creature, with pallid face and streaming eyes—and fell back as she bent her face above him.

"It was built for you, Annie, darling," he said in a hurried whisper, "and has been waiting up there for you and me all these long days. It's deeded to you, Annie, and you must—live there—with *him!* He will not mind that I shall be always near you—for it stands above—my grave!"

And he was right. In a few minutes later, when he had passed away, they did not move him, but sat by his body all night with a torch at his feet and head. And the next day they walled up the gallery as a vault, but they put no mark or any sign thereon, trusting rather to the monument that, bright and cheerful, rose above him in the sunlight of the hill. For they said: "This is not an evidence of death and gloom and sorrow, as are other monuments, but is a sign of Life and Light and Hope, wherefore shall all men know that he who lies under it—is a Fool!"

A GHOST OF THE SIERRAS

IT was a vast silence of pines, redolent with balsamic breath, and muffled with the dry dust of dead bark and matted mosses. Lying on our backs, we looked upward through a hundred feet of clear, unbroken interval to the first lateral branches that formed the flat canopy above us. Here and there the fierce sun, from whose active persecution we had just escaped, searched for us through the woods, but its keen blade was dulled and turned aside by intercostal boughs, and its brightness dissipated in nebulous mists throughout the roofing of the dim, brown aisles around us. We were in another atmosphere, under another sky; indeed, in another world than the dazzling one we had just quitted. The grave silence seemed so much a part of the grateful coolness, that we hesitated to speak, and for some moments lay quietly outstretched on the pine tassels

where we had first thrown ourselves. Finally, a voice broke
the silence—

"Ask the old Major; he knows all about it!"

The person here alluded to under that military title was
myself. I hardly need explain to any Californian that it by
no means followed that I was a "Major," or that I was
"old," or that I knew anything about "it," or indeed what
"it" referred to. The whole remark was merely one of
the usual conventional feelers to conversation,—a kind of
social preamble, quite common to our slangy camp intercourse. Nevertheless, as I was always known as the Major,
perhaps for no better reason than that the speaker, an old
journalist, was always called Doctor, I recognized the fact
so far as to kick aside an intervening saddle, so that I could
see the speaker's face on a level with my own, and said
nothing.

"About ghosts!" said the Doctor, after a pause, which
nobody broke or was expected to break. "Ghosts, sir!
That's what we want to know. What are we doing here in
this blank old mausoleum of Calaveras County, if it isn't to
find out something about 'em, eh?"

Nobody replied.

"Thar's that haunted house at Cave City. Can't be more
than a mile or two away, anyhow. Used to be just off the
trail."

A dead silence.

The Doctor (addressing space generally): "Yes, sir; it
was a mighty queer story."

Still the same reposeful indifference. We all knew the
Doctor's skill as a *raconteur;* we all knew that a story was
coming, and we all knew that any interruption would be
fatal. Time and time again, in our prospecting experience,

had a word of polite encouragement, a rash expression of interest, even a too eager attitude of silent expectancy, brought the Doctor to a sudden change of subject. Time and time again have we seen the unwary stranger stand amazed and bewildered between our own indifference and the sudden termination of a promising anecdote, through his own unlucky interference. So we said nothing. "The Judge"—another instance of arbitrary nomenclature—pretended to sleep. Jack began to twist a *cigarrito*. Thornton bit off the ends of pine needles reflectively.

"Yes, sir," continued the Doctor, coolly resting the back of his head on the palms of his hands, "it *was* rather curious. All except the murder. *That's* what gets me, for the murder had no new points, no fancy touches, no sentiment, no mystery. Was just one of the old style, "sub-head" paragraphs. Old-fashioned miner scrubs along on hardtack and beans, and saves up a little money to go home and see relations. Old-fashioned assassin sharpens up knife, old style; loads old flint-lock, brass-mounted pistols; walks in on old-fashioned miner one dark night, sends him home to his relations away back to several generations, and walks off with the swag. No mystery *there;* nothing to clear up; subsequent revelations only impertinence. Nothing for any ghost to do—who meant business. More than that, over forty murders, same old kind, committed every year in Calaveras, and no spiritual post obits coming due every anniversary; no assessments made on the peace and quiet of the surviving community. I tell you what, boys, I've always been inclined to throw off on the Cave City ghost for that alone. It's a bad precedent, sir. If that kind o' thing is going to obtain in the foothills, we'll have the trails full of chaps formerly knocked over by Mex-

icans and road agents; every little camp and grocery will
have stock enough on hand to go into business and where's
there any security for surviving life and property, eh?
What's your opinion, Judge, as a fair-minded legislator?"

Of course there was no response. Yet it was part of the
Doctor's system of aggravation to become discursive at
these moments, in the hope of interruption, and he continued for some moments to dwell on the terrible possibility
of a state of affairs in which a gentleman could no longer
settle a dispute with an enemy without being subjected to
succeeding spiritual embarrassment But all this digression
fell upon apparently inattentive ears.

"Well, sir, after the murder, the cabin stood for a long
time deserted and tenantless. Popular opinion was against
it. One day a ragged prospector, savage with hard labor
and harder luck, came to the camp, looking for a place to
live and a chance to prospect. After the boys had taken
his measure, they concluded that he'd already tackled so
much in the way of difficulties that a ghost more or less
wouldn't be of much account. So they sent him to the
haunted cabin. He had a big yellow dog with him, about
as ugly and as savage as himself; and the boys sort o' con-
gratulated themselves, from a practical viewpoint, that
while they were giving the old ruffian a shelter, they were
helping in the cause of Christianity against ghosts and gob-
lins. They had little faith in the old man, but went their
whole pile on that dog. That's where they were mistaken.

"The house stood almost three hundred feet from the
nearest cave, and on dark nights, being in a hollow, was as
lonely as if it had been on the top of Shasta. If you ever
saw the spot when there was just moon enough to bring
out the little surrounding clumps of chaparral until they

looked like crouching figures, and make the bits of broken quartz glisten like skulls, you'd begin to understand how big a contract that man and that yellow dog undertook.

"They went into possession that afternoon, and old Hard Times set out to cook his supper. When it was over he sat down by the embers and lit his pipe, the yellow dog lying at his feet. Suddenly 'Rap! rap!' comes from the door. 'Come in,' says the man gruffly. 'Rap!' again. 'Come in and be d—d to you,' says the man, who had no idea of getting up to open the door. But no one responded, and the next moment smash goes the only sound pane in the only window. Seeing this, old Hard Times gets up, with the devil in his eye, and a revolver in his hand, followed by the yellow dog, with every tooth showing, and swings open the door. No one there! But as the man opened the door, that yellow dog, that had been so chipper before, suddenly begins to crouch and step backward, step by step, trembling and shivering, and at last crouches down in the chimney, without even so much as looking at his master. The man slams the door shut again, but there comes another smash. This time it seems to come from inside the cabin, and it isn't until the man looks around and sees everything quiet that he gets up, without speaking, and makes a dash for the door, and tears round outside the cabin like mad, but finds nothing but silence and darkness. Then he comes back swearing and calls the dog. But that great yellow dog that the boys would have staked all their money on is crouching under the bunk, and has to be dragged out like a coon from a hollow tree, and lies there, his eyes starting from their sockets; every limb and muscle quivering with fear, and his very hair drawn up in bristling ridges. The man calls him to the door. He drags himself a few steps, stops, sniffs, and refuses to go farther. The man calls him again, with an oath and a threat. Then, what does that yellow dog do? He crawls edgewise towards the door, crouching himself against the bunk, till he's flatter than a knife blade, then, half-way, he stops. Then that d—d yellow dog begins to walk gingerly—lifting each foot up in the air, one after the other, still trembling in every limb. Then he stops again. Then he crouches. Then he gives one little shuddering leap—not straight forward, but up,—clearing the floor about six inches, as if"——

"Over something," interrupted the Judge hastily, lifting himself on his elbow.

The Doctor stopped instantly. "Juan," he said coolly to one of the Mexican packers, "quit foolin' with that *riata*. You'll have that stake out and that mule loose in another minute. Come over this way!"

The Mexican turned a scared, white face to the Doctor, muttering something, and let go the deerskin hide. We all up-raised our voices with one accord, the Judge most penitently and apologetically, and implored the Doctor to go on. "I'll shoot the first man who interrupts you again," added Thornton persuasively.

But the Doctor, with his hands languidly under his head, had lost his interest. "Well, the dog ran off to the hills, and neither the threats nor cajoleries of his master could ever make him enter the cabin again. The next day the man left the camp. What time is it? Getting on to sundown, ain't it? Keep off my leg, will you, you d—d Greaser, and stop stumbling round there! Lie down."

But we knew that the Doctor had not completely finished his story, and we waited patiently for the conclusion. Meanwhile the old, gray silence of the woods again asserted itself, but shadows were now beginning to gather in the heavy beams of the roof above, and the dim aisles seemed to be narrowing and closing in around us. Presently the Doctor recommenced lazily, as if no interruption had occurred.

"As I said before, I never put much faith in that story, and shouldn't have told it, but for a rather curious experience of my own. It was in the spring of '62, and I was one of a party of four, coming up from O'Neill's, when we had been snowed up. It was awful weather; the snow had changed to sleet and rain after we crossed the divide, and the water was out everywhere; every ditch was a creek, every creek a river. We had lost two horses on the North Fork, we were dead beat, off the trail, and sloshing round, with night coming on, and the level hail like shot in our faces. Things were looking bleak and scary when, riding a little ahead of the party, I saw a light twinkling in a hollow beyond. My horse was still fresh, and calling out to the boys to follow me and bear for the light, I struck out for it. In another moment I was before a little cabin that half burrowed in the black chaparral; I dismounted and rapped at the door. There was no response. I then tried to force the door, but it was fastened securely from within. I was all the more surprised when one of the boys, who had overtaken me, told me that he had just seen through a window a man reading by the fire. Indignant at this inhospitality, we both made a resolute onset against the door, at the same time raising our angry voices to a yell. Suddenly there was a quick response, the hurried withdrawing of a bolt, and the door opened.

"The occupant was a short, thick-set man, with a pale,

careworn face, whose prevailing expression was one of gentle good-humor and patient suffering. When we entered, he asked us hastily why we had not 'sung out' before.

" 'But we *knocked!*' I said impatiently, 'and almost drove your door in.'

" 'That's nothing,' he said patiently. 'I'm used to *that.*'

"I looked again at the man's patient, fateful face, and then around the cabin. In an instant the whole situation flashed before me. 'Are we not near Cave City?' I asked.

" 'Yes,' he replied, 'it's just below. You must have passed it in the storm.'

" 'I see.' I again looked around the cabin. 'Isn't this what they call the haunted house?'

"He looked at me curiously. 'It is,' he said simply.

"You can imagine my delight! Here was an opportunity to test the whole story, to work down to the bed rock, and see how it would pan out! We were too many and too well armed to fear tricks or dangers from outsiders. If—as one theory had been held—the disturbance was kept up by a band of concealed marauders or road agents, whose purpose was to preserve their haunts from intrusion, we were quite able to pay them back in kind for any assault. I need not say that the boys were delighted with this prospect when the fact was revealed to them. The only one doubtful and apathetic spirit there was our host, who quietly resumed his seat and his book, with his old expression of patient martyrdom. It would have been easy for me to have drawn him out, but I felt that I did not want to corroborate anybody else's experience; only to record my own. And I thought it better to keep the boys from any predisposing terrors.

"We ate our supper, and then sat, patiently and expectant, around the fire. An hour slipped away, but no disturbance; another hour passed as monotonously. Our host read his book; only the dash of hail against the roof broke the silence. But"——

The Doctor stopped. Since the last interruption, I noticed he had changed the easy slangy style of his story to a more perfect, artistic, and even studied manner. He now dropped suddenly into his old colloquial speech, and quietly said, "If you don't quit stumbling over those *riatas,* Juan, I'll hobble *you.* Come here, there; lie down, will you?"

We all turned fiercely on the cause of this second dangerous interruption, but a sight of the poor fellow's pale and frightened face withheld our vindictive tongues. And the Doctor, happily, of his own accord, went on:—

"But I had forgotten that it was no easy matter to keep these high-spirited boys, bent on a row, in decent subjection; and after the third hour passed without a supernatural exhibition, I observed, from certain winks and whispers, that they were determined to get up indications of their own. In a few moments violent rappings were heard from all parts of the cabin; large stones (adroitly thrown up the chimney) fell with a heavy thud on the roof. Strange groans and ominous yells seemed to come from the outside (where the interstices between the logs were wide enough). Yet, through all this uproar, our host sat still and patient, with no sign of indignation or reproach upon his good-humored but haggard features. Before long it became evident that this exhibition was exclusively for *his* benefit. Under the thin disguise of asking him to assist them in discovering the disturbers *outside* the cabin those inside took advantage of his absence to turn the cabin topsy-turvy.

" 'You see what the spirits have done, old man,' said

Bret Harte's grave in Frimiley Churchyard, England, which is inscribed:

Bret Harte
August 25th, 1839   May 5th, 1902
In faithful remembrance
M. S. Van de Velde

the arch leader of this mischief. 'They've upset that there flour barrel while we wasn't looking, and then kicked over the water-jug and spilled all the water!'

"The patient man lifted his head and looked at the flour-strewn walls. Then he glanced down at the floor, but drew back with a slight tremor.

" 'It ain't water!' he said quietly.

" 'What is it then?'

" 'It's BLOOD! Look!'

"The nearest man gave a sudden start and sank back white as a sheet.

"For there, gentlemen, on the floor, just before the door, where the old man had seen the dog hesitate and lift his feet, there! there!—gentlemen—upon my honor, slowly widened and broadened a dark red pool of human blood! Stop him! Quick! Stop him, I say!"

There was a blinding flash that lit up the dark woods, and a sharp report! When we reached the Doctor's side he was holding the smoking pistol, just discharged, in one hand, while with the other he was pointing to the rapidly disappearing figure of Juan, our Mexican vaquero!

"Missed him! by G—d!" said the Doctor. "But did you hear him? Did you see his livid face as he rose up at the name of blood? Did you see his guilty conscience in his face? Eh? Why don't you speak? What are you staring at?"

"Was it the murdered man's ghost, Doctor?" we all panted in one quick breath.

"Ghost be d—d! No! But in that Mexican vaquero —that cursed Juan Ramirez!—I saw and shot at his murderer!"

MY FRIEND THE TRAMP

I HAD been sauntering over the clover downs of a certain noted New England seaport. It was a Sabbath morning, so singularly reposeful and gracious—so replete with the significance of the seventh day of rest that even the Sabbath bells ringing a mile away over the salt marshes had little that was monitory, mandatory, or even supplicatory in their drowsy voices. Rather they seemed to call from their cloudy towers, like some renegade Muezzin: "Sleep is better than prayer; sleep on, O sons of the Puritans! Slumber still, O deacons and vestrymen. Let, oh let those feet that are swift to wickedness curl up beneath thee; those palms that are itching for the shekels of the ungodly, lie clasped beneath thy pillow. Sleep is better than prayer."

And, indeed, though it was high morning, sleep was still in the air. Wrought upon at last by the combined influences of sea and sky and atmosphere, I succumbed, and lay down on one of the boulders of a little stony slope that gave upon the sea. The great Atlantic lay before me, not yet quite awake, but slowly heaving with the rhythmical expiration of slumber. There was no sail visible in the misty horizon. There was nothing to do but to lie and stare at the unwinking ether.

Suddenly I became aware of the strong fumes of tobacco. Turning my head I saw a pale, blue smoke curling up from behind an adjacent boulder. Rising and climbing over the

280

intervening granite, I came upon a little hollow in which, comfortably extended on the mosses and lichens, lay a powerfully built man. He was very ragged; he was very dirty; there was a strong suggestion about him of his having too much hair, too much nail, too much perspiration; too much of those superfluous excrescences and exudations that society and civilization strive to keep under. But it was noticeable that he had not much of anything else. It was The Tramp.

With that swift severity with which we always visit rebuke upon the person who happens to present any one of our vices offensively before us, in his own person, I was deeply indignant at his laziness. Perhaps I showed it in my manner, for he rose to a half-sitting attitude, returned my stare apologetically, and made a movement toward knocking the fire from his pipe against the granite.

"Shure, sur, and if I'd belaved that I was trispassin' on yer honor's grounds it's meself that would hev laid down on the say-shore and taken the salt waves for me blankits. But it's sivinteen miles I've walked this blessed noight, with nothin' to sustain me, and hevin' a mortal wakeness to fight wid in me bowels, by reason of starvation, and only a bit o' baccy that the Widdy Maloney giv me at the cross-roads, to kape me up entoirly. But it was the dark day I left me home in Milwaukee to walk to Boston, and if ye'll oblige a lone man who has left a wife and six children in Milwaukee, wid the loan of twenty-five cints, furninst the time he gits wurruk, God'll be good to ye."

It instantly flashed through my mind that the man before me had the previous night partaken of the kitchen hospitality of my little cottage, two miles away. That he presented himself in the guise of a distressed fisherman,

mulcted of his wages by an inhuman captain; that he had
a wife lying sick of consumption in the next village, and
two children, one of them a cripple, wandering in the streets
of Boston. I remember that this tremendous indictment
against Fortune touched the family, and that the distressed
fisherman was provided with clothes, food, and some small
change. The food and small change had disappeared, but
the garments for the consumptive wife, where were they?
He had been using them for a pillow.

I instantly pointed out this fact, and charged him with
the deception. To my surprise he took it quietly and even
a little complacently. "Bedad, yer roight; ye see, sur (confidentially), ye see, sur, until I get wurruk—and it's wurruk
I'm lukin' for—I have to desave now and thin to shute the
locality. Ah, God save us, but on the say-coast thay'r that
harrud upon thim that don't belong to the say."

I ventured to suggest that a strong, healthy man like him
might have found work somewhere between Milwaukee and
Boston.

"Ah, but ye see I got free passage on a freight train,
and didn't sthop. It was in the Aist that I expicted to find
wurruk."

"Have you any trade?"

"Trade, is it? I'm a brickmaker, Gods knows, and many's
the lift I've had at makin' bricks in Milwaukee. Sure, I've
as aisy a hand at it as any man. Maybe yer honor might
know of a kill hereabout?"

Now, to my certain knowledge, there was not a brick-
kiln within fifty miles of that spot, and of all unlikely places
to find one would have been this sandy peninsula, given up
to the summer residences of a few wealthy people. Yet I
could not help admiring the assumption of the scamp, who

knew this fact as well as myself. But I said, "I can give
you work for a day or two," and, bidding him gather up
his sick wife's apparel, led the way across the downs to my
cottage. At first I think the offer took him by surprise, and
gave him some consternation, but he presently recovered
his spirits, and almost instantly his speech. "Ah, wurruk,
is it? God be praised; it's meself that's ready and willin',
'though maybe me hand is spoilt wid brickmaking."

I assured him that the work I would give him would
require no delicate manipulation, and so we fared on over
the sleepy downs. But I could not help noticing that, although an invalid, I was a much better pedestrian than my
companion, frequently leaving him behind, and that, even
as a "tramp," he was etymologically an impostor. He had
a way of lingering beside the fences we had to climb over as
if to continue more confidentially the history of his misfortunes and troubles, which he was delivering to me during
our homeward walk, and I noticed that he could seldom
resist the invitation of a mossy boulder or a tussock of salt
grass. "Ye see, sur," he would say, suddenly sitting down,
"it's along uv me misfortunes beginning in Milwaukee
that"—and it was not until I was out of hearing that he
would languidly gather his traps again and saunter after me.
When I reached my own garden gate he leaned for a moment over it, with both of his powerful arms extended
downwards and said, "Ah, but it's a blessin' that Sunday
comes to give rest fur the wake and the weary, and thim
as walks sivinteen miles to get it." Of course I took the
hint. There was evidently no work to be had from my friend
the Tramp that day. Yet his countenance brightened as
he saw the limited extent of my domain, and observed that
the garden, so-called, was only a flower bed about twenty-

five by ten. As he had doubtless before this been utilized to the extent of his capacity in digging, he had probably expected that kind of work, and I daresay I discomfited him by pointing him to an almost levelled stone wall about twenty feet long, with the remark that his work would be the rebuilding of that stone wall with stone brought from the neighboring slopes. In a few moments he was comfortably provided for in the kitchen, where the cook, a woman of his own nativity, apparently "chaffed" him with a raillery that was to me quite unintelligible. Yet I noticed that when, at sunset, he accompanied Bridget to the spring for water, ostentatiously flourishing the empty bucket in his hand, when they returned in the gloaming Bridget was carrying the water, and my friend the Tramp was some paces behind her cheerfully "colloguing," and picking blackberries.

At 7 the next morning he started in cheerfully to work. At 9 A.M. he had placed three large stones on the first course in position, an hour having been spent in looking for a pick and hammer, and in the intervals "chaffing" with Bridget. At 10 o'clock I went to overlook his work; it was a rash action, as it caused him to respectfully doff his hat, discontinue his labors, and lean back against the fence in cheerful and easy conversation. "Are ye fond uv blackberries, Captain?" I told him that the children were in the habit of getting them from the meadow beyond—hoping to estop the suggestion I knew was coming. "Ah, but Captain, it's meself that with wandering and havin' nothin' to pass me lips but the berries I'd pick from the hedges— it's meself knows where to find them. Shure, it's yer childer, and foine boys they are, Captain, that are besaching me to go wid 'em to the place, knownst only to meself." It is

unnecessary to say that he triumphed. After the manner of
vagabonds of all degrees, he had enlisted the women and
children on his side—and my friend the Tramp had his own
way. He departed at 11 and returned at 4 P.M. with a tin
dinner-pail half filled. On interrogating the boys it appeared
that they had had "a bully time," but on cross-examination
it came out that *they* had picked the berries. From 4 to 6
three more stones were laid, and the arduous labors of the
day were over. As I stood looking at the first course of six
stones, my friend the Tramp stretched his strong arms out
to their fullest extent and said, "Ay, but it's wurruk that's
good fur me; gin me wurruk, and it's all I'll be askin' fur."

I ventured to suggest that he had not yet accomplished
much.

"Wait till to-morror. Ah, but ye'll see thin. It's me
hand that's yet onaisy wid brickmaking and sthrange to the
shtones. Av ye'll wait till to-morror?"

Unfortunately I did not wait. An engagement took me
away at an early hour, and when I rode up to my cottage
at noon my eyes were greeted with the astonishing spectacle
of my two boys hard at work laying the courses of the stone
wall, assisted by Bridget and Norah, who were dragging
stones from the hillsides, while comfortably stretched on the
top of the wall lay my friend the Tramp, quietly overseeing
the operations with lazy and humorous comment. For an
instant I was foolishly indignant, but he soon brought me
to my senses. "Shure, sur, it's only larnin' the boys the
habits uv industhry I was—and may they niver know, be
the same token, what is it to wurruk for the bread betune
their lips. Shure it's but makin' em think it play, I was.
As fur the colleens beyint in the kitchen, shure isn't it

betther they was helping your honor here than colloguing with themselves inside?"

Nevertheless, I thought it expedient to forbid henceforth any interruption of servants or children with my friend's "wurruk." Perhaps it was the result of this embargo that the next morning early the Tramp wanted to see me.

"And it's sorry I am to say it to ye, sur," he began, "but it's the handlin' of this stun that's desthroyin' me touch at the brickmakin', and it's better I should lave ye and find wurruk at me own thrade. For it's wurruk I'm nadin'. It isn't meself, Captin, to ate the bread of oidleness here. And so good-bye to ye, and if it's fifty cints ye can be givin' me ontil I'll find a kill—it's God that'll repay ye."

He got the money. But he got also conditionally a note from me to my next neighbor, a wealthy retired physician, possessed of a large domain—a man eminently practical and business-like in his management of it. He employed many laborers on the sterile waste he called his "farm," and it occurred to me that if there really was any work in my friend the Tramp, which my own indolence and pre-occupation had failed to bring out, he was the man to do it.

I met him a week after. It was with some embarrassment that I inquired after my friend the Tramp. "Oh, yes," he said reflectively, "let's see—he came Monday and left me Thursday. He was, I think, a stout, strong man, a well-meaning, good-humored fellow, but afflicted with a most singular variety of diseases. The first day I put him at work in the stables he developed chills and fever caught in the swamps of Louisiana"——

"Excuse me," I said hurriedly—"you mean in Milwaukee!"

"I know what I'm talking about," returned the doctor

testily; "he told me his whole wretched story; his escape from the Confederate service; the attack upon him by armed negroes; his concealment in the bayous and swamps"——

"Go on, doctor," I said feebly; "you were speaking of his work."

"Yes—well his system was full of malaria; the first day I had him wrapped up in blankets and dosed with quinine. The next day he was taken with all the symptoms of cholera morbus, and I had to keep him up on brandy and capsicum. Rheumatism set in on the following day and incapacitated him for work, and I concluded I had better give him a note to the director of the City Hospital than keep him here. As a pathological study he was good, but as I was looking for a man to help about the stable I couldn't afford to keep him in both capacities."

As I never could really tell when the doctor was in joke or in earnest I dropped the subject. And so my friend the Tramp gradually faded from my memory, not, however, without leaving behind him in the barn, where he had slept, a lingering flavor of whisky, onions, and fluffiness. But in two weeks this had gone, and the "Shebang" (as my friends irreverently termed my habitation) knew him no more. Yet it was pleasant to think of him as having at last found a job at brickmaking, or having returned to his family at Milwaukee, or making his Louisiana home once more happy with his presence, or again tempting the fish-producing main—this time with a noble and equitable captain.

It was a lovely August morning when I rode across the sandy peninsula to visit a certain noted family; whereof all the sons were valiant and the daughters beautiful. The

front of the house was deserted, but on the rear veranda
I heard the rustle of gowns, and above it arose what seemed
to be the voice of Ulysses, reciting his wanderings.   There
was no mistaking that voice—it was my friend the Tramp!

From what I could hastily gather from his speech, he
had walked from St. John, N. B., to rejoin a distressed wife
in New York, who was, however, living with opulent but
objectionable relatives. "An' shure, miss, I wouldn't be
asking ye the loan of a cint if I could get wurruk at me
trade of carpet-wavin'—and maybe ye know of some manu-
facthory where they wave carpets beyant here.   Ah, miss,
and if ye don't give me a cint, it's enough for the loikes of
me to know that me troubles has brought the tears in the
most beautiful oiyes in the wurruld, and God bless ye for
it, miss!"

Now I knew that the Most Beautiful Eyes in the World
belonged to one of the most sympathetic and tenderest
hearts in the world, and I felt that common justice demanded my interference between it and one of the biggest
scamps in the world. So, without waiting to be announced
by the servant, I opened the door and joined the group on
the veranda.

If I expected to touch the conscience of my friend the
Tramp by a dramatic entrance, I failed utterly! For no
sooner did he see me than he instantly gave vent to a howl
of delight, and, falling on his knees before me, grasped my
hand and turned oratorically to the ladies.

"Oh, but it's himself—himself that has come as a witness
to me charackther! Oh, but it's himself that lifted me four
wakes ago, when I was lyin' with a mortal wakeness on the
say-coast and tuk me to his house. Oh, but it's himself that
shupported me over the faldes, and whin the chills and faver

came on me and I shivered wid the cold, it was himself, God bless him, as sthripped the coat off his back, and giv it me, sayin', 'Tak it, Dinnis, it's shtarved with the cowld say air, ye'll be entoirly.' Ah, but look at him—will ye, miss! Look at his swate, modist face—a-blushin' like your own, miss. Ah! look at him, will ye? He'll be denyin' of it in a minit—may the blessin' uv God folly him. Look at him, miss! Ah, but it's a swate pair ye'd make!—(the rascal knew I was a married man). Ah, miss, if ye could see him wroightin' day and night with such an illigant hand of his own—(he had evidently believed from the gossip of my servants that I was a professor of chirography)—if ye could see him, miss, as I have, ye'd be proud of him."

He stopped out of breath. I was so completely astounded I could say nothing; the tremendous indictment I had framed to utter as I opened the door vanished completely. And as the Most Beautiful Eyes in the Wurruld turned gratefully to mine—well—

I still retained enough principle to ask the ladies to withdraw, while I would take upon myself the duty of examining into the case of my friend the Tramp and giving him such relief as was required. (I did not know until afterward, however, that the rascal had already despoiled their scant purses of $3.50.) When the door was closed upon them I turned upon him.

"You infernal rascal!"

"Ah, Captin, and would ye be refusin' *me* a carrakther and me givin *ye* such a one as Oi did? God save us! but if ye'd hav' seen the luk that the purty one give me. Well, before the chills and faver bruk me spirits entirely, when I was a young man, and makin' me tin dollars a week brickmakin', it's meself that wud hav given"——

"I consider," I broke in, "that a dollar is a fair price for your story, and as I shall have to take it all back and expose you before the next twenty-four hours pass, I think you had better hasten to Milwaukee, New York, or Louisiana."

I handed him the dollar. "Mind, I don't want to see your face again."

"Ye wun't, Captin."

And I did not.

But it so chanced that later in the season, when the migratory inhabitants had flown to their hot-air registers in Boston and Providence, I breakfasted with one who had lingered. It was a certain Boston lawyer—replete with principle, honesty, self-discipline, statistics, æsthetics, and a perfect consciousness of possessing all these virtues, and a full recognition of their market values. I think he tolerated me as a kind of foreigner, gently but firmly waiving all argument on any topic, frequently distrusting my facts, generally my deductions, and always my ideas. In conversation he always appeared to descend only half-way down a long moral and intellectual staircase, and always delivered his conclusions over the balusters.

I had been speaking of my friend the Tramp. "There is but one way of treating that class of impostors; it is simply to recognize the fact that the law calls him a 'vagrant,' and makes his trade a misdemeanor. Any sentiment on the other side renders you *particeps criminis*. I don't know but an action would lie against you for encouraging tramps. Now, I have an efficacious way of dealing with these gentry." He rose and took a double-barrelled fowling-piece from the chimney. "When a tramp appears on my property I warn him off. If he persists I fire on him—as I would on any criminal trespasser."

"Fire on him?" I echoed in alarm.

"Yes—*but with powder only!* Of course *he* doesn't know that. But he doesn't come back."

It struck me for the first time that possibly many other of my friend's arguments might be only blank cartridges, and used to frighten off other trespassing intellects.

"Of course, if the tramp still persisted I would be justified in using shot. Last evening I had a visit from one. He was coming over the wall. My shotgun was efficacious: you should have seen him run!"

It was useless to argue with so positive a mind and I dropped the subject. After breakfast I strolled over the downs, my friend promising to join me as soon as he had arranged some household business.

It was a lovely, peaceful morning, not unlike the day when I first met my friend the Tramp. The hush of a great Benediction lay on land and sea. A few white sails twinkled afar, but sleepily—one or two large ships were creeping in lazily—like my friend the Tramp. A voice behind me startled me.

My host had rejoined me. His face, however, looked a little troubled.

"I just now learned something of importance," he began; "it appears that with all my precautions that Tramp has visited my kitchen and the servants have entertained him. Yesterday morning, it appears, while I was absent he had the audacity to borrow my gun to go duck shooting. At the end of two or three hours he returned with two ducks and— the gun."

"That was, at least, honest."

"Yes—but! That fool of a girl says that, as he handed

back the gun, he told her it was all right, and that he had loaded it up again to save the master trouble."

I think I showed my concern in my face, for he added hastily, "It was only duck shot—a few wouldn't hurt him!"

Nevertheless we both walked on in silence for a moment.

"I thought the gun kicked a little," he said at last, musingly; "but the idea of—Hallo! what's this?"

He had stopped before the hollow where I had first seen my Tramp. It was deserted, but on the mosses there were spots of blood and fragments of an old gown, bloodstained, as if used for bandages. I looked at it closely; it was the gown intended for the consumptive wife of my friend the Tramp.

But my host was already nervously tracking the bloodstains that on rock, moss, and boulder were steadily leading toward the sea. When I overtook him at last on the shore, he was standing before a flat rock, on which lay a bundle I recognized, tied up in a handkerchief, and a crooked grape vine stick.

"He may have come here to wash his wounds—salt is a styptic," said my host, who had recovered his correct precision of statement.

I said nothing, but looked toward the sea. Whatever secret lay hid in its breast, it kept it fast. Whatever its calm eyes had seen that summer night, it gave no reflection now. It lay there passive, imperturbable, and reticent. But my friend the Tramp was gone!

THE OFFICE-SEEKER

He asked me if I had ever seen the "Remus Sentinel."

I replied that I had not, and would have added that I did not even know where Remus was, when he continued by saying it was strange the hotel proprietor did not keep the "Sentinel" on his files, and that he himself should write to the editor about it. He would not have spoken about it, but he himself had been a humble member of the profession to which I belonged, and had often written for its columns. Some friends of his—partial, no doubt—had said that his style somewhat resembled Junius's; but of course, you know—well, what he could say was that in the last campaign his articles were widely sought for. He did not know but he had a copy of one. Here his hand dived into the breast-pocket of his coat, with a certain deftness that indicated long habit, and after depositing on his lap a bundle of well-worn documents, every one of which was glaringly suggestive of certificates and signatures, he concluded he had left it in his trunk.

I breathed more freely. We were sitting in the rotunda of a famous Washington hotel, and only a few moments before had the speaker, an utter stranger to me, moved his chair beside mine and opened a conversation. I noticed that he had that timid, lonely, helpless air which invests the bucolic traveller who, for the first time, finds himself among strangers, and his identity lost, in a world so much larger, so much colder, so much more indifferent to him than he ever imagined. Indeed, I think that what we often attribute to the impertinent familiarity of countrymen and rustic travellers on railways or in cities is largely due to their awful loneliness and nostalgia. I remember to have once met in a smoking-car on a Kansas railway one of these lonely ones, who, after plying me with a thousand useless questions, finally elicited the fact that I knew slightly a man who had once dwelt in his native town in Illinois. During the rest of our journey the conversation turned chiefly upon this fellow-townsman, whom it afterwards appeared that my Illinois friend knew no better than I did. But he had established a link between himself and his far-off home through me, and was happy.

While this was passing through my mind I took a fair look at him. He was a spare young fellow, not more than thirty, with sandy hair and eyebrows, and eyelashes so white as to be almost imperceptible. He was dressed in black, somewhat to the "rearward o' the fashion," and I had an odd idea that it had been his wedding suit, and it afterwards appeared I was right. His manner had the precision and much of the dogmatism of the country schoolmaster, accustomed to wrestle with the feeblest intellects. From his history, which he presently gave me, it appeared I was right here also.

He was born and bred in a Western State, and, as schoolmaster of Remus and Clerk of Supervisors, had married one of his scholars, the daughter of a clergyman, and a man of some little property. He had attracted some attention by his powers of declamation, and was one of the principal members of the Remus Debating Society. The various questions then agitating Remus—"Is the doctrine of immortality consistent with an agricultural life?" and, "Are round dances morally wrong?"—afforded him an opportunity of bringing himself prominently before the country people. Perhaps I might have seen an extract copied from the "Remus Sentinel" in the "Christian Recorder" of May 7, 1875? No? He would get it for me. He had taken an active part in the last campaign. He did not like to say it, but it had been universally acknowledged that he had elected Gashwiler.

Who?

Gen. Pratt C. Gashwiler, member of Congress from our deestrict.

"Oh!"

"A powerful man, sir—a very powerful man; a man whose influence will presently be felt here, sir—*here!*" Well, he had come on with Gashwiler, and—well, he did not know why—Gashwiler did not know why he should not, you know (a feeble, half-apologetic laugh here), receive that reward, you know, for these services which, &c., &c.

I asked him if he had any particular or definite office in view.

Well, no. He had left that to Gashwiler. Gashwiler had said—he remembered his very words: "Leave it all to me; I'll look through the different departments, and see what can be done for a man of your talents."

And—

"He's looking. I'm expecting him back here every minute. He's gone over to the Department of Tape to see what can be done there. Ah! here he comes."

A large man approached us. He was very heavy, very unwieldy, very unctuous and oppressive. He affected the "honest farmer," but so badly that the poorest husbandman would have resented it. There was a suggestion of a cheap lawyer about him that would have justified any self-respecting judge in throwing him over the bar at once. There was a military suspicion about him that would have entitled him to a court-martial on the spot. There was an introduction, from which I learned that my office-seeking friend's name was Expectant Dobbs. And then Gashwiler addressed me:—

"Our young friend here is waiting, waiting. Waiting, I may say, on the affairs of State. Youth," continued the Hon. Mr. Gashwiler, addressing an imaginary constituency, "is nothing but a season of waiting—of preparation—ha, ha!"

As he laid his hand in a fatherly manner—a fatherly manner that was as much of a sham as anything else about him—I don't know whether I was more incensed at him or his victim, who received it with evident pride and satisfaction. Nevertheless he ventured to falter out:—

"Has anything been done yet?"

"Well, no; I can't say that anything—that is, that anything has been *completed;* but I may say we are in excellent position for an advance—ha, ha! But we must wait, my young friend, wait. What is it the Latin philosopher says? 'Let us by all means hasten slowly'—ha, ha!" and he turned to me as if saying confidentially, "Observe the impatience of these boys!" "I met, a moment ago, my old friend and boyhood companion, Jim M'Glasher, chief of the Bureau for the Dissemination of Useless Information, and," lowering his voice to a mysterious but audible whisper, "I shall see him again to-morrow."

The "All aboard!" of the railway omnibus at this moment tore me from the presence of this gifted legislator and his *protégé;* but as we drove away I saw through the open window the powerful mind of Gashwiler operating, so to speak, upon the susceptibilities of Mr. Dobbs.

I did not meet him again for a week. The morning of my return I saw the two conversing together in the hall, but with the palpable distinction between this and their former interviews, that the gifted Gashwiler seemed to be anxious to get away from his friend. I heard him say something about "committees" and "to-morrow," and when Dobbs turned his freckled face toward me I saw that he had got at last some expression into it—disappointment.

I asked him pleasantly how he was getting on.

He had not lost his pride yet. He was doing well, although such was the value set upon his friend Gashwiler's abilities by his brother members that he was almost always occupied with committee business. I noticed that his clothes were not in as good care as before, and he told me that he had left the hotel, and taken lodgings in a by-street, where it was less expensive. Temporarily, of course.

A few days after this I had business in one of the great departments. From the various signs over the doors of its various offices and bureaus it always oddly reminded me of Stewart's or Arnold and Constable's. You could get pensions, patents, and plants. You could get land and the seeds to put in it, and the Indians to prowl round it, and what not. There was a perpetual clanging of office desk bells, and a running hither and thither of messengers strongly suggestive of "Cash 47."

As my business was with the manager of this Great National Fancy Shop, I managed to push by the sad-eyed, eager-faced crowd of men and women in the anteroom, and entered the secretary's room, conscious of having left behind me a great deal of envy and uncharitableness of spirit. As

I opened the door I heard a monotonous flow of Western speech which I thought I recognized. There was no mistaking it. It was the voice of the Gashwiler.

"The appointment of this man, Mr. Secretary, would be most acceptable to the people in my deestrict. His family are wealthy and influential, and it's just as well in the fall elections to have the supervisors and county judge pledged to support the administration. Our delegates to the State Central Committee are to a man"—but here, perceiving from the wandering eye of Mr. Secretary that there was another man in the room, he whispered the rest with a familiarity that must have required all the politician in the official's breast to keep from resenting.

"You have some papers, I suppose?" asked the secretary wearily.

Gashwiler was provided with a pocketful, and produced them. The secretary threw them on the table among the other papers, where they seemed instantly to lose their identity, and looked as if they were ready to recommend anybody but the person they belonged to. Indeed, in one corner the entire Massachusetts delegation, with the Supreme Bench at their head, appeared to be earnestly advocating the manuring of Iowa waste lands; and to the inexperienced eye, a noted female reformer had apparently appended her signature to a request for a pension for wounds received in battle.

"By the way," said the secretary, "I think I have a letter here from somebody in your district asking an appointment, and referring to you? Do you withdraw it?"

"If anybody has been presuming to speculate upon my patronage," said the Hon. Mr. Gashwiler with rising rage.

"I've got the letter somewhere here," said the secretary,

looking dazedly at his table. He made a feeble movement among the papers, and then sank back hopelessly in his chair, and gazed out of the window as if he thought and rather hoped it might have flown away. "It was from a Mr. Globbs, or Gobbs, or Dobbs, of Remus," he said finally, after a superhuman effort of memory.

"Oh, that's nothing—a foolish fellow who has been boring me for the last month."

"Then I am to understand that this application is withdrawn?"

"As far as my patronage is concerned, certainly. In fact, such an appointment would not express the sentiments—indeed, I may say, would be calculated to raise active opposition in the deestrict."

The secretary uttered a sigh of relief, and the gifted Gashwiler passed out. I tried to get a good look at the honorable scamp's eye, but he evidently did not recognize me.

It was a question in my mind whether I ought not to expose the treachery of Dobbs's friend, but the next time I met Dobbs he was in such good spirits that I forebore. It appeared that his wife had written to him that she had discovered a second cousin in the person of the Assistant Superintendent of the Envelope Flap Moistening Bureau of the Department of Tape, and had asked his assistance; and Dobbs had seen him, and he had promised it. "You see," said Dobbs, "in the performance of his duties he is often very near the person of the secretary, frequently in the next room, and he is a powerful man, sir—a powerful man to know, sir—a *very* powerful man."

How long this continued I do not remember. Long enough, however, for Dobbs to become quite seedy, for the giving up of wrist-cuffs, for the neglect of shoes and beard, and for great hollows to form round his eyes, and a slight flush on his cheek-bones. I remember meeting him in all the departments, writing letters or waiting patiently in ante-rooms from morning till night. He had lost all his old dog-matism, but not his pride. "I might as well be here as anywhere, while I'm waiting," he said, "and then I'm get-ting some knowledge of the details of official life."

In the face of this mystery I was surprised at finding a note from him one day, inviting me to dine with him at a certain famous restaurant. I had scarce got over my amaze-ment, when the writer himself overtook me at my hotel. For a moment I scarcely recognized him. A new suit of fashionably-cut clothes had changed him without, however, entirely concealing his rustic angularity of figure and out-line. He even affected a fashionable dilettante air, but so mildly and so innocently that it was not offensive.

"You see," he began, explanatory-wise, "I've just found out the way to do it. None of these big fellows, these cabi-net officers, know me except as an applicant. Now, the way to do this thing is to meet 'em fust sociably; wine 'em and dine 'em. Why, sir"—he dropped into the school-master again here—"I had two cabinet ministers, two judges, and a general at my table last night."

"On *your* invitation?"

"Dear, no! all I did was to pay for it. Tom Soufflet gave the dinner and invited the people. Everybody knows Tom. You see, a friend of mine put me up to it, and said that Soufflet had fixed up no end of appointments and jobs in that way. You see, when these gentlemen get sociable over their wine, he says, carelessly, "By the way, there's So-and-so— a good fellow—wants something; give it to him." And the first thing you know, or they know, he gets a promise from them. They get a dinner—and a good one—and he gets an appointment."

"But where did you get the money?"

"Oh"—he hesitated—"I wrote home, and Fanny's father raised fifteen hundred dollars some way, and sent it to me. I put it down to political expenses." He laughed a weak foolish laugh here, and added, "As the old man don't drink nor smoke, he'd lift his eyebrows to know how the money goes. But I'll make it all right when the office comes—and she's coming, sure pop."

His slang fitted as poorly on him as his clothes, and his familiarity was worse than his former awkward shyness. But I could not help asking him what had been the result of this expenditure.

"Nothing just yet. But the Secretary of Tape and the man at the head of the Inferior Department, both spoke to me, and one of them said he thought he'd heard my name before. He might," he added with a forced laugh, "for I've written him fifteen letters."

Three months passed. A heavy snowstorm stayed my chariot wheels on a Western railroad, ten miles from a nervous lecture committee and a waiting audience; there was nothing to do but to make the attempt to reach them in a sleigh. But the way was long and the drifts deep; and when at last four miles out we reached a little village, the driver declared his cattle could hold out no longer, and we must stop there. Bribes and threats were equally of no avail. I had to accept the fact.

"What place is this?"

"Remus."

"Remus, Remus," where had I heard that name before?

But while I was reflecting he drove up before the door of the tavern. It was a dismal, sleep-forbidding place, and only nine o'clock, and here was the long winter's night before me. Failing to get the landlord to give me a team to go farther, I resigned myself to my fate and a cigar, behind the red-hot stove. In a few moments one of the loungers approached me, calling me by name, and in a rough but hearty fashion condoled me for my mishap, advising me to stay at Remus all night, and added: "The quarters ain't the best in the world yer at this hotel. But thar's an old man yer—that preacher that was—that for twenty years hez taken in such fellers as you and lodged 'em free gratis for nothing, and hez been proud to do it. The old man used to be rich; he ain't so now; sold his big house on the cross-roads, and lives in a little cottage with his darter right over yan. But ye couldn't do him a better turn than to go over thar and stay, and if he thought I'd let ye go out o' Remus without axing ye, he'd give me h—ll. Stop, I'll go with ye."

I might at least call on the old man, and I accompanied my guide through the still falling snow until we reached a little cottage. The door opened to my guide's knock, and with the brief and discomposing introduction, "Yer, ole man, I've brought you one of them snowbound lecturers," he left me on the threshold, as my host, a kindly-faced, white-haired man of seventy, came forward to greet me.

His frankness and simple courtesy overcame the embarrassment left by my guide's introduction, and I followed him passively as he entered the neat but plainly-furnished sitting-room. At the same moment a pretty, but faded young woman arose from the sofa and was introduced to me as his daughter. "Fanny and I live here quite alone, and if you knew how good it was to see somebody from the great outside world now and then, you would not apologize for what you call your intrusion."

During this speech I was vaguely trying to recall where and when and under what circumstances I had ever before seen the village, the house, the old man or his daughter. Was it in a dream, or in one of those dim reveries of some previous existence to which the spirit of mankind is subject? I looked at them again. In the careworn lines around the once pretty girlish mouth of the young woman, in the furrowed seams over the forehead of the old man, in the ticking of the old-fashioned clock on the shelf, in the faint whisper of the falling snow outside, I read the legend, "Patience, patience; Wait and Hope."

The old man filled a pipe, and offering me one, continued, "Although I seldom drink myself, it was my custom to always keep some nourishing liquor in my house for passing guests, but to-night I find myself without any." I hastened to offer him my flask, which, after a moment's coyness, he accepted, and presently under its benign influence at least ten years dropped from his shoulders, and he sat up in his chair erect and loquacious.

"And how are affairs at the National Capital, sir?" he began.

Now, if there was any subject of which I was profoundly ignorant, it was this. But the old man was evidently bent on having a good political talk. So I said vaguely, yet with a certain sense of security, that I guessed there wasn't much being done.

"I see," said the old man, "in the matters of resumption of the sovereign rights of States and federal interference, you would imply that a certain conservative tentative policy is not to be promulgated until after the electoral committee have given their verdict." I looked for help towards the lady, and observed feebly that he had very clearly expressed my views.

The old man, observing my looks, said, "Although my daughter's husband holds a federal position in Washington, the pressure of his business is so great that he has little time to give us mere gossip—I beg your pardon, did you speak?"

I had unconsciously uttered an exclamation. This, then, was Remus—the home of Expectant Dobbs—and these his wife and father; and the Washington banquet-table, ah me! had sparkled with the yearning heart's blood of his poor wife, and had been upheld by this tottering Caryatid of a father.

"Do you know what position he has?"

The old man did not know positively, but thought it was some general supervising position. He had been assured by Mr. Gashwiler that it was a first-class clerkship; yes, a *first*-class.

I did not tell him that in this, as in many other official regulations in Washington, they reckoned backward, but said—

"I suppose that your M. C., Mr.—Mr. Gashwiler"——

"Don't mention his name," said the little woman, rising to her feet hastily; "he never brought Expectant anything but disappointment and sorrow. I hate, I despise, the man."

"Dear Fanny," expostulated the old man gently, "this is unchristian and unjust. Mr. Gashwiler is a powerful, a very powerful man! His work is a great one; his time is pre-occupied with weightier matters."

"His time was not so preoccupied but he could make

use of poor Expectant," said this wounded dove a little spitefully.

Neverthless it was some satisfaction to know that Dobbs had at last got a place, no matter how unimportant, or who had given it to him; and when I went to bed that night in the room that had been evidently prepared for their conjugal chamber, I felt that Dobbs's worst trials were over. The walls were hung with souvenirs of their antenuptial days. There was a portrait of Dobbs, ætat 25; there was a faded bouquet in a glass case, presented by Dobbs to Fanny on examination-day; there was a framed resolution of thanks to Dobbs from the Remus Debating Society; there was a certificate of Dobbs's election as President of the Remus Philomathean Society; there was his commission as Captain in the Remus Independent Contingent of Home Guards; there was a Freemason's chart, in which Dobbs was addressed in epithets more fulsome and extravagant than any living monarch. And yet all these cheap glories of a narrow life and narrower brain were upheld and made sacred by the love of the devoted priestess who worshipped at this homely shrine, and kept the light burning through gloom and doubt and despair. The storm tore round the house, and shook its white fists in the windows. A dried wreath of laurel that Fanny had placed on Dobbs's head after his celebrated centennial address at the schoolhouse, July 4, 1876, swayed in the gusts, and sent a few of its dead leaves down on the floor, and I lay in Dobbs's bed and wondered what a first-class clerkship was.

I found out early the next summer. I was strolling through the long corridors of a certain great department, when I came upon a man accurately yoked across the shoulders, and supporting two huge pails of ice on either side, from which he was replenishing the pitchers in the various offices. As I passed I turned to look at him again. It was Dobbs!

He did not set down his burden; it was against the rules, he said. But he gossiped cheerily, said he was beginning at the foot of the ladder, but expected soon to climb up. That it was Civil Service Reform, and of course he would be promoted soon.

"Had Gashwiler procured the appointment?"

No. He believed it was *me*. *I* had told his story to Assistant-Secretary Blank, who had in turn related it to Bureau-Director Dash—both good fellows—but this was all they could do. Yes, it was a foothold. But he must go now.

Nevertheless I followed him up and down, and, cheered up with a rose-colored picture of his wife and family, and my visit there, and promising to come and see him the next time I came to Washington, I left him with his self-imposed yoke.

With a new administration Civil Service Reform came in, crude and ill-digested, as all sudden and sweeping reforms must be; cruel to the individual, as all crude reforms will ever be; and among the list of helpless men and women, incapacitated for other work by long service in the dull routine of federal office who were decapitated, the weak, foolish, emaciated head of Expectant Dobbs went to the block. It afterward appeared that the gifted Gashwiler was responsible for the appointment of twenty clerks, and that the letter of poor Dobbs, in which he dared to refer to the now powerless Gashwiler, had sealed his fate. The country made an example of Gashwiler and—Dobbs.

From that moment he disappeared. I looked for him in

vain in anterooms, lobbies, and hotel corridors, and finally came to the conclusion that he had gone home.

How beautiful was that July Sabbath, when the morning train from Baltimore rolled into the Washington depôt! How tenderly and chastely the morning sunlight lay on the east front of the Capitol until the whole building was hushed in a grand and awful repose! How difficult it was to think of a Gashwiler creeping in and out of those enfiling columns, or crawling beneath that portico, without wondering that yon majestic figure came not down with flat of sword to smite the fat rotundity of the intruder! How difficult to think that paricidal hands have ever been lifted against the Great Mother, typified here in the graceful white chastity of her garments, in the noble tranquillity of her face, in the gathering up her white-robed children within her shadow!

This led me to think of Dobbs, when, suddenly, a face flashed by my carriage window. I called to the driver to stop, and, looking again, saw that it was a woman standing bewildered and irresolute on the street corner. As she turned her anxious face toward me I saw that it was Mrs. Dobbs.

What was she doing here, and where was Expectant?

She began an incoherent apology, and then burst into explanatory tears. When I had got her in the carriage she said, between her sobs, that Expectant had not returned; that she had received a letter from a friend here saying he was sick—oh, very, very sick—and father could not come with her, so she came alone. She was so frightened, so lonely, so miserable.

Had she his address?

Yes, just here! It was on the outskirts of Washington,

near Georgetown. Then I would take her there, **if I could**, for she knew nobody.

On our way I tried to cheer her up by pointing out some of the children of the Great Mother before alluded to, but she only shut her eyes as we rolled down the long avenues, and murmured, "Oh, these cruel, cruel distances!"

At last we reached the locality, a negro quarter, yet clean and neat in appearance. I saw the poor girl shudder slightly as we stopped at the door of a low, two-storey frame house, from which the unwonted spectacle of a carriage brought a crowd of half-naked children and a comely, cleanly, kind-faced mulatto woman.

Yes, this was the house. He was upstairs, rather poorly, but asleep, she thought.

We went upstairs. In the first chamber, clean, though poorly furnished, lay Dobbs. On a pine table near his bed were letters and memorials to the various departments, and on the bed-quilt, unfinished, but just as the weary fingers had relaxed their grasp upon it, lay a letter to the Tape Department.

As we entered the room he lifted himself on his elbow. "Fanny!" he said quickly, and a shade of disappointment crossed his face. "I thought it was a message from the secretary," he added apologetically.

The poor woman had suffered too much already to shrink from this last crushing blow. But she walked quietly to his side without a word or cry, knelt, placed her loving arms around him, and I left them so together.

When I called again in the evening he was better; so much better that, against the doctor's orders, he had talked to her quite cheerfully and hopefully for an hour, until suddenly raising her bowed head in his two hands, he said, "Do you know, dear, that in looking for help and influence there was One, dear, I had forgotten; One who is very potent with kings and councillors; and I think, love, I shall ask Him to interest Himself in my behalf. It is not too late yet, darling, and I shall seek him to-morrow."

And before the morrow came he had sought and found Him, and I doubt not got a good place.

GREAT ILLUSTRATED CLASSICS

Adam Bede—*Eliot*
Afloat and Ashore—*Cooper*
The Arabian Nights
Around the World in Eighty Days—*Verne*
Ben-Hur—*Wallace*
The Black Arrow—*Stevenson*
Black Beauty—*Sewell*
The Call of the Wild and Other Stories—*London*
Captains Courageous and Other Stories—*Kipling*
Christmas Tales—*Dickens*
The Cloister and the Hearth—*Reade*
A Connecticut Yankee in King Arthur's Court—*Clemens*
The Cruise of the Cachalot—*Bullen*
David Copperfield—*Dickens*
The Deerslayer—*Cooper*
Emma—*Austen*
Famous Tales of Sherlock Holmes—*Doyle*
Four Tales of the Sea—*Conrad*
From the Earth to the Moon—*Verne*
Great Expectations—*Dickens*
Green Mansions—*Hudson*
Gulliver's Travels—*Swift*
Hawthorne's Short Stories—*Hawthorne*
Henry Esmond—*Thackeray*
The House of the Seven Gables—*Hawthorne*
Huckleberry Finn—*Clemens*
The Hunchback of Notre-Dame—*Hugo*
Ivanhoe—*Scott*
Jane Eyre—*Brontë*
A Journey to the Centre of the Earth—*Verne*
Kenilworth—*Scott*
Kidnapped—*Stevenson*
Kim—*Kipling*
King Arthur—*Malory*
The Last Days of Pompeii—*Bulwer-Lytton*
The Last of the Mohicans—*Cooper*
Lord Jim—*Conrad*
Lorna Doone—*Blackmore*
The Luck of Roaring Camp and Other Stories—*Harte*
The Man in the Iron Mask—*Dumas*
Martin Chuzzlewit—*Dickens*

The Mill on the Floss—*Eliot*
The Moonstone—*Collins*
The Mysterious Island—*Verne*
Nicholas Nickleby—*Dickens*
The Odyssey—*Homer*
The Old Curiosity Shop—*Dickens*
Oliver Twist—*Dickens*
Our Mutual Friend—*Dickens*
The Pathfinder—*Cooper*
Père Goriot—*Balzac*
Pickwick Papers—*Dickens*
The Pilot—*Cooper*
The Pioneers—*Cooper*
The Prairie—*Cooper*
Pride and Prejudice—*Austen*
Quentin Durward—*Scott*
Quo Vadis—*Sienkiewicz*
The Red Badge of Courage and Other Stories—*Crane*
The Return of the Native—*Hardy*
Robinson Crusoe—*Defoe*
The Scarlet Letter—*Hawthorne*
Sense and Sensibility—*Austen*
Silas Marner—*Eliot*
The Sketch Book—*Irving*
The Spy—*Cooper*
The Strange Case of Dr. Jekyll and Mr. Hyde and Other Famous Tales—*Stevenson*
A Tale of Two Cities—*Dickens*
Tales—*Poe*
The Talisman—*Scott*
Tess of the D'Urbervilles—*Hardy*
The Three Musketeers—*Dumas*
Tom Sawyer—*Clemens*
Treasure Island—*Stevenson*
Twenty Thousand Leagues Under the Sea—*Verne*
Twenty Years After—*Dumas*
Two Years Before the Mast—*Dana*
Uncle Tom's Cabin—*Stowe*
Vanity Fair—*Thackeray*
Walden—*Thoreau*
The Way of All Flesh—*Butler*
Westward Ho!—*Kingsley*
The White Company—*Doyle*
White Fang and Other Stories—*London*
The Wreck of the Grosvenor—*Russell*
Wuthering Heights—*Brontë*

GREAT ILLUSTRATED CLASSICS—TITANS

Autobiography of Benvenuto Cellini
Barnaby Rudge—*Dickens*
Bleak House—*Dickens*
Dombey & Son—*Dickens*

Don Quixote—*Cervantes*
Everybody's Plutarch
Little Dorrit—*Dickens*
Short Novels of Henry James—*James*